MR. AND MRS. PENNINGTON

BY FRANCIS BRETT YOUNG

NOVELS

THE KEY OF LIFE
PROTRAIT OF CLARE
SEA HORSES
COLD HARBOUR
WOODSMOKE
PILGRIM'S REST
THE RED KNIGHT
THE BLACK DIAMOND
THE TRAGIC BRIDE
THE YOUNG PHYSICIAN
THE IRON AGE
THE DARK TOWER
DEEP SEA
MY BROTHER JONATHAN
BLACK ROSES
JIM REDLAKE
UNDERGROWTH
(*with E. Brett Young*)

POETRY

FIVE DEGREES SOUTH
POEMS: 1916–1918

BELLES LETTRES

MARCHING ON TANGA
ROBERT BRIDGES

FRANCIS BRETT YOUNG

❋

MR.
AND MRS.
PENNINGTON

LONDON
WILLIAM HEINEMANN LTD

First published 1931

Printed
in Great Britain
at the Windmill Press

To
My Friend
CHARLEY EVANS
with admiration, gratitude and affection

CONTENTS

"A few stars are known which are hardly bigger than the earth, but the majority are so large that hundreds of thousands of earths could be packed within each and leave room to spare; here and there we come upon a giant star large enough to contain millions and millions of earths. And the total number of stars in the universe is probably something like the total number of grains of sand in all the sea-shores of the world. Such is the littleness of our home in space when measured up against the total substance of the universe."

(JEANS)

CHAPTER I

BLACK LACE

I

On the night of her nineteenth birthday, at a quarter past ten on a mild May evening, Susan Lorimer stood glowering at her own cross face in an oblong Chippendale mirror. She had always hated that mirror, for its quicksilver, eaten away by time, showed irregular patches like a rash on her reflected cheeks, and its warped surface had the trick of making her face, which was quite short enough, look shorter than it really was. That was partly the reason, no doubt, why her aunt Edna Lorimer had placed it in Susan's room. The mirror stood on a mahogany Victorian dressing-table, all massive curves like the ladies favoured by Rubens, nearly filling the aperture of a window that looked down from the back of the red-brick Georgian house in Great Cornbow, at Halesby, on to a garden that sloped to the Stour and her Uncle George's warehouse. In that garden, three storeys beneath her, flowered lilac bushes emitted wafts of faint perfume into the dark. The light of a gas-jet, hissing within its spherical cage of corroded wire, threw down distant beams that glistened prettily on the heart-shaped lilac leaves. Far below, at the foot of the garden, the invisible river ran past with a subdued murmur. But Susan, at this moment, was immune from these charming effects of light and sound. She only knew that the naked light was as baffling and unflattering as it could be for a pretty girl to dress by. The moving lilacs spent their perfume in vain; and the music of water, alas, takes its mode from the mind of the hearer.

That night, in spite of the fact that the day was her birthday, Susan hated the sound of it. She was only nineteen; and she wished—how she wished!—she was twenty-one.

At the moment her life presented no single redeeming feature. To begin with she had come home late, having stayed in North Bromwich, first of all for a meeting of the University Poetry Society and afterwards to go to the Futurist (Fu-*ture*-ist, they called it) with her latest friend Muriel O'Brien, whose acquaintance she had picked up a few weeks before on the eight-nineteen. Through the fault of the slow suburban train she had found herself "on the mat." Aunt Edna, who had spitefully locked and double-bolted the door on her at ten to the tick, had traipsed downstairs in Uncle George's dressing-gown, with a candle and without her teeth, and played Hamlet at the top of her voice, to make sure that Uncle George, poor dear, heard every word of it.

"Muriel and I went to see Ivor Novello," Susan had explained.

"And who may *he* be, I should like to know?" Aunt Edna had demanded scornfully.

Well, how could you deal with such judicial ignorance? Mrs. Lorimer knew perfectly well who Ivor Novello was. So Susan had merely laughed and tossed her bright, bird-like head, though her dark eyes smouldered with indignation at being treated like a kid on the eve on her nineteenth birthday, while Aunt Edna, having pointedly, noisily, re-chained and re-bolted the front door, had dogged her upstairs in her unwieldy, flat-footed way. Even when the door of Susan's bedroom was closed with a slam of protest, the sibilant voice of Aunt Edna had still pursued her.

"I suppose you realize," she said toothlessly, "how this sort of thing's certain to end? Your poor uncle's extremely upset," she persisted, "I can tell you that!"

"He wouldn't have been upset," Susan thought, "if you'd only left him alone."

Her mind was seething now with rude and rebellious words which exploded like bubbles before they could reach her lips. She was too angry to speak— most fortunately; for Aunt Edna asked nothing better than the chance of a stand-up row, with her husband for audience. Susan refused to believe for one second that Uncle George was upset by her coming home five minutes late. She and he understood each other; all he wanted, poor dear, was to be left alone with his musty books, his pipe, his fishing-tackle, and his jumbled notes for that *History of the Wrought-iron Nail-trade,* which he was some day going to write; or to play, on the American organ, a number of hymn-tunes or the easier pieces in Mendelssohn's *Songs Without Words.* Ever since the unlucky day when that damned woman sailed into the house in Great Cornbow, she had never stopped trying to separate Susan from her uncle. And she couldn't! She knew she couldn't! That was what riled her. Indeed, on those happy occasions when Aunt Edna went, once a year, to stay with her rich sister who had married a bucket-manufacturer in Wednesford, Uncle George and Susan had had the time of their lives. Why, why had he married her? she thought. Why *did* people marry, anyway? Because they were in love, she supposed.

"Love . . . love . . . What a funny word!" she reflected as she skinned her jumper, violently ruffling the mop of her dark, bobbed hair. A blunt-sounding, ugly word, when you came to think of it all by itself. If love only meant *that!* she thought. Crawling into a mahogany double-bed every night when the clock struck ten, after putting your teeth into a glass and your hair into curlers! And calling him "dearie" and patting his bald head in a way that made everyone sick and setting his mind systematically against anyone else that he liked! "My God," Susan thought, "if that's love, they can jolly well keep it! Ugh!" she shivered and shook herself violently and saw, in the glass, her face go fierce with disgust; her smooth, white brow knitted under the ruffled hair, her cheeks hot, her teeth clenched.

"Muriel sets up as an expert at that sort of thing," Susan thought, with faint scorn, idly watching the reflection of her savage little face regain its composure and practising a smile to reassure herself that it wasn't necessarily so ugly. That expertness of Muriel's was a quality that Susan disliked and, at the same time, somehow envied. It had not been deliberately acquired, being just as much a part of her natural vulgar endowment as the tilt of her nose. When she strolled arm-in-arm with Susan down Sackville Row, in the luncheon hour, men's glances buzzed round Muriel like wood-flies. They started with her creamy face, her blue surprised eyes, then swooped down to her ankles. Those weren't, as a matter of fact, so neat as Susan's, though her heels were higher; but the flies didn't seem to mind or notice the difference; they flicked up again and settled all over Muriel, drinking in the honey of her hair, her childlike lips, devouring her creamy skin. They were really rather disgusting, Susan thought; though Muriel didn't mind. On the contrary, she throve on them. Without them, in all probability, she'd go thin and lose the magnolia complexion that meant so much to her—like flowers that have to be fertilized, Susan thought, or pearls that go sick unless they are constantly worn. "Still, *that* isn't love," Susan thought, "not what *I* call love . . ."

What was it, then? Greta Garbo or Ivor Novello? As she made this demand of the more pensive image that now confronted her, illuminated by the fish-tailed burner of gas that hissed in its cage, the atmosphere of the Futurist returned to her in the smell of cheap jasmine scent, a by-product of coal-tar, that the programme-girls, threading the gangways like fireflies, had atomized in the foul air. This perfume, clinging to her clothes and hair, reminded her of the hot-house opulence of the film they had seen that evening. *In Java, where passion blooms like a sinister orchid . . .* the caption had told them, giving place, on the screen, to a vision of vast green forests and sun-drenched mountains, the background of a super-heated *crime passionnel* contrived in a setting of luxurious hotel-suites, of huge, multi-cylindered motor-cars, of inappropriate hot sables and Paris confections and short-skirted French maids swinging ropes of indiscriminate jewels, of a sumptuous existence in which nobody, apparently, dreamed of paying for anything, in which men and women, selected from two worlds by reason of their physical beauty, spent their elegant lives in a series of passionate pursuits and surrenders. Of course the whole story underlined the moral of virtue triumphant. That was why the licenser of films had approved of it. Yet, somehow, the sound yeoman sense which Susan had inherited from her forbears in Shropshire denied her the luxury of surrendering, as Muriel frankly did, to the rich illusion. When the lights had gone up on that tawdry setting of gilt and scarlet and they had emerged, arm-in-arm, on to the slimy pavement littered with the day's conglomeration of trodden 'bus-tickets and silver paper, the spring night's drizzle had warned her, quite unequivocally, that, in North Bromwich at any rate, Passion didn't bloom like a sinister orchid. It had been difficult indeed to believe that it bloomed at all amid the hurrying stream of pre-occupied middle-class men and women, just like herself, on whose current both she and her dreams were sucked into the culvert that led to the "local" platform of the Great Western station.

No, Hollywood couldn't quite answer her question either, Susan Lorimer decided, still facing the mirror in which, as she brushed out her hair with determined violence, her eyes appraised the undeniable grace of her slim, white shoulders. "Muriel's perfectly right," she thought; "it really must be black lace. Black is always distinguished. With a thin ribbon shoulder-strap," her thoughts ran on, "and if it *is* low in the back I shan't mind in the least. Aunt Edna can say what she damned well likes. It's no business of hers. It isn't as if she'll pay for it."

II

"It," of course, was the new evening dress which she would have to buy, during the next few days, for the

B

annual dance of the College Union. She had seen the very thing—it was black lace—in Madame Allbright's window and would pay for it herself, out of her own minute independence, the two thousand pounds in War Loan which had come to her through the will her father had scribbled in his Field Service pocket-book on the night before he had been blown to atoms on the Somme. Uncle George, as trustee, looked after the capital; but the interest which he paid to Susan regularly every quarter day was the one thing that enabled her to keep her end up with Aunt Edna on awkward occasions like this. So, turning out the gas and lighting her bedside candle before she burrowed between the darned calico sheets and opened her book, the thought of the visionary black lace, linking up with her previous meditations, conjured into the space between her and the printed page the image of her friend Mr. Feilden.

Henry Feilden . . . The name was almost a coincidence. But though Mr. Feilden lectured on the Eighteenth Century Novelists and had literary ambitions he was far too refined to write another *Tom Jones*. Mr. Feilden was a tall, blond young man, with a long, ascetic face, pale blue eyes and thin lips, that weren't exactly bitter yet seemed, vaguely, scornful. He wore rimless *pince-nez*, with which, when he warmed to his lectures, he would emphasize each point that he made, waving them to and fro in his white, bony, exquisitely-manicured fingers. As a male, he would certainly fall a long way short of Muriel's full-blooded standards; but this fact, by eliminating any dangerous rivalry between them, was all in his favour. If Muriel thought him a cold fish, so much the better. Though Susan had never presumed to imagine herself in any emotional relation with Mr. Feilden in the flesh, there was no doubt but that, spiritually, he was a superior person. Not prudishly superior. His bold acceptance of the coarseness of eighteenth century fiction was anything but delicate by the accepted standards of Halesby. He never shirked calling spades spades with the starkest determination, yet his attitude toward these rude implements was always intellectual, idealistic, and so sublimely detached that Susan, who was naturally shy with most men, had no hesitation in boldly discussing with him subjects that would have suffused the cheeks of Aunt Edna—or even Muriel O'Brien—with blushes.

These discussions gave Susan a sensation—not exactly of danger but of daring emancipation; they lifted her on to a higher plane than that of her tittering and self-conscious fellow-students, whose mean ambition was a pass degree in the Faculty of Arts and a teacher's job in a Council School; they showed Mr. Feilden— if he had failed to notice it before—that one member of his class at least was capable of attaining his own spiritual altitude. His first response, indeed, had been academically correct; their converse was that of two rare and disembodied intelligences confronting abstractions in an atmosphere of Pure Thought, which was all very thrilling to Susan at first, but somewhat unsatisfying and empty as time wore on. It was only when Susan, realizing this, began to retreat, that Mr. Feilden woke up. He wasn't yet quite wideawake—however pretty and piquante she might be she was still a second year student and he a graduate—but the glances he stole through his *pince-nez* and the pink flush that coloured his pale neck when he tried to detain her in conversation, betrayed the fact that Mr. Feilden's spirit was no longer quite disembodied. However important the integrity of his career might be—and Mr. Feilden's academic and literary ambitions were grim and unbounded—it would be ungenerous and unworthy of him to despise and reject this refined and glowing creature whose quick though callow intelligence suggested that she might some day be capable of appreciating his unpublished works. So he lent her books and, later, the manuscripts of his own compositions which, they both agreed, were far above the heads of any possible audience. There was an essay, too, on *The Feminine Influence in Nineteenth Century Poetry,* which impressed on Susan the responsibility which his friendship imposed on her. He had begun to treat her, at last, very nearly as an equal. Forsaking literature they talked about the duty of "divine discontent" and "living dangerously" and "self-expression" and the purely theoretical advantages of free love. When Mr. Feilden spoke of these things his neck went pinker than ever and his long white fingers twined and untwined

themselves nervously; but he always made it quite
clear, as his position demanded, that they were skating
over the frozen surface of theory, not the thin ice of
practice, and that if the ice thawed, as with inferior,
earthbound people it might, they had only to flap their
wings and soar, hand in hand, to the glacial empyrean
of abstract intellect.

Susan didn't mind that. She wasn't in love with
Mr. Feilden, though she wouldn't have minded in the
least if he had fallen in love with her, as, sometimes,
she thought he had. She was merely, at the moment,
terribly excited about all kinds of life, as was proved
by her sudden and genuine liking for Muriel O'Brien,
whose vacuous, vulgar beauty would have frightened
poor Feilden into fits. She enjoyed the mild excitement of intellectual flirtation with Mr. Feilden. She
might equally well have enjoyed a flirtation with one
of the ardent and by no means intellectual young men
who swarmed round Muriel, though her chance of that
was a thin one, since Muriel greedily snapped up every
crumb of admiration within reach of her. And though
she had never seriously imagined Mr. Feilden in the
rôle of the great lover, it gave her a pleasant sense of
bodily and spiritual warmth to remember, as she
snuggled in bed with the print of Mr. Galsworthy's
Fraternity which he had lent her blurring in front of
her eyes, that Mr. Feilden had actually gone as
far as to buy her a ticket for the Union Ball next
week. Last year, as everyone knew, he had thought

dancing beneath his dignity.

"Yes, that lovely black lace," she thought dreamily, as she turned the page, preparing to read. Perhaps Mr. Feilden's favourite author would throw light on the problem which Hollywood had failed to illumine.

A young girl's mind is like a wood in Spring, she read.

"That sounds more like it," she thought, as she blew out the candle. But it didn't somehow, she admitted, sound quite like herself.

III

At six o'clock on the following morning, the buzzer in Bulgin's Tube and Boiler Works let out a bellow like that of a monster stabbed in its sleep. It woke, if the paid knocker-up had not called them already, the two hundred odd hands for whom its summons was intended and many others, both high and lowly, for whom it was not. The buzzer did not rouse Mr. Bulgin, its owner, for he was awake already. Man and boy, as he boasted, he had risen at half-past five. Since he had lost his poor wife in the middle of the post-war boom, on the very day, in fact, when the builders had put the last course on his big new chimney-stack, he had risen earlier than ever. He liked to take a turn in the garden and look over the Alpines before the gardeners were astir. He would walk with hands clasped behind him, a Napoleon of hardware, to the top of the isolated hill on which his house was built. There was a rustic seat on the summit commanding the two branches of the Stour that joined one another at its base. In the greater of these valleys he could gloat over the acres of roof that covered his own forges, machine-shops and rolling-mills and the grid of canal-wharves and railway sidings on which they were built. If he needed a comforting contrast to this achievement in steel and concrete he could turn, without changing his seat, to the smaller, westerly valley which fringed the red roofs of Halesby, where the moribund nailworks of his school friend George Lorimer prolonged its feeble existence like that of a chronic invalid who refused to die. For years he had contemplated Lorimer's nailworks a little greedily. The site in the Dingle was convenient, compact, yet had plenty of elbow-room, the bend of the river protected it from inquisitive eyes; it was exactly suited, in short, for the secret experimental plant which he thought of erecting. This morning, however, with the soft spring air in his blood, the ideas suggested by the sight of George Lorimer's nailworks were more romantic. Walking home in the dark from the station the night before, his eyes had followed a young woman who, most surprisingly, turned out to be George's niece, Susan. Mr. Bulgin was painfully aware that, at his time of life, the best regulated eyes were apt to notice young girls with an irritable interest. Yet that interest, in Susan's case, wasn't entirely unreasonable. Mr. Bulgin was rich, and the late Mrs. Bulgin, unfortunately, had had no family. That omission, which wasn't his fault he felt sure, might easily be remedied, and there was a lot to be said for marrying a girl that you'd known from a child. Catch 'em early, the proverb said. He believed in proverbs. It was strange, he reflected, how Susan stuck in his memory. "Something fresh and vigorous about her," he told himself. "Too young? Not a bit of it! As old as your arteries," Dr. Martock had told him. "You compare yourself," he had said consolingly, only last week, "with Solomon Magnus at Mawne. Solly Magnus, I happen to know, is exactly your age; but take my word for it, you can give him a good fifteen years."

Mr. Bulgin, brooding on matrimony and poor Solly Magnus, shook his head solemnly. He had the contempt of a man who makes things for one who merely sells them. In the distance, far down the Stour valley, he could see the trees that embosomed the stucco battlements of Mawne Hall, the mansion which Magnus, his North Bromwich stockbroker, had lately bought from old Walter Willis the ironmaster . . .

At that moment, in the ascetic dressing-room that adjoined his wife's Empire bedroom, Mr. Magnus, who had been awake since four, was shaking his head over many things. First of all his own health, for, with him, not only one doctor but many had shaken their heads already. Auricular fibrillation, they said. "What's that?" he had snapped. "Is that Latin for heart-disease? How long do you give me? That's all that I want to know." But doctors weren't business men. You couldn't pin them to facts. The last and the most expensive had smiled at his question, which wasn't a smiling matter, and asked another: "Mr. Magnus, can you tell me how International Nickels will stand in twelve months' time?" My dear sir, he had answered, "International Nickels is a speculative stock." "And so is your heart, Mr. Magnus," the doctor had told him. "If you want to insure, you'd better go slow and drop the cigars." Well, he couldn't drop the cigars; that was flat. The moment he tried to ease off his temper went ragged; and as for going slow with business. . . . In the present uncertain state of the market, with the Hatry smash and Wall Street nervy as a cat, a man with a business like his had to keep his hands on the strings. Since his brother-in-law, Hugh Levison, had died, he had carried the weight of everything. People talked about taking new partners. But whom could you trust? Not even Hugh's boy, Harry, the nephew whom he had adopted as a son. It was a mistake, as he'd always said, to send Jewish boys to Harrow. What they gained in business circles by social connections they lost by picking up extravagant ideas. His aunt spoilt him too. All women spoilt him. He had a way with them. Perhaps there was safety in numbers. But while Mr. Magnus approved this in theory, in practice he dreaded the consequences: at the

best ridiculous bills from jewellers and florists, at the
worst breach-of-promise, divorce or even blackmail.
There was a fair-haired girl in the office that Harry
was taking far too much notice of. What was her
name? O'Brien. Yes, he'd see, on the quiet, that Miss
O'Brien got a week's wages and disappeared. A week's
wages? What nonsense! Much better to give her
notice. A penny saved, he thought, is a penny earned.
If he'd guessed how tight things were going to be he
would never have bought Mawne Hall. Old Walter
Willis had got the best of that bargain. Fourteen
gardeners! Think of it! And then Laura expected
him to buy her fruit in North Bromwich! Mr. Bulgin's
buzzer lifted its voice in the distance. "Thank God!
Six o'clock, and only another hour!" Mr. Magnus
thought. . . .

At Orchard Cottage, a mile away from Halesby on
the Tilton Road, the blast of the siren made Captain
Small wake with a start. He thought he had heard the
clang of the gong that signalled a gas attack and groped
for his mask, but all his fingers found was a crumpled
sheet. He shot up in bed and made a wry grimace
with his lips. They were stiff and dry, for thanks to
the whisky and the foul air in the bar of the "Lyttelton Arms" his mouth was just awful. He screwed up
his eyes and blinked at the light which split his skull
like an axe. Captain Small had slept badly ever since
the war; so badly indeed that he almost dreaded going
to bed and sat up smoking cigarettes hours after clos-

ing-time, which, of course, only made him sleep worse
—a vicious circle! It was one of the penalties, no
doubt, of living alone. When Aunt Jane was alive she
would hear him cry out in the night and come in and
shake him; but now that she was gone he had nobody
to do things like that. Well, at any rate the old lady
had left him a roof for his head, and the fact that he
need not pay rent helped out his miserable pension.

His pension. . . . There, on the mantelpiece, he
saw the buff envelope, O.H.M.S., which had commanded his presence for a medical board in North
Bromwich that morning. "So here goes," he thought
angrily, as he heaved his game leg out of bed and
limped over to the gas ring to boil himself shaving-
water. For, in spite of the scars that furrowed the
right side of his face till it looked like a contour
map of England and Wales, he made it a point of
soldierly honour to shave every morning. Then he
rinsed his awful mouth, which still tasted like nothing
on earth, lit a gasper, and hummed out of tune, between inhalations, a song that had been in vogue in
the days when he was alive. *Pack up your troubles in
your old kit bag,* he sang as he rubbed his shaving-
stick over the crevasses. *And smile, boys, smile!* he
went on. An early cuckoo answered him from the elms
outside. . . .

Susan Lorimer did not hear Mr. Bulgin's buzzer.
She slept, with her mouth firmly closed, so peacefully
that her book lay open at the page which she had been

reading within an inch of the hand that had dropped it the night before. The morning chorus of birds had not roused her, nor yet, now that those were quiet, the determined gusts of a breeze, perfumed with blossom, which puffed the lace curtains aside and brushed her lips like an inquisitive bee. By six-thirty the floor of the attic above Susan's head was beginning to creak with the weight of Mary, Aunt Edna's cook-general, determined, at all costs, to let the household know that she got up earlier than they did. For another hour this demonstration was continued on the floors below, in the rattling of fire-irons, the brushing of carpets, the slamming of doors, and in a series of shrill, one-sided conversations with the milk-boy and the cat. All these were lost upon Susan. It was twenty-five minutes to eight when an immediate hammering aroused her to see Mary standing in the doorway with the two cups of tea, one large and one small, which she was carrying to the mahogany mausoleum where Uncle George and Aunt Edna continued to lie in state.

"Yer breakfast's spoilin' on the table, Miss Susan," she said.

Indeed, by the time that Susan had finished her toilet and put on her neat college suit of blue serge, it was spoilt past redemption. She had barely time to gulp down half a cup of an inky infusion of tannin and nibble a cinder of toast before the grandfather clock in the hall, which her uncle corrected every evening by the wireless time-signal, struck eight. Then she snapped-to the bright little clasps of the shabby attaché case in which she had already bundled her book, her powder-puff, her purse, her season-ticket and a moderately clean pair of gloves, and after one brief and discouraging glance at the oval mirror in the hat-stand, stepped out into Great Cornbow.

"What a lovely morning!" she thought, as she drew in her breath.

The soft rain of the night before had washed from the sky the particles of suspended carbon which soiled Aunt Edna's clean curtains within a week and gave the Halesby air its characteristic acridity. It was sweet and limpid now as perhaps it had been in the days before the coal-measures were bared, when Halesby had been a clean little market-town and Great Cornbow a cobbled street of brand-new brick houses, with low-silled windows and semi-circular fanlights, inhabited by gentlemen in full-bottomed wigs, skirted coats and knee-breeches. Even the sordid High Street into which she turned next seemed etherealized by the same May magic. The shop-boys were whistling as they swept clean the pavements in front of their windows or set out the red and white placards of the morning papers. (*Earthquake Disaster in Japan*, Susan read; but what did that matter?) In the beery draught that ebbed out of the "Lyttelton Arms" the barman was beating a doormat. He suspended his dusty labours for a moment to give her a wink and a smile as she hurried past, and Susan smiled back at him. In front of the

Labour Exchange a group of neckerchiefed workmen lounged gossiping already in the sun, though the doors wouldn't open till nine and jobs, heaven knew, were scarce in these days. "The unemployed," Susan thought; but somehow, this morning, the word had lost its grimness. The group burst out laughing at the joke of some cheerful humorist as she scuttled by, and, turning instinctively to catch what it was all about, she saw the tall church-spire of Halesby soaring into the blue from its nest of decrepit half-timber, and the clock-face in the tower reassured her that she could catch her train after all.

As she slackened her pace she felt her cheeks flushed with hurry; the young blood tingled in her limbs. In front of her stretched the long straight road to the station, its blue-brick pavements scattered with the familiar shapes of other season-ticket holders: a number of clerks and young men vaguely "in business," who plied their trade in North Bromwich; noisy boys with satchels, shouting and throwing catches as they went; a trio of shop-assistants flashing their flesh-coloured stockings in time; (they were much better dressed than Susan, but she never spoke to them, for in the social scale of Halesby she felt herself a cut above that) a self-conscious bevy of schoolgirls, with coltish black legs and purple-pink cheeks, who smiled as she overhauled them. All these people, whatever their age or immediate destiny, seemed inspired by the magic bred of the morning air. Whiffs of shag from the pipes of passing workmen smelt like ambrosia. The very lorries that rolled by with their loads of galvanized buckets and tubes seemed bound for a fair, so gaily they clanked and swayed. Even the curdled smoke that uncoiled from the bristling stacks of Bulgin's Tube Works blew out on the high invisible wind like banners, proclaiming the triumph and splendour of harnessed energy; and there, in the pompous gateway of the works, which their owner had built to diminish his taxable profits, stood Mr. Bulgin himself. He bowed and waved to her. And Susan smiled back at him gaily. "A kind old man," she thought, remembering how, when she was a child, he had given her chocolates.

IV

"And I don't care *how* much it costs!" Susan told herself recklessly as she swerved into the station drive: for, at that moment, the vision of the black lace dress had repossessed her—so completely, indeed, that she blindly collided with someone walking in front.

"Oh, I *am* so sorry!" she gasped.

"Not at all, not at all, Miss Lorimer." Her victim looked round. She knew his face. It was that of a man of, perhaps, five-and-thirty, yet so pitifully battered and scarred on the side that he turned to her that, before she could control it, she felt her own face shrinking with horror.

Captain Small was wearing an old grey trench-coat, spotted and threadbare, each shoulder-strap pierced by three holes in which, ten years before, had been fixed three gilt stars. His figure was sturdy, but thickened by want of exercise, for he walked with difficulty, dragging the weight of his useless leg. Though Susan knew him by sight she had never spoken to him before. If Aunt Edna had been with her she would not have spoken to him now; for "The Captain," as they called him in Halesby, was not a man one *could* know. Years before, in Susan's childhood, when he had come to visit his aunt at Orchard Cottage with his spick and span gunner's uniform and his Military Cross, he had made quite a stir in Halesby; but when, after the war, he had limped back with his mutilated body and his wretched pension to make the best of the pittance his aunt had left him, the stock of heroism had slumped. All Halesby was busy making hay in the sun of the post-war boom, and unemployable heroes had become a nuisance.

Even so, as she hurried on, Susan felt ashamed—not only of the unguarded horror that her face had shown, but of the fact that she had left him toiling so grimly behind. "I ought really to have waited and spoken to him," her conscience told her. But the engine whistled impatiently, and she could not wait.

Captain Small, plodding on, watched her vanish.

The one-sided smile, which to him was not ghastly but merely friendly, still twisted his lips.

"That Lorimer girl's pretty," he told himself. "Moves like a thoroughbred. Amazing how these kids come on!"

At that moment he thought of himself as a smart young officer with shining buttons and leggings and a chest full of ribbons, whose glance could make any girl blush. "A damned pretty girl," he thought, as he threw out his chest and twirled his ragged moustache. Yet, even as he did so, the contrast between Susan's physical neatness, her young agility, and his own maimed body swept over him; and the one-sided smile, though it looked just the same, was now one of bitterness. For Susan, as he knew quite well, belonged to a generation to whom the war was just something brutal and exciting about which men wrote books and made moving pictures. The fact that he, poor Joe Small, had spent his youth, shed his blood, and shattered his nerves for her sake, simply counted for nothing. "What these young folks want," he thought fiercely, "is another war, just to bring it home to them! Then they'd know what we service-men stand for!" he thought. But doubt whispered: "Would they?" For his "binge" overnight at the "Lyttelton Arms" had somewhat unnerved him; he grew conscious, suddenly, of his whisky-blotched face and of a pulse that laboured. The world went blank.

"No, I'm finished," he thought. "I was finished ten

c

years ago. The young ones won't look at me now, and they're damn well right. No woman has any use for me unless she's paid for it. A back number. Nothing left but the booze. God damn the lot of them!" It grew blacker still as he thought of the medical board and his threatened pension. "Economy! Cutting down everything! What about the Dole?" He gritted his teeth. "I'll tell those blighters what I think of them and their cat-and-mouse game," he was telling himself at last as he reached the platform.

"Come along, sir! Get a move on!" The guard stood impatiently, his whistle to his lips.

Captain Small only glared at him; he had come to the end of his breath. As the train gave a lurch some-one opened a carriage door and he stumbled into it. It was Susan Lorimer.

They were alone in a third-class smoker. On the platform behind them Susan saw the disgruntled face of Mr. Bulgin, who had decided at the last minute to catch the train and just missed it.

"That was kind of you," Captain Small said at last, recovering his breath. He lit a gold-flake and drew the smoke into his lungs. The fingers that held the cigar-ette trembled. They were stained to the colour of mahogany. "You're George Lorimer's niece?" he en-quired. Susan nodded. "I remember you as a kid," he went on. "Now you're quite a young lady. Time slips by, doesn't it? With us chaps who got knocked out in the war it's different, somehow. We stay where

we were when it finished. I suppose you hardly remember it?"

"Very little," she told him. "I was only six
when my father was killed on the Somme."

"July the first, nineteen-sixteen. Yes, that was a
pretty bad show. I was in it myself. Got blown up
and buried."

Captain Small's ravaged face suddenly grew taut
and grim. His mind had gone back to a summer dawn,
thirteen years ago in Flanders. The battery was moving
up into action, slowly, painfully; the limbers crunched
and jolted over the pavé of villages—ghostly villages,
falling behind them one by one. Not a light in the
windows nor even a curious face; just shuttered fronts
beneath foreign signboards—*Epicerie*. *Vins et
Liqueurs*—and, here and there, bleached shreds of a
tricolour hung out in nineteen-fourteen. Those roads
of Flanders, unending ways of his dreams, down
which, night after night and league beyond league, his
spirit wandered in sleep! It returned to them now,
wideawake as he was in the third-class smoker. The
spent cigarette burned his lip. He came back with a
start.

"Mustn't talk of it now," he apologized, though he
had not been talking. "Sounds as if I was showing
off." He glanced humbly at Susan and saw in her eyes
neither the scorn nor the pity that he dreaded.

"I think you should talk of it," she said, "if it does
you good."

He stared at her in grateful surprise. "Do you know, Miss Lorimer," he said, "that you're the first person who's said anything like that in the last five years?" She shook her head, smiling. "No, no, that's a fact," he persisted. "Do you think I don't know how people in Halesby talk of me? I mean people of your kind: the working chaps in the pubs put up with me as long as I stand them drinks. But women like you! Can't I see how they look down their noses? Captain Small? they say; that waster? You can't talk with a man who's got half his face shot away and stinks of whisky and spends his time fooling with barmaids. Well, what else can I do? I've lost the only job I was ever fit for. Even if I hadn't the house and the pension I couldn't tackle another. No nerves and no brains to speak of. I've tried Pelman. Little grey books, but no little grey matter. Cut it out! Here you are, the first decent woman I've spoken to in umpteen years. And here I am, boring you stiff!" He smiled horribly as he lit a new cigarette from the stub of the last.

Susan smiled too. "You're not boring me at all," she said, "I'm terribly interested." She was going to say "and sorry for you;" but that, she knew, wouldn't do. She saw him, at that moment, not as the waster whom Halesby people avoided, nor even as the hero with a grievance whom, in moments of swaggering exaltation, he still imagined himself to be, but as a lost and bewildered child—which indeed he was—deserving of a kind of maternal solicitude. "I *must* be nice to him," she thought.

Even so, as the train pulled up at Mawne Road Halt, her mind was divided between a guilty hope that someone else might get into the carriage to break this painful intimacy, and a cowardly dread lest that some-one might recognize her and her companion.

That hope and that dread were equally disappointed. The only passengers on the platform that morning were first-class and as far removed from her station and Captain Small's as the double-six Daimler from which they had just descended. Susan knew them by sight as the latest owners of Mawne Hall. The elder of the two was Solomon Magnus, the North Bromwich stockbroker in whose office her friend Muriel worked; the younger, his nephew and reputed heir, Harry Levison.

Mr. Magnus, in spite of the morning's mildness, was wearing an overcoat and a white silk muffler which his wife had insisted on folding round his short neck at the very last moment. In his teeth, unlit, he held the cigar which his doctor had forbidden. Above the white muffler his heavy, clean-shaven face showed a coppery pallor. The station-master opened the carriage-door obsequiously as he padded toward it with the gait of a polar bear in pursuit of his centre of gravity. Every year that he lived, Mr. Magnus looked more and more oriental; but Harry Levison, bored and attentive beside him, showed no signs of his race but a smoothness and elegance of dress and person that were, perhaps, a thought unrestrained, and full lips which, even if they were Jewish, had a certain melancholy sweetness. Susan watched him curiously—she had heard about Harry Levison from Muriel—and as she did so she found herself making unconscious comparisons between him and the other men in whom she was interested—Mr. Feilden, for example, and her odd travelling companion.

Harry Levison came out of the test surprisingly well. Compared with him, Mr. Feilden, who scorned mere externals, appeared somewhat arid and moth-eaten; whatever secret flames Mr. Feilden's shy academic rigidity might repress, Mr. Magnus's nephew made no attempt to hide anything. He was clearly spontaneous and unselfconscious to a degree. "If you find me ornate and a trifle vulgar," his manner implied, "don't consider my feelings by trying to conceal your own: I don't mind what you think; you see, that's just what I am!" Beyond this, she was forced to confess, there was something in his caressing sleekness that made an immediate appeal to a sensuous strain in herself. She felt, at a glance, that this young man understood women; with him one wouldn't have to be always explaining oneself. That made things much easier. And of course, as Muriel said, he *was* so good-looking. By mere physical standards he was Mr. Feilden's better—how much more the superior of the war-worn wreck at her side!

Captain Small, apparently, thought otherwise. He

too had been watching the Magnus group, but with prejudiced eyes; and no sooner had the train restarted than he exploded.

"Doesn't it make you see red," he raged, "to watch those Yids strutting about? They're the curse of the country, worming their way into everything. That man, Magnus, has bought Mawne Hall. You mark my words, before long they'll be on the top of us, and then look out for trouble, Miss Lorimer! Remember what happened in Russia! Jews, every one!"

Susan laughed. "Mr. Magnus is by way of being a capitalist. That's why he bought Mawne Hall. You can't have it both ways, you know."

"Well, whatever they are, they're so damned un-English!" Captain Small doggedly complained. "You've only to look at them to know they wouldn't play cricket."

Susan took him literally: "Mr. Levison does play tennis for Alvaston."

He blushed, and she could have kicked herself. *He* couldn't play tennis, poor devil, with a leg like that. All the same, though she knew next to nothing of Harry Levison and cared less, this ignorant, British intolerance made her want to defend him. A man had no right to talk violently just because he'd been in the war.

"It's not parasites of that kind, anyway," Captain Small went on hotly, "who have made England what it is."

Susan did not answer. Looking out of the carriage window she saw England as it unhappily was in the desolation of the Black Country's central waste through which they were passing. Into this desert of slag and cinder, made more mournful by the smokeless stacks of water-logged coalmines and exhausted clay-pits, the spring air she had breathed at Halesby did not enter. The face of the land was scarred and ravaged beyond recall, like that of the man beside her. In a moment of revulsion she selfishly hated both of them. To escape from the necessity of looking at either, she took out her book and began, or pretended, to read.

Captain Small, quickly scenting her stiffness, crumpled up immediately. He lit his twelfth cigarette and sat mutely staring at her like a whipped dog—like a shaggy, disreputable dog, Susan thought, that nobody cared for, with his honest, injured but rather stupid eyes and his ragged moustache. What would Muriel think of *him?* she asked herself; for at that moment, the train slowed down for Winsworth, Muriel's station. The answer was so obvious that, like the coward she was, she shrank away from the window, for there was Muriel, in her insolent blonde elegance, pacing the platform. As the Magnus's carriage passed she bowed with a quick and ravishing smile. "So that's it!" Susan thought. "She's after young Harry Levison." The reflection filled her with a curious sensation of coldness, not unlike envy. Her face showed it.

Captain Small was thinking: "What the devil's the matter with the girl? I suppose I've offended her by saying what I thought of those Yids. They're probably friends of hers. Well, I give it up. Just like my luck! Another blasted washout!"

As he sat there, grimly comparing himself with the hated and despised Harry Levison, he was forced to realize for the first time in years, his own physical decadence. "No wonder she's turned me down," he thought, "this whisky's the devil! Well, I'm not finished yet. Have another jump for the water-wagon. I can do it if I try. No drinks between meals!" Then a vision of the medical board rose up like a spectre and a panic seized him lest he had left his flask behind. No, there it was, after all—thank God!—in his trousers pocket.

"Not to-day," he thought firmly. "I'll go on the wagon to-morrow."

The train slid into the sulphurous gloom of the Great Western station. He pulled himself together. With gallant agility, he hopped out first to help Susan descend.

"I hope you'll remember me if we meet again some-time, Miss Lorimer," he said humbly.

"Remember you? Of course. Why not?"

She was smiling once more, thank heaven! Captain Small gave her a military salute and limped off, with that smile for comfort, to face his board.

V

Five hours later, as the Cambridge chimes of the Art Gallery *campanile* heralded the deep boom of two o'clock, Susan stood anxiously waiting for Muriel outside Battye's confectioner's shop. Muriel was half an hour late, as usual, and, as usual, made no apology. A new fur of dubious silver fox and a bunch of Parma violets made her look like a cinema star strayed into the orbit of the dowdy women who scrambled through lunch at the marble-topped tables, and put Susan's blue tailor-made to shame.

"Let's have something light," said Susan eagerly. "I want you to help me decide on that black lace dress. You're so marvellous at things of that kind."

"There's no hurry, darling," Muriel answered lazily. "I'm terribly hungry." As they scanned the *menu* her beautiful eyes grew greedy. She chose for herself all the richest and most expensive things; cold *consommé*, a *vol-au-vent*, lobster mayonnaise, and meringues stuffed with sugary cream. Susan, eating her cress sandwiches, couldn't help wondering how Muriel kept her figure. But she did: in all her exquisite person there was not a superficial angle or curve. When she had finished, her pink tongue licked her lips like a cat's.

"You see, darling," she sighed, "we've the whole

afternoon in front of us."

"I've a lecture at half-past three," Susan anxiously reminded her.

Muriel pursed her lips as she reddened them, smiled privately to judge the effect, then buried her newly powdered nose in the bunch of violets.

"I've got a week's notice from old father Magnus this morning," she said in her slow honeyed voice. "And, naturally, I shouldn't dream of going back to the office again."

"But, Muriel—how dreadful! What will you do?"

Muriel sighed luxuriously. "Not the faintest idea. I never meet trouble half way. First of all I shall probably take a holiday. There's no hurry. And after that I suppose God will provide. He generally does." She omitted to mention that God had already provided, substantially. "Now let's go and look at that frock," she said as she preened her new fur.

Susan approached Madame Allbright's shop with some trepidation. The "Madame" intimidated her. In Halesby nobody dreamt of buying a frock ready-made: you chose a "dress-length" and had it made up from a Weldon pattern by Mrs. Bagley, the local dressmaker. The black lace evening dress which she coveted had disappeared from the window. It had probably been snapped up by somebody, Susan thought, and her heart fell.

A discreet alarm made a buzzing sound as they entered the shop. It was empty. A dense beige carpet muffled their steps, and the scanty Directoire furniture was quite Parisian. The collection of ravishing clothes with which Susan had expected her eyes to be dazzled was not in evidence. She saw nothing but a few *batik* scarves thrown negligently on a gilt settee and a number of hats posed coquettishly on tall stands, one of which Muriel, with superb unconcern, began to try on. At that moment a tall and incredibly thin young lady emerged from the curtains at the back. She wore a clinging dress of black satin and was finishing her lunch.

"Yes, Madam? Is there anything I can show you?" she said with a porcelain smile, as she swallowed the last crumb.

Susan nudged Muriel, who, still engrossed with the effect of the hat, replied by way of the mirror into which she was gazing.

"There was an evening frock in the window. Black lace. My friend wants to look at it," she said.

"A black lace?" the young lady repeated dubiously. her finger to her lips. "Oh yes, I remember. That little Chanel," she said. She pronounced this mysterious word as though it rhymed with flannel, which made Susan imagine, by analogy, that it was the name of some new material. Then she turned and dived gracefully into a hanging cupboard from which she extracted the wisp of black lace.

"Yes, isn't it a duck?" she inquired. "Just over from Paris. Madame gets them by air, you know," she confided. Then she held it up gracefully and swayed it from side to side with the flimsy skirt trailing, like a toreador exciting the charge of an invisible bull. As she did this Susan was overwhelmed once more with a desire to possess it. "But it's far too transparent," she thought: "you couldn't possibly wear that without a slip underneath."

"Yes, it isn't so bad," Muriel said without much enthusiasm. "How much is it?"

At this blunt question a flicker of shocked surprise veiled the young lady's eyes. As a matter of form she pretended to search for a ticket. "It's a Chanel, you know," she said reproachfully. "I shall have to ask Madame. But you'd like to see it on the model, wouldn't you?"

"I think, if you don't mind, I'd rather . . ." Susan began. But Muriel interrupted her. "Yes, that will be much better," she replied, and took up another hat.

"One moment," the young lady said, retreating through the curtains with the backward smile of a ballerina who has taken a "call." Susan began to wonder what on earth the model might be. She had decided that it was probably a superior version of the full-busted wicker effigy on which Mrs. Bagley, her mouth bristling with pins, arranged the queer scraps of material she cut from patterns, when the curtains parted again and the young lady appeared standing transfigured, with one arm statuesquely raised, in the black lace dress. Then, suddenly abandoning this pose, she began to swim forward, with arched back and seductive serpentine movements of the hips familiar to travellers acquainted with the *danse du ventre* but so unfamiliar to Susan as to make her blush. She swam the length of the room, then turned and swam back again; and this manœuvre, to Susan, was so acutely embarrassing that she could see nothing of the frock which was being displayed: she saw only the spindly legs and knock-knees of the tall young lady, the sallow skin that covered her bony shoulders and chest and, through the black lace, the top of her combinations and grubby mauve shoulder straps.

The whole performance struck Susan as vaguely indecent, but Muriel, apparently, found nothing unusual in it.

"Let me see what it's like," she said contemptuously. "The line isn't bad, but the lace isn't any too brilliant," she went on as she fingered it. "It might suit me quite well, but it's rather severe for you, Susan."

"Well, it's Chanel, you know," said the seductress, as though that excused everything. "I've a draped charmeuse, a Mollynoo," she suggested thoughtfully. "That's a sweet little gown."

"I might try on the lace," said Susan, who saw it slipping away from her.

"There's no hurry, darling. Let's look at something else," said Muriel decidedly.

Susan glanced at her wrist-watch and found it was

half-past three. At that moment, in the dingy theatre, a stone's throw away, Mr. Feilden had begun his lecture on the Romantic Revival. She had never in her life cut one of Mr. Feilden's lectures. He would miss her. Indeed, he had half implied that each word that fell from his lips was intended for her ears alone. And yet, she thought, if he condescended to anything so frivolous—though she could hardly believe that he did—she was only anxious, at that moment, that her dance frock should do him credit. If Muriel hadn't been there she would have taken the black lace long ago out of sheer embarrassment.

But Muriel had no intention of being hurried: she was thoroughly enjoying herself; so they settled down in the shop for another hour in which the thin young lady robed and disrobed herself, emerging from the curtains time after time and swimming to and fro in a series of frocks—she called them creations—of a variety that made Susan's head swim.

By this time, humbled by Muriel's insolent indiffer-ence to the treasures she displayed, the thin young lady began to show signs of wear. As she minced or slouched up and down, her skin grew pallid beneath the patches of colour dabbed on her chin and cheek-bones, and the model's mechanical smile was contradicted by eyes that betrayed resentment. She was no longer a superior creature, conversant with Chanels and Molly-noos, but an irritable shopgirl, anæmic from want of fresh air and adequate meals, at the mercy of an exact-

ing and wholly pitiless customer of her own sex and
class. "Poor thing," Susan thought, "if I were she I
should have lost my temper long ago." But at that
moment the shop door opened and Madame Allbright
appeared.

She was a full-busted middle-aged woman, with a
bad complexion, a strong Midland accent, and no
claims to elegance, and her canny blue eyes took in the
situation with a glance.

"The little black lace is the thing for you," she told
Susan briskly. "You'd better try it on. Of course, it's
a last year's model—it's been copied at least six times
—and that means you can have it cheap. There! What
did I say? Just the very least lift on the shoulder!
I'll put in a couple of pins and you can alter it yourself. Now you needn't be ashamed to go anywhere.
Just wrap it up, Doris. Seven guineas, please, and
mind you, don't forget it's a bargain. Good afternoon!"

As they left the shop the Art Gallery clock boomed
five. Its bronze vibrations quivered in the white May
sky and Susan's exalted spirit drifted away with them.
As they walked along Sackville Row, past the offices
of Magnus, Levison & Co., she trod on air. It meant
nothing to her that she had missed Mr. Feilden's
lecture on the Romantic Revival. In her heart, at that
moment, was an inexhaustible fountain of pure
romance. The grimy centre of North Bromwich was
an angel market inhabited by celestial beings who

moved serenely without a care in the world. The handsome policeman on point duty who waved his gloved hands on the wheel-shaved island outside the station entrance appeared to be conducting a gay symphonic *allegro*. He held up the traffic to let them pass as though they were royalty—and indeed no princess in a fairy tale was ever happier than Susan Lorimer, with that last season's wisp of black lace in the cardboard box clutched under her arm. She carried it home to the house in Great Cornbow that evening as though it had cost not seven guineas but seven hundred. "It's a Channel," she thought. "Madame gets them from Paris by air!"

VI

Mr. Magnus went back to Mawne by the same train as Susan. His day in North Bromwich, though less exciting than hers, had been equally satisfactory. To begin with, he had purged his office of the dangerous Miss O'Brien, who had saved him a full week's salary, the equivalent of a garden boy's, by not coming back. Later on, he had unloaded a speculative holding in Transvaal platinums; lunched on a baked apple; pocketed six hundred pounds over a brisk rise in Rio Tintos; smoked three of his forbidden Cabanas and felt none the worse for them, and decided, finally, that all the doctors were fools.

Captain Small was still in North Bromwich when

Susan went home. In the morning he had rigidly determined to be what he called "a good boy" and return to Halesby as soon as his board was over. The strength of this fine resolution increased with the swig of neat whisky he had surreptitiously swallowed outside the station. Unfortunately, in the waiting-room of the Ministry of Pensions, he had bumped into a man whom he had never seen before but who had served in the next brigade to his at St. Quentin—which meant that they were morally bound to have lunch together. By the time that lunch was finished they had become such old friends that it seemed hardly polite to separate. So they decided to sit and talk over the good old times and the present bad ones in the lounge of the Grand Midland Hotel until the bar opened, to have dinner together and then go on to a show. After all, he deserved it. He was going on the wagon tomorrow.

Muriel also had dinner at the Grand Midland with Harry Levison, whom she ran into, by the sheerest chance, as he was leaving the office an hour later than his uncle. She had caviare, hot lobster, *Suprême de Volaille* with *Foie Gras* in aspic, and two *Pêches Melba*. When Harry asked her if she wouldn't have a third, she said "No, thank you," demurely. Muriel rarely saw jokes, particularly jokes about food. Harry drank half a bottle of very dry Lanson, but Muriel only drank water. Captain Small, sharing a Porterhouse steak with his latest old pal, saw them dining

together. Harry Levison reminded him of Susan and
that made him furious. "Just look at that damned
Yid," he said. "They get all the peaches!" He loathed
Harry Levison because he was rich and good-looking
and hadn't been wounded in the war and was able to
play tennis for Alvaston . . .

CHAPTER II

MR. BULGIN

I

IT was doubtless the private Providence which presided over the destinies of Mr. Bulgin's Tube Works that had prevented him from romantically catching the eight-nineteen in pursuit of Susan Lorimer. Through missing Susan he caught more substantial game in the clinching of a contract for a pipe-line in Venezuela which he would probably have lost if he hadn't been on the spot. This contract would justify his hopes of announcing an interim dividend; so he returned to his usual high tea that evening in the best of spirits, not because he felt any particular tenderness for his ordinary shareholders, but because the announcement for an interim dividend would wipe the eyes of Hingston's of Wolverbury and Willis's of Mawne, two rival concerns which had each been compelled by the present bad times to pass theirs. This good stroke of business also encouraged him to embark on a pet private project which he had had in his mind for years; the erection of a new, experimental plant on

the land now occupied by George Lorimer's nailworks
and the parallel plan of marrying George Lorimer's
niece.

In old days the families of Bulgin and Lorimer had
divided the industrial dominion of Halesby between
them. Both strangers to the district, they had dug
themselves in simultaneously at the beginning of the
last century on the two best available water-power sites
adjacent to the "ten-yard" coal-seam. At first the
Bulgin firm had shot ahead easily, carried forward by
the final impulse of the Napoleonic wars. They had
hooked themselves on to the tail of the North Bromwich gun trade, rolling scrap-iron into strips that made
roughly-welded barrels ready for finishing. The
Lorimers, on the other hand, had rolled and split slats
of iron for nail-rods.

With Waterloo won, the traffic in gun-barrels languished, and the nail trade, that plodding tortoise,
forged slowly ahead. The Lorimers' works turned out
hundreds of bundles of rods every week which were
hammered into tens of thousands of horse-nails and
rose-nails and gate-nails and spikes in the cottage nail-
hearths that surrounded Halesby with a ceaseless tinkle
of anvils and sighing of bellows. All the world wanted
nails, all the world was weary of weapons, except a few
African merchants who bartered trade-guns. In the
Hungry 'Forties the Bulgin works nearly closed, while
John Lorimer cut the price paid for hand-forged nails
and built factory sheds in the Dingle to house hearths

which he rented for fourpence a week to men who had none of their own. He moved from his original cottage into the red-brick Georgian house in Great Cornbow and filled its more important rooms with brand-new massive mahogany that would last for ever and the servants' quarters with second-hand unfashionable pieces of Sheraton and Chippendale. On Sundays he drove to church with his wife and son past his rival's door in a slap-up victoria, while the Bulgins, in long procession, trudged to chapel on foot.

Next the Bulgins sprinted. It was the age of municipal water-works. A new great light had blazed out over England with the distribution of coal-gas. Isaiah Bulgin had discovered that his plant could make gas-pipes just as easily as gun-barrels. The Crimean War brought him new contracts for guns, but he still made gas-pipes, and water-pipes. He laid the foundations of the house on the hill, which for lack of imagination he named Hill House, at a time when John Lorimer, for all his victoria, was beginning to notice the competition of the new wire nails imported from Belgium. John Lorimer, though he felt the pinch, still stuck to his principles: those wire nails, if only because they were foreign, were certain to prove a failure; they could no more replace the hand-made British article than could the machine-made iron nails that came already from Germany and lost their heads when you hammered them. He stoutly refused to contemplate making wire nails; so a new firm at Warrington made its fortune with them instead of him.

What worried the pioneer far more than this competition was the fact that his water-power was becoming inadequate; yet no sooner had he decided to fit his mills with a big beam-engine than the cost of pig-iron from the local furnaces began to rise. The deposits of ore that conveniently lay alongside the "ten-yard" coal were nearing exhaustion. It soon became cheaper to import the nail-rods from Sweden ready-made; so he bowed to reason, scrapped his mills, new engine and all, and imported them. He died, obstinately, at the age of ninety, in 'sixty-eight, leaving precious little to his son, George's father, but the works, the house in Great Cornbow, and a settled conviction that the day of the hand-wrought nail would come round again.

It didn't. The Franco-Prussian War only helped to brighten things up for the nail trade; it carried the Bulgins to a new high peak of prosperity. All Europe that wasn't fighting thought it wise to buy guns. Isaiah Bulgin set up a carriage and pair. When the war is over, the Lorimers sneered, he'll be glad to sell them. But by this time the Bulgin works were so big that they couldn't stop growing; the new plant shrieked for metal to roll and tubes to be drawn, and the fortune that favours the strong immediately invented the bicycle whose frame was nothing but tubes. The Lorimers openly sniffed and in secret bought bicycle shares over which in the following slump they dropped money; for the Lorimers were far too much obsessed with their own sagacity to ask for advice. But Isaiah Bulgin, whom a Lorimer wit had called Tubal Cain, made bicycle frames—not pans—and sold them in thousands to Coventry, and then tubes for oil, and tubes for compressed air and steam, and tubes for the insulation of cables—and tubular boilers—miles upon miles of them—until the Boer War and then the Great War in Europe called for death-dealing tubes in millions, by which time poor George Lorimer's business was dead as a door-nail, and even the cheapest door-nails were made in Pittsburg, so that the works at the foot of Great Cornbow became no more than a ruin.

As he ate his meal, two boiled eggs, a slice of fried ham, and two cups of strong tea, Mr. Bulgin remembered what he had seen when, a few weeks before, he had paid a secret visit to the Dingle site. The leat which had fed the original water-mill stood dry and crumbling, like a Roman aqueduct. The steam-plant, John Lorimer's first and last concession to progress, now cluttered the grass-grown yard with a confusion of scrap-iron. In the unroofed engine-house Mr. Bulgin's hands had been stung by nettles, above which the chimney-stack, smokeless for forty years, rose dead as a Theban obelisk.

II

"We shall have to begin by clearing out all that muck," Mr. Bulgin thought as he lit his pipe and retired to the picture-gallery.

This building, conceived in the spirit of the Albert Hall, had been added to the back of the house in the eighteen-seventies by his father, Isaiah. It was a spacious apartment, ill lighted by opal skylights, which that ambitious old gentleman, following the fashion of the age, had built to house a bargain collection that he had "picked up" *en bloc* at a London auction-room. With the exception of one, the portrait of a poodle by Landseer, the pictures were all signed old masters and none of them genuine. There were landscapes of rural scenes in Italy in which peasants disported themselves under a blighted sky that seemed more appropriate to the Black Country than to the Mediterranean; there were beer-coloured Dutch interiors fogged with smoke, and a Biblical series, in which grey-bearded patriarchs with hooked noses posed sternly against a woolly background of livestock. There was also an enormous, deathly still-life, representing a carp, a swan, a brace of pheasants, a woodcock and a bunch of small songbirds on a pewter salver, attributed to a painter called Cuyp. (Mr. Bulgin had always disliked this picture because he dared not pronounce the artist's name.) He preferred the classical piece at the end of the room, unblushingly labelled Rubens, in which a swooning, corpulent Venus, swathed in yards of butter-muslin, invited the reluctant attentions of Mars in full armour. This picture, the only visible nude in Halesby, was regarded by Mr. Bulgin, who was brought up a Wesleyan, as somewhat "spicy," and gave him, whenever he surveyed its allurements, a feeling of daring enhanced by a sense of guilt. For the rest, the polished wood floor was strewn with the yellowish skins of four genuine polar bears with red glass eyes and furnished with two circular settees, of the kind called sociable, in faded magenta plush, and a grand piano that had died in its sleep for want of use.

In spite of the funerary gloom imposed by the dead piano, the four dead bears, and, apart from the strikingly life-like poodle, the rows of dead pictures, Mr. Bulgin was proud of these surroundings, and chose them, indeed, for his liveliest meditations. As he paced to and fro that evening, with his pipe in his mouth and his mind suffused by the afterglow of the Venezuelan contract, avoiding in his promenade the nobbly heads of the Arctic monsters, he began to reflect with some satisfaction on the contrast between his own fortunes and those of his friend George Lorimer.

"Poor old George!" Mr. Bulgin thought, as he stood, sucking his pipe, in front of the Landseer poodle which, now that he came to think of it, was not unlike George himself. The man had the same bright, winning alertness of eye as the dog—which didn't, of course, imply equal alertness of brain. If George had been really alert he would never have married the middle-aged Edna Timmins. "A nice-mannered white little dog," Mr. Bulgin thought, as he pictured George Lorimer's innocent, pink and white cheeks and the shiny bald scalp, with not a suspicion inside it, and the full red lips, with their innocent smile, beneath the white moustache that his wife trimmed so badly. "A lovable fellow, not a shadow of guile in his heart," Mr. Bulgin thought, "that's why everyone likes him. But you can't go on living like that in these days," Mr. Bulgin told himself, putting sentiment firmly aside and beginning to concentrate on the best means of snatching the Dingle site from under George Lorimer's nose for less than it was worth. "It's quite possible," he thought, "that George may refuse to part with his land out of pure sentimentality." Unintelligent, soft-hearted people occasionally showed an odd streak of obstinacy, and the Dingle had belonged to the Lorimers for over a century. But that was where Susan came in. If he married Susan the Dingle need never really go out of the Lorimer property. He could make the deal look like a family alliance, instead of the forced sale which it was, and save money by paying for the property in the common stock of Bulgin's, which would never again stand as high as it did to-day. If it came to the worst, he thought, he might have to be brutal and mention the mortgage on the Dingle which he had acquired, to strengthen his position, long before the idea of marrying Susan entered his head. "But it won't come to the worst," he decided. "It'll be a walk-over. My God, it's too easy—like shooting a sitting bird!"

III

With these words in his mind Mr. Bulgin became aware of the picture which he hated, to the level of which his meditative prowlings had brought him. "C.U.Y.P. . . ." he thought, though he dared not translate the letters into sound. "Now I don't mind betting that girl knows how to pronounce it. Art's part of their schooling. I daresay there's something to be said for all this education of women provided it doesn't turn their heads. My poor Laura had none to speak of, and that's a fact."

As he left Hill House on his way to Great Cornbow his mind dwelt on the contrast between his late wife and Susan.

Except in his business Mr. Bulgin had never been romantic. According to the family custom he had married young and remained faithful to his wife. This fidelity did not imply any particular virtue in Mr. Bulgin. It was the normal conduct of a well-to-do Midland *bourgeois* amid a society unmercifully interested in the private lives of its members, and in which conventional behaviour counted as a business asset. A man who ran after women—or, far worse, after one woman—was considered to have taken the first downward step toward bankruptcy—the ultimate deadly sin. One signed the marriage register as one signed a deed of partnership; one entered into matrimony with a woman as one went into business with a man, and made profits or children, as the case might be, as a matter of course.

Looking back on that early marriage in the light of his present restlessness, Mr. Bulgin was astonished to find how much he had taken it for granted. If the society of the first Mrs. Bulgin had allayed a physical need it had certainly had for him no æsthetic significance. Even by Halesby standards, which were not exacting, the late Mrs. Bulgin had never been a beauty; but even supposing she had been beautiful, Mr. Bulgin thought, it was doubtful if he would have had time—or even inclination—to notice it.

An essentially sound point of view, Mr. Bulgin considered. He had nothing to regret. At the present moment, however, circumstances altered the case. The business, whose steps he had guided like those of a lusty, wayward child, now strode out like a giant. If it crashed to-morrow, he would still be a wealthy man. In his youth he had lived for it, as the saying went, which meant, in fact, that he had not lived at all. A man who had slaved, as he had slaved, for forty years, had a right to live. In another twenty he might not even be alive.

It was difficult, he knew, to begin living all over again at fifty-seven. Still, a man might achieve rejuvenation vicariously by identifying himself, body and mind, with another body and mind that were young and vigorous. That was why he now proposed marrying Susan Lorimer.

The very idea was enough to make him feel younger than his arteries. That morning, when he had run to the station and missed Susan's train, his disappointment had quickly given place to a superb illusion of youth. It was remarkable that he, John Bulgin, the managing director of Bulgin's Tube Works, should have abandoned his office and run like a love-sick boy after a girl of twenty. Yet the very ridiculousness of the situation had given him a greater thrill than the signing of a fifty-thousand-pound contract with the Venezuelans. He would be far more ridiculous than that before he had finished!

Just exactly how, he found it hard to say. The very indefiniteness of the programme enhanced its magnificence; yet one conviction outweighed all others in Mr. Bulgin's mind. There was nothing—nothing in the world that could not be done with money; and money, which once had meant everything to him, now meant nothing. The unusual sensation of spending lavishly would be, of itself, an excitement—much more, the symbol of a complete revolt against his old nature. By the mere exertion of signing cheques he could load his new wife with jewels, buy luxurious cars, take suites in expensive hotels, move over impoverished Europe in the style of a prince, see the world and despise it. He knew politicians. He need only build and endow a hospital like old Joe Hingston. In Halesby no kind of coronet could disguise Jack Bulgin. Well, what did it matter? There were plenty of fine old houses to be bought, for the quarter of his annual income. He could choose one quite easily within motor-drive of the works, some nice, cosy, compact estate, not too large nor too small, and settle down to the job of founding a family.

A family . . . Mr. Bulgin smiled nervously. The thought of the family—not too large nor too small, like the estate—suggested to him the intimate processes by which families were founded, and that odd, voluptuous strain which, of late, had asserted itself so surprisingly, filled his mind with ideas of a kind which he had been accustomed to repress. In spite of his twenty-odd years of married life with poor Laura, he was bound to confess that, such as they were, he had made very little of his opportunities. Well, it wasn't too late, and he wouldn't make a mistake of that kind again. He would come to marriage this time with a palate more sensitive—a virgin palate, you might almost say, yet that of an epicure. All the physical experience which in youth he had been too dull or too busy to explore might now be enjoyed with a rich and leisurely savour. It pleased him to think that Susan belonged to his own class; she couldn't attempt to pretend that she was better than he was. She was modest, not a bit like those brazen pieces all powder and lipstick who gave him the glad eye whenever he went into North Bromwich. She had known and respected him for the better part of her life. She was a child—an exquisite, pliable, innocent child. Mr. Bulgin could almost have wept when he thought of her limpid virginity. "A child and a lovely woman in one," he thought, for the moment surrendering himself to the luxury of sentiment.

At this point the sight of George Lorimer's derelict nailworks recalled him to himself, reminding him of the dual nature of his errand. His business brain had resumed its customary hardness as he mounted the steps of the house in Great Cornbow and rang the bell. The master was working, the maid said; but she showed him into the front sitting-room where George Lorimer sat poring over the notes of his obituary *History of the Wrought-iron Nail-trade*. Mr. Bulgin felt thankful that Susan wasn't there, and annoyed by the fact that Mrs. Lorimer was. She rose from her knitting and welcomed him with a hostile smile.

"Well, this *is* an honour!" she said in a tone that irritated him although he agreed with her. George Lorimer also looked up from his work and smiled; but in his smile there was nothing but innocent goodwill.

"Sit down, John, sit down. You're quite a stranger," he said.

Mr. Bulgin sat down heavily. He was anxious to get to business at once, but couldn't, first of all because that damned woman refused to budge as a woman should do, and next because it was against all business etiquette in Halesby to come to the point.

"Caught any good baskets lately, George?" he

asked sympathetically; for he knew that George Lorimer's passion was fishing for slimy, inedible roach in the pools and canals near Halesby.

George Lorimer smiled. "Close season for coarse fish," he said. "Doesn't open till June the fifteenth—that's another month."

"Well, that just shows my ignorance, doesn't it?" Mr. Bulgin replied with humility. "I'm no sportsman, you know. In fact I've never had time for it."

"I wonder what he's after this time?" Mrs. Lorimer was thinking. "Lovely weather for the time of year, Mr. Bulgin, isn't it?" she said with a smirk.

"Lovely weather," Mr. Bulgin repeated without enthusiasm. Why didn't the woman grasp the fact that she wasn't wanted? She did grasp it: that was the trouble. Like an anxious hen she spread her wings to shield her chicken from the impending kestrel. As John Bulgin angrily swooped to a new point of vantage he saw on the mantelpiece a photographic enlargement of Susan's father, and the uniform suggested a tactical diversion.

"Saw that fellow Joe Small going into North Bromwich on Susan's train this morning," he said.

"Poor chap," said Lorimer. "I'm afraid he's as good as finished."

"Poor chap, indeed!" Mrs. Lorimer replied indignantly. "It's a positive scandal to Halesby, the way he goes on!"

Mr. Bulgin didn't even listen to this outburst. He

E

cleared his thoat. The conventional five minutes of small talk were over. He must come to the point.

"There's a matter of business I want to discuss with George, Mrs. Lorimer," he suggested pointedly.

Mrs. Lorimer smiled but held her ground. "That's good news," she replied.

"So I think, if you don't mind, Mrs. Lorimer, I'll say good-bye to you," Mr. Bulgin continued firmly. "We can talk it over in the drawing-room, can't we?" he said, as he tapped George's shoulder.

"There's no need for that," Mrs. Lorimer answered in a voice cold with fury. "If George wishes me to go, I'll go." George Lorimer smiled weakly. "I think, my dear . . ." he began; but she knew what he thought. With a queenly gesture she picked up her knitting and left them.

"Well, what is it now, John?" George Lorimer timidly inquired.

"There are two small matters I've had in my mind," Mr. Bulgin began. He took out his empty pipe, as his habit was, and emphasized the words that he spoke by waving the stem to and fro. "Now look here, George, you know that it's no use bluffing. The nail trade is finished. It was finished before the War. If you tell me the truth you'll admit it and say no more."

George Lorimer flushed slightly; beneath the white ragged moustache his full lips trembled. It was true, of course, but of course he wouldn't admit it. "Well, what if it is?" he inquired.

"I've just been having a friendly look over the Dingle," Mr. Bulgin said with a jerk of his pipe.

"The devil you have!" George Lorimer was growing uneasy; but he said it with such a gentle little laugh and looked at that moment so very like the white poodle that Mr. Bulgin went on:

"Last Sunday week. That's your fault. If you don't want folks to get in you should mend your railings. Now the Dingle, as you know and I know and everyone else knows, is not, in these hard times, what you'd call saleable."

"I dare say it isn't," said Lorimer quickly. "What's more, John, it isn't for sale."

"Now don't cut up rough, George," Mr. Bulgin answered soothingly. "I know you can't *say* it's for sale, because naturally you wouldn't be such a fool as to let anyone know that you wanted to rid yourself of it."

"I don't want to rid myself of it," said Lorimer bluntly.

It'll get rid of you if you don't look out, Mr. Bulgin thought grimly. He said: "Look here, George. We're old friends. Supposing I told you now that I'd heard of a customer? I imagine it's yours to sell? I mean there's no mortgage or anything?" Will he lie? Mr. Bulgin thought. George Lorimer didn't.

"I've told you it's not for sale and never will be as long as I live," he said, evading the question.

Oh, won't it? Mr. Bulgin thought angrily, that's all *you* know about it! "Look here, George," he said.

"You and I have been friends for the best part of fifty years and I'm going to be straight with you the same as I am with everyone. I repeat: the nail trade is finished; the Dingle's unsaleable; but I want it, I fancy it, what's more I'm ready to buy it, and I'll pay for my fancy— give you far more than it's worth."

George Lorimer shook his head. "Nothing doing, old fellow. We've had it a hundred years, and I'm going to stick to it. The business . . . well, that will fade out as you say. I don't mind. I've enough to live on." He blushed as he spoke. His last words, of course, were not true.

"Now, George, don't be obstinate," Mr. Bulgin proceeded tenderly, as a patient parent might coax an idiot child. "There's no reason at all why the business shouldn't drag on as long as you can make it. You're only a distributor now. All you want is a warehouse. As far as that goes, I'm prepared to buy the whole thing as a running concern, ay, lock, stock and barrel. I'll arrange to have it absorbed as a department of Bulgin's and pay you for it in shares of our ordinary stock."

George Lorimer shook his head mulishly. "No good. Nothing doing."

"Wait a moment. I know how you feel. You're saying to yourself: 'No, I'm not going to see the old Dingle go out of the family.' Well, you needn't. We'll keep it inside the family. What about that?"

George Lorimer said: "I'm sure I don't know what you mean."

"You don't know what I mean!" Mr. Bulgin echoed playfully. "You don't know what I mean? Well, I'll tell you. What I mean's Susan!"

"Susan? Susan?"

"Now don't get excited, George," Mr. Bulgin pleaded. "What I mean is this: If Susan and I got married I'd settle it on her."

"If Susan and *you* . . ." George Lorimer began, then stopped suddenly.

"Well, you've nothing against me, I hope, George," Mr. Bulgin broke in, confidently.

"You've not spoken to Susan about this?" George Lorimer spluttered. His pink and white cheeks grew red; the flush spread to his scalp; even his ragged moustache seemed to bristle. Mr. Bulgin laid a hand on his arm but the little man bounced away from him.

"Of course I've not spoken yet."

"I forbid you to speak to her." George Lorimer's voice rose to a squeak. "Do you hear? I forbid you! I've never heard anything so monstrous. To sacrifice a child like that! A man of your age! Why, you're old enough to be her grandfather. I say it's monstrous, monstrous—and you ought—you ought to know better. I tell you . . ."

"Now, George, do be reasonable."

"I refuse to be reasonable!" George Lorimer danced up and down—ridiculously for a man of his age and build, Mr. Bulgin thought—"And I tell you again," he screamed, " the idea is monstrous. You can ask her of course. Unluckily I can't stop you doing it. But not in this house—not here. Please understand that!" He snatched up Mr. Bulgin's hat and stick as if he hated them, and thrust them violently into Mr. Bulgin's unwilling hands. Then, still flaming, he swung open the door and held it wide. Mr. Bulgin went out, with a smile. There seemed to be no alternative.

As soon as he had gone, George Lorimer sat down and stared at his papers. It was the first time in years that this equable, easy-going little man had lost his temper. Even now he didn't quite know why he had lost it so wildly. It was jealousy, he supposed, just unnecessary violent jealousy. The thought of Susan in Bulgin's gross arms made him lose control. Yet Bulgin, as he realised now that the storm was over, was not a man one should quarrel with. He was ruthless and powerful; as he went his smile had been ugly. George Lorimer shook his head and ran his fingers through his white fringe of hair. When he thought of the Dingle the shadow of the mortgage fell black on him. If Bulgin knew anything about that, he might well turn nasty. Was it possible that he knew? One question he had asked half suggested it. "This would never have happened," George Lorimer thought pitifully, "if Edna hadn't left me alone with him."

In her room, three storeys above, Susan sat enraptured, with bare arms and shoulders, altering the black lace dress. She had fluttered upstairs like a jackdaw carrying some glittering treasure to his nest. Its presence transfigured not only her own warm heart but the mean little bedroom. She smiled as she sewed. She could see herself swimming forward, with the undulant, sensuous gait of the thin young lady, to the amazement of all her acquaintance at the Union Ball. There wouldn't be anything to touch it; she was quite sure of that; in fact it was almost too good for poor Mr. Feilden. She had no idea, at that moment, that neither Mr. Feilden nor the Union Ball would ever see it; that its brilliance was reserved, in fact, for another conquest. Yet she might have been warned. As she sat at the window, sewing, Susan Lorimer sneezed . . . three times.

At the moment, long after midnight, when Captain Small reached the door of Orchard Cottage, having triumphantly navigated the curves of the garden path, and full of sublime resolutions, she woke and found herself shivering.

<h2 style="text-align:center">IV</h2>

Captain Small, as he assured himself constantly, was a man of his word. When he said that he was going "on the wagon" he almost meant it. For more than a week after the day of his satisfactory Medical Board in North Bromwich he drank nothing but beer, cider and an occasional glass of port. He could hardly persuade himself that he felt any better for the change; there were moments of black emptiness when he would have given the world for a valid excuse to release himself from his rash resolve. Time hung on his hands, for he had never acquired the habit of reading, and the number of people who were willing to discuss the War with him was limited and dwindling. To steady his nerves he smoked more cigarettes than ever. Bereft of the narcotic influence of whisky he slept atrociously. People said that fresh air and strenuous physical exertion would make him sleep better; so, in spite of his useless leg, he pledged himself to take two long walks every day. He limped along the level road to the station in the morning when people were hurrying for the eight-nineteen and in the afternoon at the time when the five-thirty arrived from North Bromwich; but never, in all the next week, did he catch a single glimpse of Susan Lorimer.

For the best of reasons. Susan was safely in bed with what Dr. Martock, who hadn't got it himself, described as a trifling infection. She had lain there hopefully with aching limbs and numbed head for three days before she realized that going to the Union Ball was out of the question and that her black lace creation might just as well never have been bought. She was lonely, and bored by reading *Paradise Lost* which, however symbolical of her present state, failed to divert her. Not a soul came near except Dr. Martock, who made misplaced little jokes about germs to which she rose

with difficulty, and Mary, the cook-general, who grudgingly stumped upstairs to fling her meals at her. Uncle
George had not even dared to enter the room. Whenever he ran the risk of catching a cold, Aunt Edna
enveloped him in figurative cotton-wool and an actual
aura of eucalyptus. This protective devotion, Susan
had to admit, was the one good thing about her. Only
once, when she went calling, had Uncle George ven-
tured to steal upstairs on tiptoe and poke his pink and
white face round the corner of the doorpost with nods
and smiles and whispered condolences. Aunt Edna herself had appeared in the doctor's company twice, standing well out of range, with a handkerchief under her
nose and affronted eyes. Aunt Edna was never ill herself, and therefore regarded illness in others not as a
misfortune but as a deliberate crime against society,
atoned for by a scandalously inadequate punishment.

Yet illness had compensations. In the garden beneath Susan's high bedroom delayed spring broke into
riot. Under veils of sun-glistening rain blade and leaf
expanded; from their running green flame a smell of
growth mounted to the window like burning incense in
a myriad molecules of perfume pervading the languid
eddies of air. Lightly brushing nerve-endings as she
breathed them, their stimulus flashed into her blank
convalescent brain the hope and tenderness of a world
gay and virginal beyond words, beyond music even,
unless it were caught, once for all, in the hollow flute
of a thrush that hung on the dusk, like the ghost of a

sound, when all others were silent. That exquisite note, too pure for melancholy, released in her mind a torrent of eager desires and vague aspirations. Youth burned in her idle blood like a vestal fire, white and unquenchable. She grew suddenly hungry for life—and, perhaps, for love.

On the fourth day of her illness Mary brought up her morning mail on the breakfast tray. None of Susan's friends wrote to her at Halesby. She preferred her letters first-hand, uncensored by Aunt Edna's eyes. On the top was a picture postcard of the Grand Midland Hotel, over-scrawled on both sides by Muriel's bold round hand. Muriel never wrote letters; she scribbled all her correspondence on postcards provided by the hotels where she was taken to lunch, in odd moments when her escorts were paying their bills or getting their overcoats. When she had finished she would say, "Oh, *do* be an angel and slip this in the post for me"—which meant, of course, that they had to provide the stamps. She would have preferred to conduct all her correspondence by wire, for words were not a medium in which she expressed herself easily; but you had to know a man awfully well before you could land him with telegrams. The postcard which Susan now saw had been written on the previous day after lunch at the Grand Midland and stamped and posted by Harry Levison. It said: *Here I am again! Haven't seen you for three days. What's wrong? Am popping off to Brinton-le-Sands this day week. What*

fun! Why don't you come too? and was left, as usual,
unsigned. Aunt Edna's curiosity, Susan reflected
maliciously, must have been pricked by the lack of a
signature, though, for anybody who knew Muriel, one
was hardly needed, so expressive of that lovely, lazy,
sensuous vacuum was the round, florid script in which
it was written.

Of an opposite nature, yet equally characteristic, was
the writing—the calligraphy one might justly have
called it—of the letter beneath Muriel's postcard. Mr.
Feilden's innermost nature was manifest in the careful
characters of his address. It was minute and precise
and scholarly to the last degree, each letter the symbol
of a spirit refined and repressed to attenuation; the
Greek "e's" so perfectly formed and the words so
strictly aligned that, from the first glance, Susan knew
she could never live up to it. Not even in the letter enclosed did Mr. Feilden unbend. On the contrary, his
style was more eighteenth century than usual. He was
astonished, he wrote, that she had not been present at
his final lecture on the Romantic Revival, but the loss,
his manner implied, was hers, not his. He was equally
surprised and sorry to learn from her postcard that she
was ill and would be unable to go to the Union Ball
with him, but sorry in such an impersonal way that she
couldn't help feeling he thought she was shamming.
Between the lines he made it quite clear that the defec-
tion of a young person so completely unworthy of his
condescension did not disturb him. Just to show her

where she stood he added a brusque little postscript in which he asked her to return the lady's ticket together with the book he had lent her, very much as a Lord Chamberlain might withdraw a Royal Warrant from an unsatisfactory tradesman.

Susan blushed as she read. "He's welcome to his ticket," she thought, annoyed that she had given him the chance of asking for its return. At this moment she could have kicked herself for ever having been seriously impressed by Mr. Feilden. Each line of his letter bespoke the superior person, and she wasn't, quite frankly, and never would be a superior person herself. Mr. Feilden could never have loved her; he was in love with books and his arid literary self. She could never have loved Mr. Feilden; she was in love with life—with life rich and vulgar; life, full of laughter and vanity, and that rash, purely physical savour, transcending Art's pallid images, which mounted to her head like wine and quickened her heart on the wings of the vernal air. All that Mr. Feilden stood for, all that she had shared with him, had been sterile, cerebral, zestless, and alien to her true self. If she faced the truth she had more in common with Muriel—Muriel, frankly inferior as she was!—than with Mr. Feilden. On the whole, she confessed, she preferred inferior people, with generous human passions and human feelings. "Like poor Captain Small," she thought, as her mind was snatched back to that odd encounter. "He may be a waster," she thought, "but at any rate he's ten times more of a man than Henry Feilden." So contemptuous indeed was her revulsion from all that he stood for that before she knew what she was doing she had torn Mr. Feilden's letter to pieces. "I'll send him his damned ticket this evening," she told herself as she picked up the remaining letter. "What on earth can this be?" she thought.

It was enclosed in an oblong buff business envelope and bore a typewritten address. She immediately supposed that it must have been intended for her uncle and slipped on to her tray by mistake. But the typed address was explicit: "Miss Susan Lorimer." She opened it curiously. The enclosure was written in a bold business hand under the printed heading of *Bulgin's Tube Works, Ltd.*, and conveyed, in business-like terms, the offer of Mr. Bulgin's hand. As she read it her convalescent body went hot and cold by turns with embarrassed astonishment. She could hardly believe that she wasn't asleep and dreaming; yet the terms of the offer were as direct and precise as Mr. Bulgin's practised commercial style could make them. He began, quite bluntly, with a statement of fact: he wanted to marry her. No doubt the idea would be novel to her and, possibly, surprising. He was fifty-seven, but sound in wind and limb. The mere fact of his age would assure her that his offer was not impulsive or frivolous. He had thought it all over, and taken his time about it. His financial position, he hardly need tell her, was more than secure: he would give tangible proofs of that in a generous marriage settlement. He took it for granted that she did not love him and had, indeed, never thought of him in this connection; but as a man of experience he could assure her that this made no odds: in the majority of happy unions love came after marriage, as it undoubtedly would in this case. She must be prepared for objections on the part of her uncle, to whom he had mentioned this matter already. He advised her, as a genuine friend, to take no notice of them; in fact she would oblige him if she didn't discuss this proposal with George. He had waited so long before coming to this decision that she need not hurry to answer. She had better think it over for a week or so before she replied. He was not a poet, he added, with a touch of pride, but when he told her that he loved her he meant what he said as usual. And with kindest regards, awaiting her favourable reply, he remained her affectionate friend, Jno. Bulgin. In the left-hand bottom corner of the sheet Mr. Bulgin, out of sheer habit, had added the word "Copy."

It took Susan's breath away. Mr. Bulgin's phrasing, as dry and formal as Mr. Feilden's reproaches, seemed so incongruous with the subject that her first impulse was merely to laugh. She did laugh. This proposal, of course, was ridiculous in itself apart from the way in which Mr. Bulgin had put it. But the impulse of laughter died quickly. This letter was serious. It contained, after all, a proposal of marriage, and, however unwelcome, the first she had ever received. She felt

rather ashamed that her sense of the ludicrous had got
the better of her. On that quarto sheet Mr. Bulgin had
recorded his decision on a matter of important business,
the most important in life. In writing those words,
however surprising they might be, Mr. Bulgin had
opened his heart, and the last thing he could have suspected would be that she should find the contents of it
laughable.

Yet, however she tried to remember the gravity of
his mood, she couldn't treat it as anything but prepos-
terous. She found it impossible to detach it from the
image of Mr. Bulgin himself as she had seen him four
days before when he waved and smiled at her from the
grandiose gates of his tube-works; a stocky, thin-haired
figure with a budding paunch and a closely-clipped
iron-grey moustache revealing a mouth that even when
he smiled was hard and pugnacious. She remembered
once, when he had given her chocolates as a child, he
had kissed her by surprise; she could still recall the
rasping sensation of his grey-stubbled chin on her cheek
and the smell of his plug tobacco. If actual contact with
him had revolted her then, the idea of a similar experience now repelled her doubly. She shivered when she
thought of it. And marriage didn't end with kissing.
The idea of the sequel sickened her. She remembered
his hands—not bonily sensitive like Mr. Feilden's nor
stained mahogany with tobacco like Captain Small's, but
blunt, crude members incapable of any gentleness.

As she lay with closed eyes the thought of those

hands made her shudder.

Still, however acute her instinctive distaste might be, this letter could not be evaded. It would have to be answered seriously and on its merits. She read it again and again; and as she did so, deliberately stifling her feelings, a different image of Mr. Bulgin emerged. It was one by which Mr. Bulgin himself would hardly have been flattered: that of a rather pathetic old man, in whose age no question of arteries was involved, who had done her the highest honour he could pay to a living woman and was, no doubt, proud of the fact. At his advanced age he couldn't be suspected of not knowing his own mind. However much it disliked him, the world respected him. Even Uncle George. He had spoken to Uncle George first. How very old-fashioned! And Uncle George, apparently, had felt strongly about it. "I suppose the poor darling was jealous," she thought: and she smiled; she couldn't help loving him for being jealous.

"Poor Uncle George!" she thought. Although they had been schoolboys together he was always a little on the defensive with Mr. Bulgin. Mr. Bulgin was inclined to be patronizing because his works were so big, because he was so rich.

So rich! The idea of Mr. Bulgin's wealth had only just occurred to her, though that phrase about a generous settlement was intended to remind her of it. It would be lovely to be rich; to walk into Madame Allbright's without being intimidated or having to put up with a last year's model; to buy Channels and Mollynoos just in from Paris by air! "Why not hand him over to Muriel?" she thought. "That part of it would just about suit her."

But she couldn't see even Muriel facing the other part, or settling down to the sombre routine of life at Hill House. She remembered awed visits in her childhood to Isaiah's picture-gallery; the air of a mausoleum embalming the four dead bears, the ghostly old masters, the perpetually silent piano. That chill room, where one entered on tiptoe and spoke in whispers, had always given her the creeps. And the rest of the house was hardly less depressing, being charged with the slowly-fading atmosphere of the first Mrs. Bulgin, an unimaginative woman who had died before Susan was born. "It's just like a prison," she thought; "I should suffocate in it. I should always be longing to escape."

Could one ever escape? "In ten years," she thought, "when I'm thirty, which isn't really old, he'll be nearly seventy. He'll probably have to take cures at places like Droitwich and Harrogate. He'll go to Torquay or Bournemouth for a month or two in the winter." She could see herself walking sadly to and fro keeping pace with short invalid steps or crawling along beside a man who pushed a bath-chair; and her physical revolt against Mr. Bulgin as he was became trifling compared with her dread of what, in a few years, he would be. It brought to her mind a story in a novel she had read during her illness about two manacled convicts who had

F

escaped from the mines in Siberia—how one of them had died, and the survivor had been compelled to continue his flight still dragging his dead companion by a length of chain.

"That's just how I should be," Susan thought; and her horror of this prospect, enhanced by the rebellious zest of her convalescence, made her finally expel Mr. Bulgin's proposal from her mind. "I can deal with it later," she told herself, "when I've spoken to Uncle George. Aunt Edna, of course, would be only too glad to get rid of me. That's only another reason for saying 'No'."

v

She returned to Muriel's postcard, and with it there came to her a vision not of Torquay or Bournemouth but of Brinton-le-Sands. For more than twelve months Susan's subconscious mind had been prepared to receive this impression by the cumulative suggestions of an up-to-date publicity-agent who, having succeeded in vulgarizing a number of southern seaside resorts, had been bribed, at enormous expense, to make Brinton outdo their vulgarity. Every morning at Halesby Station and at every other stopping-place on the local line her eyes had been assaulted by a series of flaming posters that proclaimed the extraordinary fascinations of Brinton-le-Sands. *Come to Bracing Brinton,* they shouted, *on Britain's Bluest Bay.* And the posters had shown her a vast sheet of ultramarine under turquoise skies, and white gulls wheeling above a youthful female figure in a skin-tight scarlet bathing-dress whose smiling lips seemed to repeat that blatant appeal to a bronzed young man who hovered in the middle distance. *Come to Brinton for Bathing,* they yelled. And the same young lady in the same scarlet bathing-dress was displayed in a deck-chair of scarlet striped canvas, with a neglected book on her knees. At her feet, in admiring attitudes, sat the bronzed Apollo and a bright little Sealyham, as white as the wheeling gulls. *Come to Brilliant Brinton,* they whispered. The sea lay in moonlight beyond the indigo sweep of the Promenade; but lights suspended among palm-trees showed dancing in progress, and the same young people, who had exchanged their bathing-suits for "faultless evening dress," stood romantically close to each other gazing seaward. *Book the Bairns for North Bromwich on Sea,* the fourth poster said jokingly. And there, on the golden sands, sat the identical couple miraculously blessed with a bouncing family of three!

That inspired phrase, *North Bromwich on Sea,* had been the making of Brinton. It had given North Bromwich a proprietary interest in Brinton which was comparable to that of Mayfair in the Lido or Cannes, implying that all the best people went there for their holidays automatically. So persuasive, indeed, were the posters' reiterated suggestions, that when Susan heard that Muriel was actually going to Brinton she was filled with envy. The Brinton of her desire was precisely the Brinton of the posters, a place where the sun always shone, where it never rained, where one basked on the sands or was braced by ozone all day long, where the nights were so mild that one danced under fronds of palm-trees, or stood gazing over moon-lit seas, in a black lace dress, with a bronzed young man at one's side. She felt once again the convales-cent's impulse to escape, to free herself from the stale surroundings of illness, to start life anew on another, richer plane.

"Why don't you come too?" Muriel had written. Well, why on earth shouldn't she? Her amateur en-thusiasm for English literature had waned with her interest in Mr. Feilden. She had only "gone in for" it because girls of her class "went in for" those sort of things nowadays. That was one of the advantages of being ill; it gave you time to know your own mind, made you see things more clearly. She saw Mr. Feilden now with devastating clearness in the new light shed by his prim, refined little letter, and she wouldn't mind much if she never saw him again, for in any case the black lace would have been wasted on him. Yes, why shouldn't she have a good time with Muriel at Brinton? After a sharp little attack of fever like this she deserved a holiday. She could afford it; it wouldn't cost much. Indeed it would probably come cheaper for both of them if they shared a bedroom. She would write to Muriel at once and arrange to go with her. A

week from to-day! She'd be quite fit to travel by then.
"And I'll wear the black lace frock after all," she
thought.

By the time she had finished her reply to Muriel's
postcard she was quite exhausted. Such a series of excitements as that morning's post had been too much
for her. Disinclined to read she lay back in her bed
luxuriously and breathed the soft air that welled from
the silent garden. It was marvellous, she thought, to
be young, and just over influenza, and going to Brinton.
She felt rather excited now, and a little light-headed.
The least thing in the world would have made her
laugh or cry. And this odd emotional state brought
with it an intuition, persistent as it was inexplicable,
that something was going to happen. She hoped something would.

CHAPTER III

YELLOW SANDS

I

THE "Sea View" hotel was not exactly an hotel and it
had no view of the sea. Muriel O'Brien had chosen it
in preference to the admittedly smart "Brinton Palace"
on the recommendation of Harry Levison, who had
struck it a few weeks before when another girl friend
of his in the chorus of a *revue* had happened to stay
there. Brinton-le-Sands was Mr. Levison's happy
hunting ground. He could buzz down to Brinton from
North Bromwich in less than four hours on Saturday,
in the canary-coloured Bentley which his friends on
"change" had nicknamed the Yellow Peril, for a couple
of nights at the "Palace," where everyone knew him
as a dashing young man very free with his uncle's
money. It was the fact that everyone knew him at the
"Palace" which made him prefer to install his various
lady friends at the more modest "Sea View," where
nobody of his own financial standing in North Bromwich would be seen dead. If he took them to dine or
dance at the "Palace" they were less conspicuous than

76

if they had happened to be staying there and fewer questions were asked. What was more, his ally, Miss Lengel, the proprietress of the "Sea View," understood his feelings and kept a sharp, motherly eye on his lady friends when he was away.

It should not be supposed that the "Sea View" hotel was an ill-conducted establishment, or that Miss Lengel herself was anything but a mirror of propriety. On the contrary, though it drew many patrons from readers of *The Era* and *The Stage*, it was also a favourite resort of family parties and even clergymen, who enjoyed the liberal table which Miss Lengel advertised in the *North Bromwich Courier* and took no exception to Miss Lengel's liberal ideas.

"We may be Bo'emian," she declared, "but there *are* limits! I like my little bit of fun, but none of *that!* My house is Liberty Hall," she proudly maintained; but the meaning of the word liberty was sharply defined, and nobody in his senses would dream of taking one with Miss Lengel.

Miss Lengel was a "character." In her person she had the build and beam of a dreadnought, protected, from bust to hip, by an armoured belt of corsets. Her face resembled that of an Amazon figure-head, roughly hewn and considerably battered by stormy voyage, but handsome still in a bold and masculine way. Her eyes were exceedingly small and of a bright, hard ruthless blue. They stared at one from under a henna-coloured fringe detached from a mop of bobbed hair, of the same coppery hue, except at the roots which showed a modified iron-grey. Her neck was throttled to the chin by a stock whose compression might possibly account for the florid complexion to which a layer of talcum powder gave a violet tinge. From her waist, tightly girt with a belt of red patent leather, hung a very short skirt of white drill, much creased at the back. Beneath this there appeared occasionally an area of pink-stockinged thigh and knee. Out of doors she wore a straw hat, encircled, though she did not know it, by an *I Zingari* ribbon. She habitually stood with legs wide apart like a man, but this masculine pose was modified by a pair of soft, plump hands, heavily loaded with jewels which looked most improbable. Her voice, too, was low, with a mysterious, husky quality which seemed, somehow, to belong to another and more alluring body; but the loud, ringing laugh, into which she often exploded, renewed the impression of a pantomime male comedian equipped for the part of an ugly sister in *Cinderella*.

It was this apparent confusion of sex which made Miss Lengel so sympathetic with men. She preferred men to women, in fact, just because she was so entirely feminine. Men felt, from the moment they met her, that she knew what they wanted. She did. With elderly invalids she would talk by the hour of old times and old songs; she would humour their fanciful stomachs, and wrap woollen mufflers round their necks when they tottered out for a stroll on the front. With

middle-aged men she would sympathize in hushed confessions of domestic inquietude, agree with complaints
that their wives were frigid and didn't understand
them, and tactfully introduce them to lonely women
who weren't and would. With young men, whom she
liked best of all, such as Harry Levison, her attitude
was half that of a mother, half that of a procuress, and
wholly indulgent. The pleasure she found in "throwing young people together" made her equally flattering and charming at times to guests of her own sex
whom, in fact, she despised and regarded primarily as
instruments of comfort or amusement for the other.
She received their confidences and seconded their
desires with a shrewd mixture of sympathy, worldly
wisdom and tolerance that won their hearts. "People
came to 'Sea View' for a holiday," she would say.
"What they want is change. Why not? What the eye
doesn't see, my dear, the heart doesn't grieve over.
And, thank God, we're all human, I hope!"

Miss Lengel was not only human, but anxious that
her guests should share her humanity. She sat in the
centre of her hotel like a benevolent spider, extracting
vicarious romance from the finest vibrations of the
emotional gossamer that bound them to herself and
each other. If a single thread failed to vibrate she felt
something was wrong and crawled out to repair it.

That was why she was troubled, at the moment,
about Mr. Pennington. He had booked his room for a
fortnight well in advance in answer to her standing

advertisement in the *North Bromwich Courier*. He had been at "Sea View" already for three days without showing a single sign of emotional awareness, and Miss Lengel was distressed to feel that his holiday was being wasted, all the more because he was just the kind of young man she fancied. He stood nearly six foot, with the loose-limbed poise of an athlete. He spoke nicely —as far as he could ever be persuaded to speak— without any accent, and habitually wore the colours of a reputable, third-rate public school in the Midlands. He wasn't, by Lengy's standards, in the least good-looking, in the way that that naughty boy Harry Levison was. His features, in fact, were thoroughly undistinguished, surmounted by a mass of untidy light-brown hair; but his skin, as Miss Lengel noticed, was clear and fresh and liable to engaging blushes, and his teeth, when his frank smile displayed them, were regular and sound as a strong young animal's. From the moment of his arrival Miss Lengel had set him down as a potent and desirable male; yet never, so far, had she seen him address a word of his own accord to a woman.

This puzzled and annoyed Miss Lengel. It wasn't as if Dick Pennington had anything in common with those "nancy" young men whose growing numbers disgusted her in the post-war generation. His tastes were those of the normal open-air man. He bathed twice a day in the icy Brinton sea regardless of weather. He played violent tennis on the municipal courts and went for long windy rides on a motor-bicycle which, Miss Lengel regretfully noticed, was not supplied with one of those brackets designed for a female companion. When he came back to the "Sea View" at night he looked happy and burnt with fresh air; but as soon as dinner was over he retired from the family circle to a detective story, that he appeared to read rather negligently, and an enormous briar pipe which he clenched in his admirable teeth.

On the first night Miss Lengel had thought he—and she, vicariously—were in for some fun. She had purposely put him to sit by little Miss Froggat, who was dark and demure, and really quite pretty when she took off her spectacles. "That poor child," Miss Lengel thought, "deserves a morsel of fun; what's more, she won't put the wind up him." But she did. Though carefully coached beforehand, Miss Froggat, to whom Lengy had offered her new guest as a refreshing tit-bit, appeared to inspire the young man with positive terror. He had bolted to his book like a shy colt as soon as the meal was over. "What *he* wants," Miss Lengel had thought, "is someone with a touch more mustard." So she changed his seat and put him beside the "Sea View" vamp, Mrs. Everard, a provocative grass-widow with tastes that were not vegetarian and whom the waiters had been heard to describe as "pretty 'ot pastry." Mrs. Everard, as she afterwards confided, had done her damnedest, proposing a moonlight walk and a visit to the pictures. "When I touched his foot, Lengy," she complained, "that boy jumped as if I'd

stung him. You may take it from me he's no more use
to a girl than a Frigidaire. He'll probably write home
and complain to mother about it," she said as she
freshened her moist lips to the hue of a fly-eating
sundew.

As a matter of personal honour Miss Lengel declined to accept a defeat. She tackled Dick Pennington
herself as man to man, and found him, on neutral
ground so to speak, completely natural and even forth-
coming. He was, it appeared, the son of a country
parson—"Well, that's a good start," she thought—but
both his parents were dead. He was a clerk in a
merchant's office in North Bromwich and hoped, in
good time, to work his way up in the business. He lived
in cheap lodgings in Elm Road, Winsworth, a dreary
suburb. He was keen on all games; played hockey in
the winter and cricket in summer; he liked walking and
birds and fast-riding, and wished he could afford to
fly; he didn't like films or theatres, because they were
stuffy and expensive, and rarely read a book unless he
was bored. When he spoke about things he cared for
he became almost handsome, which seemed to Miss
Lengel a criminal waste of good material.

"You're not much of a lady's man, are you?" she
asked him teasingly. "A boy like you could have any
amount of fun. You don't know your luck."

At this Mr. Pennington smiled and blushed quite
charmingly.

"Well, you know," he said, with a serious, engaging

innocence, "I can't possibly afford to marry as things are now."

"Oh, I didn't mean *that!*" said Lengy with her loud, ringing laugh.

"And I'm horribly shy," he confessed, "in any case."

"Well, the sooner you stop it, my child, the better for everybody. It's not natural, what's more it's not 'uman!" Miss Lengel told him. "You just wait a bit. *I'll* find you a nice girl-friend by the end of the week. A good-looking boy like you! *I* call it a crime!"

"You ought to have gone more gently," she told Mrs. Everard afterwards. "He's all right! Wait and see!"

"Yes, you'll wait a long time," Mrs. Everard answered scornfully. "I know that kind when I see them."

"Oh, go on! He's only a boy," Miss Lengel replied. She went away chuckling obscenely in luxurious anticipation.

II

When Muriel O'Brien invited Susan to go with her to Brinton-le-Sands she hadn't really meant it. The words were just as much a matter of form as the rest of her postcard. But when Susan wrote back enthusiastically to say that she was coming, Muriel didn't discourage her. She never discouraged anybody who might conceivably be useful.

There was nothing sentimental about Muriel. She knew to the fraction of a farthing the value of everything, her own integrity included. Though a number of young and elderly men had contributed to her appetite and her personal vanity, she was still what people in Winsworth called "a good girl," being able to mop up everything, like a hygroscopic salt, but never disintegrating, like most hygroscopic salts, in the process. At the moment, she had decided—though he little suspected it—to marry Mr. Henry Levison. That was why she had promised to meet him at Brinton-le-Sands; and that, when she came to think of it, was where Susan came in.

She liked Susan, partly because she liked everyone who admired her and partly because Susan was so entirely unlike herself. Susan was modest, and a lady, and cultured; Muriel could pretend to none of these qualities. Susan was dark and vivacious—a perfect physical and mental foil to her own passive blondness, and not at all likely to queer her pitch. Susan would share her bedroom at Brinton—to say nothing of the cost of it—and thereby constitute an economy, an unimpeachable chaperon, and a stimulus for bringing Harry Levison up to the scratch. Susan's presence or absence could be used, as occasion prompted, for keeping Mr. Levison off or drawing him on. Even so, she had no intention of travelling to Brinton with Susan in a third-class railway carriage. It would be cheaper for her and far more comfortable to let Harry drive her down after a choice little lunch at her favourite "Grand Midland." The fact that she was expensive would make him appreciate her more. So she dropped Susan a line on a postcard to say she would meet her at dinner, and Susan travelled alone.

When she finally took her seat in the corner of the through-coach to Brinton she could hardly believe it was true. The last week of her convalescence at Halesby had had the same unreal quality, coloured as it was by her own weakness and the subdued yet ever-present excitement of the approaching journey. To begin with, she had felt herself bound to deal with Mr. Bulgin's proposal. She had talked it over, contrary to Mr. Bulgin's advice, with her Uncle George, not at Great Cornbow, where Aunt Edna's ears were always jealously pricked to overhear their confidences, but in his seedy office at the nailworks, where she went on the pretence of taking a walk, and found him engrossed in the untangling of his fishing-tackle. When she handed him Mr. Bulgin's letter he had shown extreme embarrassment. His pink cheeks had gone crimson; his eyes swam with sudden tears. "I was afraid this was coming," he wailed as he shook his bald head from side to side.

"I want you to help me to answer it, darling," she told him. "Of course it's impossible."

When she said this the tears brimmed over, but his face glowed with joy.

"Thank God for that, Susie!" he said. "Thank God

for that! I couldn't have borne it."

So they sat down side by side at the roll-top desk littered with casts, floats and fishing-hooks and, between them, composed Mr. Bulgin's momentous answer. "You needn't offend him, you know," Uncle George insisted. "John Bulgin's a very strange man and he might turn nasty. You never know."

"But he can't do *me* any harm," Susan said.

"No, no, you're quite right," Uncle George hurriedly assured her. "He's a very queer man, all the same," he added pitifully.

"Do you mean he can hurt *you?*" she asked. "If I thought for a moment . . ."

"No, no, my dear child, don't consider it," Uncle George answered bravely. "Do you think I'm afraid of him? Let him do what he likes! I don't care! As long as you're happy there's nothing that matters in the least."

He stood gazing at her with his little eyes red and a tremulous smile on the full lips beneath his ragged moustache. He kissed her, and she knew that this odd little man, so innocent and full of goodness—there was no other word for it—was the person she loved most of all in the living world. She felt it even more when she compared him with Mr. Bulgin, on whom his half-spoken fears had cast a sinister light. It was incredible that even he could dream of being unkind to Uncle George.

When the letter was finished she felt so tenderly

toward him in his pathetic shabbiness that she could hardly bring herself to face the second part of her errand, which was to ask him for an advance of money to pay the expenses of her holiday. The fact that the money was really her own made no difference. It seemed to her almost like holding-up a child with a loaded revolver.

Nor was the figure fantastic. When she casually spoke of her needs he gave a visible jump, and his cheeks flushed again as if her request had surprised some guilty secret—which, of course, was entirely ridiculous. "Ten pounds will be plenty," she added hurriedly, though she had meant to ask for fifteen.

"Ten pounds?" he repeated. "Of course. Are you sure that will be quite enough?"

He unlocked a drawer in the roll-top desk and took out the key of the safe, an enormous armoured affair that had been built into the wall in those ample days when the Lorimers' business had flourished. As a child she had always been impressed by the idea of the wealth it contained; but now, as he opened it, she saw nothing but bundles of dusty documents and worm-eaten ledgers which, ages ago, had meant business. As she peered over his shoulder Susan saw that his neck was flushed; his plump hands trembled as they opened a drawer inside—a drawer that was almost empty, from which he extracted a thin wad of notes and slowly counted out ten, one by one. Of course, in these days, she told herself, people didn't use safes to

G

keep money in; when they wanted cash they drew a cheque on the bank. But the sight of this meagre store, like a squirrel's hoard, in that vast, rusty emptiness, made her so ashamed of her own careless extravagance in going to Brinton—when Uncle George, as she knew, hadn't taken a holiday for years—that she could almost have burst into tears and begged him to take the notes back and lock them in again. But by this time, whatever might have disturbed him, Uncle George was his smiling self.

"You'd better count them," he said. "Mistakes will happen, you know, in the best regulated families."

She smiled as she told him not to be foolish, but still she could only see him as a poor little grey round-shouldered squirrel robbed of its hoard.

"There, now you'll be happy, Susie," he said with a sigh. The door of the safe sighed too as he closed it. When he had locked it he turned suddenly and took her in his arms and kissed her. She felt proudly certain that he didn't kiss Aunt Edna like that. But you never knew. Marriage was a mysterious state. However deeply you loved people you couldn't see into their hearts.

"Yes, I *am* happy now; he was right," she thought, as the Brinton train slid out of North Bromwich station. All the hallucinated atmosphere of her illness, of that strange interview with its odd sense of something concealed or unspoken on his part, of Mr. Bulgin's surprising letter, of her break with Mr. Feilden, seemed now to belong to some other person in another life. She was not only alone in the compartment but, somehow, alone in the world—in a new world, full of incalculable possibilities, into which this romantic coach was swiftly transporting her. "I suppose I'm really just the same," she told herself; but, not being quite sure, though deeply interested in the problem, she rose and stood weakly gazing at a mirror on the opposite wall as the carriage swayed and jolted.

And indeed, when Susan came to consider herself, she seemed to have changed. Her face was pale; it had lost with its colour a little of its natural pertness; it looked, she decided, not nearly so healthy but much more interesting. Her eyes, too, were less bright, but bigger and softer. What they had lost in sparkle they had certainly gained in pathos. Her thinness had made her whole face look longer, which was what she had always wanted, and her mouth made a solemn line, to which, in vain, she had been aspiring for years. Having been cast by nature in the mould of a brisk and jolly soubrette, Susan naturally dramatized herself in languid and tragic rôles. The present effect satisfactorily reminded her (unless the mirror were at fault) of a number of heroines in novels of a type whom she greatly admired—of women who had erred impulsively and suffered and emerged the sweeter for it, but a little sad. At the moment, with her hat off, she looked just like the *Dame aux Camellias*.

Yes, no doubt her appearance had changed. She

looked older and more mysterious. It seemed almost as though the receipt and rejection of Mr. Bulgin's proposal had added to her dignity. She noted, with satisfaction, that her pallor would set off the black lace dress.

That virgin miracle lay folded with the utmost care in the fibre suitcase, made to look just like leather, that a porter had hoisted on to the luggage-rack above her head. She now saw, as she looked at it fondly, the label which Uncle George had written for her in his book-keeping copper-plate. *Miss S. Lorimer,* she read, *Passenger to Brinton-le-Sands.*

"To Brinton-le-Sands!" she thought. "Yes, I'm actually going there!"

As the express gathered speed and went hurtling through local stations with a contemptuous snarl, she saw, on the platforms, momentary shapes of less fortunate people who stood idly gazing, as she herself had gazed so often, at the coloured posters inviting them to visit Brinton.

"But they'll only go on dreaming about it," she thought pityingly, "while I shall actually be there in four hours' time."

And she saw that wide bow of ultramarine, the white gull wheeling, and herself, much taller and slenderer than ever before, in the scarlet bathing-dress which she would certainly have to buy.

At Brinton, no doubt, the perpetual sun was shining. All over the Midlands, however, it had begun to rain.

Harry Levison, much against his will, had just been compelled to jump out of the yellow Bentley and put up the hood for the sake of Muriel's perishable hat and complexion. He was not in the best of humours. Only that morning he had had an unpleasant talk with Mr. Magnus about his small overdraft. He hated pulling up on the road in any case; for he had meant to do the run down to Brinton in record time without stopping for tea. The same storm, as Susan saw it, moved blackly eastward, diagonally cutting the sky into cubes and triangles behind Staffordshire smoke-stacks. After Crewe it enveloped her, splashing the carriage window panes with a sooty compost of rain and engine-smoke, which blurred her view of the trim, red-brick suburbs of Wigan. At Preston a ticket-collector suddenly woke her. He said "Brinton-le-Sands? No change, miss," with a friendly smile.

"Yes, Brinton-le-Sands," she repeated with conscious pride.

And there, of a sudden, came the sea—or rather, the sand: or both, for you couldn't be certain where sand ended and sea began, so subtly were both of them blended in levels of delicate light. At a distance sky, sea and sand seemed compact of the same unsubstantial stuff. "Like a pastel," she thought; but their hues were too translucent for pastel or even for water-colour. It was as though a master had dipped his brush in a wash of moist air, in vapour rather than water. But the foreground was virgin sand, incredibly smoothed by a tide so tired and languid that it left no trace behind but a wavering fringe of weed and sponges and driftwood, so that where the twin tracks of a cart or of sunk human footsteps were seen, they gave a sense of the intrusion of something brutal. From time to time the train crossed tidal channels where fresh water ebbed slowly to lose itself in the sand or the salt. They went coiling away into the distance like sleepy, silvery snakes that had swarmed down to drink; on their shining banks sat vast congregations of sea-fowl with all their heads turned one way, so intent on their mysterious life that they took no heed of the train thundering past over bridges and culverts.

The sea didn't, of course, resemble the halcyon sea that the posters had promised her. Its surface was silken and grey and pearly, like the bloom on the wings of a moth; but the very emptiness of those expanses of light, swimming over the edge of the world on one side and bounded on the other by the sun-smitten crescent of stucco lodging-houses that was Brinton, a thin line dividing the immensities of sea and sky, was enough to give Susan's adventurous spirit wings. She threw open the carriage window and put out her head. The wind that rushed through her hair smelt not only of smoke, but of rotting sea-weed. *"Come to bracing Brinton!"* she thought ecstatically. "Why, you can actually smell the ozone!"

An extension of this exalted mood possessed her as she descended from the train. At that time of the year the Brinton season had hardly begun, and the platform was drowsily emerging from its long hibernation. Outside stood a number of dejected hotel omnibuses and two sleepy four-wheelers, but the gasworks and red-brick villas overlooking the station yard seemed not very different from those which she knew at Halesby. But the streets through which her cab passed on her way to the Grand Parade were lined with small shops offering for sale the rubbish which trippers buy on their holidays: spades and buckets and seaweed—barometers and guide-books and diminutive shrimping nets and shilling novels and heraldic porcelain, and mugs with a blurred imprint of the Pier Pavilion and the legend *A Present from Brinton* on them in gold lettering; and Susan, seeing this trash, experienced the authentic thrill of a trip to the seaside.

She felt somewhat disappointed, it is true, when the cabman, after crawling the length of the Grand Parade, turned away from the view of the sea into the street where the "Sea View" hotel was situated; but the "Sea View" hotel itself wore a holiday air, with open bay-windows from which a contortionist might catch a glimpse of the sea and the garden railings and balconies in front festooned with gritty towels and bathing-dresses. It gave her the right marine atmosphere too to feel under her feet on the front-door steps the scrunch of fine sand. And Miss Lengel, who welcomed her, fantastic as she was, seemed a friendly person.

"No, your friend hasn't turned up yet," she said,

"but that makes no odds. You just go to your room, dear, and have a nice wash and tidy your hair and come down to tea when you hear the bell. We don't stand on ceremony here. We're all pals together, as the song says. So you needn't be shy even if your friend hasn't come."

As she closed Susan's door behind her Miss Lengel stood thinking.

"I've got it! The very thing!" Miss Lengel thought.

III

Dick Pennington whizzed home on his motor-bicycle late that evening. He had spent the afternoon lying and scorching the skin off his nose in the heather on the top of the fells and had had words with a gamekeeper who cursed him for disturbing young grouse, which made him decide to vote Labour next time, in spite of his Tory traditions. Dropping down from the hills he had seen the same watery transfiguration of sea and sand as Susan, and rejoiced to think that the weather was picking up at last; for his holiday, so far, had been, literally, rather a washout. He, too, had been tricked into coming to Brinton by those romantic posters, and found it an empty, lonely, "dud" sort of place; but not being a grouser by nature, he had made the best of it. This evening, for once, the tide was high; the dun waves actually beat on the base of the promenade. So he propped up his motor-bike at the kerb in front of the "Sea View" hotel and rushed breathlessly upstairs to get his towel and bathing-dress.

On the landing he collided in his hurry with a strange young woman, a dark, slender girl with a pale face and big eyes. He said: "Oh, I beg your pardon!" and she: "I'm sorry: it's my fault." And then, for no reason, they stood smiling at each other and both of them blushed. "I'm just dashing off for a bathe," he explained quite unnecessarily. She said: "How lovely! I hope you'll enjoy it"—and that was all. He went flying downstairs, for he hadn't much time to spare, to find the garden path blocked by two other new arrivals; a dapper young man with an Harrovian tie, who appeared to be in a hurry, and a dazzlingly pretty fair girl who wasn't in the least. At the kerb, impeded by his own motor-bicycle, stood a canary-coloured Bentley. When Dick Pennington moved aside to let them pass the second pretty girl smiled and said "Good evening," as if she knew him.

"Now who the devil is *she?*" he thought, breaking into a double with his towel draped round his neck. That face was familiar somehow, but he couldn't just place it. One kind of make-up was much like another to him. As a matter of fact he never took much notice of blondes; they weren't his type; he preferred 'em dark, like the first girl he'd met on the landing. He was swimming on his back with the setting sun in his eyes when Muriel's identity dawned on him. She lived, he remembered, at number fifteen Elm Road, a few doors away from his own lodgings in Winsworth. Her parents were the woman who always sat in the window like a fat black cat, and that handsome, seedy, theatrical-looking Irishman whom he had often seen coming out of the pub at the corner. Yes, he had passed her a hundred times on his way to business, though she wasn't the kind he would ever have dared to speak to. Now what was she doing at Brinton, he wondered, in a yellow Bentley? No good, he'd be bound! A car like that didn't exactly fit in with the "Sea View" hotel, much less with fifteen Elm Road!

Having pickled in brine the nose which the sun had already scarified, he doubled back to the hotel with a tearing appetite and changed for dinner. He put on a blue serge suit and his old Brunstonian tie, and plastered down his hair with a brush dipped in water. The unusual smartness of his appearance this evening matched his oddly high spirits. He wondered if the girl he had spoken to on the landing would be downstairs.

At the dining-room door Miss Lengel stood with her legs wide apart and her hard blue eyes on the waiters serving the soup. She smiled at Dick Pennington: "Hurry up, young man, you're late. I've put someone else in your seat, by the way," she whispered. "Go over there in the corner, at the little table along with those two young ladies." He said, "Thank you, Miss Lengel," and moved forward through a clatter of soup-spoons. At the corner table sat not only the girl of the landing, but the formidable Miss O'Brien—he had got the name now—from Elm Road. They were both very elaborately dressed by "Sea View" standards; the fair one in white satin and the dark one in diaphanous black lace. Their elegance was so forbidding that, at the last moment, Dick's courage failed him. So, before he reached them, disregarding Miss Lengel's violent signals of disapproval, he shied and slipped into a vacant chair at another table, and began to talk fluently, to hide his confusion, with the astonished Miss Froggat, who thought he must have been drinking and edged away from him.

Muriel's eyes, which missed nothing, had seen this little comedy and hardened with disappointment. "What a let-off!" she whispered to Susan. "I thought we were going to be landed with that dreadful young man!"

"How do you know he's dreadful?" Susan said. "He looks rather nice."

"My dear! You can see he's a bounder at a glance. As a matter of fact I know him by sight. He lives a few doors away from us in Elm Road."

"What is he?" Susan asked.

"Oh, a clerk or something, I suppose," Muriel answered contemptuously. "Nothing that matters, anyway. You're bound to get all kinds of queer people in a place like this."

That, in point of fact, was exactly what Dick Pennington was thinking. It was a shame for that nice dark girl, so modest and delicate, to be forced to sit next to that painted O'Brien creature who, instinctive wisdom told him, was no fit company for her. He began to wish that he had had the courage to butt in, if only to protect her. "A nice girl like that, all alone! It's a damned shame," he thought. "After dinner," he decided, "I'll go and talk to her; that meeting on the landing is as good as an introduction."

"How red your nose is, Mr. Pennington," Miss Froggat remarked reproachfully. It was red, she thought, with the drink that made him so unusually talkative.

"It's burnt with the sun and the air, I suppose," Dick Pennington replied; but his blush confirmed her suspicions. Till that moment he had actually been rather proud of his sunburn; it was the hallmark of a holiday-maker's emancipation; he had hoped that his office pals in North Bromwich would notice it when he returned; but now, in view of his possible interview with Susan, it had become a blemish. He took a sly, sideways glance at her; she was talking eagerly with Muriel; a quick flush of excitement coloured her cheeks, and the hair that curled at the nape of her neck was adorable. "My God, how pretty she is!" he thought. And at that moment another wild thought rushed into his mind: "That's the girl I'm going to marry!"

"You should wear a hat, you know," Miss Froggat advised him. "No need to waste money on a reel

Panama," she said. "You can get a white linen one for two shillings or two and threepence in that shop at the corner."

She stopped, for she saw that he wasn't listening. How rude! Now she knew for certain he must be intoxicated. And he was. At that moment his brain was drunk and reeling with the sweet poison of that unwilled, undreamed-of idea. "I'm in love," he thought, and all his surroundings, Miss Froggat included, dissolved in a rosy mist, for he had never spoken such words to himself before. It was Miss Froggat's frigid, affronted eyes, staring stonily forward through her *pince-nez*, that brought him back to his senses.

"I'm terribly sorry," he stammered, "I got lost for a moment."

"It was really of no consequence, Mr. Pennington," she answered coldly. "Drunk! Brutally drunk! What beasts men are!" Miss Froggat was thinking.

After dinner Dick ran upstairs to tidy his hair again, and see, in the glass, if his nose was as red as she had said. When he returned to the drawing-room his breath came short and his limbs were tremulous.

For one dreadful moment he thought that she wasn't there. It was possible, though surely improbable, that she might only have called in for dinner. Then he saw them both through the leaves of a specimen aspidistra. He had imagined that they had been sitting at the table together by chance; but now they were talking like old friends, and Dick Pennington became half jealous and half scandalized to see her still with Muriel, for he couldn't believe that she was that sort of girl. If she *were* that sort of girl, of course, it would be ten times as easy to make love to her; she would almost expect it, in which case he would lose all interest, or ought to, anyway, because he had high ideals in matters of that kind. Perhaps, on the other hand, she was only being polite, and Muriel wouldn't stay long with her. So he slunk round the room in an odd, restless manner, picking up old magazines and looking at them and putting them down again and taking occasional furtive squints at himself in various mirrors, until Miss Froggat, who was watching him, became more than ever convinced that he was suffering from alcoholic aberration, and felt that she really ought to warn Miss Lengel.

At that moment Harry Levison dashed in. He was in evening dress, and made straight for the table where Muriel and Susan were sitting. "Well, that's torn it!" Dick thought, for, although he had already once seen Harry in Muriel's company, he couldn't believe that anyone looking at the two girls together could help being more attracted by Susan. In his sporting tweeds Harry Levison had seemed quite a decent fellow. Evening dress, on the other hand, brought out the physical worst of him; he was just a trifle too handsomely sure of himself; his shirt-studs and cuff-links were too shiny; his butterfly tie too big and his waistcoat cut too smartly. There was a moment of dread when he stooped—"Like a blooming foreigner," Dick thought—over Susan's hand. Then, confirming Dick's deep conviction of his lack of taste, he nodded casually to Susan and swept Muriel away with him. "I'll try not to wake you when I come in, darling," Muriel said.

This smile of fortune nearly robbed Dick Pennington of his senses. His first instinct was to flee; but something stronger than instinct drove him forward and plumped him down on the chair that Muriel had vacated.

"Do you mind if I sit here?" he said.

"Of course not," Susan replied. "Did you have a nice bathe?"

She had actually recognized him!

"Oh, the bathing's not terribly good here," he explained. "You see, unless it's high tide you've got to walk miles to get to the sea. I suppose you've been here before?"

She hadn't. It was her first evening. And that gave him the opportunity of hiding what he really felt under a spate of commonplace information about Brinton. The concert-parties at the Pier Pavilion were pretty good. (Her eyes in this light looked almost more grey than brown!) By taking a twopenny tram ticket you could ride all the way to St. Bride's. (How demure she looked with that firm little wrinkling of the brows!) Oh no, there was nothing particular to see there; you just took another twopenny ticket and came back again. (They were blue, after all! God! what a delicious mouth!) He didn't know much about dance bands; they weren't in his line. (Now why *did* I say that? I could easily have taken some lessons!) As a matter of fact, he confessed his game was Rugger— yes, the one with the oval ball; the other was quite different. (The ring, thank heaven, wasn't on her engagement finger!) Well, soccer was professional, you see; and Brunstone—he fingered his tie self-consciously—was a Rugger school.

She was thinking: "What a dreadful mess the poor lamb's made of his nose. It just shows how extraordinarily unselfconscious men are. I should like to give him some face cream; when it peels it'll be even worse. But he has quite a nice skin," she thought, "and nice eyes and awfully nice teeth. He speaks nicely, too: he must be a public school man; but how shy he is! He doesn't even know what to do with his hands!"

At that moment, indeed, Dick Pennington had furtively taken out his pipe with his right hand and was polishing the bowl of it in the palm of the left.

"If you want to smoke," Susan said, "please don't mind me."

"Thanks so much," he said gratefully. "I'm afraid I can't offer you a cigarette. . . . Unfortunately . . ."

"I don't smoke," said Susan, although she did.

"I say, I think that's perfectly splendid of you," he said. "The girls you meet nowadays . . ."

"Oh, it isn't *that*," Susan told him. "It makes me cough. No, your smoke won't, I promise you. I like the smell of it, really. Yes, quite sure. But if Brinton's so dull," she went on, "what on earth do you do with yourself? I suppose you must read quite a lot?"

Now, she thought, I can show him how truly cultured I am. But the question, which might have put him to shame, did nothing of the sort. "Read?" he laughed. "Well, of course, I sometimes pick up a detective story. I like travel books, too. But books generally don't mean much to me. You see, I'm not that sort of chap. And as for novels—all this modern stuff about sex. . . . You can't tell me, honestly, you like it?"

Susan hedged a little. That depended, she said, on how they were written. His nice simple eyes held hers. It was flattering to think how much he respected her opinion. "The story's not everything," she explained. "You see, there are things like atmosphere and style and poetry."

"Now there you've got me!" he laughed. "I'm afraid I'm not much of a poet."

Just like Mr. Bulgin, she thought, but otherwise, how different! And how very different from Mr. Feilden, too!

"You see," he went on, excusing himself, "I'm mad on open-air things. I was born in the country. My pater was a parson in Shropshire."

"In Shropshire?" she repeated. "How funny! Why, my mother came from there too."

"That explains why I wanted to speak to you the

H

moment I saw you," Dick managed to say.

"Well, you did—the very first instant—after nearly knocking me down. But do tell me what part of Shropshire. My mother was born at a place called Lesswardine."

"At Lesswardine? Lesswardine?" he cried. And the whole man glowed. He was no longer awkward or apologetic or even commonplace. A beautiful enthusiasm for simple things which he loved transfigured him; he seemed to shake the dust of the workaday world from his feet as he spoke, and the valley of Teme, as he remembered it now, shone through his lame words with a tender, mystical radiance. Not a pool that he didn't know, not a rabbit-hole he'd not had his arm down! And the timbered farms and the golden-green Tenbury cider! And shaggy otter-hounds crashing under red cliffs! And church bells on a Sunday evening, and the sound of bubbling water! "For the sea, you know, isn't water," he said—profoundly, she thought.

As he spoke with this lyrical passion he seemed to Susan to make life sound so sweet and sane, so much nearer to its holy source than it had ever appeared to her before; till, the rhapsody suddenly ceasing, he burst out again: "What on earth are you and I doing in a rotten little hole like Brinton—a made-up place that's been stuck down on the sands without any real reason—when for half the money we might be on a farm in Shropshire? We've come here because we're just like a lot of sheep, because we've been told to; that's the honest truth! But, do you know, you're the first person who's ever made me see it? And I don't even know your name!"

It was Susan Lorimer, she told him.

"Susan Lorimer. What a pretty name! Mine's Dick Pennington," he said.

"It suits you, I think."

He laughed. "That's what I meant about yours— when I said it was pretty, I mean. But, you know, in a place like this we're just wasting our holiday," he went on seriously. "The hills inland from here are fine wild country—the fells they call them. You can breathe decent air up there, though the heather's not out yet. There are heaps of buzzards, and I heard a curlew to-day."

"I've never heard a curlew," she said, "though, of course, I've read about them."

"It's a topping sound, quite different from these screeching gulls. Look here, Miss Lorimer, I'm going to ask you something. If you hate the idea I shall quite understand. Of course, you don't know me. I've a motor-bike here. Will you come for a ride to-morrow, right up in the fells? I'll promise you shall hear a curlew for the first time."

"Why, I'd simply love to," she said. "I'm afraid I'll fall off, though."

"Oh, don't worry about that," he replied. "I'll be as careful with you——" He hesitated, then added lamely—"as if you were my sister! Shall we say eleven o'clock?"

When Muriel came home yawning from the Brinton Palace at one, she found Susan safely in bed, but still awake. Miss O'Brien was not in the best of tempers, for Harry had not suggested their having supper, and a girl at the next table was eating oysters, for which she had a passion. In spite of this she felt it incumbent on her to apologize to Susan for leaving her.

"I'm afraid you won't see much of me during the next few days," she said. "You see, Harry only stays till Tuesday, and he'll expect me to go with him everywhere. I'm afraid you'll be lonely. As far as I can see, there's not a soul here you can talk to."

"Oh, you needn't bother your head about me. I shall be all right," Susan told her.

But she was careful not to mention why she would be all right. She remembered the contempt with which Muriel had spoken of her new friend. She wasn't exactly ashamed of him, and yet, and yet. . . . It was much more exciting, anyway, to keep him a secret.

CHAPTER IV

LIVING DANGEROUSLY

I

DICK PENNINGTON was over the sky when he woke about daybreak next morning. He jumped out of bed and leant through the window looking into the empty street. The pavements were dry, he saw, and a faint haze presaged a brilliant day. "I love Susan Lorimer," he thought, "and I'm going to marry her. She's not only lovely; the strange thing is that she understands everything. How splendid life is!" He could hardly contain himself until it grew light enough for him to get up and bathe. The image of Susan so filled his brain that there was no room in it for anything else; not even for such practical considerations as how the deuce he was going to marry anyone on his present screw. He took it for granted that she hadn't a penny of her own. It would spoil things, in a way, if she had, he thought; for, never having known what it felt like to have money himself, he distrusted and despised it. He had no idea that such things as marriage settlements existed. No member of his own family had ever

owned anything of much value; they had just stuck to
their jobs in the church or the humbler professions and
got paid enough to live on—or very nearly—and
managed to instil into their offspring the same modest
ideals of moderation and content. When they fell in
love, well, they married as soon as they could afford to,
or cheerfully faced a long engagement if they couldn't.
As for divorce or irregular relationships of any kind—
in their sort of life such things were not even dreamt
of. From generation to generation this family life had
persisted in an orderly, unambitious, and, as some
people might think, dull procession of quite undistinguished creatures with big bones and loose joints and
fair hair and wide-set blue eyes like his. The Pennington stock didn't run much to beauty, or indeed, at the
moment, to anything; for the war had wiped out Dick's
two uncles, both his parents were dead, and his only
living relation, as far as he knew, was a little old lady
who lived, heaven knew how, in a cottage near Ludlow.
It was better on the whole, he thought, for a marrying
man to have no relations; for marriage, after all, was
a fellow's own affair and one other person's: a new
start in life, a clean cut. . . .

The clock on the landing struck seven. At last! So
much to be done! He tore off his pyjamas and stripped
to his skin, his torso astonishingly white beneath the
tanned neck. Then he put on a bathing slip, a pair of
gym shoes and an old raincoat, snatched up a towel,
stiff with salt and sand, and ran like a colt let loose to

the brink of the sea. Coming back from his bathe he
stopped at the garage where his motor-cycle was kept
and opened his heart to a sleepy mechanic.

"Well, of course, *some* only use cushions," this
expert advised him. "No, nothing special. Any old
cushion'll do. You don't even 'ave to tie them on: the
lady's weight keeps 'em down. If you want one
permanent-like it's another matter. . ." Dick hoped
to heaven he would want one permanent-like. "Well,
in that case," his adviser went on, "there's two alterna-
tives: either the regular bike-seat, the same as the one
you sits on yerself, or what *we* calls the flapper-bracket.
Of course, that costs more; but there's no denying it's
more clarssy. Yes, I think we could manage to find
one. Ten-thirty? O.K.! Very good, sir. And fill up
the tank, of course?"

At five minutes to eleven when he pushed his motor-
bike round to the front of the "Sea View" Hotel, Miss
Lengel was enchanted to see a romantic addition to its
amenities. Dick Pennington also was proud. It gave
him a feeling of gallantry to have damned the expense,
even though funds were running short and it nearly
broke him. He had reason for pride. The bracket was
a virgin bracket. No flapper had ever sat on it. It
enchanted him to think that no flapper ever would.

Susan was ready, waiting. They set off together on
the tick of eleven. She was wearing a bright blue
feather-weight mackintosh and a beret of the same
colour. Dick Pennington, on the other hand, wore a

kit like that of an Arctic explorer, and his beret was black. Susan, balanced on the seat behind, felt terribly conspicuous; she thought everybody must be looking at her, though nobody did. The few who noticed them at all simply took them for granted; these two were just like hundreds of other grotesque young couples who went tearing up and down England in this grace-less fashion—the young man gazing grimly ahead through his goggles and the girl perched behind like a frog. But for Susan the abominable stuttering machine with its foul exhaust was a vehicle of supreme romance. This method of transport, moreover, was not only perilous, but intimate. When they swept round corners she was forced to clutch at Dick's shoulders or be flung in the gutter, until she caught the trick of countering the centrifugal force whenever he swerved.

The bicycle hummed through the air like a flying projectile, and the vacuum that their speed created caught her breath. As the town fell behind and they reached a main road he opened the throttle cautiously; they flew faster and faster. She was actually frightened now, imagining newspaper headlines: *Another pillion tragedy: Unknown couple killed.* "You're going too fast," she shouted.

But Dick Pennington, who only caught the last word, thought: "Fast, is it? By Jove, you're a sports-man."

"I can't make her do more than sixty," he shouted back; but he made her do sixty-two.

"Slow, slow!" Susan cried.

But this time he was going too fast to hear her at all. "Even if I'm going to be killed," she thought, "I can't do anything." She laughed at death with the superb, light-hearted detachment of youth. "I shall be found with my arms tightly clasped round a stranger's waist!" On the whole, she decided, she couldn't have chosen a pleasanter fellow-victim.

Approaching another cross-road he slowed down to what seemed a snail's pace. He said: "Well, Susan, how do you like it?" The Christian name was a challenge; but she didn't accept it. "I'm loving it, thank you," she said. "Do we really have to go as slowly as this?"

By midday they were already approaching the crown of the Pennines. On either side of the road lay miles of dark, velvety heather. The sun shone fiercely, but the air was crisp and cool. They had lunch in the shadow of a wall of lichened, lilac stone. They talked lazily, easily now, while Dick smoked his pipe. He didn't even touch her hand, as he might have done quite easily by accident. They spoke a great deal about themselves, as though each were anxious that the other should start on even terms in this sudden, strange friendship. Then they fell into silence, and she suddenly saw he was asleep.

But Susan stayed awake. "How odd," she thought, "that I, Susan Lorimer, should be sitting here on the top of the world by the side of a sleeping man!"

While he slept she was able to examine him closely without feeling shy. "How strong he must be," she thought, "and yet how gentle!" Her heart went out to the helplessness of his sleeping strength. For all his bodily force he was in her power at that moment, and the consciousness of that power filled her with a tenderness which she had never experienced before for a human being. "He's not very clever," she thought, "and he's not really handsome; but there's something simple and straight and sound about him which makes things like that unimportant." She smiled in spite of herself as she gazed at him, then checked her smile. "If I go on like this," she thought, "I shall begin to imagine I'm in love with him. And I'm not. I won't be. That would be too terribly *banal*. A young man at the seaside!" At this point she became aware of his hands. She had always cherished a theory that hands were a reliable index of character; and his, though nobody could call them sensitive, were brown and firm and capable and, somehow, kind. She compared them with Mr. Feilden's and Mr. Bulgin's, to the great disadvantage of both. "I'm becoming sentimental," she thought. "This will never do!" So she decided to look at them no longer, and closed her eyes, till the sun and the singing air which rang with the infinitesimal bells of wind-swept grasses and heather threw a spell on her senses, and she too fell fast asleep.

Dick Pennington woke her at last. Her sleep-dazed

eyes saw him standing hugely above her, and she blushed, for she knew that he had been watching her asleep as she had watched him, and might even have kissed her without her knowing.

"Do you realize it's nearly five?" he said. "We ought to be moving. I do hope you're not cold. If you are, I'll lend you my coat."

But she wasn't, she told him; so they went drifting downward to the plain with the silent flight of a planing bird——(he had shown her the curlews)——of a bird dipping down to the sea with rigid wings. The bright sky was golden about them; the sands and the sea were gold, and the same aureate air suffused their spirits with rich content, compelling silence. "How marvellous it would be," Susan thought, "if all life were like this."

That evening Muriel only appeared for a moment when she dashed in to dress. "I'm terribly sorry to leave you again," she apologized. Susan wasn't sorry in the least. After dinner, when, to Miss Froggat's disgust, Dick took Muriel's place, they went out together to listen to the concert-party. Dick laughed a great deal, far more than Susan thought proper, at the jokes of a coarse comedian, and two of the party sang a new duet about *A Room with a View—and Yew*. A woman sitting behind them whispered loudly that this was the Prince of Wales's favourite song, which impressed them both, and when the concert was over the tune stuck in Susan's memory, beating time to their steps and to the waves which spilt over the sand with a creamy phosphorescence, attributable, some people said, to the Brinton drainage system. As she undressed that night she found herself humming it.

That day ushered in a golden week of which this tune became a kind of *leit-motiv*. They were hardly a moment apart. When Harry Levison shot back to North Bromwich in his Bentley, Muriel joined them. Though her original frostiness toward Dick Pennington melted and she was prepared to annex him for want of anything better, Dick's loyalty never wavered. He obviously disliked the O'Brien, and she, by way of revenge, never tired of telling Susan in private how boorish she found him.

Susan didn't mind in the least. It was providential that the motor-cycle, unlike the Bentley, could only carry one passenger. Every day she and Dick—he was no longer Mr. Pennington—set out on long, lonely voyages of exploration. The colour which she had lost came back into Susan's cheeks. In the sun of his admiration her beauty bloomed with new radiance. They bathed together before breakfast and after their rides. When he was stripped of his Arctic cycling-kit and his baggy home-spuns his athletic body lost all its awkwardness, and Susan's slenderness was adorable to him, however she clothed or unclothed it. He had shed all his shyness, too; they were able now to laugh in each other's eyes, and the touch of her hand, though it thrilled him still, no longer made him blush.

Toward the end of the week he became tragic. His short holiday was nearly over.

"It isn't only the thought of having to leave you," he told her. He stopped, and she said: "Well, what is it, Dick?" For she saw that he needed encouragement. But it wasn't what she thought.

"It's that Muriel O'Brien," he said. "I've been thinking so much about this that I simply must get it off my chest. I can't bear the thought of leaving you with a girl of that kind. You're so different from her in every way. It's all wrong. The thought makes me sick."

Susan stiffened. "You've no right to say that. She's my friend. I find her amusing. If it weren't for her, you know, we should never have met."

"I know all about that," he grumbled. "That's just the worst of it. But her Influence . . ."

"Can't you trust me?" she asked.

He became humble. "Of course I can trust you. It isn't that. But you . . . you're so . . ."

"Really, my dear, I'm not quite a baby; it's awfully kind of you to choose my friends for me, but not a bit necessary. As a matter of fact, Harry Levison's coming down to-morrow, so I shan't see much more of her."

"There you are!" he cried. "Harry Levison! That's a rotter if ever there was one."

"Do you think so?" she answered coldly. "I don't suppose he admires you either."

After all, she thought, what right has he to dictate

to me like this? It will do him good to realize that I'm not to be bullied. But his face fell so piteously at her coldness that she was forced to relent and to talk, as though nothing had happened, about their next and last expedition.

"Yes, we'll go to the fells," she said, "and hear the curlews again."

Something shadowed that day from the first. The doom of separation hung over them. At dawn a dense bank of fog enveloped the sands and the sea. Then something went wrong with the carburettor, and Dick came round nearly an hour late, his face flushed with exertion and his hands all smothered in oil. He found Susan cold and irritated.

"I've been waiting here ages and I'm frozen," she told him. "Don't you think we'd better give it up? The fog is so thick."

"It's only a sea fog," he told her. "It'll be quite clear inland. The garage man says it means heat."

"What does *he* know about it?" Susan thought. But Dick's face was so fussed and anxious that she had to take pity on him. "All right," she said. "Don't let's stand here quarrelling, anyway."

They set off slowly. The fog lay in drifting banks. At one moment they could see half a mile in front of them, at the next a few yards. Inland, as Dick's counsellor had prophesied, it grew steadily clearer. The ghost of a sun shone out like a luminous lamp. As they climbed the range the mist fell away beneath them, a soft blanket of woolly vapour hiding the land. In this light the uplands seemed wilder, more lonely than ever. Invisible curlews whinnied in the sky. Below, in the white silence, startled sheep stampeded, their fleeces beaded with dew like September gossamer.

"Oh, I'm cold!" Susan wailed, "and I know it's long after lunch-time. Can't we stop somewhere, Dick?"

He stopped. The mist clung in fine globules to his eyebrows and his woolly muffler. They had travelled so slowly that when he looked at his watch they found it was three o'clock.

"No wonder I'm starved!" she complained.

They sat down together and ate their lunch silently in the lee of a wall. Before they had finished the mist had increased in density to such a degree that the bicycle, strutted at the side of the road a few yards away, was scarcely visible.

"I think we'd better go home," Susan said disconsolately. "It gets worse and worse."

"I'd looked forward to this so much," he said.

"So had I," she answered irritably, "but it's no good looking like Hamlet."

He didn't really look like Hamlet. In her heart she knew he was awfully good and patient, and that she herself was behaving abominably; but she was feeling so cross and cold that she had to take it out of somebody. She straddled her seat and they set off again slowly. The engine made a disconsolate popping sound in the mist. For a long time he spoke not a word.

"What is he thinking?" she wondered. "I suppose I've offended him. How horribly sensitive men are!"

She was just on the point of breaking the silence herself when he burst out suddenly:

"I've been thinking about that girl again."

"Which girl?" she asked.

"Muriel O'Brien. Susan, I do wish to goodness you'd drop her."

"Oh, don't start *that* all over again," she cried. "You know nothing about her. You've no right to talk to me like this. I was friends with Muriel months and months and months before I was even aware of your existence, so you needn't be jealous."

"I'm not jealous," he said. "It's only that I can't bear to see you . . ."

"Oh, for God's sake shut up!" She was really angry now. "You can talk for a month, but it won't make any difference to me. Let's get home; that's all that I care about. Can't we go faster?"

"No, I daren't. It's too thick in front. We might run into something. I can't help it."

Of course, she knew quite well that he couldn't help it. Every moment now the mist grew denser and denser. It was difficult to see the stone walls that defined the road on either side. The fells were an empty whiteness. During the last half-hour they had not seen a living creature—not even a sheep. A new and horrible suspicion began to assail her.

"Are you perfectly sure you're on the right road?" she asked.

"The right road? Of course I am."

"Well, I'm not," she told him.

"This is the road we came along, anyway."

"You might easily have missed a turning."

"I don't think I have."

"Don't *think*?"

"Well, I'm practically sure I haven't. You needn't worry."

"I'm not worrying," she answered coldly. But she was—like the devil. "When we come to a signpost," she said, "we'd better look at it. For all you know, we may be going miles and miles out of our way."

"Well, we're bound to get somewhere," he said.

"I don't want to get somewhere. I want to get back to Brinton."

"All right. When we see a signpost we'll stop," he agreed; "but you won't see many up here."

They popped on for another half-hour. Then, suddenly, the road divided. In front of them a melancholy signpost raised three arms into the mist. Two yards short of it he stopped and Susan dismounted. Her limbs were stiff; her eyes smarted with fog. At close quarters she found the post rotten and shagged with lichen. It was impossible to read a letter of what had once been painted on the arms. Dick stopped the engine and joined her. The two roads into which their own had divided seemed equally important. He climbed up the post to examine the blurred directions more closely, but could decipher nothing.

"Drawn a blank," he reported cheerfully. "We'll keep to the left all the same. I'm sure that's the direction, roughly speaking, of course, if we *were* on the right road before."

"Aren't you sure we were on the right road?" she demanded querulously.

"I *was* sure," he told her, "before you began putting me off."

"Oh, blame me for everything, of course!" she cried.

He smiled. "I'm not blaming you. You know I'm not blaming you. We'll keep to the left."

"How d'you know where that leads?"

"I don't." He was laughing now. "But we can't stay here, can we?"

Though the question was reasonable enough, his laughing hurt her. She was colder than ever and beginning to get rattled; he oughtn't, she thought, to treat such a grave situation with levity.

"If you'd only thought of bringing a map," she said.

"Well, that wouldn't help us either," he replied serenely. "Come along. Jump up, my child. Let's try our luck."

She obeyed him grudgingly. He folded the strut and applied all his weight to the kick-starter. The engine turned over violently, but refused to fire. He tried it again and again with no result. By this time he was red in the face with exertion and annoyance.

"What is it?" she asked.

"I don't know. I shall have to find out. Do you mind hopping off for a second? You're sitting on the tools." As he unstrapped the oily roll in which they were wrapped he went on talking—to himself, it seemed, rather than to her. "The engine's cold," he was saying, "but I guess it's the plug—the same old game as this morning: they get sooted up."

He screwed out a sparking-plug and scraped it with a pen-knife, then washed it with a rag soaked in petrol and put it back again. She watched him with the complete detachment of technical ignorance. "Is that all?" she said. "Do you want me to get up again?"

"We shall see in a second," he told her.

In a second they saw that things were no better than before. In spite of all his exertions the engine declined to start. Dick stood panting and gazing at it with puzzled eyes. "You can't force it to go by staring at it," she told him acidly.

"I was thinking," he said, with an injured air. "You see, it might be the magneto."

"Well, for heaven's sake find out if it is!" she snapped. She hated herself for the tone of exasperation; but by this time, in spite of herself, she felt like crying. He sat down in the road and examined the points of the magneto. "I don't see much wrong there," he said. He began to scratch his head with an

oily finger, and that, too, irritated her. At the moment
it seemed as if he could do nothing that didn't. His
slow, methodical movements, his puzzled eyes, even
the unruffled good humour of his face began to get on
her nerves. Once more he stamped violently on the
starter. Once more the engine, revolving, sucked in
mixture, but failed to explode it.

"Perhaps it's the carburettor," he mused, with a new
inspiration. Susan moved away down the road. At a
little distance his Arctic shape loomed gigantically
through motionless fog. The wind had now dropped
completely, the silence was absolute; not a whisper
moved from the unending expanses of coarse grass
and heather. Looking back at that vague, laborious
figure, now stooping, now standing upright beside the
obstinate machine, she felt her resentment melting
away; his virtues, which had merely acted as irritants
before, resumed their real values, and even his defects
began to count as virtues. After all, this idiotic fiasco
was no more his fault than hers; she must treat it with
humour, in spite of her frozen feet. As she turned to
approach him, armed with the resolutions of a minister-
ing angel, the engine started with a roar. He waved his
arms wildly. "Come along, come along! All aboard!"

"Was it the carburettor after all?" she asked, with
penitent interest.

"I'm damned if I know what it was." His voice was
shaken by vibration. "I just flooded her and she went.
We'll soon be home now."

"If we're on the right road," she thought grimly; but this time she held her peace. And, on the whole, it was as well that she did; for no sooner had she framed the words "How clever you are!" than the engine began to misfire and then, suddenly, stopped.

"Oh, you poor dear!" she cried. "Will you have to do it all over again?"

He appeared not to hear her. At that moment a dreadful suspicion had entered his mind. He unscrewed the cap of the petrol-tank and dipped in a stalk of bracken.

"Bone dry!" he said glumly. "They forgot to fill it this morning. That's done it!"

"You mean . . ." she began.

"I mean we shall have to walk home."

"But we're miles from anywhere!" she cried.

"God knows. I don't. I'm terribly sorry, Susan."

He was so helpless now that she simply couldn't be angry with him or even reproach him for his carelessness. She looked at her watch. It was now nearly half-past six, and the mist-throttled light was failing. "No wonder I'm hungry," she thought; but the necessity of playing the game tied her tongue. They walked on together; he pushing the unwieldy bicycle, she plodding beside him. They walked for an hour, maybe, and almost in silence. As her feet grew warmer they began to ache. The fog seemed to curdle; the low sky darkened above them; and in all that hour—though sometimes the road descended and sometimes he panted, pushing the lifeless machine up a rise—their surroundings seemed just the same, a wilderness of black heather, an ever-darkening silence.

"We might just as well stop where we are," she said at last; "this road leads nowhere."

"It *must* lead somewhere," he said.

"To Rome, of course."

But he wasn't seeing jokes at that moment. He panted: "What did you say?"

"To Rome," she almost screamed.

"Oh, I see," he replied. "Do you mind if I rest a moment?"

She was past minding anything now; but when they re-started the road took a turn for the better, winding gently down hill. "If you'll get up behind," he told her, "I think we might coast for a bit."

They coasted. It was worth while, anyway, resting her feet. The slope grew steeper; the bicycle ran down it as though it had actually come to life again. Then suddenly it stopped again. They had reached the pit of a valley. In front of them another hill rose, incredibly steep, a small stream gurgled under a bridge, on their left stood a small, dilapidated, barn-like building.

"This hill looks a brute," he said cheerfully. "I think I'd better go and prospect." In a few moments he returned defeated. "It's like the roof of a house," he reported. "I doubt if I can manage it."

"Well, what are we going to do?"

"I don't know. What can we do? I suppose we'd

better throw up the sponge. That's all. I'm terribly sorry," he repeated.

Susan wished he hadn't. Apologies didn't mend matters, and she felt like telling him so.

"At any rate, there's cover," he said. "Let's look inside here."

The interior of the barn was stacked with last year's dead bracken, reasonably dry. It smelt sweet and aromatic, and was pitch dark inside. Dick struck a match.

"Be careful, for heaven's sake!" she cried. "You'll set it on fire."

"Don't get nervous, Susan," he told her.

Nervous, indeed!

"You see," he went on, "it's quite warm in here. You can lie on this stuff and cover yourself if it grows colder at night. There's bound to be a farm or something to which this belongs. I'll dump the bike here and walk on to see if I can find it. If I once know where we are I can probably manage to get some petrol."

The prospect filled her with sudden, unreasoning terror, for her nerve, by this time, was breaking.

"No, no, don't do that. You mustn't leave me!" she said.

"Well, come along with me then."

"I can't do that either. If you only knew how sore and tired my feet are!"

"You poor darling!" he said. It was the first time

he had called her darling, and in spite of her distress, the word filled her heart with strange sweetness, softening it so much that she suddenly wanted to cry. "This will never do," she told herself, "I'm not really a coward."

"Look here," he was saying, "if your feet are as bad as that, you'd much better bathe them. Come down with me to the stream."

They went, and he knelt to undo her shoe-laces. His knightly humility touched her. It was like a romance, Susan thought, but it made her shy. Some conventional modesty rebelled against the idea of taking off her stockings in front of him. It was ridiculous—hadn't they bathed together a dozen times? Yet feet, somehow, were different. So much more intimate and not in the least romantic. She dreaded the disclosure of a hole in the foot of her stocking; one's feet, after all, were not meant to be seen at close quarters.

"I can manage quite well by myself," she told him, as kindly as she could.

He took this exclusion from the mysteries of her toilet rather well. Susan sat on a very damp boulder and dabbled her feet. The water was icy cold, but it took the ache out of them. When she had dried her toes on a handkerchief and pulled on her stockings they felt much better. "I could go and explore with you now," she told him cheerfully; but now it was so dark that it hardly seemed worth while.

"I've made you a sort of nest in the bracken," he said. "It's quite cosy in there; you'll be warm as a toast in no time."

With a sigh of relief she settled herself down among stiff, brittle fronds in the sleepy odour of fern. It wasn't exactly comfortable, and the back of her mind was haunted by the suspicion that rats or fieldmice might have made their nests in it. She was happy to think that Dick was standing beside her; but when next she spoke he did not answer, and she realized with alarm that he had gone.

"The conventional fifteen minutes' grace," she thought, "like a married couple."

Up to this point she had been so deeply concerned with her own distress that the proprieties and the associated romantic possibilities had not even entered her mind. Now they came to her suddenly. She, Susan Lorimer, was going to spend the night with a man, a pleasant young man who was clearly attracted by her and had even—once—gone so far as calling her "darling." A situation of this kind could never have arisen in Halesby; it belonged to the upper regions of high romance. For the first time in all her life she was Living Dangerously, and faced with the opportunity, if not the duty, of Self-Expression! The situation filled her with an exquisite panic, amid which she proceeded to dramatize herself in a series of scenes suggested by the works of fiction on which her imagination had been fed. She saw herself cold and distant: *with a single glance she froze him.* It was difficult to freeze anyone, she reflected, with a single glance in the dark, and they were, both of them, frozen already. She saw herself making dignified appeals to his better nature: *"My honour is in your hands," she said, and looked him straight in the eyes.* She saw herself fighting tooth and nail, to defend that honour: *His brutal hands were closing on her white flesh, his hot breath seared her cheek.* She saw herself finally yielding. *With a shuddering sigh her body relaxed and he took possession of her . . .*

Twenty yards away down the darkling road Dick Pennington walked to and fro, his mind in a similar turmoil. He was thinking: "She'll probably imagine I did this on purpose, and never forgive me. What a damnable piece of bad luck! Bad luck? Don't you see, my boy, it's the chance of a lifetime? Any fellow with guts in him would make the best of his opportunities! She's a modern girl: ten to one you'd not be the first," he thought, and his brain went hot. "No, no, that won't do! She's different; she's not that sort; it's a crime to imagine it. . . . Rot! All women are the same: she's a friend of that creature O'Brien; they've both of them come down here for a bit of fun; if you don't try to bring it off she'll only think you're a dud. But suppose she *is* different? In that case, you'll look a damned fool! Look here, she's a lady. You can't honestly pretend that she's ever led you on. And you, by the way, are supposed to be some kind of a gentleman. Public school and all that. It's up to you to behave like one." For a moment he began to wish to God that it wasn't. A fellow like Harry Levison wouldn't be bothered by scruples. It was the devil. "And the worst of it is," he thought, "that I'm actually in love with her and going to marry her. If I weren't, it would be quite a different kettle of fish. The poor kid's in my power; I can do pretty well what I like with her; and that's just the reason why, in the end, I shall have to do nothing. But to-morrow, to-morrow, whatever happens, I'll speak to her!"

Through the mist he heard a faint cry. She was calling. He hurried toward her. She was standing in the door of the barn.

"Dick, Dick, where are you?" Her voice was agonized. "Please, please don't leave me alone!"

"I'm sorry, Susan," he said.

"Aren't you coming in here?"

"I'll stay just outside," he said, "and smoke a pipe."

"You'll be frozen."

"No, no. It's quite warm. I might set the whole place on fire."

"Do you want to smoke dreadfully?"

"I'll sit down by the door. We can talk just the same."

"Oh, very well. If you want to. . . . You're very unsociable, aren't you?"

"It's not that. I'm quite comfortable here."

"I'm glad to know that. I thought you were merely

being honourable and noble. You can be all those things just as well inside here as out."

He lit his pipe in silence. The flare of the match illuminated Susan's face. The great shadows made her eyes and hair look curiously wild, and so lovely that his heart beat faster; but her smiling mouth was petulant and scornful as she turned on her heel.

He smoked doggedly in silence. From within she could see the rhythmical glow and fading of his pipe-bowl. She lay on the bracken watching it. "How strange men are!" she reflected. The silence lengthened until she could stand it no longer.

"Are you frightened of me?" she asked suddenly.

He was frightened of himself. "I'm not going to quarrel with you."

"I'm quite harmless, really. I see what it is. You think I want to seduce you. Is that it? Well, I don't."

"You know I thought nothing of the sort," he proclaimed indignantly. "Such a thing never entered my mind."

She laughed. "You're not awfully complimentary, are you, Dick?"

He refused to answer. It seemed to him sheer sacrilege that she should speak of herself so lightly. He lit another pipe solemnly and realized, with a feeling of being completely disarmed that he had used the last match. After this, for a long time, she was quiet—so quiet that he believed she must surely have fallen asleep. The night was now of a pitchy blackness; not a single star showed itself. With each minute the air felt colder; his body grew as stiff as if it were slowly freezing.

"If she's really asleep," he thought, "I might just as well go inside."

So he entered the hut with cautious steps and lowered his weight on to the bracken as silently as he could in a corner far removed from that in which he had left her. He performed this manœuvre, as he thought, with signal success, then stretched out his aching legs on the fern luxuriously. In the absolute silence that followed he became aware of a sound of soft regular breathing not far from his ear. He trembled to think that she was nearer to him than he had imagined; this warm, breathing creature whom his crude idealism had invested with a beauty of body and spirit so far transcending actuality. It enraptured him to think of her sleeping there, so near, so help-less, so innocent. It filled him with a strangely exalted pride in his own restraint and delicacy that he had not even attempted to kiss her, and this sense of virtue was even more flattering because he had wanted to kiss her so much and so often. He felt, in fact, that he was being extremely manly and wise and magnanimous. And he hoped that when Susan woke she would realize this.

Susan Lorimer, who, of course, was not even drowsy, much less asleep, regarded his admirable conduct differently. To her it seemed stupid, childish, and above all unenterprising. It was not that she had the least intention of letting his enterprise go too far. Her reading of popular fiction had taught her the theory of this game; she knew stratagems adapted to counter the most dangerous gambits, but had no knowledge of how to deal with an opponent who simply declined to move. The pricks of faint irony with which, at first, she had tried to stimulate him, had merely made him dumb and obstinate. However chivalrous his attitude might be, it was certainly anything but complimentary to her own charms. It was the first time that she had ever put herself into such a humiliating position with a man, and it was what she herself had done rather than what he had refused to do that made her angry, because, as likely as not, he would misunderstand her motives. Harry Levison, she didn't mind betting, would never have behaved so clumsily. He might be a dirty little Jew, as Dick said, but he did understand women. If Dick got pneumonia he deserved it. Although she quite definitely didn't want him to make love to her, she *did* think he might have tried.

When Dick, having struck his last match, crept into the barn, she held her breath, for she thought he was going to apologize or make amends in a more practical way. Her heart gave a sudden wild flutter as he groped his way toward the very spot where she lay and sank down in the fern beside her. "If he speaks to me now," she thought, "I suppose I shall have to forgive him."

Her heart was beating so furiously that she felt he must hear it. But, to her enormous surprise, he didn't speak one word. He settled his big limbs cautiously, carefully, within a foot of her own, then turned over in the opposite direction with a stifled yawn and began to breathe as softly and evenly as if he were already asleep. Not a whisper of the conflict that divided his mind as he lay there beside her could penetrate hers. All that she heard was the gentle sound of his drowsy breathing.

And now, as she compared him again with Harry Levison, Dick's simplicity, his childishness—if that were the word—appeared to her in another light. He was so big, so strong, so direct, so clumsy, so obviously, translucently guileless, and herself, by contrast, so full of theatrical moods, complications and every kind of despicable littleness, that her sense of grievance was lost in an odd new emotion of shame for herself and of admiration, not unmixed with pity, for him. She remembered the solid patience and good humour with which he had met this unfortunate emergency and her own querulousness. However she had railed at him and taunted him he had never said a cross word. During all the long hours they had spent together he had been just the same; the soul of goodness and gentleness and kindness and—yes, though the word had a priggish sound—of honour. You didn't, she told herself, often meet men like him in these days.

"Of course he's not clever or cultured," she

thought, "like Mr. Feilden; but then there's another thing: he doesn't show off; there's nothing superficial about him; he's sound all through, and so humble about things of which he's a right to be proud. What he really needs," she thought, "is somebody to make the best of him—someone understanding, like me . . ."

The confession gave her a shock. Yet this mood, half maternal, gained upon her as she lay there thinking in the dark; and the thought of fostering his simple strength with her own frail subtlety filled her mind till there was no room in it for anything else—till, all of a sudden, there leapt into her consciousness a new and shattering conviction. "Good heavens! I might be in love with him!" she thought. "So it's come . . . at last!" This overwhelming tenderness, this new humility could have no other meaning. The wonder ran through her like flame till all her body and mind were deliciously aglow. "I love him, and he loves me," her heart cried. "It was for this that I was born, that I'm living at this moment, unless it's all a dream."

As though to assure herself of reality she stretched out her hand. Her fingers fell on the clammy sleeve of Dick Pennington's waterproof so lightly that he did not feel them. Then, cautiously, tenderly, they strayed downward till they reached his hand. "Poor darling, how cold he is!" Susan thought. Dick moved in his sleep as her warm hand crept into his. His fingers closed on it gently. But he did not wake. The situation

now struck her as so ludicrous that she was compelled
to laugh. And that didn't wake him either.

II

It was after four o'clock in the morning when
Muriel O'Brien returned to the "Sea View" hotel,
bowed down with a burden of conscious virtue. She
was not very pleased with herself, and even less with
Harry Levison. That gentleman, whose understanding of women Susan had admired, understood them
only too well. This evening, feeling that the time of
her stay at Brinton was running short, Muriel had decided to force the pace. All the skill she possessed had
been used to extract a proposal from him; and indeed
a proposal had come—but not a proposal of marriage.
At this she had appeared to be not only affronted, but
shocked. She made it quite clear to Harry that he had
made a great mistake. But Harry had merely smiled
in his debonair, mocking way. He knew perfectly
well that he himself had avoided making a greater.
There were plenty of other pebbles on the beach, he
implied; and she knew it was true—the foreshore at
Brinton was notoriously pebbly. "You can take it or
leave it," his manner suggested, and, reluctantly, she
had left it, for she knew, by the way in which he looked
at her when she pretended not to be looking at him,

K

that she still had power over him and that a day might come when he would be glad of a harder bargain.

She entered the bedroom on tiptoe and began to undress in the dark. She didn't even trouble to rub off her make-up, for her instinct was secretive. She preferred not to let Susan know how late she had come in, and hated explanations anyway. The thought of her friend, so innocently sleeping away there in the other corner, filled her mind with mingled feelings of envy and contempt. Susan's visit, by Muriel's standards, had not been a success. She was a soft little thing, incapable of making the best of her chances. Her lack of proportion was shown by the way she had taken up with that Pennington boy, a fellow (with Muriel young men were generally "fellows") who obviously hadn't and never would have a bean. "If she's fool enough to marry him," Muriel thought, "she'll deserve all she gets, and that won't buy anything at Woolworth's. Well, it's not my fault anyway," she thought, as she turned over to sleep.

But she couldn't sleep, somehow. Her want of success with Harry Levison rankled. She felt that for once she had played her cards badly, but couldn't discover just how or when. And then, to make sleep completely impossible, the damned wind rose. It roared through the open window—Susan never would close it—and flapped Miss Lengel's lace curtains. Then the casement swung to with the crash of a broken pane. "Well, that's torn it," she thought, "and I'm blest if

I'm going to pay for it. The silly little fool deserves to be wakened, anyway."

"You'd better hop out and fasten that window," she called.

No answer. Not even an easy conscience could excuse sleep as heavy as that. Perhaps Susan was foxing. "I'll make her shut it," Miss O'Brien thought angrily. So she slid out of bed and switched on the light and saw, with a gasp of surprise, Susan's empty bed.

"Well, I'm damned!" she said and stood staring, her mouth wide open. "Just to think of it! Susan! Of all people! Well, this is the limit."

As she fastened the window viciously and ran back to bed her surprise gave place to a righteous scandalization. To drift in at four was a thing that might happen to anybody; but to stay out all night with a fellow—it just wasn't done. Such an escapade must reflect on her own unstained reputation. She would have to apologize to Miss Lengel for having brought Susan with her, to explain that she never suspected she was *that* sort of girl. With a fellow like Pennington, too! That just put the lid on! She decided, there and then, that when once she had told Susan at length what she thought of her she would never speak to her again.

At that moment, thirty miles away on the top of the fells, the gale howling in from sea woke Dick Pennington to a consciousness of something extremely odd in his surroundings. On his eyelids a strange dawn shone through the door of the barn. Stranger still, in his listless hand lay another hand. When he opened his eyes and looked he saw Susan sleeping beside him. She slept the drugged sleep of complete exhaustion, the wind had not wakened her; and Dick Pennington's heart, as he gazed at her helpless figure, was swept by an emotion stronger than the wild wind. The miracle of the hand which, himself unknowing, had crept into his and lay there so trustfully was the symbol of one even greater. If he dared to interpret it at all it meant that she loved him, and his incredulous eyes, as they devoured in the dusk that face which was all his heaven, grew dim with the tears of an infinite gratitude.

"Perhaps she did it in her sleep," he thought, "and doesn't even know that she did it. How lovely she is! My God, I don't deserve it. I must be gentle. I won't even wake her."

So, with infinite caution, he loosened the fingers that held Susan's hand and stole out into a dawn more miraculous than any in all the world's story. The air was cleaner and sweeter than any he had ever breathed. Overhead, in the windy dusk, the curlews were crying. Torn shreddings of mist, the last wisps of the milky coverlet that had smothered them, whirled past on the wings of the gale; and he, in his ecstasy, felt as strong and clean as the wind blowing in from the west; his own amazed soul and body assimilated its speed and its power. He spread wide his arms to embrace it, it blew through his tousled hair, he opened his mouth to inhale that free, fierce element streaming and leaping invisibly to meet the dawn. As he stood there, entranced, the blood tingling in his wind-whipped skin, the eastern sky lightened momently; a tawny streak defined the black arc of moorland. And there, beneath it, poised on the lip of the stream, stood a low, grey farmstead, with peat smoke whirling away from its slated chimney. It had lain there all night, a couple of hundred yards away from them, lost in the mist, and a cart-track approached it diagonally from the road on the further side of the stream.

In the increasing light he examined the road surface eagerly, and discovered, at a point where a muddy runnel crossed it, the track of a motor-car's tyres. "That means a good chance of petrol," he thought triumphantly, "but I won't wake her yet. Thank heaven we didn't know of this last night."

In the farmyard he discerned a human shape moving slowly among the conical mounds of harvested bracken. "Can you spare me a gallon of petrol?" Dick asked. The man stared at this apparition with half-awakened eyes. "Nay, lad, thee might just as well have asked for a gallon of beer. We've no motor-folk hereabouts, though you're not the first by a long way as has been caught up here. Nay, but now that I coom to think on it," he said—and his slow Yorkshire voice brightened suddenly, "ah'm not speakin' the truth: there's a tin in th' shippon as our Agnes's young man brought up for her to clean her blouse with at Whit, but I doubt you'll find more than a drain there. If you do, you can take it and welcome."

Dick thanked him. He returned to the barn in triumph with a two-gallon tin half-full of petrol that had already been used on our Agnes's blouse in one hand, and in the other a pannikin of milk still warm from the byre.

"Susan, Susan!" he called.

She came to the door, her eyes blinking, for now it was daylight; her dark hair was dishevelled and her face flushed with sleep.

"Have some milk," he said, "while I fill up the tank. By the time that I've carried the tin back to the farm you must be ready to start."

She watched him striding away with the wind behind him. He was as gay and strong and boisterous as the wind itself. "No, it isn't a dream after all," she thought. "I'm in love. How marvellous!" And she hurriedly finished what toilet she could to make herself fit for a lover's eyes—an unnecessary precaution, not only because lovers are blind, but since the thought of love itself had already transformed her and made her lovely and glowing. Yet, strangely enough, through all the long homeward ride, sweeping down to the coast like birds wheeling in a swift aerial courtship, no word of love passed between them, though each was deliciously conscious of the other's nearness.

When they reached the "Sea View" hotel not a soul was stirring, for it was Sunday morning and even the servants "lay in." They laughed in whispers over this amazing piece of good luck. "I'm afraid I'm not compromised after all," Susan whispered jokingly. "Nobody will know that I've been away all night except, possibly, Muriel; and Muriel, who lives in a glasshouse, can't throw stones at me. She'll probably think I came in just after she fell asleep."

"How soon shall I see you again?" he pleaded. As he spoke Susan thought: "Why, he's really quite handsome!"—for he, too, had been physically transfigured by an equal magic. " Don't forget it's my last day," he said.

She frowned: "Oh, why *did* you remind me?" But her heart said: "This is not the last day; it's only the first, the beginning of both our lives, so there's plenty of time to spare. And in any case," she thought prudently, "I mustn't make myself cheap." So she answered his tragically intense demand with a tolerant smile. "I should have thought that you'd seen enough of me to last for the rest of the year," she said. "If you're not going out we shall meet at lunch as usual. I can do with a couple of hours' sleep before anything else."

At the luncheon table they met. Susan had not slept; she had had it all out with Muriel, whose envy of this comparative success took the form of shocked bitterness. She assumed that the accident was a put-up job and that the worst had happened, and Susan, divining the jealousy beneath her righteous pose, found a wilful, unhallowed joy in leading her on. It was something of an achievement to be able to shock Muriel O'Brien. "The more she is shocked the better," she thought, remembering how deeply Dick disapproved of their friendship. "I shall have to break with her, anyway." If it were a matter of choosing between him and Muriel, the choice was easy.

"A one-eyed donkey could see what's happened to *you*, so don't try to kid *me*," said Muriel scornfully. "Why, your eyes are like saucers. But one thing I *must* say. I should never have dreamt it of you."

Susan laughed. "Do I really look like that?" She didn't care if all the world saw how happy she was. Miss Lengel certainly did. Waking early, she had heard in the road beneath her bedroom the stutter of Dick's motor-bicycle. She had peered through the window and seen that adventurous return. "That's better," she had thought, as she nodded her head with approval; for she liked, as she vulgarly said, to see the young pups rolling together.

At lunch, with the curious eyes of the whole room fixed on her, and Muriel's offensive propriety at her side, Susan wanted, most of all, to see what Dick really looked like; she wondered if he was actually as nice as she had imagined him in the hours between. He came in late, as self-conscious as Susan herself in the limelight of Miss Lengel's approving smiles. He was dressed in a blue serge suit, which struck her as much less becoming than his burly motoring-outfit. He looked somehow diminished; his hair was too smoothly brushed and he had gashed his chin badly in shaving. Not even the most prejudiced eye could have considered him handsome now. But his awkward attempts to appear at his ease and the studied stiffness with which Muriel frustrated them aroused Susan's protective instincts again and threw her more violently than ever on to his side.

"As soon as we get a chance let's escape," she whispered to him. "Oh, Dick, how I loathe all these people!"

So, when luncheon was over, they slipped away together. If he had asked her to risk another night on the fells she would have consented; but all he proposed, in fact, was a stroll along the front. They paced up and down the windswept asphalt of the promenade, under the eyes of a series of surfeited lower middle-class visitors like themselves, who sat sucking their teeth after lunch and gazed idly seaward from boarding-house windows. Though his heart was bursting with the unspoken heroics which he had carefully planned during the morning, Dick found himself dumb. It was Susan who did all the talking. She listened to herself being pert and silly and excitable, but couldn't help it. It was Susan, again, who finally took his arm.

"I shall be blown away if I don't," she excused herself boldly. "Do you mind?"

Did he mind! "Let's sit down somewhere out of

the wind," he said. His voice trembled. They took shelter in a hollow amid dunes of blown sand, as remote and secret as their mist-wreathed sanctuary of the night before. There, at last, he succeeded in finding his tongue.

"I can't bear to think that this is our last day," he told her. "When I leave here to-morrow I suppose I shall never see you again."

"What on earth do you mean?" she said. "You'll still be in North Bromwich. Surely we can do something about it."

"About what?" he asked eagerly.

"About us. You and me."

"You don't mean . . ."

"Oh, Dick, don't pretend like that. You knew all the time."

"My God!" He went pale. "I never dared to believe it. I love you too terribly, Susan."

"You needn't be so rough," she protested, though she was glad that he was rough with her and he, too, felt rather proud of it.

"My darling," he said, "I've waited so long for this. I can't think why we waited last night."

"Nor can I," she whispered. "It wasn't my fault, you know."

They lay silent in that windless solitude, clasped in each other's arms, unconscious of any sound but the boom and hiss and withdrawal of waves that pounded on sand—unconscious, above all, of several other equally amorous couples who had found shelter near-by. The sand filled her hair and Dick's pockets and the shoes of both of them. When they came back to consciousness Susan had to empty her shoes, and when Dick knelt at her feet to tie up the laces she was no longer shy. They had tea together in a lonely, wind-swept cottage that smelt of the sea and tanned nets and lobster-pots. Susan poured out the tea and was proud to remember his two lumps of sugar (what a baby he was!) while he picked her shrimps clean for her. Then he lit his pipe and they walked miles together over the hard smooth sand, exclaiming at shells and dead starfish and sponges that the tide had left behind; and once, where an ebbing runnel of water impeded their path, Dick picked her up in his arms and carried her and would not release her till she had paid a full toll of salt kisses incredibly sweet.

All that afternoon they only lived in the light of each other's eyes, and at dinner, thank heaven, they found themselves alone at the table, for Muriel, in spite of her rebuff, had no intention of forgoing a final expensive meal with Harry Levison. Dick and Susan sat facing each other, entranced. It seemed sheer waste of time to be sitting there, among all those un-fortunate people, pretending to eat. A wild impatience for solitude possessed them both; so, as soon as it was decent, Susan disappeared to fetch her coat and they strolled out again, under Lengy's benevolent eyes, to the deserted sea-front.

The wind had fallen; the night air was as mild as milk; a faint luminosity of clouded moonshine made the sky pale, and gave just enough light for them to look into each other's eyes. They sat on an iron seat at the edge of a concrete basin of slimy fresh water, on which, in the daytime, children sailed their toy boats. Between them and the sky a municipal palm-tree, like those on the railway posters of Brinton, shivered dolefully.

"Heaven knows how long we shall have to wait," Dick was saying. "You see, business is bad and I'm lucky to stick in a job at all. I can't keep a wife on three pounds a week. Never mind. We won't be long. I promise you I'll work like the devil."

"Could you keep one on five pounds a week, darling?" Susan asked him anxiously.

"Five pounds? I should just think I could! But if you think I'm going to allow you to work you're badly mistaken."

"You see," she confided gently, "I've a little money of my own. About a hundred a year. That makes it quite possible, doesn't it?" He was silent. "What's the matter, Dick darling?" she asked. "Why don't you answer?"

"Of course, it's too wonderful," he said. "Yet, somehow, I wish that you hadn't. I'd no idea . . . You see, it's my business to look after you. I suppose it's a matter of pride."

She laughed. "You ridiculous child!" But she

loved him for it. "Very well, if you don't want to marry me until you're rich . . ." she teased him.

"Susan! How can you! I'm just staggered to think that it's even possible. Of course we'll be married as soon as we can. I suppose it'll have to be in Halesby Church. We must put up the banns."

"I hate Halesby so much," she said. "I'd much rather people didn't know there. What's wrong with a registry office?"

He hesitated. "I'd much rather be married in church," he said.

"How odd," she thought. It was the first mysterious thing she had met in him.

"I can't help feeling like that," he went on. "You see my father was a parson."

"Do you mean you're religious, Dick darling? How funny! Those things mean nothing to me. Are you *really* religious? The Thirty-nine Articles, and all that?"

"I know nothing about those. Only . . . Well, it feels safer, somehow. After all, it's a terribly serious business, isn't it? A sort of . . . sacrament."

"If two people love each other as we do it seems just the same to me. But of course, if you feel like that, darling . . ."

They sat whispering, huddled together, leagued against time. The moments went by so swiftly and each was so precious. They sat there, with hands tightly clasped, gazing over the dim, stagnant water.

On its surface in the middle distance there suddenly appeared a luminous patch that held both their eyes.

"What is it?" Susan asked him.

"I don't know. I suppose it must be the reflection of the moon shining down through the clouds."

"But it can't be the moon. It's moving," she said. "Oh, look, Dick darling, it's a swan!"

Like a ghost the great bird came gliding into the bank and peered at them curiously with head aslant. Its placid beauty filled Susan's mind with ecstasy. There was no loveliness in the world that did not seem more acute for the surplus of beauty that brimmed her heart that evening, and it seemed to her odd and a little disquieting that Dick did not share her immediate rapture.

"There's just one thing I'd like to tell you, Susan," he was saying. He hesitated. His tone was so serious that her heart felt a sudden chill. "He's going to tell me," she thought quickly, "that he's been involved with some other woman. But I don't mind. He's mine now. Though I'd rather he wouldn't mention it. Confessions are so painful."

"Yes," she said, and she lowered her eyes so as not to embarrass him.

"I don't know how to say it," he answered clumsily. "I want you to know that . . . well, just that you'll be the first: I've never had anything to do with any other woman. And I'm terribly glad of it, somehow."

Susan laughed with relief. "Is that all? Well, of course I'm glad too." It was in her mind for a second to tell him jokingly that she, too, had never slept with a man before last night, but his face was so earnest that she refrained from this irreverence. His attitude toward her partook of a mystical idealism which seemed to belong to a younger and simpler world. It made her feel old and hard and grossly material. And, though she was equally innocent herself, she felt his innocence touching. It filled her again with that odd, protective feeling which apparently played so large a part in this strange thing called love. Such a situation, she reflected, could never have arisen in the case of Harry Levison. She had no business to be thinking of Harry Levison at all.

CHAPTER V

HOLY MATRIMONY

I

MR. BULGIN had been genuinely shocked to receive Susan's letter of rejection, which began so politely and ended like a slap in the face. He blushed as he read it. He would never have thought it of her. No sensible young woman, he felt, could have thrown away such a chance on her own initiative. And yet, when the first shock of surprise was over, he had no feeling against her.

"George Lorimer's in this," he decided. "In spite of my telling her to keep it dark she's gone and told him, and the old boy's cracked jealous—that's what's the matter with *him*."

Though George Lorimer was exactly the same age as himself, Mr. Bulgin always thought of him as either childish or senile, and this latest symptom of decadence confirmed his contempt. "If he's such a damned fool as not to see on which side his bread's buttered," he thought, "it's no fault of mine. I've given him his chance, and I reckon he won't get it again.

This frees my hand. Poor old George!"

Mr. Bulgin smiled and wagged his head compassionately. But the smile was an ugly smile. Although, as he had proudly admitted, he was not a sportsman himself, Mr. Bulgin regarded the friend of his boyhood with the interest—even the affection—which lovers of blood-sports frequently feel for the creatures they are about to hunt and hope to destroy. He would have been the first to admit the sentimental appeal of George Lorimer's innocent obstinacy—as a hunting man gives full marks to a fox that has given him a rousing run or a fisherman approves the gameness of a salmon that has all but broken him. But these generous admissions by no means tempered his ruthlessness. As he shook his head over poor old George he rang for his confidential clerk. "I want all those papers about the mortgage on Lorimer's Nail Works. Look sharp!" he said in a business-like tone.

It was just as he thought. Even in trifling matters, when they were connected with money, Mr. Bulgin made few mistakes. The mortgage on the Dingle expired on Midsummer Day. "He'll have more than a fortnight to think it over," Mr. Bulgin reflected as he dictated a letter to his lawyers, Wilburns', of North Bromwich, instructing them to let George Lorimer know that the mortgagee had decided not to renew.

"That'll make poor old George put his thinking-cap on," he thought, with the half humorous grimness of a keeper who has stopped the last hole in a covert.

L

"This'll make him sit up," he chuckled to himself as he signed the letter and passed on, with the ghost of a smile, to matters of more serious import.

The letter that came three days later from Wilburns' filled George Lorimer with panic. Ever since his scene with John Bulgin he had been living on tenterhooks—not because he had suspected that the counter-attack would come from that quarter, but because he knew that any man in Halesby who had offended John Bulgin had reason to feel insecure. Even now he didn't suspect that Bulgin was personally responsible for the present emergency. He merely felt that the fact of his quarrel with Bulgin prejudiced his chances of meeting it.

Trade was bad. Although he had strenuously denied it, he felt at the bottom of his heart that it might easily grow worse. The small, specialized market for which he catered was steadily contracting. His old customers, hard-hit as himself, were demanding long credits, and one of the biggest of them had lately gone bankrupt. The pitiful emptiness of the safe at the works which had so distressed Susan was a symbol of his financial state. As for finding two thousand pounds, within fourteen days . . .

At a pinch, of course, he vaguely supposed he could raise it. The house in Great Cornbow and its contents were still unencumbered and worth a good deal more than that—though whether anyone would be willing to lend him as much on them was another matter. In any case the idea of raising money on his home was distasteful to him. It had been in the family, after all, for more than a hundred years. He had actually been born in it, and so had his father before him. Every brick of its structure (the walls at the back needed pointing alas, and the roof new slates!), every stick of furniture inside was as much a part of himself as his skin and his bones. He was too old, far too old, he told himself, to begin life all over again in a smaller place. Besides which, he had never regarded the house as his own. It was a family possession. In his will he had made careful provision for its disposal. His wife would have a life-interest only: on her death it would pass to Susan and Susan's children, who, he thanked heaven passionately, would never now be John Bulgin's.

There was nothing that George Lorimer hated more desperately than facing facts. He had managed not to do so, with some ingenuity, for forty years. But these facts must be faced. What was more, he must face them alone; for Aunt Edna, much as he loved her, was apt to be downright and even harsh when she found him wanting. He liked to feel she was proud of him as no one else was proud, and in this case he felt that she couldn't be. So next day, without telling her anything, he shut up the works and stole into North Bromwich by train to see the lawyers.

On his way to the station he very nearly turned back. Since the bad times began he had been nervous of showing himself in Halesby, and that morning it seemed to him that everyone regarded him with contemptuous pity. The day was oppressive and windless; there was thunder in the air. The black smoke unfurling from the chimneys of Bulgin's Tube Works draped the sky like a funeral pall—a sinister omen! As he approached the Wilburns' office in Sackville Row he began to feel like a criminal. A defaulting debtor wasn't, after all, very different. He had dealt with the firm in his young days when business was good; but the last of the Wilburns had died soon after the war, and the new partners were strangers to him. Not only strangers, he felt, but instinctively hostile.

He was received—as a favour, it seemed—by a junior partner, a smart, wooden-faced young man in tortoiseshell spectacles, who made him feel shabby and soft, an off-handed young man whom he did not know and who, obviously, was not anxious to know him. The name of Lorimer, which had once commanded respect, meant nothing to this generation. George, stammering, ingratiating, had to explain who he was; and when he had done so the lawyer wasn't impressed.

"Oh, that mortgage," he said at last, with a contemptuous nod. "I thought that the situation was perfectly clear. I dictated the letter myself. At the moment," he said, as George doubtless realized, "money was tight" (George nodded: Didn't he just!) —"and his client had urgent need of the small sum involved. As far as he remembered the terms of the loan were explicit."

"Oh, I don't question *that*," George eagerly agreed. "I was merely wondering——" He hesitated. A word so indefinite as "wondering" seemed out of place in that office where no odd scrap of paper escaped strangulation by red tape. The lawyer impatiently twirled a stick of sealing-wax as George Lorimer plunged again. "Do you think," he asked timidly, "that you could interest any other client in this mortgage of mine? I've been paying six per cent., as you know. Well, I'm willing to pay seven."

The owlish young man shook his head. Money was tight, he repeated. What was more, in the present condition of trade the market was glutted with factory sites. Modern sites, already equipped with railway sidings and canal wharves, could be had for a song. "As a matter of fact," he went on, "I think you're extremely lucky to have raised two thousand. You'll never get half as much again. If you want to know my candid opinion," he added, remembering the hint that Mr. Bulgin had dropped him over the telephone, "you'll be wise to let the property go. The mortgagee lent his money on a valuation that no longer holds good. To part with it now is equivalent to having sold it at the top of the market. Why don't you let my client foreclose?"

George shook his head feebly. "It's rather hard to explain. It's a matter of sentiment . . ."

"Oh, well, if you put it like that!"

The wooden-faced young man washed his hands of him; the law was not sentimental. George tentatively returned to the attack with a fainter heart.

"Have you anyone interested in house property?" he nervously enquired.

"Any client, do you mean? What kind of house property?"

"It's a Georgian-style house—rather large, I'm afraid. It's in Halesby."

"A large house? In Halesby? My dear sir, you must surely be joking!"

"Thank heaven!" George thought. "If he *had* known of anyone and said 'yes' I couldn't have done it." He rose limply. "In that case," he said, "I don't think I need trouble you any longer. I shall endeavour to pay by the end of the month. Many thanks."

Outside, in Sackville Row, he stood with his hat in his hand and mopped his bald head. He found he had more than an hour to spare before his train left for Halesby. On the grilling pavements of North Brom-wich amid the roar of market-day traffic he felt singu-larly rustic and helpless. His head ached, his eyes smarted with petrol vapour and dust. Times were bad, they all said: yet the streets were crawling with costly motor-cars, the jewellers' windows crammed with luxurious rubbish. Mechanically he made his way to a shop which he knew in a humble side-street that catered for the modest extravagances of local coarse fisher-men. He stood under the shade of an awning peering critically at the stuffed shapes of specimen roach and perch in their cool glass cases, examining the latest varieties of rods and tackle and creels and infallible ground-baits. Yet not even the apparatus of his ruling passion could soothe his distracted mind. The contents of the window seemed to waver; they went dim before his eyes; and he saw, instead, a ghostly reflection of himself on the dusted plate-glass.

It was the first time for years that George Lorimer had been made aware of his personal appearance. The vision shocked him. However ageless his spirit, he saw that his body had suddenly grown old. Could this odd, huddled, plump little figure in the wrinkled coat and baggy trousers, with the ragged moustache and the wisp of grey hair escaping from under the billycock's brim, be himself? Was he, young George Lorimer, really as shabby as that? He gazed at the dim reflection with doubtful, fascinated horror. He contorted his face into a ghastly smile to disprove its reality; the figure grinned back at him in grim confirmation of the worst. "Good God, if I look like that," he said to himself, "no wonder that lawyer fellow treated me like dirt. I really must try and pull myself together." He did so, and momentarily assumed an erect and truculent air; but bold as he made himself feel, the reflected figure remained as ludicrous as that of a clown at a circus. He fled from it across half the width of the town to the station refreshment-room, where, in desperation, he gulped down a double whisky and soda. Then, tired out, bewildered, but—thanks to the alcohol—a little elated, he ran for his train.

In the opposite corner of the third-class smoker Captain Small was planted. That morning, having drawn his pension, he had paid a visit to North Bromwich to get his monthly hair-cut. He was brimming, at the moment, with conscious virtue, having successfully resisted the temptation to make a night of it. At the newsagent's stall he had bought the day's *Times* and a copy of the book called *Fraternity*, which he had seen Susan Lorimer reading in the train three weeks before. To tell the truth he couldn't make very much of it; but as soon as he opened *The Times* an advertisement had caught his eye.

"No, he's not quite the man that he was. He finds everything too much trouble nowadays," the caption told him, then went on to describe in a sinister crescendo the lamentable degenerative results of moderately excessive indulgence in spirituous liquor. "I suppose I'm what you'd call a moderate drinker," he decided cheerfully. At any rate the fellow who had written the advertisement knew a devil of a lot, though there were one or two points on which Captain Small, out of personal experience, knew rather more. Those dreams, for instance. The chap didn't even mention them, or the headache either, though that of course was shell-shock. But the loss of appetite, of memory for names and power of concentration—well, didn't he just know them! A nice, sympathetic fellow, not a bit

self-righteous and all out to be helpful. If you filled in the form at the foot of the paragraph he would send you particulars of a Sure and Secret and (all but) Gratuitous cure for this tiresome failing. Was it really worth while? Captain Small reflected. *Loss of Power of Concentration,* the advertiser suggested scornfully. No doubt that was why he was hesitating. *Everything's too much trouble nowadays.* So he tore out the column of newspaper—rather furtively, for, somehow, to be taking a secret cure for drink seemed much more shameful than open drinking—and stole a shy glance at the man in the opposite corner to make quite sure that he hadn't been caught in the act. "Well, I'm damned," he thought to himself, "if it isn't George Lorimer!"

"Afternoon, Mr. Lorimer," he said cheerfully.

George Lorimer jumped at the sound of his own name like a shot rabbit. He nodded, smiled nervously, and then, in an agony of self-consciousness, looked out of the window. He had hoped to avoid seeing anyone who knew him on the afternoon train. Now that Small had recognized him the news of his visit would be known and discussed in every bar-parlour in Halesby. Halesby people were always interested in their neighbours' business. Time enough for them to talk when they heard the report of his bankruptcy. Two thousand pounds . . .

Captain Small, vaguely conscious of a rebuff, was thinking, "What a queer little cuss! Who on earth would imagine that a seedy bloke like that had anything to do with Susan?" He glanced at George Lorimer. "Too good to speak to me, are you?" he thought. "We'll see about that! I'm as good as you are, anyway. What part did *you* take in the war?" he thought indignantly. Aloud, and extremely politely, he enquired:

"How's your niece getting on?"

George Lorimer gave another jump. "Oh, she's quite well, thank you. I mean, she's been ill. Gone to Brinton-le-Sands for a holiday."

"Oh, I say, I'm sorry to hear that, Mr. Lorimer," Captain Small replied, "about her illness that is," he hurriedly explained. He wasn't sorry in the least. He was thinking: "Brinton! She's at Brinton. So that's why I haven't seen her! It isn't that she's been avoiding me. I'm flush at the moment. I could easily pop down there myself next week-end. A breath of the briny, by Jove! and the chance of seeing her. One glance at that girl would do me more good than all the cures in creation." And he staged for himself (for the hair-cut had made him feel smarter than usual) a casual encounter on the palm-shadowed esplanade as portrayed on the railway posters; long talks on the sand or the front at night; (no nonsense, mind you—always the officer and the gentleman!) a frank interchange of confidences, genuine friendship. "Is she staying there long?" he enquired.

But George Lorimer didn't answer. He, too, was

troubled with a sudden vision of Susan—of Susan standing behind him in the office while he delved in the empty safe. He remembered how thankful he had been to find her satisfied with ten pounds instead of fifteen. The rest of her allowance would be due on Midsummer Day—the very same date as the mortgage.

Two thousand pounds! It came to him in a flash that the capital which he held in trust for Susan amounted to this figure precisely. Two thousand pounds! In Savings Certificates and War Loan. A bearer scrip as easily negotiable as Bank of England notes! Two ugly words, made vaguely familiar to him by the newspaper reports of defaulting solicitors, popped up in his memory. *Fraudulent Conversion.* It was to escape the penalty for this that poor Ernest Wilburn had shot himself in the days before the war. But in his own case, his simple mind argued, there need be no conversion. All he had to do was to lodge the scrip with his bank as security for an overdraft. The money would be just as safe there as anywhere else and carry the same interest. As for fraud . . . Well, that question didn't arise either. The transaction would amount, in reality, to a loan—from Susan's estate to his—a temporary loan, amply covered, as nobody could deny, by the value of the Dingle site and that of the house in Great Cornbow. After all, when you came to think of it, Susan's capital and the Halesby property were essentially interchangeable parts of the same estate. Both would ultimately come to her. He could

set off the value of the house—the wooden-faced
young man was talking through his hat when he questioned that—against the government securities. It
was all, on the surface, a little confused, demanding,
for full comprehension, a mathematical mind. The
main point was that however much he might gain,
Susan didn't stand to lose a penny by this arrangement.
He could pay her her income quarterly, just as before.
The only difference would be that the money he paid
would represent her interest in the works—no, that
wasn't right either: the bank would get that—say,
rather, her interest in the house which he had already
willed to her. The question of handing over the
capital would not arise for two years at least. "Yes,
that's it," he decided triumphantly, "now I've got it
quite straight!"

George Lorimer's mind, as his record had proved,
worked somewhat illogically in matters of money.
This inspired solution of his difficulties struck him as
masterly, though a real business brain, like John
Bulgin's, he supposed, would probably have tumbled
to it at once. Its saving grace was that the arrangement
would merely be temporary. The long lane of business
depression must come to a turning. He remembered
his father's deep-rooted faith in the ultimate recovery
of the wrought-iron nail trade. Machines were all very
well, his father had said, but sound material and honest
handicraft must win through in the end. Trade, like
everything else, obeyed the law of averages. As surely

as day followed night the slump would give way to a boom. And then . . . well, of course, then things would be just as they'd always been: Susan's money, the Dingle, the house, in their proper places—and something to spare for the dear child's future as well.

In spite of the gross economical fallacy on which they were based, these plausible conclusions seemed irrefutable to George Lorimer's mind. Though people might misunderstand the arrangement, nobody need know. In a moment the opaque situation became clear as crystal. Instantaneously his clouded mind recovered its serenity. And there, like the puff of smoke that hangs in the air when a shot has been fired, the faint echo of Captain Small's last question demanded his attention. What was it? He chuckled to himself. He had quite forgotten.

"I beg your pardon," he said. "I was dreaming. I believe you asked me something?"

"I asked you how long Miss Lorimer was staying at Brinton," Captain Small repeated grimly. People were perfectly right. Her uncle was no more than an idiot. Sitting there and gazing at nothing and chuckling to himself! *Lost Power of Concentration,* indeed!

"Do you know," George Lorimer blithely confessed, "I haven't the faintest idea!"

He was thinking: "I'm too late to-day. The bank closes at three. But to-morrow at ten they'll be open. I'll go down there at once after breakfast and settle everything." He smiled unconsciously as he thrust the whole matter behind him. "If I'd had any sense," he thought, "I should certainly have bought a bag of that patent ground-bait." And he envisaged a corner of the mill-pond with a gravelly bottom where once, it was said, a man named Parker had caught a perch weighing exactly three pounds. He imagined an equivalent tiger-striped monster with its red spine erect set up in a glass case. He saw in this day-dream the black varnish inscription beneath it: *Perch. 3lb. 2oz. Caught by George Lorimer, Esq.* "Yes, I'd been after that brute for years," he would probably explain to his angling friends.

Captain Small watched him sourly. He knew nothing of this innocent exalted dream nor of the nightmare which had preceded it. He interpreted George Lorimer's abstraction as a deliberate slight on himself. "You self-righteous little swine!" he thought bitterly. "You blasted bourgeois! Is there any wonder that the Midlands are rank with Bolshevism with employers like you about? It'll come, sure as fate, and then you'll be licking the boots of any fellow like me who can handle a machine-gun!"

With this acrid conclusion he took up the book called *Fraternity* and turned over the pages savagely. He had bought it because of a vaguely romantic idea that the written word might lead him nearer to the sweet, mysterious recesses of Susan's mind; but when he came to read it the story seemed to lead nowhere. It was all about a lot of high-brow blighters, artists and such like, and a doddering old gent who wore a Wotan blue collar. How the devil could he be expected to know what Wotan blue was? An artist's model. . . . That was rather more in his line. "But give me old Sapper or Edgar Wallace," he thought.

II

At one-twenty-five p.m. on Saturday, the ninth of July, the Reverend Charles Pearson, Rector of Halesby, bolted his last morsel of Cheddar and biscuit, cleared his throat, wriggled into his cassock, jammed on a crumpled mortar-board, and hurried, with long, athletic strides, across the strip of graveyard that separated his vicarage from the vestry wicket. That wasn't the only kind of wicket on which, at the moment, his thoughts were centred—as might be judged from the blazer (of Keble College, Oxford) which his cassock concealed and the yellowish flannel trousers that occasionally showed beneath it. Within half an hour he was due to catch the motor char-à-banc that would transport him with the rest of the Halesby eleven to Stourton; but fortunately, as he told his wife, the duty that was making him run it so close was not a funeral. It was merely a wedding. And weddings—particularly unimportant ones—didn't take long.

Mr. Pearson felt pleased with life. His digestion was excellent. The day had turned out sunny, but not sultry. The grass of the ancient churchyard, whose spurred seeds clutched at his sweeping cassock and clung to it, bowed under the breeze in satiny ripples and smelt of summer. The vestry had a cool smell of coconut matting, and stone and piled hymn-books more ancient than modern; the familiar, enveloping odour of his holy vocation. He felt at home in it. The looking-glass on the wall reflected his face, middle-aged, but perpetually boyish, and flushed at the moment with food and the pleasant anticipation of an afternoon's cricket. He enjoyed marrying people; he heartily believed in marriage as the sunny, contented state which his own experience had found it. He smiled in the glass as he smoothed down his strong sandy hair and slipped on his surplice. As the chime in the tower struck half-past one he composed his features to gravity and passed, with a stride of modified swiftness, from vestry to chancel.

At the western end of the nave the wedding-party awaited him, a small group, dwarfed by the soaring arches and clerestory. It consisted of the bride, the bridegroom, two witnesses and Bagley the verger.

Mr. Pearson beckoned them towards him, and the whole group timidly advanced. Nice young people, he thought. How splendid to be young and in love! He knew the bride slightly by sight. Though she wasn't, regrettably, a member of his congregation, he was glad she had at least had the decency to be married in church. As she advanced to the chancel rail he noticed her cool zephyr frock (a trifle too short in the skirt,

Mrs. Pearson would have said) and the neat little figure inside it.

"Why, she might be a school-girl," he thought, "but that's all to the good." (He approved of early marriages.) "A pretty girl, too," he thought, "and as cool as a cucumber. So completely composed. They're most of them like that nowadays. The tearfully modest bride has quite gone out of fashion. Very different indeed," he thought, as the group continued to advance, "from the fortunate bridegroom. A well set-up young fellow: blue serge suit; old Brunstonian tie. Not a bad school, Brunstone: I wonder if he's keen on cricket. If he's coming to live here he might be a useful man; we want more of that kind; but the poor boy looks just as scared as if this were his trial show in his first school eleven."

Mr. Pearson smiled kindly. His smile was the equivalent in facial gesture of an encouraging slap on the back, but it could not penetrate Dick Pennington's aura of nervous agony. He stared straight at the parson, or rather through and beyond him; his hands hung down tightly clenched; his face was as pale as death, and, from time to time, he nervously moistened his lips.

"I know just what it feels like," Mr. Pearson thought sympathetically. The smile which he had intended for Dick Pennington glanced sideways and found its mark in the scared eyes of George Lorimer, who moved forward on tiptoe touching the arm of the

M

bride. George Lorimer looked even more awed and pallid than his prospective nephew. He was visibly sweating in the grip of a cut-away coat that had been made for him in the distant days before he had lost his figure. In his left hand he carried a top hat of the same remote period, the crown marked, in its lower two-thirds, by the removal of the crape band which he habitually wore at funerals. The other hand wandered nervously, from time to time, to his waistcoat pocket, in which, as Mr. Pearson knew from experience, the ring was hidden. As he caught the wan smile that George Lorimer returned to him Mr. Pearson's face stiffened. The Lorimers, he knew, had once been big people in Halesby. As a matter of tradition, George ought to have been a prominent churchman. And he wasn't. On Sundays, Mr. Pearson knew by report he went fishing in a punt; and the fact that he was *that* kind of fisherman was almost as great a crime in the eyes of the rector, who was a dry-fly purist, as his Laodicean attitude toward the established church.

Apart from the bride the only persons in the group who appeared not to be embarrassed were the verger, who scented a handsome tip, and George Lorimer's wife. Mrs. Lorimer, conceding nothing to fashion, was clothed in a hot-looking dress of black satin. Her face, which had once, no doubt, been handsome, wore an expression of triumph, content and determination. "Thank Heaven I'm not married to a woman like that," Mr. Pearson thought. "No wonder poor

Lorimer looks scared. If he crossed her in any way his life simply wouldn't be worth living, and I don't mind betting that girl's hasn't been too easy. She's probably glad to be out of it. You can see that her uncle's fond of her."

By this time the party had reached the steps. Mr. Pearson briskly cleared his throat and began:

"Dearly beloved, we are gathered together here in the sight of God and in the face of this congregation to join together this man and this woman in Holy Matrimony, which is an honourable estate. . . ."

His voice, an admirably modulated voice of which he was reasonably proud, drifted away melodiously into the echoing vaults of nave and transept. The words tripped slickly from Mr. Pearson's tongue, for he knew them by heart. But he meant what they said all the same, and even felt it, being a generous man to whom Christian marriage was a genuine ideal. As he spoke his eyes met those of the bride. They were wide, dark, solemn. Her composure, he decided, was not that of unconcern, but of natural, habitual gravity. She was facing this solemn moment and the future, he felt, with a seemly, clear-eyed seriousness; and his voice, which really sounded exceedingly well in the empty church, grew more intimate and human, as though, indeed, he were addressing a sister in Christ and she were listening. He hoped, from the bottom of his heart, that these two would be faithful and happy and have a large family, though education, as he knew to his cost, was a problem in these days.

Susan Lorimer, in spite of her appearance of rapt attention, did not hear a word. She was thinking: "So this is what it's like. I'm actually being married. It can't be true—not just yet. What on earth am I doing? But it *is* true," she thought. "When it's over, in five or six minutes, I shan't be what I was any longer. I'm going to be a married woman. How strange life is!"

"*The procreation of children . . .*" Mr. Pearson said bluntly. Susan caught at the emphasized words, and they shocked—not her modesty (she knew all about those things)—but her sense of physical security. A red signal of danger, betokening pain and, possibly, peril, flashed into her brain. She felt suddenly frightened and doubtful, so insecure that for the first time since they had entered the church she stole a swift glance at the man she was marrying, half in fear, lest she should find him even more of a stranger than her momentary panic persuaded her. That glance reassured her. After all, he was only Dick Pennington. She saw him for an instant in profile; his lips were set tight, his hands nervously clenched, and his face, beneath the Brinton tan, showed the deathly pallor of intense emotion. He seemed even less imposing at that moment than she had previously imagined him. Compared with the amplified, surpliced figure of Mr. Pearson he looked a stripling, a schoolboy, a mere child; and this odd diminution in the man, of whose strength her own body in those last three weeks of

acute enchantment had been so proudly aware, filled
her heart with a sudden flood not of pride, as before,
but of overwhelming tenderness and loyalty and protective courage.

"He's mine," she thought, almost fiercely. "He belongs to me and to nobody else. He's good and simple
and gentle and lonely. He loves me; he needs me, and
I . . . why, I'm not fit to black his boots. I'm an
ignorant, selfish, sensual little bundle of conceit. I'm
a sham, but he's real all through. And some way or
other—Heaven knows how—I've got to live up to it,
and I will!"

A moist hand clasped hers. Dick was speaking. His
voice was steady, but so low she could scarcely hear it.
Her own hand tightened. "I am here," she was saying.
"I'm yours. We're in this together." Then she felt a
conviction that George Lorimer, behind her, was crying.
"Poor darling!" she thought. Dick's voice ceased, and
now she herself was echoing Mr. Pearson's an octave
higher in syllables that, though her tongue formed
them clearly and confidently, did not belong to her.

*"I, Susan, take thee, Richard, to be my wedded
husband, to have and to hold from this day forward,
for better for worse, for richer for poorer"*—(We
couldn't be much poorer than we are, she was thinking)—*"in sickness and in health; to love, cherish and
obey till death us do part, according to God's holy
ordinance, and thereto I give thee my troth."*

The ring, damp and sticky from George Lorimer's

anxious hand, was placed upon her finger. Next she heard Mr. Pearson say: "Lord have mercy upon us"— an imprecation that Aunt Edna echoed in a tone which implied her conviction that His mercy would shortly be needed. Then, it seemed, the ceremony was over. Mr. Pearson, who believed in the adequate solemnity of the liturgy and remembered his waiting char-à-banc, spared them an address. His innocent smile, of itself, bespoke his goodwill.

In the vestry Dick suddenly turned and kissed Susan with blundering timidity; he was smiling tremulously and very red in the face. Susan kissed him again. It was a different kind of kiss from any she had given him before. Then George Lorimer, between laughing and crying, kissed her, too. Mr. Pearson, having doffed his surplice and his sacerdotal manner together, got in a word with Dick on the subject of cricket, picked up his cassock and was off like the wind. Aunt Edna also kissed Susan. "I only hope," she said, without much conviction, "that you and Mr. Pennington" ("Why not Dick?" Susan thought) "will be as happy as your uncle and me." The verger was smiling in the background, waiting for his tip. The scent of graveyard grasses blew in through the vestry window. Outside the church a hired car was waiting for them. "I expect the driver 'll be getting impatient," Dick hurriedly suggested. Susan nodded and flew back again to kiss Uncle George.

"I shall see you next week, uncle darling," she said.

George Lorimer smiled and shook his head help-lessly. It seemed kinder to leave him. At the church-yard gate stood two women in shawls; one was nursing a baby and the other expecting to do so. Three ragged children shouted and waved and ran after them as they drove away. They sat side by side, too dazed to speak or touch one another's hands.

(It is popularly supposed that marriages are made in heaven.)

George Lorimer and his wife plodded back to Great Cornbow through the heat. The pressure of his top hat, by a natural association of ideas, continued to con-vince him that it was Sunday, not Saturday, and that he had been to a funeral. There was an awful void in his life that none of his usual resources could fill. He hadn't even the heart to go fishing that afternoon, to do anything, indeed, but play funereal hymn tunes on the American organ or moon about the summer garden in the grip of his festal clothes. But that night, when his Susan lay in her husband's arms in the Winsworth lodging-house that was to be their first married home, George Lorimer, after eating far more than usual and drinking two bottles of Astill's Entire ale, dreamt he was a perch. A coarse, invisible hand gripped his striped body and clipped off his crested dorsal fin and put him on a snap-tackle attached to a green and white float, then cast him far into the middle of the mill-pool, where he swam round and round in feeble circles as a well-behaved live bait should, and Mr. Bulgin, with a face like a pike's—or rather a pike with a face like Mr. Bulgin's—watched his conscientious evolutions with a hungry grin in leisurely anticipation of the moment when he should gobble him up. "But if you get *me*," George Lorimer cunningly reflected, "you'll only be caught yourself." And so great was his hatred of John Bulgin that he strained every nerve to make himself appear helpless and appetizing, till suddenly, in a swirl of mottled olive, his enemy swooped on him. He felt his bones go crack in John Bulgin's scrunching jaws and woke, gasping, to hear the clock in the hall below strike two and to know a dark loneliness such as he had never felt before.

III

Married people expect to receive calls, and are bound by politeness to return them. Neither Dick nor Susan had ever possessed a visiting-card; so, to save expense, Susan had fifty printed (while she waited) for both. The type was so neatly set that it looked almost like copper-plate. It announced them, indissolubly, as:

Mr. and Mrs. Pennington.

CHAPTER VI

A ROOM WITH A VIEW

I

On a Saturday afternoon three months later Mr. and Mrs. Pennington alighted in the main street of Tilton from one of those Midland buses that threaded the weft of streets between North Bromwich and Halesby like flying vermilion shuttles. The force which impelled them thither, though they were not aware of it, was identical with that which had brought them severally to Brinton-le-Sands and each other's arms: the cumulative suggestion of advertisement hoardings that proclaimed the advantages of Tilton as a place of residence. They were feeling extremely adventurous and a little nervous, for Susan had made an appointment to view a house without consulting Dick, and Dick was quite sure they couldn't afford to take it. With equal assurance, to his embarrassment, she was capable of entering a shop and asking the price of something she had no intention of buying.

"But really, Dick darling," she was saying for the hundredth time, "there's no harm in *seeing* the place.

You don't understand. A woman can't call her soul her own when she's living in lodgings. Mrs. Wallis means awfully well, I know, poor dear, but you've lodged with her so long that she feels you're her property and that I'm a temporary intruder. I can't do a thing for you without feeling that she disapproves it. After all, you're my job. You *do* belong to me, don't you? I feel at an absolute loose end. And it's not only that—there's no earthly need for us to go on living in Winsworth. Those dingy streets get on my nerves, and I hate being so near Muriel. That awful mother of hers sits in the window and watches like a cat over a mouse-hole. When you've gone to the office I simply daren't put my nose out. I stay moping indoors all day surrounded by awful lodging-house furniture: if you move a thing Mrs. Wallis takes it as a personal insult, and if you open a window she shuts it as soon as your back's turned." She drew a deep breath. "Oh, dear, how delicious this air is! It's as if we'd escaped from a prison. And really nobody can say Tilton isn't convenient either. Twenty minutes to Sackville Row and only eighteen—just think of it— to poor Uncle George's. I know he'd be happier, Dick, to feel we were near. I wonder if 'Chatsworth' will be as nice as the advertisement says. If it is, the rent sounds quite ridiculously low."

Dick walked beside her, her hand clutched his arm and reinforced each disjointed sentence with eager movements. He didn't trouble to answer her, and indeed no answer was expected. In the early weeks of their married life he had been astonished by the way Susan "rattled on"—she who at Brinton had been so demure and silent. It was as though she had been waiting all her life for someone to talk to, but by now he had grown accustomed to her spate of rapid inconsequences. Her mind was like a restless butterfly, thrusting its slender proboscis into a dozen blooms and never the one on which he expected it to alight. After all, this quality of mind was only a part of the mysterious physical difference which underlay their mutual infatuation. If she had thought or spoken as he did his life with her would have lacked the element of surprise which made half of its enchantment. When he came back from the sombre world of the office and the sober calculable reactions of men, it ravished him to find Susan fluttering round like some bright captive bird, so gay and perky with her pretty posturings, her quick movements, her easy laughter. It didn't matter much what she said. For him it was delight enough to hear the sudden, tender inflections of her voice; to know that this ardent being, so different and so various, was there beside him; to realize in flashes of wonder and with a sudden stirring of the blood, that by virtue of some miracle she was his not only to worship, but also to protect and possess.

Even now as she clung submissively to his arm while he steered her across the road through a momentary gap in the half-holiday motor traffic that gushed through this western faucet of North Bromwich in an almost continuous stream, Dick felt himself transported by the contrast between his own slow solidity of body and mind and Susan's impulsive frailty. Even now he glanced sideways at her, secretly, proudly, bewildered by the discovery that she was his wife.

"And then, darling," Susan went on breathlessly, "I've always loved Tilton—even when I was a funny little girl, and we used to drive into town on the top of the Halesby bus. It was always a sweet little village. Uncle George told me once that when he was a boy his father showed him the field where they used to tilt at the quintain. But of course it's quite different now—so brisk and awake. Don't you feel that everyone you see here looks happy and young? It must be full of people like us just starting life. Don't you love that feeling? Don't you think it's terribly attractive? All these new little shops, so gay and venturous, with everything one can possibly want! I'm certain that things will be twice as cheap here as they are in Winsworth. And no smoke! Oh, *why* don't you say something, Dick?" She waited. "How slow you are!"

He laughed and pressed her arm to show that however slow he might be, he worshipped her. Although he had no intention of taking a house there, he too remembered Tilton before the war: a hamlet consisting of no more than a whitewashed, abandoned tollhouse with Gothic windows, a discreet little church and a score of red-brick cottages. In those days the expan-

sion of North Bromwich on its western edge had been
checked by the discouraging smugness of upper-
middle-class Alvaston. The war, with its quickening
inundations of easy wealth, and the internal combustion
engine, which made formidable distances negligible,
had changed all that. Under these twin stimuli the
Iron City had developed the encroaching activity of a
cancer cell, overleaping the barriers of Alvaston,
thrusting greedy tentacles of brick and mortar and
steel and cement into the healthy countryside, until
now the sleepy street of Tilton echoed continually
with the grinding of gear-pinions and the stutter of
exploding petrol, and its ancient buildings with their
air of formal grace had become encysted (as it were)
in reticulations of staring new brick: a red and rodent
ulcer eating its way into the soft green tissue on either
side of a broad arterial road where a series of jerry-
built shops and petrol-stations, a concrete cinema, a
galvanized iron estate-office, and a showroom exhibiting appliances for the use of municipal gas and
electricity, had made Tilton, that shy, individual
hamlet, no different from hundreds of other debauched
villages on the outskirts of a Midland industrial town.

"Do let's look in that window," Susan pleaded.
"We've plenty of time, and the agent's sure to be
late. Oh, look at that little jumper, Dick darling!
Don't you think it's too sweet? I priced it last week,
but now it's reduced. I should have to pay five
shillings more than that in North Bromwich."

It was sweet, he agreed, without much enthusiasm. This was another of the astonishing things he had discovered about Susan: the passionate interest and enthusiasm that clothes excited in her. The things she desired were endowed with affectionate diminutives: they became sweet "little" hats, "little" frocks, "little" belts, "little" overalls. For himself he had always taken clothes for granted. With Susan on the other hand—particularly since marriage had deprived her of her academic outlets for energy—the problems of dress had become a predominant interest. He didn't even attempt to understand it. To him, dressed anyhow or nohow, she was equally ravishing. Yet gradually, in his desire to give her happiness, he had been coaxed into an affectation of sharing this passionate absorption until now he appeared to give it the importance it had with her. Her very enthusiasm for colours and fabrics quickened her own glowing beauty; she could achieve as much ecstasy from the perusal of a mail-order catalogue with its rough cuts of elongated female figures in frocks and underwear as an artist could find in the contemplation of a masterpiece. The least change in the *mode*, as she called it, would excite her to frenzied scheming. The length of a skirt or the width of the crown of a hat were more momentous to her than the fate of nations. "I've nothing to wear, darling," she would tell him pathetically at a moment when, it seemed to him, her wardrobe was almost bewilderingly full.

"I've nothing," she really meant, "that I haven't already worn." And this puzzled Dick, who habitually wore the same suit for five years on end.

Yet, against all reason and always with a half-hearted rebellious consciousness of his own weakness, he constantly found himself surrendering to Susan's point of view. Her clothes—not only those which were outwardly visible, but the diaphanous under-garments which it was his sole privilege to see—were part of the feminine mystery to which the intimacy of marriage had admitted him. He had even begun to master the jargon of bastard French associated with them, to realize the gulf that separated *georgette* from *taffeta;* and though he was alarmed at first by the aggregate of the small sums which she lavished on frail fripperies, whose charms were apparently as evanescent as the bloom on a flower, he was so much in love that the thought of questioning the wisdom of her acquisitive passion rarely entered his mind. After all, the money she squandered so carelessly was hers, and in other economies she sometimes showed a surprising keenness for what she called "bargains." Even so, as Susan stood glued to that shop-window at Tilton, her soft eyes greedily fastened on the mutilated remnant of artificial silk which, at that moment, had become the centre of her existence—and therefore of his—he couldn't help remembering, doubtfully, that they had only married on the strength of their con-joint incomes, and that her sense of the value of money had not been developed in the strict school he had known.

As to this mad scheme of taking a house—a whole house for two people. . . . But the house, for the moment, was forgotten.

"You see," she was saying, "it would go too perfectly with my blue check skirt. Of course, I should need a new hat to match it, shouldn't I?—unless I sent this green one to Pullars' to be dyed," she added reflectively, "though, in that case, of course, I'd have nothing to wear with that bottle-green coat with the nutria collar. How difficult life is! It seems a shame, doesn't it, to miss the chance of saving five shillings? Do you think I could pop in, just for one minute, and slip it on? It may be too small, and then we needn't think about it."

Dick looked at his watch and discovered, to his great relief, that they hadn't time. "Mr. Duke's appointment was made for five-thirty," he told her, "and we really oughtn't to keep him waiting."

Being late, he thought, wouldn't matter so much if their visit had been serious.

"Well, five minutes won't hurt him," she answered, almost petulantly. However, we shall know at once if we like the house, and we shall just have time to look at the jumper afterwards, shan't we? They won't close till half-past six." She hung on his arm reluctantly. "Don't you think I'd better tell her we're coming back later, and ask her to take it out of the window? Just in case . . . ?" she pleaded.

He laughed, for he knew by experience that the jumper was as good as bought, and waited good-humouredly, hearing the tinkle of the shop bell and her eager voice whispering instructions to the woman inside, till she returned, her cheeks glowing with triumph and her dark eyes smiling. "I'm so sorry to have kept you, darling," she said, as she slipped her warm hand into his; and again he wondered how so slender an emotion could transport her and make her more beautiful.

Ada Road, the object of their visit, was the pride and crowning achievement of Mr. Duke, the milkman. His local patriotism, which, apart from a shrewd acquisitive instinct, was his ruling passion, took the shape of a vandalistic relish that amounted to genius. His conception of the landscape of heaven, if he had one, would undoubtedly have been a rectangular net-work of asphalt roads bordered by bungalows each equipped for the reception of the post-war social unit —a young married couple, a dog, and a baby Austin— ancillary to a milk-bottle embossed with the words "Duke's Dairy" on every front door-step. Mr. Duke had begun business in a small way in the Penningtons' childhood with a pony-drawn second-hand float, in which, at dawn, he personally collected milk and eggs from the farms on the Halesby escarpment. By the time that his sons came back from the war, he was already a man of substance, with a dairy, two motor-

N

vans, and an idealistic faith in milk as the sole com-
modity necessary to mankind in health and sickness,
from the cradle to the grave. By this time, envisaging
life as one grand milk-round, he had begun to be irked,
like Alexander of Macedon, by the unexpansive nature
of his field of activities, and it was this that had
tempted him to risk his modest fortune in real estate
by going into partnership with his wife's brother, a
mason turned speculative builder.

The first-fruits of this unholy alliance had been Ada
Road. In the flush of his original inspiration other
names had been canvassed—from the downright
"Duke's Road" to a modification "The Dukeries";
but an affected modesty tempered by an unaffected
sense of insecurity in what, after all, was an heroically
rash speculation had (not inappropriately) watered
down these claims on immortality to a more domestic
consistency. The new road had eventually been named
Ada Road in honour of his only daughter and his
partner's niece, while a delicate allusion to its
originator's surname had been perpetuated in the
designation of the houses that composed it, which
ranged from "Haddon," "Clumber" and "Belvoir" to
"Welbeck" and "Goodwood."

The latest built of them all and the object of the
Penningtons' visit had been labelled "Chatsworth."
Mr. Duke, having once, on a day trip to Derbyshire,
visited the august original, had kept this name up his
sleeve in reserve for his masterpiece. Dick and Susan

found him that evening waiting at the point where his road debouched on the main route to Halesby. He was an agile little man with wiry grey hair, a walrus moustache, and beady brown field-mouse eyes beneath a low brow, whose corrugations gave them a puzzled expression, as though the magnitude of his achievement were still not quite believable. He wore a gold Albert watch-chain across a little round paunch that stuck out like an inflated tennis-ball, and seemed to be detached from the rest of his spare anatomy. As they picked their way in his company over the surface of rutted clay in which brick-ends and builders' rubbish were deeply embedded, Mr. Duke's mean figure swelled like that of a pouter pigeon.

"These 'ouses of mine, they're every one different: not one like another, if you take my meaning," he explained, as he pointed to the variously coloured composition tiles with which they were roofed—and, indeed, the houses in Ada Road had nothing in common but an extreme degree of ugliness — "Yes, we've developed a lot of first-rate ideas since the days we built 'Welbeck' and 'Bel-voyer,' though I say it as shouldn't. Each 'ouse a picture in itself, and yet you can't say they're not 'omely. Though it's the men that foots the bill, it's the ladies we have to consider. That, if I may say so, is why we went nap on bungalers. No stairs to walk up means no brass stair-rods to polish, and no risk, when it comes to that, of kids falling out of the window—though I doubt if you've reached that

stage, ma'am," he added apologetically. "Still, you
never know, do you?" he continued, with a ribald wink
that made Dick feel awkward, "and, family or no
family, a young married woman likes things to 'er 'and
and all up to date. There's nothing old-fashioned 'ere.
Sanitation's our slogan, as they say, in the 'ome as well
as the dairy, and if you knew the figure we've poured
into the plumbing, so to speak, you'd be fairly staggered. The only thing is"—he held up a grimy-nailed
finger—"if you're thinking of settling on 'Ada' you'd
better look sharp. These bungalers of ours, they've a
way of getting snapped up before the plasterers are
out of them. I'm not pressing you, mind—though
there's applicants standing in queues, you might say—
but a nod's as good as a wink, and you may as well
know. What's more, I may tell you in confidence-like,
we're not laying another brick, Mr. Hodgetts my
partner and me, till the council comes up to the scratch
and takes 'Ada' over. So now you see where you stand,
and that's best for both parties."

He paused, not for breath, but to wave his hand
dramatically, and stepped aside into a puddle in order
to allow the splendour of his latest creation to sink into
Susan's eyes.

"There it is, ma'am. . . . There's 'Chatsworth,'"
he cried, with pardonable pride. "Now I've plenty else
to look after. Don't mind me, Mr. Pennington. You
walk right in and look round as if it belonged to you."

To walk right in was easier said than done, for the

garden gate, on which a nailed strip of embossed copper lettering obscurely suggested the house's name, was blocked at its lower edge by an impacted brick-end. It was slung on wooden posts painted with strong-smelling creosote, from either side of which ran two strands of galvanized wire enclosing a double row of puny privet-shoots, some of which had already perished. The desolation of recent building activities lay on the potential front garden, a minute plot of trampled earth strewn with lime and mortar and sodden wood-shavings. The path that led up to a porch recessed between the front rooms was paved with pounded rubble, and the floor of the porch itself, under a semi-circular arch of bricks, consisted of pressed tiles of the shade known as bullock's blood. Flanking the door-way, backed perilously by the side-lights of the out-jutting front-room windows, ran a wooden bench, on which an exceptionally spare human being might con-trive at a pinch to sit sideways.

"Very useful them benches," Mr. Duke encouraged them from the distance where, having made a feinted retreat, he now stood watching their movements with the eyes of a kestrel hovering over a pair of enamoured voles. "Very 'andy to leave the milk on," he bawled. "You can sit there and 'ave a quiet pipe on a Sunday evening and look at the view."

The view from the porch consisted, in fact, of Mr. Duke's earlier masterpiece, "Welbeck," from the curtained bow-window of which, as they turned in response to his call, the tousled head of an interested female spectator abruptly appeared. At the same moment, in the front garden of "Belvoir," the arched back of a corpulent gentleman who had apparently been weeding behind his own privet hedge upreared itself, like that of a hippopotamus emerging from its wallow, to be followed by a turnip-shaped face, with sparse sandy hair and moustache, plethoric by nature, yet made even more red by stooping.

Mr. Duke, whose eyes missed nothing, acknowledged their presence. "Good evenin', Miss Maples. . . . Good evenin', Inspector!" he shouted in either direction. "New neighbours, you see! Now didn't I tell you with my own lips that a week wouldn't pass without 'Chatsworth' being snapped up?" He dropped his voice suddenly, and spoke behind his hand to Dick. "Miss Maples is a monthly nurse," he whispered significantly. "I merely mention that as a fact worth remarking. You never know, do you? And Inspector Frome, he's 'igh up in the North Bromwich Police, which means that we don't get worried with hawkers and gipsies and such-like. Walk in, Mr. Pennington, walk in!"

Dick pushed at the door. It was even more tightly wedged than the garden gate. When he put his shoulder to it Mr. Duke was seized with alarm. "Gently, gently!" he cried. "Easy does it. You don't want to strain yourself. You just wait. I'll pop round to the back and ease it from inside." He skipped off with an agility extraordinary for an elderly man. They heard him panting and tugging and scratching like a terrier at the bottom of the door. Then, suddenly, with a screech, the raw deal gave way and revealed him devoid of breath, but triumphant. "Just shavin's," he puffed. "That's all it was. Just shavin's got wedged underneath." He swung the protesting door to and fro. "Now that's what I call a good fit. If it's snug, it's a fault on the right side. No draughts could get under that. As I always say: you can plane off what you can't put on, if you take my meaning." He breathed heavily. "Now this, as you see, is the entrance 'all. No space wasted. One width of lino will cover the lot. Just room for an 'at-stand and a drain-pipe for sticks and umbrellas. As to that I shouldn't wonder if my partner couldn't find you a drain-pipe. Two-penn'orth of paint and you've got something useful, simple and tasty. Now this 'ere"—another new door gave way with a screech—"this 'ere, according to my manner of thinking, though, of course, that's a matter of choice, ought to be the droring-room or parlour, as some people call it, and I'll tell you why. To tell you the honest, this room don't get much sun. Well, what does that matter? A droring-room doesn't need it. You're not likely to set foot in it except of a Sunday afternoon after dinner or to play the piano supposin' you want a tune, and who does that nowadays, with wireless and gramophones and such? As I say to my partner, if it wasn't for the fashion I'd cut out droringrooms. Now *this*, as you see"——he opened the opposite door——"is my idea of what a living-room should be. Sun, morning to night, and a butler's 'atch, as they call it, though we don't keep many butlers in 'Ada.' Well, it speaks for itself. This 'ere, if I may say so, is a *room*."

"I like those shelves," Susan whispered.

Mr. Duke, who had heard the last word, caught at it suspiciously.

"Them shelves?" he repeated. "Well, really, in a manner of speaking, they're bookshelves. But you can use them for ornaments, you know," he added, consolingly.

"Oh, my wife's very fond of books," Dick assured him proudly.

"Well, some are and some aren't," Mr. Duke replied. "There's no doubt they do a lot of 'arm," he added darkly. "But that's neither here nor there," he went on. "No need to waste time on it. I know what the lady's thinking of. The kitchen. Well, 'ere it is, ma'am, and if this isn't a beautiful kitchen I'll eat my 'at. Mrs. Duke, my missus that is, she often says that she'd give her eyes for a leg-saving kitchen like this. Everything to your 'and. Why, a lady could prepare and cook all her Sunday dinner and wash up as well without stirring a foot; and the feet——you know that, ma'am, as well as I do——is what suffers in 'ouse-keeping. As for larders: well, look"——he dragged open another door——"like an ice-'ouse this is in the 'ight

of summer. If you take in your milk from that bench
in the porch as soon as my man leaves it there and put
it in 'ere, I'll warrant its keeping sweet for twenty-
four hours. That's our full-cream milk, understand!
I say nothing of other dairies. The milk that some
dairymen sell in Tilton—I mention no names, mind—
well, the less said about it the better. Mr. Duke pursed
his lips with disgust and shook his head regretfully as
he passed on to display what generically he described
as the "Sanitation": a miniature bath and wash-hand-
stand enamelled in the bluish-white hue of watered
milk, both clogged with dust and shavings, and a
minute dank dungeon of a water-closet, walled with
olive-green cement, in whose upper third a galvanized
iron cistern gurgled dolefully. Mr. Duke turned on
the taps of the one and pulled at the flush of the other
to prove that both were what stage directors call
practicable, then pointed, with pardonable pride, to the
garage shed and the dog-kennel which he, as a pioneer
of suburban life, had first made "standard in Ada."
"I've been keeping the bedroom till last," he told them
cunningly, "because that, if I may say so, is me and my
partner's 'igh water-mark. When you come to think
of it, the 'ealthiest people spend up to a third of their
life in bed, and in sickness unfortunately more. Now
this bedroom's a bedroom. Night or day it's a pleasure
to lie in. It's a bedroom. I'll say no more. You can
see for yourselves."

The chamber to which Mr. Duke introduced them

so impressively did not, at first sight, appear very different from those they had examined already. It smelt, like the rest of the house, of damp plaster and unseasoned deal. The white paint on the woodwork had been so sparingly applied that it gave—like the sanitation's enamel—the effect of well-watered milk. The corners were clogged with collections of shavings and lime. The floor, the electric fittings and the window-panes had been marked by small, pear-shaped splashes of hastily spattered distemper. Round the central light-bulb disconsolate flies wheeled moodily like homeless ghosts in an outer circle of purgatory. But, as they turned to survey it, the prospect that met their eyes through the dusty window took their breath away. It was as though they had suddenly been permitted to gaze into another world. From this viewpoint not one of Mr. Duke's improvements on the Worcestershire landscape was visible. Not a brick, either old or new, not a single trace of recent human activity met their enchanted gaze. Beyond the unbroken back garden and its ragged hedgerow stretched mile upon mile of a still, sweet-breathing countryside asleep in misty bloom of September sunshine. Tall pillars of golden elms and domed beech-trees rose like plumes of smoke from the autumnal smoulder of hedgerow brambles and rusty hawthorn, while beyond, transported to an unnatural distance by the haze of moist air, the undulant line of the Clents, that fragment of wild Wales stranded east of Severn, whose

domed shapes had dominated Susan's childish imagination in Halesby, hung blue and cloud-like along
the line of the westering sun. As they gazed, the
words that came to their lips were checked and
silenced. Not only the beauty, but the mysterious
peacefulness of those wide expanses caught at their
hearts. The narrow preoccupations of their urban life
in the Winsworth lodging-house no less than the
financial doubts that haunted them fell away from
their minds. They stood hand in hand, recapturing a
larger emotion than any they had known since those
rapt days of courting in Brinton, and each of their
hearts was warmed by the secret glow of the other's.
This was one of the moments, rare as they be, that the
dullest of human beings are destined to remember.
Susan's hand clutched Dick's tightly. "Oh, Dick,
darling!" was all she said.

"They might build another house," he reminded
her.

"But they won't. He said so," she answered eagerly.
"Let's enjoy it while we can. We're going to live here.
We must. Whatever it costs."

"Well, of course, we can think it over. The furniture. . . . The rent . . ."

"Oh, Dick, what a coward you are! We need only
furnish two rooms at first," she whispered.

"He mightn't like that."

"I could put up some curtains, darling. He'd never
know. I'd buy them instead of that jumper."

He laughed. "It's not only that. We ought to look round. We mustn't jump at the first thing we see."

"You jumped at me, didn't you?"

"Yes, and look what I've got!" he teased her.

"Are you terribly sorry?"

"Oh, Susie!" He glanced round quickly. Mr. Duke had tactfully disappeared.

"Don't, darling. How dare you? He'll see us," she laughed, as he kissed her quickly. "Oh, Dick, don't you see . . . don't you *see?* It's a Room with a View."

II

Those bright September days suited Captain Small no end. He liked to feel the nip in the morning air, to see the diminutive lawn of Orchard Cottage silvered with ground frost or fine bejewelled webs and strands of nocturnal gossamer; to watch the leaves of the damson trees in the wet orchard (his aunt had always been celebrated for her pickled damsons) shining out like golden fruit; to smell chrysanthemums and trodden horse-chestnut fans and the smoke of the first scutch fires. The sultry summer days made life rather hard for him, for the weight of his useless leg made him sweat like a pig when he walked, to say nothing of catching cold afterwards, and one part of his cure for *Immoderate Indulgence in Alcohol* consisted, according to the book, of moderate exercise.

He had followed the régime religiously for over three months, taking regular doses of the capsicum mixture prescribed before meals and working in the garden which, since his aunt's death, had been sadly neglected. On the whole, he decided, the cure had been a success. Though the fear of appearing priggish or unsociable had let him in for an occasional binge, especially when he went into North Bromwich to get his hair cut, he had managed, as he put it himself, to keep fairly straight, circumventing the craving which still periodically assailed him by the cunning stratagem of allowing no liquor to enter the house when the supply that was in it when his treatment began had been exhausted, and never taking a drink unless he had earned one. This restriction had been enforced by a secret device known only to himself by which he recognized in his own mind the existence of four distinct persons: the first a rollicking free-handed youth, weak, of course, to a fault, but with no real vice in his nature; the second a fatherly middle-aged man, sympathetic and deeply versed in the weaknesses of human nature, who regarded the first with the paternal severity of an experienced company commander toward a wayward recruit who meant no harm and might some day make a good soldier; and a third impartially keeping the ring, so to speak, for the struggle between the one's sense of discipline and the other's frailty, whom a fourth Captain Small (or all the Captain Smalls together) regarded as commanding officer. By this happy convention, which owed its symbolism to the only kind of life he really understood, his mind had become a kind of perpetual orderly room in which the three divided personalities formally conversed:

"What? Small here again? Usual thing, I suppose? Have you anything to say for yourself?"

"I'm sorry, sir. It just happened to be my birthday. It won't occur again."

"Very well. About turn! Next time you won't get off so easily."

And next time: "You remember what I said, Small. Three days C.B. And you may think yourself damned lucky not to have got field punishment."

However childish this plan might seem, it had justified itself. Generally speaking, the "crimes" were becoming less frequent, for he took the pamphlet's instructions as well as the medicine quite seriously. *Take regular exercise,* it said, *short of absolute fatigue.* So he worked every day in the garden at Orchard Cottage, with more visible benefit to himself than to that tangled pleasance. He threw himself into this so vigorously that by the time he had finished he often felt disinclined to walk down to the "Lyttelton Arms" as usual. His tiredness induced a sleep too profound to permit the invasion of dreams; he awoke in the morning as one wakes from an anæsthetic, with a wondering sense of perils survived and no fear of the future. *Use tobacco in moderation,* it said. That was much more difficult. When a cigarette burnt his fingers his hand went out automatically to light another from the stub. He returned to the pipe which he had abandoned when he lost two front teeth, and rejoiced to find that the mechanical difficulty of using it made him smoke less. He was also delighted and proud to notice that, roughened by gardening as they were, his fingers no longer showed the mahogany discoloration which he had taken for granted, and that they trembled less when he carried a match to his pipe. His eyes, once angry with the fumes of burning cigarette paper, became clearer and unsuffused. His flabby muscles grew firmer. He was so conscious of this change for the better that he decided to encourage it by a regular morning spell of "physical jerks" which he performed, with virtuous satisfaction, in front of an open window; and this pride in his body extended itself to his dress. He found to his surprise that he had more money to spare and bought a new trench-coat, in whose shoulder-straps, for his own satisfaction, he pierced three holes for the stars that denoted his retiring rank. *Cultivate new intellectual interests,* the pamphlet urged him. That was even more difficult. Intellect wasn't his line. But he made a shot at it, all the same, with the help of a dictionary. Unluckily the small library which his aunt had left at Orchard Cottage consisted for the most part of evangelical books of devotion, and he couldn't make headway with those. But he read, for the first time, Scott and some tattered volumes of Dickens, in which he discovered to his delight a world whose values were very near to his own, a recognizable world of sawdust-strewn tap-rooms and hard-drinking ostlers and jolly good fellows with hearts of gold and charmingly familiar frailties, to say nothing of pure-minded young women (whom he identified, sentiment-ally, with Susan Lorimer) and touching renunciations, like that of Sidney Carton, who loved and lost and "took a drop" like himself. Encouraged by the suc-cess of these literary adventures he took a plunge into the muddy spate of war-books which began to appear at that moment, and the fury which these chronicles aroused in him enhanced his own growing self-respect and self-esteem by emphasizing the contrast between himself and his comrades-in-arms and the neurotic, disillusioned conscripts who wrote them. *He* wasn't disillusioned by anything—thank God!—but the meanness and sloppiness of the generation for which he had shed his blood—the internationalists and Bolshies and Conchies who now emerged from their funk-holes. The fellows with whom he had fought had more guts than that. And the conviction that he himself belonged to a sterner race with (relatively) clean minds and a simple, untarnished faith in the British Army and the villainy of all its enemies, made him hold his head high, according with the ideals of his tentative reformation. It was up to him, clearly, to show the new world what the men of the old B.E.F. were like. He would march out in face of its ill-veiled contempt with banners flying. And when the time came, as it would come . . .

So he thought, rather truculently perhaps, that September evening as he limped out, in his brand-new trench-coat, to take his appointed exercise—an hour's hard walking—on the road to Tilton. If he finished up at the "Lyttelton Arms" for a drink he would certainly have earned it. He didn't now, as in the bad old days, bribe loafers on the dole to talk with him in the bar by indiscriminate treating. He had his half-pint or pint—no whisky nowadays—in his own special corner. If he spoke at all it was when they got on to politics, with a few home truths, collected from the *Daily Express*, on the way that the working man was being duped by organized labour. They could like it or lump it as far as he was concerned. What the post-war world wanted, as he often told them, was discipline; more work and less whining. He believed they respected him more for calling a spade a spade.

Yes, however doubtful the times might be, he himself had gained a new confidence. It was part of the game to reiterate this, again and again. In this brisk evening air of September, tramping along as they used to march in the halcyon autumn of nineteen fourteen, he had less need than usual of self-assurance. There was only one blank in his present life that remained obstinately unfilled. He was a male, after all—his

recrudescence of physical energy made him sharply
aware of it—and needed, even more than he dared to
confess, the society of women. In the ordinary course
of human events he should have been married by
now, though in his present condition he wasn't much
of a match for any woman. There were times when he
sat alone reading in his cottage at night when his half-
occupied mind would suddenly become aware of that
want, so acutely that had it not been for his newly-
erected standards of decency he would have fortified
himself with a drink and pushed off to North Bromwich, determined to pick up the first "bit" that took
his stimulated fancy—not so much, if the truth were
told, to assuage a physical need as for the extraordinary
spiritual relief that these paid relationships afforded;
the rich joy of giving pleasure, of being generous to
another human being, the luxury of finding a listener
for thoughts intimate and childish, of being trivial and
natural and foolish and human and forgetting himself.

The women of the streets, at any rate some of them,
instinctively understood this craving of the lonely man.
They knew loneliness of another kind themselves.
They too, far, far removed from this sordid business,
had lives of their own, small financial schemings, dear
aspirations, a hidden yearning for tender domesticities
from which fate, chance, or perhaps the compulsions
of heredity divorced them. They knew that many men
who paid to possess them felt the want of more than
possession, of a friend as much as a mistress, and did

their best to supply this unrealized need by abandoning far more than they were paid for, admitting the casual possessor to secret, small intimacies of their lives, maternal or sisterly, as occasion dictated. It was contacts and communions of this kind that Captain Small missed most of all in his reincarnation; and that, he sometimes reflected half bitterly, half proudly, was Susan Lorimer's fault. That train journey into North Bromwich with her, during which, for the first time in years, he had opened his heart and been listened to by a woman who hadn't been paid to listen, had been the first real check in his slow downward career. It was the memory of her physical refinement, her soft voice, her pitying eyes, the astonishing birth in his consciousness of an ideal devotion, that had made him suddenly forswear commercial loves. Only once, illogically incensed by the shock of Susan's wedding, an infidelity that justified retaliation, had he broken loose in a fit of blind madness and returned to his former ways, with a resulting sense of emptiness and degradation more painful than the fury which had driven him to it. Yet, all the time, though the thought of one woman who could never be his obsessed him to the exclusion of all others (and indeed, since her marriage, he had never once set eyes on her) he couldn't help wondering if there wasn't, somewhere in the world, another who, by her resemblance to the ideal Susan of his memory, might fill the void in his present empty life. The sting of keen autumn air, so bright and invigorating after the languors of summer, more suggestive of youth and vigour than of approaching extinction, was almost as provocative and emotionally unsettling as that of spring. He felt it stir in his blood, like some creature awakening from æstivation. It made him think often of Susan—not Susan, the woman, herself—his old-fashioned middle-class principles reverenced marriage —but of all the feminine perfections that Susan stood for. Day after day on his evening walks he would catch sight in the dusk of some figure that brought his heart into his mouth by its resemblance to her or to what he remembered of her, as often as not in the company of some young man. Of course they were never anything like her, even if they had been un-escorted he wouldn't have dreamt of addressing them, for his attitude toward respectable women was that of a "sahib," and if once, by some miracle, he had actually met her, alone or with Dick, he would probably only have mumbled a gruff "good evening," blushed hotly, and limped on his way. Yet the mere fact of Susan's existence sweetened life somehow. He wasn't, in theory at any rate, jealous of Pennington. Though he had never met the fellow, he gave Susan credit for enough discrimination not to have thrown herself away. No doubt he was a solid young English-man, the kind who turned out good regimental officers. If he made Susan happy, more luck to him! If he ever used her badly, the dirty dog! Captain Small's brain blazed up, his hand gripped his walking-stick, he saw red at the very thought of it. And because he was an incurable romantic he forgot what he was and where he was going, imagining himself the central figure of a scene in which, like the Disinherited Knight in *Ivanhoe*, he figured as Susan's champion, prepared to lay down his life for her in mortal combat, and finally receiving the gage of her gratitude if not of her love.

"But that's all my eye, she's probably forgotten me," he told himself, returning from high romance to the Tilton Road. And there, at the turn, came one of those visions of happy lovers that so often disturbed him: a slim girl, just like Susan at a distance, in a bottle-green, fur-collared coat, with a tall young man at her side. They walked arm-in-arm and came swinging along toward him at a tremendous pace. Their short steps rang on the road in unison. All the vigour and freedom and hope of youth were in their movement. They talked rapidly, excitedly together, their speech broken by quick laughter echoing in the brisk September air and happy glances meeting each other's eyes. They were so absorbed in the separate world that they carried with them that they didn't even see Captain Small's plodding figure in their path. They pulled up just short of a collision and stood laughing like school children.

"I'm *so* sorry . . . Why, it's Captain Small!" Susan cried. "We're always running into each other."

"Not at all, not at all, Miss Lorimer," he stammered, so suddenly transported that he didn't know what he said.

She laughed again. "I'm afraid that won't do, Captain Small. My name's Mrs. Pennington now. Of course you don't know my husband. This is Captain Small, Dick."

The two men shook hands, while Susan still clung to her husband's arm. Dick smiled in the charming, shy way he had, his handclasp was frank and firm.

"Not so bad," Captain Small thought critically. "Well-made fellow, a bit on the soft side; a year in the army would make a man of him. Funny to think of a man like that getting married though. Lucky devil! Of course she's worth ten of him." They stood and gazed at each other with the mute hostility of two leashed dogs on their best behaviour.

"You see, we're both terribly excited," Susan broke in, "we've just taken a house."

The cheek of her! "Oh, I say, look here," Dick protested, "we haven't *taken* it."

"But don't be ridiculous, darling! Of course it's as good as taken."

"We don't know if we can afford to furnish it," he answered obstinately.

"That's half the fun! You don't have to pay for furniture in these days, do you, Captain Small? They deliver it free of charge, in plain vans, with a life insurance policy gratis. So even if you die before it's paid for nobody's any the worse. We shall be quite near neighbours. It's right at this end of Tilton. You must promise to come and see us as soon as we're settled."

Dick was pinching her arm as a signal of irritable impatience. Susan took no notice. She was sorry for Captain Small, and so full of high spirits herself that she felt it her duty to be nice. It was obvious from Dick's manner that he was cross and didn't much like the look of him. Well, it would do him good not to have his own way for once.

"We're going to my uncle's," she said. "Do walk part of the way with us."

Captain Small flushed with pleasure. "Oh, may I?" and they set off down hill together; but even down hill he found it difficult to keep up with them. He walked thrillingly close to Susan, quite unaware of the signals of distress and impatience which Dick continued to impress on the arm he held. "He's much nicer than I imagined," Susan was thinking, "and much smarter in every way; he must have had that awful trench-coat cleaned or bought a new one; he has a nice voice, too, and he doesn't speak like a man who's drinking heavily." In a way, Captain Small's improvement took some of the virtue out of her charitable condescension. To annoy Dick she talked about the relative convenience and cleanliness of carpets and rugs.

"Give me rugs every time, Mrs. Pennington," Captain Small panted, for even their modified pace was growing too hot for him. "You can find 'em everywhere. The fellows that came back from Mespot brought 'em home by the dozen. They're glad to get rid of them nowadays, poor devils, for what they'll fetch."

"But if we have rugs," Susan said, "we shall have to stain and polish the floors."

"Never mind about that," Captain Small gasped enthusiastically. "That's a job of work I'd be only too glad to take on. Just my ticket! Leave it to me. You drop me a postcard whenever you want me and I'll be there."

"Isn't that sweet of him, Dick?" Susan asked with charming maliciousness.

Dick growled something inaudible. Her complete disregard of his signals had begun to make him dislike Captain Small. It was bad enough anyway losing time on the road keeping pace with this old, maimed vagrant. A fellow with a face like that wasn't any too safe, and he'd be damned if he was going to have him mooching round "Chatsworth" when he wasn't there, even if they *did* take it. He would make that quite plain. At this moment he was fortunately saved from positive rudeness by the fact that they reached Orchard Cottage. Captain Small clutched eagerly at this chance of stopping to recover his breath.

"I won't keep you two back any longer," he said. "These are my quarters. Not a bad little billet. Old-fashioned, like me, and no frills. Let me have your address, Mrs. Pennington. If it isn't too late I'd like to send you a wedding present."

"How kind of you!" Susan smiled.

"Not at all. Not at all. And those floors. . . .
When you want me to lend you a hand you've only to
say so."

He shook hands vigorously with both of them and
disappeared. The gate clicked behind him; but as soon
as their backs were turned he stole cautiously up to the
hedge and gazed after them. They appeared to be
whispering, their heads close together.

"Youth, youth!" he thought bitterly, as he watched
their retreating figures. "Yes, youth, damn and blast
it!"

"Who on earth is that blighter?" Dick asked coldly
as they walked out of earshot. "Is he a friend of
yours?"

"Not exactly. Would you mind if he was?" Her
tone was provoking. "His name's Captain Small. I
told you that when we met him."

"Well, anyway, I don't much like the look of him,"
he answered grimly.

"You showed that pretty clearly, my dear."

"I daresay I did. Why not? He's an ugly customer.
What's the matter with his face?"

"He can't help that, poor thing! It was shrapnel or
something. He got smashed up in the war."

"Oh, the war!" said Dick Pennington irritably.
"I'm sick of the war. Those old soldiers just feed me
up. What's the war to do with *us*, anyway?"

"Nothing much. My father was killed in it, of course."

"Oh, Susie—I'm sorry."

His distress was so genuine that she had to forgive his bearishness. "I suppose you're just jealous," she said.

"Me? Jealous of *that*? My dear child!"

"I suppose a mixed compliment's better than none," she said with a sigh.

He slipped his arm round her. They kissed in the empty lane. "Come along," she said briskly, "I'm dying to tell Uncle George about 'Chatsworth'. Isn't it exciting?"

III

Not only exciting, Dick thought, but somewhat bewildering. It was no easy matter, he had discovered, to live with a woman of temperament. Before their marriage his emotional life had been curiously even, while Susan's, at all times, in its swift succession of moods, resembled a barometric graph of the English climate. Now, since all his happiness depended on hers —and he was so much in love that the slightest deliberate coldness on her part annihilated him—he was always trying, laboriously, to keep pace with her sudden vagaries. It was her feminine privilege, she implied, to exercise her caprice despotically, and there was

nothing in which she displayed it more than in matters
of money. He excused her, of course, and even smiled
at her recklessness. This celestial being, nourished on
light and air, knew nothing, naturally, of the hard
school in which he had been nursed. The careful
accountancy with which, every evening, he balanced his
daily expenditure, and of which he was rather proud,
only sharpened her impatience. At that moment there
flashed through his mind the memory of a little dispute
they had had some evenings before this wild scheme
of moving to Tilton had begun to obsess her.

"Oh, Dick, what a bore you are with your old
accounts!" she had cried.

"Well, I like to know where we stand," he had told
her. "We're not millionaires. After all, we jolly well
ought to."

"But it comes to the same in the end," she had said
with irrefutable logic. "It isn't as if we *were* millionaires. We're living from hand to mouth. If we've
money in our pockets we can spend it. If we haven't
we can't, and that's that."

"I've always been taught to look out for a rainy
day," he had told her.

"Yes, darling, you're always meeting trouble half-
way, and it's most depressing."

"Well, you never know, do you? Supposing we had
a kid . . ."

"God forbid!" She touched wood. He blushed.
He was always a little shocked whenever she said

"God." Not because he was narrow or priggish, he told himself: he just didn't like it. And the way in which she took the possibility of their having children wounded him too. He had always secretly imagined seeing Susan with a baby of his in her arms as soon as they could afford it. It seemed to him unnatural, unlike her, that she should shrink from the idea with such horror. She saw at once that he was hurt and passed on quickly.

"Of course we don't know," she had said. "That's half the fun of it. If we did life would be even duller than it is."

"Is our life so dull, then?" he asked her seriously.

"Oh, my child, don't be so pathetic. You know I don't mean that. What I mean is: for heaven's sake let's get all the fun we can out of it while we've the chance."

Then, seeing the tokens of surrender in his puzzled face, the inevitable end to any conflict between them, she had flown to his arms and salved the wounds of defeat by a sudden, tender childishness. "Do you love me, Dick darling?" she had whispered. "You do love me, don't you? I can't help being what I am, and it's no use my pretending. How I loathe all this talk about money! If we love each other nothing else matters, does it?"

No, nothing else mattered, he told himself, as they walked down from Tilton. But he knew, in the back of his obstinate mind, that many things did. There were a number of doubts in connection with his work which he hadn't shared with her. She was too lovely and childish and innocent to be burdened with his forebodings. He knew, for instance, that the firm for which he worked was feeling the pinch of bad times, as was shown by an increasing irritability on the part of his employers: long faces in the office, a tightening on all expenditure, the consciousness of depression issuing like a miasma from behind the closed doors where the heads of the firm deliberated. Once or twice of late there had been talk of reducing the office staff and the rate of wages. In black-coated jobs like his you couldn't fight and bargain as if you were a trade-unionist. It was always a case of the devil taking the hindmost; and though Susan professed to think him a commercial genius and looked forward gaily to a partnership, Dick Pennington had no illusions as to his own capacity. He knew himself for a decent, hard-working fellow, well up to the average, thank heaven, but a bit on the slow side and as likely as anyone, in an emergency, to get the sack. After all, the position of a weekly wage-earner was none too secure. Though the heads of the firm had a fancy for public-school men, who were good at games and gave "tone," it was said, to the office, he had no reason to suppose they would go on paying for their fancy. And if he did get the sack or have his wages reduced Susan's charming theories of life would certainly have to be modified, for the expense of getting married and the innumerable small extravagances into which his weakness for gratifying Susan's adorable whims and vanities had betrayed him had already played the deuce with his meagre savings. Supposing. . . .

"You're awfully silent. What's the matter, Dick darling?"

"Just thinking."

"About 'Chatsworth'?"

He laughed. "Not I!" He supposed he must satisfy her. "I was feeling sorry I'd been offhand with that chap Small."

"Oh well, that's all over."

Yes, that was the trouble. It was the general sense of being dragged into this "Chatsworth" business against all his judgment on the tail of her pretty enthusiasm that had made him awkward and bearish. Of course he hadn't been jealous, as her mischief suggested. But the airy way in which she had calmly announced that they had taken "Chatsworth" and even talked about details of furniture at a moment when politeness toward a stranger disarmed him, was just not "cricket." He might have expected it. Their sublimely impudent lack of what he called sportsmanship was one of the surprising things he had learnt about women from Susan during the last three months. And the devil of it was, he couldn't make her see it. If he tried to do so by reasoning she'd fly off at a tangent. If he tied her to the point, well, life wouldn't be worth living. And there you were! His only hope of outside support in this unequal contest was George Lorimer, who, although Dick knew very little about him, was presumably a business man and sufficiently interested in their finances as her trustee to be able to put the brake on. "I shall have to get hold of him alone and talk it over; for I'm *not* going to take that house," he told himself firmly.

IV

Dick Pennington didn't succeed in having an intimate talk with George Lorimer that evening. Before Susan and he approached the house in Great Cornbow the lights in the formal front room had been lit, and Mr. Bulgin installed in George Lorimer's most comfortable arm-chair. Mr. Bulgin was in excellent form. That morning, thanks to Solomon Magnus's shrewdness, he had realized and re-invested a lot of money.

Nobody could have been more surprised by this visit than George Lorimer himself. He had congratulated himself on his luck in avoiding Mr. Bulgin since their scene over his offer of marriage to Susan and his own miraculous escape from the loss of the Dingle site. The announcement of Mr. Bulgin's arrival threw him into a sudden, irrational, vain desire to escape. He couldn't believe that this visit wasn't inspired by some sinister purpose, and not even Aunt Edna's protective presence could restore his sense of security. As Mr.

Bulgin heartily plumped himself down before the empty fireplace—Mrs. Lorimer would never allow the front-room fire to be lighted before Michaelmas Day —George Lorimer's attitude was that of some timid antelope surprised at a water-hole when lions come down to drink, though Mr. Bulgin's intentions, by his own account, were anything but carnivorous.

"Just thought I'd pop in and have a chat with you, George," he said with a beaming smile, full of charity, interest and friendliness. "I haven't set eyes on you for months."

"You look pretty spry, John."

"So I ought to. Just come back from Harrogate. How's sport and how's business?"

George Lorimer was perfectly aware that John Bulgin cared nothing for sport and knew better than he did that business couldn't be worse.

"Well, I can't complain, John," he answered with a smile of timid defiance.

"Oh, you can't complain, can't you?" Mr. Bulgin echoed. "Well, well . . . Fancy that now. I congratulate you, George. That's the first cheerful note I've heard in the last six weeks. Well done! Good old George! You won't mind if I smoke, Mrs. Lorimer?" Without waiting for a reply he filled his briar pipe, then went on meditatively. "Now that's very inter*est*-ing, that is. What you said just now only confirms what I've been thinking myself. I've been thinking a lot about what you said last time we two had a chat *re* the hand-wrought nail trade. There's a deal of horse-sense in your views, and after a lot of careful enquiries, I've come round to your way of thinking." He paused. "You don't mind all this business talk, I hope, Mrs. Lorimer?" he enquired politely. "When old pals like George and me get together it's only natural. Isn't that so, George? What d'you want to go prowling around like that for? Why don't you sit down like a Christian?"

It was natural, George Lorimer wanly agreed. This excess of friendliness and courtesy filled him with foreboding. He had known John Bulgin long enough to be certain that neither the scene over Susan nor the salvation of the Dingle was forgotten. Yet nothing could have been more engaging than the frankness with which Mr. Bulgin pursued his theme.

"I've come round to your way of thinking," he repeated. "The nail trade's all right. I don't say there's much money in it, mind you; but as long as there's a horse left in England, wrought-iron nails 'll be needed. What's more, it's not overcrowded, and that's all in its favour. Lovely weather we've been having, Mrs. Lorimer. A bit nippy, though, evenings."

"Don't you think we might have a fire, Edna?" George Lorimer hurriedly suggested, jumping up from his chair to avail himself of this first chance of escape.

"No, no. Not at all. I'm not cold. If I am, I'll tell you. Sit down, George. Whatever's the matter with you? Now what was I saying? Ah yes, I remember: about the nail trade not being overcrowded. As a matter of fact, apart from your own concern, which I suppose is the oldest of the lot, there's only three firms turning out wrought-iron nails. We've got Holland's at Wolverbury and Baker's at Stourton and Higgs's at Mawne. Correct me if I'm wrong."

"You're perfectly right. You know that as well as I do," George Lorimer said quickly.

"Well, I'm dead nuts on facts, as you know, George." Mr. Bulgin knocked out his pipe on the empty fire-grate. "That's my first rule in business. To come down to brass tacks I've been looking into this matter. The trouble with you chaps is you're too individualist. I know that the wrought-iron nail's an old-fashioned product, but that don't imply it ought to be produced by old-fashioned methods. What the trade wants just now is reorganization on modern lines. Sales as well as factories. It's top-heavy. Instead of squinting at each other out of the corners of your eyes and slitting each other's throats, you should get together and cut down the overhead and work out some plan of marketing. Now don't get excited: I'm only saying this for your good."

"I'm not getting excited," George Lorimer almost screamed. "I was merely going to say . . ."

"Let me finish what I'm saying first," Mr. Bulgin blandly intervened. "Now listen: things being what they are, and happening, at the moment, to have a

couple of thousand to spare——" George Lorimer
went hot at the mention of this significant figure, and
hotter when he saw a flicker of amusement in Mr.
Bulgin's eyes—"I've decided to try my hand at setting
this business to rights on up-to-date lines. Now how
does that strike you?"

It struck poor George Lorimer's brain like a
thunderbolt. "That depends what you propose to do,
John," he answered defensively.

"I'm not proposing to do anything. I've done it,"
said Mr. Bulgin. "Signed the papers yesterday. I've
bought Holland's and Baker's and Higgs's. I'm form-
ing a new company. Within a few months I shall have
all those concerns under one roof and under my eye.
Now this is your chance, George. I'm holding out the
hand of friendship. You'd better come in with us.
Supposing we get down to business? That is, if Mrs.
Lorimer don't mind," he added benignantly.

Mrs. Lorimer did mind. "I don't think George
ought to say anything till he's thought it all over and
taken the best advice," she declared emphatically.

"Quite right, ma'am, quite right," Mr. Bulgin
agreed with enthusiasm. "It's advice that I'm giving
him. I want him to realize his position, if you'll give
me the chance."

George Lorimer realized his position. It was precisely that by which he had been tortured in his nightmare. He saw himself again, a live-bait hooked to a
snap-tackle with his back fin clipped off, swimming

round in pitiful circles, greedily watched by the yellow eyes of an enormous, voracious pike. In his dream he had consoled himself with the thought that if it gorged him the pike would be landed. In real life, unfortunately, Mr. Bulgin stood to lose nothing. His mind was so paralysed by the confusion of helpless rebellious thoughts which surged through it that he scarcely listened as Mr. Bulgin went on lucidly.

"You see, it boils down to this. If you refuse to come in with us you'll just have to take the consequences. With our new organization prices are bound to come down. If you choose to compete with us . . . well, try it! You just try it; I've no objection. If you do come in, on the other hand, of course you'll be welcome. We'll take over your business in a friendly manner on a reasonable valuation: one valuer nominated by you and one by us and a neutral referee. That's fair all round. It goes without saying you'll get a seat on the board, same as Holland and Baker, with the usual director's fees, as well as your share of the profits. And when we're all under one roof . . ."

George Lorimer emerged from his dream. "What about the Dingle?"

"You and your Dingle!" Mr. Bulgin thought. "Rum little cuss!" He wrinkled his brows in token of momentary incomprehension, then relaxed into a broad smile. "The Dingle? Why, to tell you the honest truth, George, it's never entered my mind. As I've said, the root idea of this new concern is to concentrate everything at one works. That's only logical, and I may say that the others agree with me. We'll find some use for the Dingle. Don't you worry about that."

"You will, will you?" said George Lorimer bitterly. "That's where you're mistaken. I've no use for combines. I prefer to be my own master. I'm not going to have my business swallowed by Holland or Baker or you or anyone else." Mr. Bulgin nodded his head sympathetically. "And as for your threats," he went on . . .

"Threats? Come, come, George!" Mr. Bulgin protested.

"Aren't you threatening to undersell me?" George demanded indignantly.

"Undersell you? Of course we shall do that. You bet we will," Mr. Bulgin chuckled.

"Well, do it, then, and be damned to you!" George Lorimer cried, suddenly transported. Mrs. Lorimer laid a restraining hand on his arm. "George, George dear," she whispered. George Lorimer bounced away from her. He was white with hatred and fury. He snatched up a book from the table and waved it wildly. For a moment it looked as if he were going to fling it in Bulgin's smiling face. Mrs. Lorimer jumped up in alarm to take it away from him. Mr. Bulgin, with superb unconcern, proceeded to knock out his pipe. The tap of the briar on the grate was echoed by a knock at the door and followed by Susan's voice: "May we come in?"

"Yes, come in," gasped Aunt Edna, eagerly thankful for any interruption.

Susan had walked into the house, as was her wont, without ringing. She had heard, as they hung for a moment in the hall, the unrecognizable drone of Mr. Bulgin's voice, broken suddenly by George Lorimer's outburst. Dick checked her tactfully. "I say, sounds as if there's a row on; we'd better clear out of this." But his tact weighed little with Susan. Inside there someone, it didn't matter who, was worrying her poor Uncle George. Before Mrs. Lorimer's sentence had left her lips Susan was in the room, with Dick hovering awkwardly behind her. What they saw, in effect, was a charming social reunion: Mr. Bulgin expansively posed with his back to the fireplare, smiling and polishing the bowl of his pipe on a magenta silk handkerchief; Mrs. Lorimer positively brimming over with an unusual welcome; Uncle George apparently engrossed in the middle of Nuttall's invaluable dictionary which, a moment before, he had nearly hurled at Mr. Bulgin's head. It was left to Mr. Bulgin, by reason of his business experience the most accomplished actor of the three, to carry it off superbly.

"Why, it's Susan. . . . Just fancy that. Looking pretty as a picture, too. Old buffers like us are allowed to pay little compliments, aren't we, George?"

George Lorimer closed his dictionary with the satisfied air of a man who has just confirmed an important reference. He laughed nervously and spoke

in a high, jerky voice. "Yes, that's about all we *can*
do. You don't know Dick Pennington?"

"Of course not," Susan interposed gaily. "This is
my husband. Mr. Bulgin's a very old friend, Dick."

"I've heard of you, sir," Dick said shyly as the two
men shook hands. Was the sentence as innocent as it
sounded? How much had he heard? Mr. Bulgin was
flattered at first to be called "sir"—even workmen
tended to drop that nowadays—but on second thoughts
he wasn't quite sure that it wasn't meant to emphasize
the difference in their ages, and a quick resentment
seized him to think that this puppy had actually been
preferred to himself.

"*You* look as if marriage suits you, anyway, young
man," he said.

"I can't complain, sir."

Mr. Bulgin laughed loudly.

"Here's another optimist, George! This is no place
for me. One thing's clear. He can't be in business."

"But he is," Susan answered quickly. For her, at
least, the situation was richly romantic. Of the five
people present only three were aware of the recent
emotional relationship of Mr. Bulgin to herself. In
the mantelpiece mirror beyond Mr. Bulgin's shoulder
she had caught sight of her own face, small and pale
in the gaslight above the fur collar, with huge tragic
eyes, and had realized how perfectly cast she was to
hold the stage in this *scène à faire*. With an instinct
that never deserted her on such occasions she proceeded

to dramatize herself and "show off" for the benefit of the other actors, George Lorimer and Bulgin, and to the bewilderment of an audience, ignorant of the scene's inner meaning, consisting of Aunt Edna and Dick. Accordingly, for Dick's sake she became seductive with Mr. Bulgin, for Mr. Bulgin's affectionate with Dick, while for Aunt Edna she staged a version of "Cinderella," in which the ill-treated heroine returned to flaunt the independence of a brilliant marriage and the obvious devotion of every available male before the grimmest of "Ugly Sisters." For Dick again, since the stage was set, she mischievously decided to clinch the move to Tilton with Uncle George who, she knew, could never resist her in her fantastic moods.

"Dick and I are so excited, darling," she told him breathlessly. "We've taken a house."

"A house? You've taken a house?" George Lorimer gasped. "What sort of a house?"

Susan laughed. "Just an ordinary house. The kind people live in. It's in Ada Road, Tilton, only eighteen minutes from here. It's got rather a grand name: 'Chatsworth.' Poor Dick thinks we can't afford it. But you know how unenterprising he is." And she launched herself into an extravagant account of their visit to "Chatsworth," letting her fancy run wild in comic descriptions of Mr. Duke's milky obsession and his pride in his sanitation. The fact that three men, all variously attracted by her, were hanging on her words and bewitched by her physical presence, spurred

her on to an intoxicated assurance, almost as though
the complete surrender of her modesty in marriage
had freed her body and mind from all other shyness.
All her audience—except Aunt Edna, who really
didn't matter—were moved by this odd abandonment.
Mr. Bulgin went red in the neck; for he knew that the
little devil intended to provoke him; George Lorimer,
who adored her in any case, was transported out of his
own distress by the joy of seeing her high-spirited
happiness; while all Dick's reservations were swept
away once more by his wonder and pride in the fact
that this brilliant, desirable creature was actually his.

"The only thing that frightens poor Dick, uncle
darling," she explained, "is the cost of the furniture;
but I've told him that's nonsense—in these days nobody dreams of paying for everything at once, and it's
nothing to do with him anyway. It's *my* house. We
could start quite nicely on a hundred pounds—or perhaps a hundred and fifty. You could sell some of my
war-loan or lend us that quite easily, couldn't you,
darling?"

George Lorimer smiled weakly. He was tortured
by a conviction that John Bulgin, standing there with
his plump red neck and his greedy eyes fastened on
Susan's figure, knew his shameful secret and was waiting for him to confess. "Well, you see," he began,
"a trustee's position is difficult. I shall have to consult . . ."

"Come on, George, be a sport now," Mr. Bulgin

broke in maliciously. "Tell you what—I've never given you a wedding present, Susan. If you take that house you can put me down for a bedroom suite and send in the bill."

"Mr. Bulgin, how lovely of you!" Susan exclaimed. "Isn't that marvellous, Dick?"

"That'll touch the old devil up!" Mr. Bulgin thought.

George Lorimer shivered. He felt positively certain now that John Bulgin knew everything; and this certainly spurred him on to angry bravado. After all the new combine was going to ruin him in the end. One might just as well be hanged for a sheep as a lamb. The situation demanded a gesture. He achieved one magnificently.

"All right, Susie," he said, and his head spun round as he spoke, while his weak eyes glared at Mr. Bulgin's sinister smiling face, "I think you can count on me . . . for two hundred, anyway."

"Now what did I tell you, Dick?" Susan cried triumphantly.

v

Mr. Bulgin left first. He was feeling pleased with himself and at peace with the world for a number of reasons. To begin with he had had the satisfaction of getting even with George Lorimer and twisting his tail. Poor old George's wrigglings, even that last quick show of spirit, gave a sporting zest to the game; they could no more influence the end of it than the squeal of a little white poodle in the jaws of a mastiff. The assurance of victory had cost him nothing in any case. To have cleared two thousand pounds on a mortgage which he had cleverly bought for eighteen hundred, when the property pledged could not possibly have fetched two-thirds of that sum on foreclosure, was pretty good business to start with. As for the nail-making combine, that would probably just pay its way. Whatever line George Lorimer took he was going to be ditched. If George chose to see reason the Dingle site would pass automatically into his, Mr. Bulgin's, control. If George elected to fight the combine he would certainly be broken—so much the worse for him!—and the Dingle site could be bought in the liquidation for a song.

"There's nothing that brains and brass can't do— not only in business, either," Mr. Bulgin reflected. He was still a little thrilled and pleasantly disturbed by Susan's friendliness. There was no doubt that marriage had added to her allurement, and her manner toward him that evening had been almost provocative. "That show won't last long," he told himself sagely, think-ing of Dick Pennington. "Not a bad type of chap, but he don't carry guns enough for our Susan. She'll lose patience. That's what'll happen." With the memory of her soft warm handclasp still in his mind,

he could fancy himself in a rôle more suited to a man
of his age than a husband's—in that of a sort of safe,
benevolent father-confessor, a friend of the family,
made free of all kinds of charming, titillating intimacies. "Not so safe as all that by long chalks," Mr.
Bulgin reflected luxuriously. When he had offered his
wedding present, just to touch up old George, he could
have kissed her, he didn't mind betting, if nobody else
had been there. The future, in fact, was rosy with
possibilities.

As Susan rode home that evening in the last 'bus
from Halesby, she did not give Mr. Bulgin a single
thought. She had been flattered, of course, by the
presence of her rejected suitor, and flirted instinctively
with Dick just to show him how much he had lost.
She had let her hand rest in John Bulgin's a little
longer than was necessary, because she felt sorry for
him and touched by his generosity. He could continue
to be generous with pleasure, as far as she was concerned. Her head was awhirl with the excitement of
furnishing "Chatsworth." But now that they were
alone together, she was too tactful to presume on her
victory. She was gentle and subdued and full of
genuine tenderness for her poor, simple Dick, who had
taken the surprise she had sprung on him so well. She
had got her own way and could now afford to be
generous. So, concealing the tumultuous enthusiasm
that burned within her, she sat by his side with her
hand in his as quiet as a mouse, proclaiming herself a

playful, wayward creature, with whom, however wild her caprices, he couldn't really be angry because she was always his little love, his Susan. And Dick, his heart melted by this sweetly submissive reincarnation of virginity, was so moved that he trembled when she crept into his arms that night. It seemed to him that their love had never before been so passionately rare, so beautiful . . .

The least happy of them all was poor George Lorimer. When Susan had thanked and kissed him again and again and he had closed the front door behind her and Dick, his smiling face fell. As he lingered in the dark hall, determined to pull himself together, he became aware of the ticking clock. It was ten past nine. He had missed his usual time-signal. He stood for a moment, gazing at the clock's blank, solemn, moonlike face, listening to the slow tick of the pendulum. It had gone on ticking like that, neither hurried nor checked by emotion, since the day it first stood there, fifty years before he had been born. It would go on ticking, he supposed, for years and years after he was dead. Well, what did it matter? If only the human heart were made like that! He shook his head pitifully and escaped from that mocking reminder of human frailty to the room they had left. Mrs. Lorimer was on her knees before the fireplace, brushing up the ashes that had fallen from Mr. Bulgin's pipe; the crouching position made her middle-aged hips look enormous. She spoke, without turning.

"Is that you, George?" As if it could be anyone
else! "If John Bulgin were my husband, I'd teach him
to dirty the fireplace. What's all this about the new
combine? It sounds sensible to me. I suppose you
ought to go into it like the rest of them. Why on earth
did you lose your temper, I should like to know? You
gain nothing by behaving like that."

He grew agitated again. A sudden recklessness
urged him to tear up the whole drab tissue of their
conjugal life and tell her the truth. He wanted to say:
"I've nothing to gain or to lose. Whatever I do, John
Bulgin's determined to smash me. And that doesn't
matter either. Nothing matters. I'm a criminal. I've
been guilty of fraudulent conversion, and you may as
well know it!"

The words died on his trembling lips, and the
momentary dislike of her that surged up behind them
was checked by another rising emotion of pity for her
ignorance of the truth, almost of tenderness. He saw
that he had done Aunt Edna a grave injustice by
marrying her. He had only done it, mistakenly, to
give Susan a mother. It wasn't her fault, poor woman,
that that hadn't been a success. To be married to a confirmed bachelor like himself was rough enough luck,
without her knowing that the man she had married was
a criminal bankrupt! Receiving no answer she turned
round and gazed at him enquiringly. When he saw
her plain, high-coloured face, which he had once
thought handsome, his pity became so acute that he

dared not look at her. He must either escape or burst
into tears, so twisting his lips into a smile, he murmured
something about "a breath of fresh air" and made for
the garden. It was dark there, and dank, and of an
almost holy stillness. A falling apple plopped on the
ground and startled him. Mist lay white in the Dingle
above the murmur of the river; his disused chimney-
stacks pierced it like broken obelisks. "Dead, dead,"
he thought. "But what does that matter, either?" He
sat down on a rotten bench which, with the vague
aspirations of domestic felicity, he had put up in the
year of his marriage, and wept till he began to feel
better.

When he re-entered the house the hall clock was
striking ten, and Mrs. Lorimer, according to her habit,
had gone to bed. She knew by experience that when
George was worried it was better to leave him alone,
but in her heart she felt just as sorry for him as he
had been for her, though the expression of such an
emotion in words was beyond her. Yet when, having
secretly watched him undress and slip into his cotton
nightshirt, she heard him blow out the candle, she
turned over in bed toward him and gathered him to
her arms as a mother gathers her child.

CHAPTER VII

"CHATSWORTH"

I

THE occupation of "Chatsworth" afforded as much entertainment to Mr. Duke's other tenants as does the arrival of a new boy in a preparatory school. Whenever the Penningtons emerged from the still unfurnished house the female inhabitants of Ada Road betrayed an interest in their front gardens as sudden and unanimous as if they were following a time-table; front windows were abruptly thrown open, babies arbitrarily snatched up from their prams, and shadowy forms might be observed in a state of agitation adjusting lace curtains.

Miss Maples, of "Welbeck," was not under the necessity of resorting to any of these brazen artifices. From her straight-backed chair in the drawing-room bow-window—the equivalent of a seat in the middle of the front-row stalls—she was able, without subterfuge or impoliteness, to witness every stage of the Penningtons' installation. It was unfortunate and fortunate at once, that during the whole of that month she hap-

pened to be disengaged. She was feeling the pinch of
hard times, like everyone else, through the medium
of the declining birth-rate, but found some consolation for her enforced stay at home in being able to sit
through the whole of this gratuitous spectacle and to
communicate its details, in the vivid style she had
copied from broadcast descriptions of cup-finals and
boat-races, to her invalid mother, who sat in a wheeled
chair crippled with rheumatism, and draped in a Shetland tippet, close to the fire. This diversion, at second
hand, did old Mrs. Maples no end of good. Her
daughter, on the other hand, was interested for more
serious reasons. Young married couples meant babies
(or ought to mean babies: Miss Maples' attitude
toward contraceptives was unequivocal) and babies
meant work for herself. Her trained eye noticed regretfully the uniform slimness of Susan's figure, but
took comfort from the fact that the "Chatsworth"
garage held nothing more grand than a motor-bicycle;
for the baby car, as she knew by experience, was a
particularly deadly competitor, being as incompatible
with the human baby as grey squirrels with red or
limestone with rhododendrons. As Miss Maples sat
at the window pretending to knit lamb's-wool boots for
the babies of prospective patients, her mother riddled
her with a quick fire of questions. No detail of this
pantomime was too small to engage the old lady's
curiosity. She wanted an exact description of everyone
who entered or left the house, from the time of the

Q

Penningtons' first hurried visits, weighed down with brown-paper parcels, through the grand transformation scene, when the motor furniture-vans swayed and floundered and stuck in morasses of October mud, to the slap-stick harlequinade of red-faced men in baize aprons, who light-heartedly smashed two panes in one dining-room window and scraped permanent weals in the paint of the front door-posts.

The character of those furniture-vans was the crux of the whole situation. Their precise size and colour were as important to Mrs. Maples as their contents.

"Can you see any name painted on the side of them, Maud?" she anxiously enquired.

Miss Maples couldn't. "Then get your glasses at once," the old lady commanded. "Of course it's possible the name may be printed on the board they let down at the back."

"I can't see the back from here, mother," Miss Maples told her.

"Then go to my bedroom, and notice particularly too if the men have any names on their caps."

Miss Maples patiently obeyed. There wasn't, she reported, a trace of a name on either.

"Ah, I thought as much!" Mrs. Maples declared triumphantly. "That confirms my suspicions. It means that they've bought the whole lot on the hire-purchase system. Remember the advertisements: 'Plain vans and no uniformed porters.' That settles it. I told you before the young woman spent far too much money on her back for my liking. We must warn Mr. Duke immediately he'd better be careful. He ought to insist on having his rent in advance. It's a great mistake to trust people who furnish on credit. Easy come, easy go. I was afraid we should be disappointed."

"There's a beautiful walnut bedroom suite just gone in," her daughter told her.

"Yes, and just as likely as not you'll see it come out again in a year or two's time," said the old lady grimly.

"Why, there's Mr. Bulgin's car, I do believe," Miss Maples cried suddenly.

"Mr. Bulgin's dead," her mother firmly corrected her. "I suppose you mean John. Are you perfectly sure?"

"Yes, and there's John Bulgin himself."

"Well, that is a surprise. His father and your dad were great friends. Mr. Bulgin was a strong Wesleyan and extremely artistic. Your dad and I once went to see his picture gallery. There was one by the great painter, Landseer. You'd have thought that dog was going to jump out of the picture. Who'd have imagined that those young Penningtons were as well connected as that? Perhaps you may have been mistaken about the vans after all, Maud. You're very short-sighted, aren't you?"

Though Miss Maples confessed that she might have been, she was not mistaken. The furnishing of "Chatsworth" had been undertaken by the Bromwich Furnishing Emporium, a concern widely advertised as the Young Married Couple's best friend. Susan had been brought to their doors (as she had been attracted to Brinton and even "Chatsworth" itself) by the lure of advertisement, and had found Mr. Bellis, the manager, entirely helpful and charming. For one thing Mr. Bellis had obviously succumbed at first sight to her personal attractions, and betrayed her conquest by an intimacy that never overstepped the bounds of respectful propriety and a shy disinclination to talk about money. "Of course our usual terms," he had said, "are thirty-three per cent. down and the remainder in instalments; but with people like you and your husband, Mrs. Pennington, I'm quite sure we can make them much easier. Shall we say one-fifth—that's twenty per cent. down—and the rest spread over four years? No, don't thank me. It's a pleasure, I assure you." Though he casually mentioned a number of aristocratic mansions which the firm had lately furnished, he made it quite clear that the Penningtons' order was nearer to his heart.

"How lucky we went to them," Susan confided to Dick.

Within a week of their visit to Great Cornbow George Lorimer had somehow contrived to produce the two hundred pounds he had promised her. Mr. Bulgin had promptly sent her another twenty-five and a receipt to sign for it. She had opened an account at the new Tilton branch of the Midland Bank and re-

ceived a cheque-book, the possession of which gave her
a feeling of limitless wealth. Now Mr. Bellis's immediate surrender to her charms made it quite unnecessary to give money another thought. She was free
to indulge what Mr. Bellis admitted to be her
exquisite taste.

"It's a privilege to deal with a lady like yourself,
Mrs. Pennington," he confessed. "The majority of
customers they've no more idea of what elegant pieces
are than the man in the moon. To tell you the truth,
they're pitiful to a man who loves furniture like I do;
so why waste time over them? As for taste . . . Well,
you know what I mean, they're the kind that'll mix up
their periods as soon as look at you—put Tudor and
Hepplewhite and Louis Cans all together, in the very
same room, mind! Now in public I don't pretend to be
anything more than a salesman myself, but speaking
privately, I know good taste when I see it. You've
only to look at a lady's clothes to see if she has it."
And he stole an admiring glance at the jumper from
which Dick had dragged Susan away on the day of
their first visit to "Chatsworth." "With a lady of
taste," he went on, "I hesitate to offer advice; but from
what you tell me of the style of the residence, I can
see exactly what you want. Take the dining-room
suite, for instance: well a bungalow dining-room ought
to look solid. It oughtn't, if I may say so, to give an
impression of flimsiness. There's only one thing for
your dining-room as *I* see it, Mrs. Pennington—

though of course it's for you to choose—and that's
(Susan listened eagerly), that's Jacobean, or, as some
people call it, Baronial. If you put in one of our
Baronial suites in black oak, with genuine deep carving, you can't go far wrong. As a matter of fact we've
only one left, and the model won't be repeated. Remember, the fine pieces of to-day are the antiques of
the future."

"Don't you think it might look rather heavy for the
size of the room?" Susan timidly enquired. "You see,
it's only fourteen by sixteen."

"Fourteen by sixteen?" Mr. Bellis repeated. "No,
honestly, no. The room's on the small side, of course,
but Baronial would give it dignity. If you could pick
up a bit of old pewter or a pair of antlers, now . . .
But don't think I'm persuading you."

He made this so clear from the start that in the end
Susan was quite convinced that the "Chatsworth"
furniture was entirely the product of her own unerring
taste. That the judgment of an acknowledged expert
like Mr. Bellis should so often coincide with hers was
a proof of its instinctive fineness. When she disliked
anything he suggested, he almost invariably agreed
with her. "On second thoughts," he would say, "I
believe you're right. Take it away, George. We won't
even look at it." Then he would glance secretly at
Dick with a nod and a smile, which implied: "There
you are! She's taken the words out of my mouth
again." "You know, Mr. Pennington," he once whis-

pered in Susan's hearing, "your wife's missed her
vocation. She ought to be an interior decorator. She's
got what the French call flare. That's a thing you can't
learn. You've either got it or you haven't. I shouldn't
be surprised if one of these days she didn't go into
business."

Susan laughed happily when Dick passed on to her
what Mr. Bellis had said. "Go into business, indeed!
As if it wasn't a full-time job looking after a husband.
Why, you'd never change anything unless I put it out
for you."

By the end of a week she and Mr. Bellis were such
good friends that she began to wonder if they really
oughtn't to invite him and his wife, if he had one, to
visit "Chatsworth." You could tell he was a gentleman by the way he dressed. (So much better than
Dick. Indeed, his cutaway coat and white slip reminded her of snapshots of peers at Ascot and royal
garden-parties.) And the fact that he didn't even look
at her cheque when she paid her deposit. In her pursuit of perfection she had spent nearly half as much
again as they had planned to spend; but the terms were
so easy that that didn't really matter.

Nevertheless, the day when the furniture came into
"Chatsworth" was devastating. Its unexpected arrival
caught her standing over the charwoman who had
been hired to scrub the floors and sweep up the dust
and shavings. On this peaceful scene Mr. Bellis's van-
men broke in like a riotous mob. Before she had

bustled the char out of the house with her broom, her swabs and her buckets, they made the floors quake with their stampings. When they staggered and bumped down the hall with the black oak sideboard Susan felt that the flimsy partition-walls on either side must surely give way. She saw the newly-scrubbed floor befouled with mud and torn with hobnails and littered with flakes of plaster. She heard, with a sinking heart, the crash and tinkle of broken glass from the dining-room window. A hanging lampshade went smash. Disasters of this kind, it seemed, were all in the day's work for Mr. Bellis's men. "Easy there, Jim," was all the comment that the foreman made, while Jim stared, with a smile on his sweating face, at the naked bulb swinging, and trod the splinters of the shade into the floor underfoot.

In the midst of this turmoil Mr. Bulgin arrived. "Thought I'd just look you up," he said cheerily, "but it seems you're busy." "Busy" wasn't exactly the word to describe her mind's chaos, but the thought of the walnut bedroom suite compelled her to gather her wits and show him not only his own wedding-present, but the rest of the house. She had never, Mr. Bulgin thought, looked more desirable than at this moment, her cheeks hot with excitement, her dark hair abandoned, her body so deliciously alive and slim in the thin print overall. It was a bit of rare luck, he thought, that her husband wasn't there. As they stood alone, approving the walnut bedsteads, he half wondered if it wasn't his duty to snatch a fatherly kiss in payment on account, so to speak. After all, this was only the beginning of their new, delightful relationship; so he contented himself with putting his arm round her warm young waist and patting her cheek paternally, and his next move, whatever it might have been, was prevented by the arrival of the foreman with some vexatious enquiry about the kitchen linoleum.

"Will you excuse me?" she asked pathetically. So he made his farewells. "I'll pop in again when you're settled," he said reluctantly. "Don't forget, if you're in any trouble you know where to come. By the way," he called back as he put on his hat in the porch, "if you see your uncle you might give him a message from me. Just say I'm still waiting for his answer. He'll know what I mean."

Susan promised that she would. "Thank heaven," she told herself. "I thought he'd never go! It was sweet of him to come, though."

The linoleum was too short. Dick must have mistaken the measurements. How like him! She had begged him to go over everything twice, but he, in his superior masculine way, had only laughed at her. Well, it couldn't be helped. The piece had been cut and they must put it down as it was.

There were many things that couldn't be helped that day—such as the broken window, the dents in the woodwork and plaster, the scraped paint, the indelible marks of hobnails on the new linoleum. Mr. Bellis's men left a track like that of a hurricane behind them wherever they went. She hadn't even time to boil a kettle for tea. It was unjust, she thought, that Dick hadn't been at home to take his share of it—quite apart from his having made such a mess of the measurements. "There he is," she thought, "calmly enjoying himself in his beastly office, while all the donkey-work falls on me. Yes, that's married life all over!"

And so it went on. The climax of the eruption was reached about five o'clock, when the light was failing. As she worked in the bedroom, feverishly trying to reduce the confusion of parcels and new furniture to order, she heard, in the hall, a series of dull impacts louder than any before, accompanied by sounds of hard breathing and spitting and voices raised in apparent altercation. A moment later Mr. Bellis's foreman appeared in the doorway.

"It's that dining-room table," he explained. "I guessed we'd have trouble with it. That's why we left it till last."

"Why, what's wrong?" she asked in alarm. "It's not broken, is it?"

"Oh no, it's not broken. But you see, we can't get it in nohow. It's too big for the 'all—or the 'all's too small, whichever you like."

"Well, what are you going to do?"

"That's just what I was saying to Jim. It'll have to go through the window. That's all about it."

"Well, put it through the window. I don't mind

what you do as long as you get it in."

Considering the havoc they had already made, it seemed to her that the foreman was showing unusual delicacy.

"But you see, ma'am," he went on kindly, "we can't do that either. These 'ere casement windows is awkward. We should 'ave to take out the 'ole frame."

"Well, do that then," Susan innocently suggested.

The foreman appeared to be staggered by the suggestion. "It's gone five o'clock. My mates and me ought to 'ave been back at our teas by this time. What's more, that's a carpenter's job. We're not tradesmen, we aren't."

"I'm sure Mr. Bellis wouldn't mind."

"Mr. Bellis is not my boss," said the foreman haughtily. Having paid cash down for his own furniture, he had a profound contempt for people who didn't.

"I suppose," Susan said, "you'd better take the table back to North Bromwich."

"They wouldn't thank me for that. Our people reckon to do a job like this on one journey. We could shove it in the garridge."

But Dick had the garage key.

"Well, the best we can do," the foreman decided at last, with the air of making an unusual concession, "is to leave it outside covered up with a bit of tarpaulin till you get in a carpenter."

"The rain might spoil it."

"Oh, the rain won't 'urt that," said the foreman. "If the stain washes off you can always dab a bit more on."

He said good-bye gruffly. The best class of customers always gave him a tip, if only out of relief at his departure; but Susan was too much distressed and exhausted to think of such things. She picked her way through the tornado's path to the disordered kitchen, where she sat down on a packing-case and burst into tears.

Dick cheerfully arrived in the dark at six-fifteen to find the garden-path blocked by the tarpaulined hulk of the Baronial table.

"Hello, darling," he called. "Has the furniture come? How topping! Susan, Susan! Where are you? Good Lord, what a mess!"

He found her sitting on her packing-case, small and desolate. She gazed at him savagely out of her tear-reddened eyes. His heart fell suddenly. "Why, darling, what on earth's the matter?"

"They've got to take out the window," she said, and burst into tears again. "And you hadn't even the sense," she complained, "to leave me the garage key."

"Well, that's all right, darling," he said, "here it is."

"You'd have thought it all right," she sobbed, "if you'd been here all day and heard them smashing up everything and . . . ruining the paint!" On the last words her voice broke completely, rising to a pitiful wail. He had never before seen her quite so upset. In an ill-advised moment he rashly implored her to be reasonable. That made things far worse. It took him ten minutes to bring her round again.

"I've had nothing to eat all day," she told him piteously.

"We'll get something to eat in Tilton."

"Don't be silly. It's early closing day. I'm too tired to eat anything, anyway."

With enormous effort, by the light of his bicycle lamp, they succeeded finally in lugging the Baronial table into the garage.

"Now we'd better go home," he said tenderly. "Come along, Susie darling."

"I'm too tired to go home," she protested. "Let's sleep here in blankets."

She allowed him to unpack the blankets and lay them out. He was hungry himself, and there seemed to be no chance of supper. She lay limply stretched out on the mattress of their large single bed. He lay down beside her, though it was barely eight o'clock. Neither slept; but when Dick wanted to make love to her she was quite annoyed.

"Well, I really do think you might have more consideration than that," she said. "If you knew what a day I've had!"

He took her refusal mildly. There was nothing else

for it. The rain beat on the roof; the sanitation gurgled unceasingly. And thus they began their first night in the Room with a View.

II

The Baronial dining-table remained in the garage for a whole week, at the end of which Mr. Duke's carpenter solved the problem of getting it inside by ruthless dismemberment. "Them legs is only screwed on," he said, "and the wood's as soft as butter. You leave it to me, ma'am, I'll fix you."

Susan was puzzled. "I thought oak was hard."

"*And* it is," said the carpenter. "But the only thing oak about this table is the stain—and that's creosote."

A rough working-man could hardly be expected to know as much about high-class woods as Mr. Bellis, who owned to a passion for them; and whatever the table was made of, the overwhelming effect of the Baronial suite, with its genuine deep carving, was undeniable. Though the sideboard and table left very little space for six chairs and did make the room rather gloomy, the right word was the one which Mr. Bellis had employed: it was "stately." Sitting down for the first time at one end of the table, separated from Dick at the other by eight feet of dark wood, Susan felt like the châtelaine of an old-world country seat in a novel. The illusion lacked nothing, indeed, but the service of a noiseless, white-whiskered butler ("Perks has been in the family for centuries!") to whisper "Hock or champagne, madam?" beneath the approving eyes of painted Jacobean (some called it Baronial) ancestors. Determined to live up to it, she had insisted, at first, on Dick's wearing dinner-dress, while she herself had slipped on her "little" black lace; but the incongruity of dishing up sausage and mash in this attire and the agony that Dick bore in the grip of a boiled shirt finally forced her to abandon this elegant fashion of dining. From the strain of the Baronial style they gravitated first to the living-room and thence, a few weeks later, to the little kitchen, which was not only much more convenient, but always warm, reserving the dining-room suite as a museum piece for exhibition to visitors and for those *chic* little dinner-parties that Susan was some day going to give, and for which even now she cut out menus of dainty dishes from the daily paper.

They were so busy, indeed, during those first months at "Chatsworth," that the bitter Midland winter passed by almost without their being aware of it. Until Dick saw the pride and labour that Susan lavished on the house, he had not realized how deep-seated was the instinct that it satisfied. She hugged it to her heart as a child hugs a cherished doll. There was no detail in its cleanliness or order or embellishment that failed to engage her passionate interest. The symmetrical set of a curtain, the position of a vase or candlestick, the angle at which a chair must be set or a cushion negligently thrown, had become as absorbing to her decorative zeal as the fashions of dress which had formerly engrossed her. She was so proud of these nice variations, so eager for him to share in her little triumphs, that Dick, who, except in his early boyhood, had never known anything nearer to a home than lodgings and asked very little more of life than an easy chair and a table to put his pipe on, became infected, in spite of himself, by her restless enthusiasm. She would ponder and scheme and debate for hours over details that in former days would have seemed to him quite unimportant. She "took in" illustrated magazines that dealt technically with houses and gardens and labour-saving devices, revealing dozens of ways in which such things as soap-boxes could be adapted to household uses. Her passion embraced not only the æsthetic side of suburban life, but the utilitarian. The nose for "bargains" she had formerly exercised in matters of dress now smelt out the cheapest jams and currants and potted eggs and packets of self-raising flour, which she would drag home in triumph from the grocer's in her string shopping-bag and miraculously convert into cakes and scones and sponge sandwiches, which, in spite of a few sad failures, were more delicious, Dick declared, than any he had ever tasted. She pursued economy, in fact, not so much for its own sake as for that of revealing her domestic virtuosity, treating the theme of Sunday's roast beef to as many dizzy variations as a famous violinist displays in a concerto's cadenza. In this process Dick's stomach was subjected to a series of what doctors call "test meals," which, being extremely robust, it survived without permanent damage.

"Now isn't this delicious?" she would ask him, with glowing eyes.

"Yes, it's topping. What is it?"

"That's my secret. You'd never guess, and I'm not going to tell you," she would say. "As a matter of fact," she conceded, "it's French. That's why it may taste rather strange."

"Not strange, darling—perhaps unusual," he loyally protested.

Though Dick, for his own part, much preferred the lodging-house regimen of a fried chop and chipped potatoes with stewed fruit and rice pudding to follow to any of the made dishes that satisfied Susan's craving for the exotic, he was proud of her ingenuities, and even boasted of them to his friends in the office. "My wife," he would say—and the words still thrilled him strangely—"she's a marvel at cooking. Got all sorts of French ideas. If you gave her an old boot she could make it taste like a fillet."

"Lucky dog!" the office wag told him. "If business goes on in the way that it's going now, that's just about what we shall all be eating next year. Boiled upper for supper, my boy!"

As a matter of fact, this new domestic activity pro-

R

vided Susan with the kind of romantic expression for which she yearned. The devotion to literature which she had assumed for Mr. Feilden's benefit in a previous dramatization had never gone very deep. It was an interest too static, too impersonal. It allowed her imaginative nature too many opportunities for vague, exalted dreaming which bred nothing but discontent. Her idle life in Dick's lodgings at Winsworth had afflicted her with a similar restlessness. Her work at "Chatsworth" was too absorbing for that. It suited her. Her mind was contented; her body throve on it. She had never been so lovely, Dick thought, as now, when she bustled about in her overall, with flour on her arms to the elbows and even on the tip of her nose, and her healthy cheeks red with the heat of the kitchen range. She actually complained, good-humouredly, that she was putting on flesh. "It must be the result of the Tilton air," she said. "I'm always famished. I eat twice as much as you do."

When she had finished her work Dick found her deliciously lazy and complacent. But she had never really finished. There was always something that lacked the last touch of her fingers. After the Baronial suite had been abandoned to its monumental dignity, her eager mind concentrated all its energies on the sunny room opposite, in which, except when they ate in the kitchen, they spent most of their waking lives. Its contents suggested an even compromise between Dick's interests and hers. On the walls Dick scored

heavily, with a series of purplish framed photographs
of house—and form—and team groups at Brunstone,
over the most important of which—the one that represented him sitting paralysed on the captain's left with
colossal fore-shortened knees—was suspended the most
important prize of his school career: a tasselled skull-
cap composed of alternate segments of puce and canary
velvet. Susan's only contribution to the walls was
Aunt Edna's wedding-present—an engraving, after
Watts, of Hope in difficulties with the terrestrial globe.

The mantelpiece, again, asserted her husband's pre-
ponderance, being mainly occupied by three silver cups
won at Brunstone, a tobacco-jar blazoned with the
School arms and the motto *Floreat Brunstonia,* and
a battery of manly pipes, including a clay church-
warden, all completely dwarfed by Captain Small's
contribution—the brass cylinder of a British field-
gun's shell-case. This present, it may be said, had
caused Susan considerable embarrassment. She might
have used it in the hall as a single umbrella-stand if
that function had not already been provided for by the
drain-pipe, generously supplied by Mr. Duke's partner.
It might, again, as Captain Small himself suggested,
have been converted into a dinner-gong; but since they
had taken to dining in the kitchen, a gong was superfluous. Its bulk made it as difficult to dispose of as a
murdered body. So there it stood, dominating the left
end of the mantelpiece, a sacrifice on the altar of
friendship, neither beautiful nor useful—for even as a

mirror, Susan quickly discovered, it made her look
awful.

The shelves flanking the fireplace were Susan's un-
disputed territory. Though she had turned up her nose
at Mr. Duke's suggestion of using them for "ornaments," her personal library did not suffice to fill them,
so the two uppermost were occupied by effigies of comic
animals in various materials symmetrically disposed on
either side of an electro-plate rose-bowl and a clock
which, resenting the plaster-damp air of "Chatsworth," persisted in the assertion that it was half-past
two. To fill the others she had rifled, with George
Lorimer's connivance, the recesses of the glass-fronted
Chippendale book-cases at the house in Great Cornbow.
Her haul consisted for the most part of late Georgian
and early Victorian sermons bound in half-calf, and
might have suggested that her interests were mainly
theological if that body of evangelical opinion had not
been leavened by her private possessions. Dick contemplated these evidences of culture with awe, and
frequently made Susan blush by mentioning them to
visitors; but a more skilful observer might have extracted from their confusion a synthesis of Susan's
intellectual horizons. There were few of those fan-
tasies on which the children of the leisured classes in
England are reared. The foundations of the library
consisted of ink-splashed school books, primers of
history, geography and elementary mathematics, with
a sprinkling of Shakespeare's plays and novels by Scott

set for holiday tasks. There followed a section representing the indiscriminate romantic idols of adolescence
—*Lorna Doone,* the collected poems of Longfellow
and Tennyson in bindings of padded morocco, the
elevating works of Ella Wheeler Wilcox and Laurence
Hope, and no less than three copies, the gifts of world-
weary school friends, of FitzGerald's *Omar Khayyám*
—while the sensual ferment of those callow years
found its proper medium in such highly coloured
romances as *The Garden of Allah, The Green Hat,*
and the passionate experiences of seduced or seductive
heroines created by Miss Victoria Cross and Mrs.
Elinor Glyn—all of which had been read in secret
and concealed from Aunt Edna's eyes. Mr. Feilden's
influence had seasoned this adolescent's tipsy-cake with
the harsher condiments of Fielding and Smollett. He,
too, was responsible for cheap editions of Conrad and
Henry James (given up in despair); those Bibles of
youth, *The Way of All Flesh* and *Ann Veronica;* odd
plays by Shaw, Strindberg, and Galsworthy; *Love's
Coming of Age,* by Edward Carpenter; two popular
presentations of the theory of Psycho-Analysis; D. H.
Lawrence's *Kangaroo* and *Women in Love;* Shaw's
Intelligent Woman's Guide to Socialism, and beside it,
unblushingly displayed to the world at last, Dr. Marie
Stopes' rapturous guides to the adventure of Birth
Control.

Dick's sensibility had been deeply shocked by dis-
covering these. Though Susan had begged him to read

them, because she thought he ought to, he had found it impossible to do so in her presence. One day, when she was busy in the kitchen, he had furtively skipped through them. He had found their technical enthusiasm so embarrassing and felt so oddly ashamed that he had ended by deliberately hiding them behind the innocent row of school books. It hurt him to see, next day, that Susan had replaced them in a prominent position, but he was far too shy of opening the subject to protest.

Though Susan was proud of these relics of her Feilden phase as evidences of a clear-eyed, courageous, modern outlook on life, their perusal had never influenced her thoughts very deeply. She had adopted them at that period and ostentatiously carried them about with her hoping to shock somebody, in much the same spirit as, when first she knew Mr. Feilden, she had heightened her air of studiousness by equipping herself with an entirely unnecessary pair of imitation tortoiseshell spectacles, which she had abandoned as soon as she discovered that they didn't suit her. Though she liked to be thought an emancipated example of what Mr. Feilden called the *intelligentsia,* and Dick the Highbrows, her natural attitude towards life was as old as Eve's: emotional, subjective, sensual, and anything in the world but detached, as was shown by the undisguised relish with which she devoured the fiction of A. S. M. Hutchinson and Gilbert Frankau and the thrills she extracted from the

crudest of human relationships as presented by Hollywood. These frank appetites fortunately had no
further need of concealment since her capture of a
husband, toward which end, unconsciously, her former
poses had been employed.

For the rest the living-room at "Chatsworth" was
as comfortable as her zeal for tidiness would allow it
to be, and Dick, who had been somewhat intimidated
at first by its smartness and Susan's forbidding attitude
toward the mud he brought in from the unfinished
surface of Ada Road and his bachelor disregard of
tobacco-ash, soon settled down into it and to a life, of
Susan's creation, more like that of a home than any he
had known before.

It was a placid routine, uncomplicated by anything
but small household emergencies—as when flues would
not draw or the sanitation went wrong or a cow
wandered into the garden—and Dick, by nature a
highly domesticated animal, found it wholly satisfying. It was wonderful, he thought, to wake up warm
in the morning and look out over those wintry fields;
to fetch in the milk from the porch and set the kettle
boiling on the gas-ring; to talk, while he shaved in the
sanitation, to Susan rapt in the mysteries of her toilet
in the bedroom; to help her prepare the breakfast
and read little snippets of news from the morning
paper.

"It says they had thunder at Stourton yesterday, the
main street's under water," he would announce.

"Well, now didn't I *tell* you I heard thunder, Dick?"

"Yes, that's what it says. It's going to be colder to-day, though, according to the forecast."

"Well, there! I had to pull up a blanket last night."

He never had to worry now about missing the bus. All through breakfast Susan would keep glancing at her wrist-watch and warn him when he ought to start. She would find him his hat and his coat and his stick and give him a good-bye kiss on the door-step, unless a bright morning tempted her to walk with him to the end of the road. It was marvellous, Dick thought, to have someone to kiss you good-bye every morning, and stand looking after you and waving as you reached the turn. And when he came back from North Bromwich what a joy it was to see from a distance the lights of "Chatsworth" and think of the red fire's reflection flickering in Captain Small's shell-case and the sweet smell of home and the sweet smell of Susan, too, as he buried his face in her hair and kissed her warm lips. She would bring him his slippers and sit cuddled up on his knee in the big arm-chair and tell him all the exciting things that had happened since he had left her.

Everything that happened at "Chatsworth" in those early days was exciting, according to Susan, if it were only the visit of a hawker or a rag-and-bone man. She made Dick laugh with her mimicries and exaggerations and pretended to be hurt when he didn't take them seriously.

The hour of whispers and kisses and long silences and baby-talk in the dusk was very precious to him; but towards eight o'clock Susan's mind turned to a more serious matter, the evening meal, which, though at first it had been "dinner" they now called "supper." She would turn on the red-shaded reading-lamp and leave him to the *Evening Courier* that he always bought at the corner of Sackville Row when he left the office. He would turn first of all to the "sporting" page, for although he had been far too busy to play games since his marriage, he always "kept up with them." He read the police-court news as well and reports of week-end motor-car smashes, but, like most of his friends, he was not much interested in politics, and made no attempt to understand them. While he read the paper he would be vaguely and pleasantly conscious of the patter of Susan's quick steps as she bustled about the kitchen, or listen to her singing disjointed phrases of songs they had heard at Brinton; and sometimes these evidences of her existence, suddenly realized, made him feel what a lucky devil he was and how little he had done to deserve it.

When supper was finished and everything washed up, Susan turned on all the lights in the sitting-room, to make things more cheerful, she said. A friend of Dick's at the office had built them a crystal wireless set out of cheap components. It was generally out of order, but when it wasn't they would settle down solemnly on either side of the fire with ear-phones over

their heads and "listen in" to the News Bulletin and
the Weather Forecast (which Dick had already read in
the *Evening Courier*) and S.O.S. messages about missing people who were supposed to have lost their
memories. When an S.O.S. message came through
Dick always made notes—"Albert Hall—five feet six
—eyes blue—scar on left cheek—drab weather-proof
coat and cloth cap—report Chief Constable, Southamp-
ton, or any police-station"—because, as he said, you
couldn't tell; Albert Hall might even be discovered
in a fainting condition on the door-step of "Chatsworth," though he never was.

Incidentally they listened to a great deal of Modern
and Classical Music, which Dick confessed he could
make neither head nor tail of, but which Susan said
she enjoyed. As he sat there, dutifully deafened by
those odd elaborations of sound which were supposed
to be sublime, he found some satisfaction in thinking
how sensitive and cultured she was to understand them.
If Dick couldn't approve the quality of the music he
could feel its loudness.

"I say, Susie, it's coming through top-hole to-night,"
he would say.

"That's Wagner," she would shout in answer. "*The
Ride of the Valkyries.*"

"Now how the deuce did she know that?" he asked
himself proudly. "How clever she is!"

But more often the thought that came into his mind
was: "How lovely she is!--the music that beat on his

unresponsive brain being no more than a half-heard accompaniment to the passion that swayed him as he gazed on her sitting there, so small and so precious, with the grotesque apparatus clipped to her ears.

As a matter of fact, Susan only pretended to enjoy Wagner—as much to herself as to him. Though well-marked rhythms stimulated her and made her beat time with her foot, she was almost tone-deaf, as Dick might have judged (if he had not been similarly afflicted) from the dance-tunes and theme-songs she hummed out of tune in the kitchen. The only music that really moved her was that oily drooping note of the saxophone combined with the negroid, nasal whine of Broadway Jews which had imposed itself in those days, through the medium of the sound film, on the whole British Empire, from Inverness to New Zealand. Even this appealed to her senses less as music than as the accepted accompaniment of her ideals of fashionable life and romantic love. She was happiest, indeed, when the Queen's Hall closed down and the Broadcasting Corporation's arbiters of elegance "took her over" to the Savoy Hotel, whence she could hear the clapping of the dancers' hands when the saxophone ceased to whine and almost feel she was taking part in those brilliant gatherings where "titled" men and "society" girls (in the latest Chanels and Mollynoos) performed the most difficult modern steps with an "easy nonchalance" in a "gala atmosphere" of coloured balloons and paper streamers and popping champagne-corks. She could imagine all that quite easily, for Muriel O'Brien had once seen the New Year in at the Savoy with Harry Levison, and had told her all about it. What a brilliant, care-free life men like Harry Levison must lead! To dance in *chic* rendezvous, without having to think about money. . . .

But by this time Dick had knocked out his last pipe and was beginning to yawn, so, banishing these envious dreams from her mind, Susan took off her ear-phones.

"I expect you're sleepy, darling," she would say. "You'd better lock up."

While he went to the front door and opened it before he finally locked it, inhaling the sharp air and scanning the frosty sky for some confirmation of the weather he'd read of in the *Courier* and heard about in the forecast, Susan would have a last look round the kitchen, just to see that everything was in place. Dick would join her there, slip his arm round her waist and draw her along with him, and while she completed her relatively elaborate bed-time toilet she could see him in the mirror, first stripped—what odd shapes men had!—and then kneeling down in pyjamas by the side of Mr. Bulgin's walnut bed. It was strange, she would sometimes think, how some part of his mind which she could not enter compelled him, even now, to say his prayers every night. That was one thing in which he still remained a stranger to her. When he had finished his prayers he would jump into the creaking bed and lie watching her, rather impatiently. He often thought

that her white shoulders were the loveliest part of her.
But when she switched off the light and ran to find
warmth in his arms with an affected shiver, they were
strangers no more. They were both still passionately in
love; and this moment of sudden darkness, when their
bodies lay close together, was still a miracle, whose
wonder never grew stale.

III

George Lorimer frequently came to see Susan at
"Chatsworth" — far more often than Aunt Edna
imagined; though, since that last skirmish with Mr.
Bulgin, he had been so unlike himself, mooning about
the garden, prowling upstairs and down all over the
house like a ghost and starting as if he had been shot
whenever she spoke to him, that she was almost thankful to see the back of him. All her attempts to make
George talk about his business troubles had failed. If
she even hinted at them he went red and stole away in
a frightened, elusive manner. Nor had there been any
further mention of Mr. Bulgin's combine save once,
when Susan had passed on an equivocal message. Mrs.
Lorimer consoled herself by reflecting that this odd
secretiveness was the usual attitude of business-men
toward their wives. "Tell 'em nothing," the Midland
proverb ran. She supposed most men conformed to it.
In any case, being a spinster in everything but name,

she knew very little about them.

The thoughts that pursued George Lorimer during those months were so clamorous that he scarcely heard his wife when she spoke to him. His mind was one small confusion of dancing figures, as disordered as the blotting-pad on which he scribbled vain calculations when he sat, with knitted brows, on his high desk-stool at the office. He was entirely incapable of preparing systematic defences against the new combine's attack. Having heard, perhaps during the war, that the most disconcerting form of defence was an unexpected offensive, he decided to make the first move and book advance orders at prices cut to the finest shaving of profit. It would make that move more impressive, he thought, if, instead of sending out circulars or the single decrepit salesman whom he had inherited from his father, he paid personal calls on all his important customers. They would surely be flattered to receive a personal visit not from Lorimer's paid representative, but from Lorimer's principal.

They were not flattered at all. George's person, in fact, made less impression than if he had substituted a smart new traveller for the old one. His generous offers of cuts in the price of nails were only received with suspicion. Though John Bulgin's combine was not yet in being, all his customers had heard of it. The seasonal slackness of trade, they told him, made it quite impossible to place large orders in advance. They were actually waiting, he knew well enough, for the price reductions which the combine were certain to offer them, and he returned from his tour with his order-book so empty that he was ashamed to show it to his salesman.

Throughout all these vain excursions in search of trade, he had been embarrassed by the problem of ful-filling his rash promise to provide two hundred pounds for Susan's furnishing. As he mooned about the house in Great Cornbow it had suddenly occurred to him that some of the useless eighteenth-century furniture that cluttered the attics might fetch fancy prices with dealers. The idea had transported him until he began to reflect not only that he knew nothing about the value of furniture and would probably be cheated, but that he couldn't remove a single piece from the house with-out exciting his wife's curiosity and being cross-examined on his reasons for doing so. His final solu-tion, like most inspirations, was simple in the extreme: he realized the cash-surrender value of a life-insurance policy which he had taken out many years before. The sum was considerably less than the amount of premiums he had paid, but it was some relief to know that he needn't bother to pay any more; and the fifty odd pounds that remained after Susan's cheque had been paid so filled him with a sensation of affluence that he actually bought a new spinning-rod, designed for the capture of pike.

Those fishy incarnations of Mr. Bulgin's voracity should now have been at their best. The first nip of frost had killed the weeds and sharpened their appetite. But, somehow or other, George Lorimer couldn't settle down to his fishing that autumn. There were days, under sulky grey skies, when the pike in the mill-pool grew equally sulky, refusing to feed. As he sat in his leaky punt, growing colder and colder, his empty mind, which in former days had been the playground of small vagrant fancies, became invaded by the turbulent pack of financial worries. They stole in one by one till his wretched brain was so maddened by their snapping and yelping that he could do nothing but pack up his rods and tackle and tramp up the hill to "Chatsworth." Miss Maples, of "Welbeck," first seeing him arrive with his bundle of ferruled rods (two for pike, one for roach) mistook him for a plumber and told her mother that something must have gone wrong with the drains at "Chatsworth." It gave her a shock to see Susan kiss him on the door-step. Even if he were a relative (which she doubted), she hated that sort of thing.

George didn't tell Aunt Edna when he went to see Susan, not for fear of making her jealous, but because he hated explanations. Through all this distracted voyage, the living-room at "Chatsworth" was the one haven on all that iron-bound coast where he knew that the running sea could not reach him. Its small, cosy compass made such a contrast to the chilly, ill-lighted, sepulchral rooms of the house in Great Cornbow. However glum he might feel he knew he was always

welcome in that bright little room, as clean as a new-
minted shilling, with its gay-patterned chintzes, its
cheerful fire, and the air of light-hearted youth and
active hope that pervaded it.

Susan's mind was so thronged with the immediate
excitements of her new life, so proud, and so anxious
for him to share in her pride, that, for hours on end,
he would forget the grim deeps of Halesby that lay
brooding beneath them in the valleys under the smoke-
pall of Bulgin's chimneys. He had grown fond of
Dick Pennington too. Though they hadn't very much
to say about it, George Lorimer felt they two had
established a mute understanding, and Susan, of course,
did quite enough talking for both of them. He would
often have liked to stay on at "Chatsworth" all evening, but fear and duty together always compelled him
to be back at Great Cornbow with his rods and tackle
soon after dark. But he returned to Halesby with the
darkened mind of a boy going back to school, leaving
all that he cared for most in the world behind him.

George Lorimer wasn't by any means Susan's only
regular visitor. There were two others, both, as Miss
Maples took occasion to tell her mother with regret, of
the opposite sex.

"Times have changed, Maud," the old lady said
spitefully, "since you were a girl."

There were moments when Miss Maples actually
hated her mother—never more so than when she threw
her age in her face. It was unnecessary: all her forty-

eight years were in it already, and if she did show their scars they were honourable scars, the signs of her selfless devotion to this exacting old lady. If it weren't for her mother she might have been married once and knitted boots for babies of her own, instead of other people's.

"I dare say times have changed," she primly replied, "but not for the better. I should think it's unusual even now for a young married woman to make a habit of receiving men when her husband's away. I don't say it's wrong, Mamma, but I do think it's extremely thoughtless. I can see everything that they do!"

"You haven't been paid to watch," Mrs. Maples said acidly.

"How like you, Mamma! You know perfectly well you'd hate it if I didn't tell you. It's the third time this week she's been visited by that strange lame man in the trench-coat!"

Since the day when he first timidly limped up to "Chatsworth," carrying his shell-case, Captain Small's store of courage had swelled miraculously. Susan encouraged his visits, not only because he patently (yet so respectfully!) adored her, but because it was useful to have a man in the house when Dick was away. First of all Captain Small had fulfilled his promise of staining and polishing the floors. Later on she could always find some odd thing for him to do with nails and a hammer or a paint-brush. He performed all these tasks with the brisk, smart, barrack-room air of an officer's servant; the mere fact of being near Susan made him radiantly cheerful. When he had finished his job he was always humbly ready to go, but his face was so wistful that she often asked him to stay to tea, and it was almost worth the occasional inconvenience when she saw the gratitude and joy with which his eyes brightened. They would sit through the fading wintry afternoon and talk in the firelit dusk—Susan never switched on the light for fear of staring at his face, though, little by little, she was beginning not to notice it—while Captain Small, encouraged, and carefully avoiding the war as much as he could, poured out his confessions—or all confessions but one.

He told her about his trouble with the drink and how he was conquering it, without mentioning the part her existence had played in his reformation. He told her, quite frankly, of surprising romantic adventures on leave in London during the war, and his later disasters in trying to run a garage when the war was over. He made nothing heroic of these experiences, and was never more amused than when the laugh was against himself; but what touched her most was the deference to her wisdom, her innocence, her beauty, implied by all these confessions—a deference so humbly pathetic that when he was talking to her she accepted his own naïve valuation of all these qualities and felt like a queen. Oddly enough he acquired virtue of a sort in her mind by the very vices to which he confessed. She wasn't quite sure that Dick wouldn't have been more human for a little of the lurid experience which she associated with Captain Small and with Harry Levison. Yet, in many surprising ways, Joe Small's attitude toward life was nearer to Dick's than to hers. She concluded that all men were pretty much cut from the same material, a sound homespun, compact and durable, but of a pattern by no means exciting —very different from the flimsy, shimmering gossamer of which she was made.

Sometimes, when he came home at night, Dick found them still talking. Then Captain Small would clumsily hoist himself up on to his stiff leg. The promptness with which he surrendered her to Dick annoyed her.

"There's no reason to rush off like that," she would say. "Dick's not going to eat you, are you, Dick, darling?"

"Yes, stay and have a drink, Small. Why not?"

Captain Small was adamant. "No, thank you, old chap. Haven't earned one to-day. Two's company, eh? No, it's time I was pushing off to my bachelor billet. You fellows have all the luck! So long! Cheerio!"

"He's really far nicer than I thought, Dick," Susan explained, "and so useful in the house. I wish you two would make friends."

"We might, if he'd give me a chance."

"He's so terribly shy. It takes hours to get under the surface."

"Well, you've more time to spare for that sort of

thing than I have. Dig away, but don't encourage the fellow too much. You see, people might talk. That woman over the way . . ."

"Dick, what do you mean? He isn't the kind of man who would dream of taking a liberty."

"I should damned well think not!"

His sudden heat made her mischievous. "Well, darling, if he did, I probably shouldn't tell you."

He stared incredulously. "Susie . . . what are you saying?"

She laughed. "My dear child, this isn't the Nineteenth Century. Don't look so foolish and serious. Come and kiss me! If you really love me I expect you to love my dog—such a pathetic, shaggy creature, so different from you!" she said, as she nuzzled his cheek with her soft face.

IV

It was curious that neither Dick nor the watchful Miss Maples harboured the faintest doubt as to the desirability of Susan's other male visitor, Mr. Bulgin. Mr. Bulgin was no raffish ex-officer, but a man of substance. When he came to "Chatsworth" he didn't slink in through the dusk. He approached it openly in his Phantom Rolls-Royce, with headlights blazing. For Miss Maples it was enough that her mother approved of him and that he owned a Landseer, though he never visited "Welbeck." She watched his arrivals not with suspicion but with faint envy, and Susan, equally, was flattered by the impression his opulent approach must make on her neighbours. No other car quite so big and no man so rich frequented Ada Road. She didn't mind how many men appeared to admire her: the more the better!

Mr. Bulgin also had been exceptionally busy that winter. After Susan's rejection of his suit there had been a short period in which he had begun to feel his age. Now that climacteric was over. He appeared to have taken on a new and extensive lease of life. Thanks to Solomon Magnus he had escaped the catastrophe in which Wall Street crashed like a skyscraper. The contract for the pipe-line in Venezuela had encouraged others of the same kind. His tubes were beating the Americans at their own game. With the object of evading the tax on excess profits he had bought up a derelict tin-plate works in South Wales and equipped it lavishly. This establishment was nearer to the coast and to his prime materials. He didn't mind betting the day would come when all the rough processes would be done there and the old works at Halesby reserved for refinements of machine work. As a minor diversion he had amused himself by organizing his nail-making combine. It had been called The New British Nail Company, and this name, quite by accident, had provided him with an advertising catchword or "slogan" as he called it: *N.B.—Use N.B. Nails!*

With this pressure of affairs in his head it came as a great relief, when the office closed, to sit back in the car and drive majestically to take tea with Susan at "Chatsworth." He made no attempt to conceal his visits, for the best of reasons. It was one of the penalties of wealth and local celebrity that a man like himself couldn't stir a yard without being recognized, so one might just as well go comfortably in the Rolls, Mr. Bulgin thought. His conduct toward Susan, in any case, was extremely correct. If he brought her expensive presents—such as chocolates from Bond Street and exotic flowers from North Bromwich—it was well worth the money to see her face light up with greed and delight. He was sufficiently shrewd, moreover, to associate Dick with these bounties. He came to "Chatsworth," he implied, just as much to see Dick as to see Susan: a rather sad figure, in spite of his enormous wealth, with no children of his own to spoil, he found some compensation in picking up the crumbs of happiness that fell from their table. He even affected a benevolent interest in Dick's commercial career, and questioned him about his work.

"You're doing the right thing, my boy," he would say, "starting right at the foot of the ladder. I did that myself; I know just what it feels like. All you've got to do, Dick, my lad, is to keep plugging on. And don't you forget, I've always got my eye on you."

Susan thought this remark extremely significant. Who knew what beneficent scheme underlay Mr.

Bulgin's words? "Isn't it wonderful, darling," she said, "to think of an important man like him being interested in you? He might offer you a directorship some day. Only think of it!"

Dick, too, in a milder way, was excited by these hints of patronage. He shared Mr. Bulgin's fruit and chocolates and cigars without the least qualm of conscience, and only the faintest twinge of jealousy pricked him when he saw Mr. Bulgin's paternal arm about Susan's waist and the ceremonial kiss, smelling faintly of brown Windsor soap and lavender-water, with which he bade her farewell. Old men had their harmless privileges, and Mr. Bulgin, in Dick's young eyes, was unconscionably old. He was too highly flattered to notice how, even when he spoke of his work, Mr. Bulgin's glance hovered greedily over Susan from neck to ankle; nor, fortunately, did he know of the less perfunctory embraces with which Mr. Bulgin greeted her on his arrival.

As for Susan, she now regarded Mr. Bulgin with favour, quite apart from his potential usefulness to Dick and his luxurious presents. It was characteristically perverse of Uncle George to dislike him. The fact that he had asked her to marry him and that she had refused him gave their intercourse—particularly when they were alone—a tinge of sentiment. It pleased her to think of Mr. Bulgin as being nobly resigned to a hopeless passion. His glances, which made her feel hot, subtly flattered her; the kisses which she yielded so frankly did no harm to anyone and obviously gave Mr. Bulgin acute satisfaction. Their new relationship, in short, was familiar to her—if not actually on the screen—in the social picture of Hollywood. In the vulgar phrase of that world Mr. Bulgin was her "sugar-daddy," though that term implied an intimacy the mere suggestion of which would have shocked and offended her. She was always more than usually affectionate with Dick when Mr. Bulgin had kissed her.

For the rest, though the electric bell had "gone off" at the end of six weeks, few visitors, male or female, knocked at the front door of "Chatsworth." Once or twice Dick brought hearty young men from the office to be impressed by the Baronial suite and stare in frank admiration at Susan; but the inhabitants of Ada Road, as a whole, were not given to calling. New "dormitory" suburbs such as Tilton knew nothing of the old village life. They were inhabited by a shifting population, drawn thither by the industrial magnet, with nothing in common but the road in which they happened to live and the patronage of Mr. Duke's milk-van; no deeper roots in the soil than the houses they occupied.

By the end of the winter Susan had achieved no more than a nodding acquaintance with most of her female neighbours. When she came back from shopping she would sometimes pause for a moment in front of "Welbeck" and raise poor Miss Maples' hopes of a consultation. Mrs. Duke, indeed, had called formally and left one of Mr. Duke's business cards with an "s" added on to the "Mr." and everything about milk crossed out. She was a very grand lady, with a structure resembling a rockery in full flower balanced on her head and a high-mettled set of teeth controlled with masterly decorum; but her call was less in the nature of a visit than a visitation with the object of satisfying herself that the amenities of "Chatsworth" were not being abused. "You've got to travel far to find reliable tenants in these days," she informed Susan sternly, "what with hammering nails in the walls and letting the doors slam. Why, naturally, plaster won't stand it." It was clear that she found the furniture hardly worthy of its ducal setting, till at last, very diffidently, Susan exhibited the "Baronial" and, for once, its stateliness justified its existence with a crashing success. Mrs. Duke was floored. "That's a lovely suite, that is: you keep your eye on it," she said—as though it were quite on the cards that a burglar might whisk it away in the night, which, considering the struggle they had had to get it inside, Susan thought unlikely. "You've not dug the garden yet, I notice," Mrs. Duke said, at parting.

The premature florescence of spring in Mrs. Duke's hat had the effect of spurring Nature on to swift emulation. All through the winter a solitary robin had hopped round the backyard at "Chatsworth" like a familiar spirit and cocked a bright jet-black eye at Susan when she shook out the crumbs. Now the air thrilled at dawn with the wildest, most soul-subduing music. One morning, blinking idly out of the window when first she woke, Susan saw that the farmer had turned out lambs into the field at the foot of the garden. These tiny creatures filled her heart with an aching tenderness. She longed to pick them up and kiss their little faces and press her nose into their silky, curled astrakhan. Their vague, tottering movements entranced her attention for hours; and later, when they found their weak legs, she would call on Dick to hurry and look at them bounding in the air, like mechanical toys, and kicking out their legs behind to try their strength. Once, cautiously slipping through the hedge, she surprised a lamb and caught it up in her arms.

"Oh, Dick," she cried rapturously. "There's hardly any wool; it's all solid lamb, the darling!"

Though he couldn't quite share her rapture, he found it beautiful. "How lovely she would be," he thought, "with a baby in her arms instead of a lamb!" But he didn't dare say so. Once or twice, when he had hinted at such a possibility, she had made it quite clear that with her the practical aspects of child-bearing had more weight than his easy sentiment. So he let it pass.

When he came home now in the evening it was quite light and he had time on his hands. He didn't play games any more, because that would mean leaving Susan. So, following the example of all the other suburban householders in Ada Road, he was stung with the ambition to "make a job" of the garden.

"It seems a shame," he said, "with all this land on our hands not to have any flowers. I think I'll start with a rockery."

That peculiarly English form of æsthetic expression was all the fashion in Tilton. Every garden of Ada Road at that time of year broke out into billows of arabis and purple aubrietia. The hierarch of this cult was Inspector Frome, the tenant of "Belvoir," to whom, rather timidly, Dick applied for advice. Inspector Frome's outward appearance was anything but sleuth-like to Susan's eyes. The word suggested something sinuous and slinking, with a touch of the sinister. The inspector was far too solidly built to slink through any-thing, with a clean-shaven, freckled face, thin sandy hair, light-blue opaque eyes, like those of a china doll, and a charming smile. As he shook hands with Susan he apologized for the soil with which they were stained and for the carpet slippers he wore. "My work's very hard on the feet," he explained, "and I always wear them off duty." When she spoke to him he stared at her fixedly, and paused for three seconds before he replied, as though, for lack of his usual notebook, he were committing her words and precise appearance to memory.

"You'll be surprised to hear how little I know about gardening," Dick modestly told him.

Inspector Frome shook his head. "People in my line," he said, "are never surprised at anything, Mr. Penning-ton. You never know," he added dreamily. "You never know. Still gardening's a great opportunity for thinking things over," he continued, his eyes intently fastened on Dick. "I should never have hung Garside, the Wednesford murderer, if it hadn't been for gardening. It's my only passion, you may say, apart from crime, and one sets off the other."

Of the two, Susan told him, she considered his profession the more interesting, but he didn't, it appeared from his answers to her eager questions, regard it romantically. All was grist that came to the mill of the law. Just as the eye of a doctor sees and notes instantaneously, mechanically, without surprise or emotion, the clinical signs of trivial or mortal disease, so Inspector Frome contemplated the whole long gamut of crime, from murder and rape and blackmail to riding a bicycle without a lamp one hour after sunset. It was only at the end of his visit, when he had carefully instructed Dick in the propagation of cuttings, that he pandered in any way to Susan's acute curiosity. At this point, slowly, mysteriously, he took from his waistcoat pocket a little tin box and opened it.

"You might like to see that," he said. "I don't often show it to civilians."

Susan saw a small twisted cylinder of string-coloured material.

"What is it?" she asked.

The inspector paused. "That's hemp," he said shortly. "That's hemp," he repeated, "that's part of the actual rope with which they hanged Garside."

Susan shuddered. He turned sharply on Dick as he closed his reliquary. "*You* ought to be interested in that, you know, Mr. Pennington."

"I? Interested? Why?" Dick asked. He too had been shaken.

"Because Pennington hanged him. It was Pennington gave me the rope."

"What d'you mean?" Susan cried.

The inspector smiled slowly. "Don't you know, Mrs. Pennington," he said, "that your husband's got the same name as the executioner—the hangman as some people call him? No relation, I suppose?"

"No, no, not in the very least," Dick assured him hurriedly.

"It isn't a common name," said the inspector, staring fixedly at Dick, as though he took it for granted that he was lying. "What's relations, anyway? I understand from the papers we're all more or less descended from William the Conqueror, every jack man of us. That makes you think, doesn't it? Criminals and bishops and all. That explains a lot, that does. As I was saying: you never know!"

He shambled away in his carpet slippers, apparently unaware of the sensation he had created. If Susan had asked for thrills she had got them with a vengeance. The shadow of the inspector's macabre exhibit lay black on her all that evening. There was another shadow, too.

"I wish you hadn't asked him to come," she said.

"He must be a horrible man to carry that rope about with him."

"But be reasonable, darling. You know perfectly well that things of that kind can never possibly touch *us*."

"Yes, I know. But that makes no difference. It was like an omen."

"Oh, well, if you're superstitious . . ."

"Don't be silly. I'm not superstitious. Can't we change our name, Dick? I thought it was such a nice, dignified name; but now I can't bear it—it's awful!"

"You'll forget all about it to-morrow," he told her. "Let's go to bed."

"I shall never forget it . . . *never*."

That night, for the first time in all their married life, Susan couldn't sleep. As Dick held her in his arms he could almost feel the tensity of the nerves inside her. Long after midnight he was wakened by a strange sound that penetrated his dreams. She was crying like a baby. There was something dreadfully alien and detached about this crying. It didn't fit in with the Susan he thought he knew; it almost frightened him.

"Susie, Susie," he said, "what's the matter? Do tell me, sweetheart."

She couldn't answer him. She was able to cry more loudly now that she knew he was awake. The bed shook with her sobbing.

"Tell me, Susie. You're surely not going on worrying about that wretched man? Is there something else?

There must be something else."

She shook her head violently in denial. But there was something else, though even now she rebelled against believing it. She had never been quite so scared and miserable in all her life.

v

Mr. Bulgin, on the other hand, had had a delightful evening. That day he had celebrated the nativity of The New British Nail Company. In honour of the occasion, instead of his usual high-tea, he had staged a little dinner-party at "Hill House," to which he had invited the new board of directors, Mr. Holland, Mr. Baker and Mr. Higgs. Though he sedulously cultivated a reputation for unostentatiousness in public, there was nothing Mr. Bulgin liked better in private than showing off to his humbler contemporaries. The dinner, though lavish, had been incontrovertibly English, consisting of oysters (there's an "r" in April, thank God!), grilled soles ("these come straight from Ramsgate, Baker"), a crisp saddle of lamb (Mr. Bulgin was not sentimental about lambs), and cabinet pudding to finish. With their dinner the party drank champagne (or, rather, Saumur), and after it port— not his very best port, but a perfectly drinkable wine matured in cask—for at the end of the meal (or even, for that matter, at the beginning) not one of them would know the difference.

"This is some of the real stuff. Don't light your cigars till you've tasted it, gentlemen," he implored them.

When the decanter had passed his untasted glass four times, Mr. Bulgin led his guests by way of the cloak-room to the picture-gallery, where Mr. Higgs, who up to this moment had not opened his mouth except to gobble the dinner, proclaimed loudly and suddenly that the Rubens Venus was "a bit of all right." Encouraged by this overture, Mr. Baker, a tall, thin man with a big Adam's apple, who looked like an undertaker, began to tell bawdy stories which made Mr. Higgs slap his thighs and Mr. Holland, on whom alcohol had a stringent effect, look down his nose and pretend to examine the beer-coloured backgrounds of the Dutch interiors. Mr. Bulgin, meanwhile, sat solitary in one of the bays of the sociable settee, vaguely thinking of Susan Pennington as he puffed at his pipe, and waiting for the clarification of his directorate's brains, like a surgeon watching his patient come out of an anæsthetic.

When Mr. Baker had reached the end of his repertory and Mr. Higgs had laughed himself dumb, they held an informal meeting over the dining-room table, which had now been cleared. Mr. Bulgin produced the proofs of the new advertisements which the publicity department of the tube-works had already prepared for insertion in all the agricultural journals. They

T

were "snappy" and impudent and quite unlike anything his partners had used before.

"The bulk of our stuff," he explained, "is used in the rural districts. If you get at the farmers direct, the ironmongers 'll be forced to stock it. You needn't worry about them."

"Ay, that hits the nail on the head," Mr. Higgs declared with enthusiasm. Mr. Bulgin smiled. "Not so bad, Higgs. Another slogan!" He made a short note on his blotting-paper:

N.B.

N.B.'s new prices!

They Hit the Imported Nail on the Head.

"What about our new prices?" Mr. Holland dolefully enquired. "We haven't settled them yet."

"Oh, haven't we! Take Rose Nails." Mr. Bulgin passed him the paper carelessly. "We're offering a shilling cut all round—that's eleven and sixpence a hundredweight."

"Eleven and sixpence a hundredweight!" Mr. Holland cried in alarm. "Eleven and sixpence? It can't be done, sir."

"I know it can't," Mr. Bulgin answered laconically. "That's why I'm doing it!" He thought: "That fellow Holland can carry a damned lot of liquor!" "Look here," he said firmly, "I know much more about big business than any of you do. The first thing a new firm's got to do is to collar the market. You've got to make N.B. nails a household word the same as my tubes, so that when a chap sees an iron nail he thinks N.B. When once you've done that the rest of it's easy as winking. You can push up your price bit by bit without the fools knowing. When they've once got N.B. in their heads they won't notice the difference. It's a question of establishing a habit. That's the meaning of salesmanship."

Mr. Holland remained obdurate. "There's the personal factor, Bulgin. Now my salesman, Timmins, he knows every one of our customers. He drops in for a quiet talk, as you might say, and asks after the family. . . ."

"Then the sooner we fire Timmins the better," Mr. Bulgin replied contemptuously. "We're not pedlars, we're nail-makers on a large scale. Just get that in your head! If you sent Timmins buzzing round England in a six-litre Bentley for twelve hours a day, with no time off for meals, he wouldn't reach half the folk that this list's going to hit in the eye. You leave that to me, Holland. I know all about prices, thank you! You may get cold feet the first quarter, but at the end of the year you'll be thanking me."

When the party had dispersed, Mr. Bulgin sat on over his papers. The atmosphere of the room was cloudy and foul with stale cigar-smoke; he needed a breath of fresh air to clear his head. As he stared at the printed price-list a slow smile stole over his lips. He slipped the advertisement into an envelope and carefully addressed it to George Lorimer. Then,

putting on his hat, he strolled down the hill through
the still spring night. The air was so mild, so sweet, so
vaguely disturbing, that he dallied on his way, recalling sentimentally April evenings of his boyhood
(he, too, had once been a boy) and all the sharp
savours of youth. With another, triumphant emotion
he skirted the Dingle. Most triumphantly of all he
slipped the envelope into George Lorimer's letterbox.
It tickled his humour to be inviting George Lorimer to
buy Rose Head Spikes at a price which he knew to be
lower than George's cost of production.

CHAPTER VIII

FORCED INTERLUDE

I

WHEN George Lorimer found Mr. Bulgin's envelope in the letter-box next morning he recognized the writing and was on the point of opening it at once to get the worst over, as he did with income-tax envelopes; but at the moment when he began to do so Aunt Edna appeared unexpectedly, so he slipped Mr. Bulgin's letter into his pocket—an unreasonably guilty gesture —and entering the room with a jaunty air, ostentatiously laid the rest of his mail on the breakfast-table.

"Any letters for me this morning, George?" Mrs. Lorimer enquired.

"Letters? Really I haven't looked at them. Nothing important, I'm sure."

How important the letter he had slipped in his pocket was he didn't realize till he opened it on his way to the office. It was only the advertised prices of N.B. nails, but the figures so overwhelmed him that when he reached his desk he couldn't think how he had

283

got there. Mr. Pound, the decrepit salesman who had scored so heavily over his employer's travelling-round, was waiting for instructions before starting on another trip.

"Here you are, Mr. Pound," George said, and handed him Bulgin's price-list.

Mr. Pound put on steel-rimmed spectacles. "H'm, that's it, is it?" he said. "Well, what are we going to do about it?"

"Come down to seven and sixpence the same as them," said George Lorimer valiantly.

Mr. Pound folded his spectacles away in a cardboard case. "Can't be done. And you know it can't."

"It's got to be done," said George Lorimer, violently opening and shutting ledger after ledger in sheer agitation.

"I've been with Lorimers' forty odd years, Mr. George, long before you came into the business," Mr. Pound said bitterly. "If I sell at this price it'll mean the end of my job."

"It'll mean the end of your job if you don't," George Lorimer replied with a final slam. "All the stuff in this warehouse is going to be sold at those prices," he added briskly. "After that I don't know . . ."

"Well, I do then," said Mr. Pound.

"You know a damned lot," George answered with unusual acidity.

Mr. Pound caught the nine-five bus to North

Bromwich at the foot of Great Cornbow. At a quarter past nine Dick Pennington was running for all he was worth along Ada Road to board the same vehicle at the Tilton cross-roads. He was going to be late at the office for the first time in his life, but that wasn't what worried him. He had had a perfectly dreadful night with Susan. It was nearly daylight before she had fallen asleep, and then, of course, they had both of them overslept. When they woke she seemed fairly composed, but haggard to a degree.

"You're sure you're not ill?" he asked anxiously.

"Of course I'm not ill. I'm only upset."

"I'd better take your temperature, anyway."

"Don't be silly. I've told you I'm all right."

"Well, you'd better have breakfast in bed, darling."

"All right, Dick. I don't want much, though."

"That's the trouble with you. You're so frightened of getting fat that you starve yourself while I'm away."

So he brought her fried bacon and an egg he had broken in the cooking, and sliced his cheek with a safety-razor that wouldn't shave, and finally, leaving his first cup of tea untouched, kissed her tragically and made a desperate bolt for the bus. "Such a topping spring morning!" he thought. "But it's all lost on me." It was strange how, when one was married, the least thing wrong with the other person put the whole world out of tune. A nervous crisis of the kind he had passed through last night wasn't in keeping with

Susan. He had heard that women were subject to "turns" of this kind. But Susan, he felt convinced, wasn't like other women. There must be something more serious. He wished to goodness now that he had insisted on taking her temperature.

As soon as she heard the latch of the front-door click behind him, Susan got out of bed and examined herself in the glass. Apart from the streak of blood that Dick had left on her cheek and a certain hollowness of eye, the result of her restless night, she looked much as usual. The sight of Dick's cold cup of tea aroused feelings of faint remorse. There was really no need, after all, to have been so dramatic. Finally, feeling a little light-headed for want of sleep, she bathed, dabbed colour on her cheeks and rubbed it off again, put on her best *crêpe-de-chine* underclothes and her second-best frock, and, somewhat tremulously, crossed the road to "Welbeck."

"No, I don't think I will after all," she thought as she reached half-way; but at that moment Miss Maples threw open the front-door to sweep the steps, and Susan's intention was so obvious that she couldn't pretend to change it.

"Good morning, Miss Maples," she said. "Can you spare me a moment?"

"Well, what does *she* want now," Miss Maples thought, "and why bother *me?*" She said: "I won't be a minute, Mrs. Pennington. I'm just sweeping these steps."

"I'll come inside if you don't mind," Susan said. "I . . . I want to consult you."

"Oh, really?" A greedy look came into her eyes. "Step into the drawing-room, please—the one on the right." At that moment Susan became aware of a dull knocking on the wall. "It's only mamma," said Miss Maples confidentially. "She's so curious I'll have to satisfy her." Susan heard her whispering loudly in the opposite room: "Yes . . . Mrs. Pennington . . . I don't know . . . I expect it is." Returning, Miss Maples shut the drawing-room door like a trap.

"Excuse me. I have to humour her. How long did you say?" she began.

"Eight weeks," Susan told her. "The first time I took no notice. You see I thought it couldn't be possible."

"Oh . . ." Miss Maples said disapprovingly.

"Well, it might have been a chill or something, you know. And then . . . Last night . . . It almost looked as if it must be. But it can't be, Miss Maples, unless . . ."

"There are no 'can'ts' about it," Miss Maples thankfully declared. "And you ought to be glad. There's nothing to be frightened of, anyway."

"Oh, it isn't that. It's only . . . Well, I just can't believe it, because . . ."

"I quite understand," Miss Maples broke in. "You'll soon know if it is," she said darkly. "Do you mind just stepping this way? The bedroom is more private."

"Then when do you think . . . ?" Susan said at last.

"I make it November the fifth."

"Guy Fawkes day? How awful! It sounds a terribly long time."

"No, the usual time, Mrs. Pennington," Miss Maples said firmly.

"I suppose I really should let Dr. Martock know?"

"I'll tell him myself if you like. The nurse generally does. And I'll keep myself free for November the fifth," she added gaily. "So convenient to be handy, isn't it? Mamma *will* be pleased!"

When Susan re-entered "Chatsworth" the house seemed to have changed. There was an odd hushed feeling about it, although it had always been quiet. She didn't quite know what she was doing, so, for want of anything better, changed back into her ordinary underclothes. From this slightly dazed condition a more definite emotion emerged. She felt mortification and anger—a bitter tense fury against Dick. It was just like his blundering to go and let her in for this. He wouldn't mind in the least. He had always hinted that he wanted one. Men were like that. He'd probably be quite delighted for her to lose her figure: like an artist who smashes the mould when he's taken a single bronze of his masterpiece. Rotten selfishness!

She might still, of course, do something about it—

there were women in North Bromwich and even shady
doctors who helped girls who were in trouble; Muriel
had told her about them. But the fact that she'd been
such a fool as to let Miss Maples into the secret
queered that pitch. She supposed she would have to
go through with it. It was no good standing there
staring out of the window at nothing, anyway, with the
bed waiting to be made and the rooms to be tidied and
the breakfast things washed up.

She opened the bedroom casement, and there
entered not only a waft of sweet air, but a torrent of
bird-song. In these nesting days the thrushes and
blackbirds sang from dawn to sunset. A sunny shower
swept the field; a rainbow flashed suddenly on its
scintillating tissue and faded. "Hope . . ." she
thought. The whole earth was tremulous that morning with stirrings of increase, with buds swelled to
burgeoning and warm rain searching the roots of the
springing grass, with light airs spilling the pollen of
blackthorn blossom and bees in the arabis bloom of
the garden next door. She saw the lambs skipping
and shaking the drops of rain from their pretty heads,
then racing madly to butt at their mothers' udders and
wagging their tails ecstatically. The ewes didn't seem
to mind. The fecundity of green things and birds and
animals seemed so easy, so gay, so natural. "That's so
much less complicated," she thought. "Still, I'm not a
sheep."

She set about her work mechanically, still nursing

the same resentment, which swelled at times to a white-hot anger, against Dick. The first thing that softened her was the sight of his cold cup of tea, which made her remember his white, anxious face and the cut on his cheek. No doubt he was still wondering if she was really ill. There was no denying that he had been awfully patient with her in spite of his distress. It wasn't fair to put all the blame upon him. "The best regulated families . . ." Proverbs weren't much use after the event.

Still this sudden revulsion of tenderness in Dick's favour relieved her tense feelings. She sat down on the floor and cried softly and much less hysterically than the night before, and when she had finished crying she felt quite different. "I suppose I shall just have to make the best of it."

Her instinct told her to make the best of it dramatically. So, later, when the usual hour of Dick's homecoming drew near, she composed herself in the still, sublime, expectant attitude which she remembered having seen painted in a number of Italian pictures of the Annunciation. The exigencies of the modern short skirt made these poses difficult. She had a feeling, also, that she ought to be holding a lily, and it was hard to invest her pert and so English features with the classical repose of the best renaissance models. But she did her best, and when Dick arrived at six, a hush that was almost religious possessed the little living-room. As a rule she would leave whatever she happened to be doing and run to meet him, and the silence that met him was so unexpected that fear chilled his heart. He entered the room on tiptoe, with anxious eyes.

"Thank heaven!" he said as she put up her face and he kissed her clumsily. "It was so awfully quiet I thought you'd fainted or something. How are you, my darling?"

An imp of humour tempted her to say: "As well as can be expected," but she checked it firmly. "Oh, I'm quite all right now, Dick," she said, with a hushed placidity.

"Only overtired, I expect. Have you just got up?"

"No. I got up as soon as you'd gone this morning. You left your tea."

"Yes, I know. I was horribly rattled. What have you been doing?"

"Nothing much. I went over the road to 'Welbeck' to see Miss Maples." Now it's coming, she thought.

"Miss Maples? You must have been bored! Whatever did you want to see that old cat for?"

"The usual thing. You know what she is."

"But what . . . Susie! You don't mean . . . ?"

"Yes, I do."

"Good God!" It was the first time she had ever heard him say that. He went very white.

"Radiant fatherhood!" Susan thought.

"But, darling, you never . . ." he began.

"Well, I didn't know. I just hoped . . ."

"That explains last night, I suppose. Partly, any-way."

"Yes, I suppose so. I'm quite all right now."

"But, Susie, it's impossible . . ."

She smiled. "That's just what I said. Apparently it isn't. Anyway, there it is. You don't look very pleased, do you, Dick?"

"I'm just dazed," he said. "It's . . . It's a bit of a knock-out, isn't it?"

"For you? I don't see that *you*'ve got much to worry about."

He blushed quickly. "Susie, that's not fair. You know that anything that affects you means a lot to me."

"Yes, I do, darling. I'm sorry."

Both were silent for a moment. Dick sat down heavily opposite to her with his hands clasped tightly.

"There must be some mistake," he said. "I can't believe . . ."

"Oh, don't go on talking like that. Of course there's been a mistake. That's the trouble. But Miss Maples is positive. She knows."

"I suppose she does," he admitted reluctantly. "When is it going to be?"

"November the fifth. You'll be able to let off fire-works. Guy's rather a nice name for a boy."

"Guy?"

She began to laugh. It was the only alternative to crying again at that moment. "I simply have to be flippant," she told him, "when you look so solemn.

Don't tell me you feel this the proudest moment of your life. Oh, let's forget all about it and go and look at the lambs."

He kissed her again. He had often imagined this moment in the terms of the few sentimental novels that he had read, but he could never have guessed that it would work out anything like this. In a flash Susan's heartless mood had changed to a high-pitched vivacity which she over-acted a little, as she always did in moments of excitement. She became at once melting and gay and tender, like the April day. Her swift changes of colour dizzied him. Beneath them all he couldn't forget the impression she had first deliberately imposed on him; the rapt and serenely innocent pose of an *Annunziata*. When he thought back on it there remained with him a vision of hushed and holy expectancy more real than the levity of her present mood. The memory compelled him to reverence. He hardly dared touch her for fear of smirching or breaking the fragile vehicle of this miraculous conception.

And though she had joked about the cant phrase he *was* proud—overwhelmingly, unreasonably proud. After the first shock of surprise and incredulousness that swelling emotion had mastered all others. Up till that moment he had been nothing but a boy, he told himself. Now he was a father . . . Very nearly a father, anyway . . . and the sudden augmentation of dignity and responsibility so filled him with triumph that his first impulse was to let the world know that he, the previously undistinguished Dick Pennington, of "Chatsworth," Tilton, Worcestershire, had achieved this thing——not exactly single-handed or intentionally ——but with unique success. The fact that the population of the North Bromwich district was approximately a million did not cheapen the achievement. He wanted to tell all his friends, particularly those at the office, in a casual way. He imagined himself, for example, refusing an invitation to a bachelor meal: "No, sorry, old chap, I can't manage it. Got to settle down now. You see my missus . . ." "You don't say so? Congratulations! Lucky devil! Wish *I* could afford it!"

When later in the evening, however, he urged this desire on Susan he found her point of view entirely different.

"I suppose we ought to let Uncle George know about this," he said.

"Uncle George? Why on earth Uncle George? It's no business of his."

"I expect he'd be bucked about it."

"He'll guess quite soon enough. So will everyone. You don't know what a sight I shall look. I'd much rather keep it private as long as I can. Besides, something might happen."

"I hope to goodness it won't!"

"So you really are pleased, Dick?" she teased him.

"Of course I'm pleased."

"You've been terribly clever, haven't you? I wish you'd been a bit cleverer!"

Did she really wish he'd been a bit cleverer? Even then she wasn't quite sure. When the first phase of futile, rebellious anger had passed she began to find some consolation in the fact that her condition was "interesting" and dramatized it accordingly. Apart from her first nervous crisis she felt none the worse for it, on the whole; indeed, rather better; but that didn't prevent her from seeing herself as a romantic heroine; and though the gaze of an awed and admiring public was not yet fixed on her figure, she contrived, in private at least, to keep well within focus of a spot-light. The exclusively feminine mystery of the whole affair compelled Dick's reverence, and it pleased her to encourage this attitude by immediately becoming—not exactly an invalid, but a delicate creature whose condition (entirely due to Dick) demanded unceasing consideration and gentleness, whose least caprices must be humoured, whose most extravagant desires must be gratified without question. This situation, the result of "living dangerously," gave opportunities for self-expression (at Dick's expense) which she had never enjoyed before. Dick suffered them willingly, and Susan, who had originally adopted this variant on the Annunciation-pose as a dramatic experiment, became so engrossed that she ended by believing in it herself and losing the sense of humour which was her most valuable private possession.

While Dick did all that part of the housework which was disagreeable to her, Susan "rested" on the living-

u

room sofa and looked pathetic. When once the first shock of surprise and revolt was over she had become not only resigned to maternity but interested in it, as she had been interested before in her college curriculum and in domestic science. The idea of evading her fate had been long since abandoned. After all, she supposed they would someday have to have children—or at least one child—and it was better to get those things over early in life. That point was insisted on in all the pseudo-scientific books which she had made Dick obtain from the City Library in North Bromwich and studied attentively. Most of these volumes approached the subject from a mystical, sentimental, romantic angle, which accorded with her own inclination. There was one book which dwelt in particular on the importance of pre-natal influences in the development of the super-baby. It was not only essential that this creature's expectant mother should cultivate physical placidity, but also that her eyes should be surrounded by natural beauty and her intelligence nurtured on the sublimest manifestations of Art. Susan took these instructions seriously; and the nascent soul of superbaby was subjected to a course of carbon-dioxide and Burne-Jones in the North Bromwich Art Gallery, to the Eighteen Twelve Overture, and Liszt's Second Hungarian Rhapsody as rendered, through crashing atmospherics, by the massed Guards' Bands, and to the literary influences of Wordsworth (highly recommended but wearisome) and Mr. Galsworthy.

Dick was also enjoined to read poetry aloud when he came home at night. He read poetry without understanding, but also without affectation: in a word, rather well—but it always sent Susan to sleep.

As for Nature—there was always, of course, the Room with the View. Susan lay on her bed for hours and gazed at it lazily, acquiring placidity. The hedges quickened; the beech lost its vernal traceries and hung heavy with leaf; oaks, lately wrapped in a mist of gold, darkened in a night; the lambs grew stubby and awkward and shed their graces; they no longer clung to their mothers, but packed, like grouse in September, and butted each other savagely or scampered about in droves. An orange-tip butterfly fluttered limply against the window-panes; when it settled the light shone through its marbled green underwings. It was June—but November still seemed a long way off.

II

According to one of the books this time should have been the happiest in Susan's life. It wasn't. The mornings were awful—so alarming to Dick that he ran over the road and called in Miss Maples. Nothing out of the ordinary, Miss Maples declared. There was something sadistic in her satisfaction that made Susan hate her. "I ought to have gone to a woman who had had children herself," she told Dick. "I believe she enjoys it." Dick called in Dr. Martock, who met George Lorimer on the road and gave him a lift in his car to "Chatsworth," so the secret was out.

George Lorimer showed himself a little hurt that they hadn't told him before. His feelings were on the surface just then. He always felt aimless and out of a job during the close season for coarse-fish, and in spite of his reckless gesture in price-cutting, sales continued to fall. Even at the price which he quoted on the ruinous level set by Mr. Bulgin, nobody wanted his nails. The whole world of buyers appeared to be hypnotized by the New British Nail Company's "slogans." "N.B. Nails are the the Best Nails," Mr. Bulgin shouted so persistently that they all believed him. George Lorimer, though he had no faith in advertisement, tried his hand at it: *The Old Firm: the New Prices*, he announced, with a modest footnote to the effect that Lorimers had been making nails for more than a century; but buyers in the nail-trade were already aware of that, and the farmers who read agricultural papers asked for N.B. So this infinitesimal deadly struggle went on, as little noticed beneath the surge and clash of the world's industrial war as that of insects in a ditch on the Somme under the barrage of the July offensive. George Lorimer, now fighting not only for his beloved Dingle but for sheer commercial existence, could not give his enthusiasm to the prospect of a new life at "Chatsworth" as wholeheartedly as he might have done; but he did think they might have told him about it all the same. In his present despair he could see nothing hopeful in anything, and Susan's baby was no more than another hostage to fate.

By this time the secret was an open secret to anyone who was not blind. Dick told Captain Small, who received the confidence with tears and a silent, manly hand-clasp. They both told Mr. Bulgin what he had already suspected. His reception of the great news was brusque; it appeared to embarrass him; the prospect of becoming a grandfather to Dick's child allured him much less than being a father to Susan; her solemn and sweet Annunciation pose fell exceedingly flat with him; his visits to "his little girl" and his presents became much less frequent.

So June passed, and the time of Dick's annual holiday came round again. He found it hard to persuade himself that only a little more than a year had elapsed since the day when he first collided with Susan on the boarding-house landing at Brinton. A year ago he had been nothing but an irresponsible schoolboy; and here he was now, a staid married man, with a wife, a Baronial dining-room and (very nearly) a family! He would have been glad, for financial reasons, to forgo his holiday this year. His employers, on the other hand, seemed unusually anxious for him to take it, and even suggested three weeks instead of the usual fortnight—the third, of course, without pay.

In the winter evenings Susan and he had made plans

to revisit Brinton. It would be such fun, they decided, to stay together as a legally-married couple in a house which had seen the beginning of their romance as furtive lovers. The new situation naturally altered all that. For himself—and again from the point of view of expense—Dick would have been perfectly content to spend his three weeks at "Chatsworth"; but Susan was restless; she needed a change more than he did, and to remain at "Chatsworth" would be no holiday for her. They had hoped, in the spring, to fit a new side-car to the motor-bicycle; but that, too, with the expense of Miss Maples and the doctor impending, was out of the question now. The machine had not even been licensed.

"If we can't go to Brinton," Susan told him, "I should like to stay at a farmhouse and have plenty of milk. The books say that's most important. And really there's no cream at all on Mr. Duke's milk; you can almost see through the bottle . . . Somewhere quite near," she said, "that we could get to easily by train without being too tired or spending too much on the fare."

It was at this point that Dick recalled the existence of his aunt in Shropshire. Though he hadn't seen her or heard of her since he was a boy and didn't even know if she were still alive, he vaguely believed that she lived in a village named Lesswardine, near Ludlow. He wrote to her there, on chance, asking if she knew of a farm where he and his wife could stay

cheaply. Three days later he received a reply. Judith
Pennington had left Lesswardine some years before
and was now established in a house called the "Old
Parsonage" at Chapel Green, on the Radnorshire
border. *My cottage is quite tiny,* she wrote, *but I have
a spare room with a four-poster bed that belonged to
your great-great-grandmother, and if your wife is not
too grand I should like you both to stay with me, at any
rate until you have found suitable farmhouse lodgings, which should not be difficult. I believe you are
actually the only living relative who bears my name.
The war took a heavy toll of us. You must come by
train to Llandwlas on the Teme Valley Line, and Mr.
Evans will meet you with the pony-trap.*

Susan opened Aunt Judith's letter on its arrival,
before Dick returned from North Bromwich. It was
written on cheap blue pad-paper, of the kind that one
buys at a village shop, in a thin, slanting, pointed
script that seemed somehow to belong to an older and
more formal world. At the bottom of the first page
Aunt Judith had written the first word of the next: a
custom that had gone out of fashion at least half a
century ago. The whole tone of the letter, though
warm, was restrained, and suggested that, if they *did*
go to Chapel Green, they would have to be on their
best behaviour. She didn't mind that, provided that
she had a little time in which to transpose her clothes,
her manners and her conversation to this new key;
indeed, a fortnight in Cranford might even be a rest-

ful change. While she waited for Dick's return she
tried to imagine just what Aunt Judith and her tiny
house would be like and to evolve a new dramatization
of herself appropriate to the scene. Her speech and
bearing and clothes, she decided, would have to be
equally quiet. The day would probably begin and end
with the reading of prayers. She would have to remember not to sit down at meal-times until grace had
been said, and not to say "damn" or "God"—especially together. If she took any books with her she must
certainly choose them with care. On the whole it
might be safer to cut out books altogether and concentrate on knitting or crochet-work or sewing the baby's
layette. One would have to be careful, also, not to
eat too much—which might be a nuisance; her appetite
now was so voracious as to demand apologies—for, in
view of the notepaper, it seemed almost certain that
Aunt Judith was poor, though obviously, since she
lived in a house of her own, she must have independent
means: a point to be remembered, if only because
Dick was her only relation and presumably her heir.
When Dick came home that evening he found that she
had been looking out all her longest skirts and
roughest shoes and least exiguous hosiery: a stage-
wardrobe, in short, to fit Mr. Evans's pony-trap. Her
ordinary holiday attire was much better adapted for
pillion-riding.

"I'm awfully glad you've taken to the idea," Dick
told her enthusiastically.

"You can't look a gift-pony in the mouth, darling, can you?" she said.

"But apart from all that you'll enjoy it," he replied, without smiling. "And the change will be good for you. I'm afraid it'll be a big fare."

"If we're really as poor as that," she said, "we might go on the motor-bike."

"I'm taking no risks of that kind," he told her firmly.

"Well, if you don't like it, I can always feel seedy. Her letter's a little stiff, don't you think so, darling?"

"No. I think it's a topping letter. You imagine so many things."

His whole face brightened at the idea of visiting Chapel Green, not only because it would take them into the country he had known and loved as a boy and spare his small bank-balance, but because he was so proud to exhibit Susan to one of his own "people" and flaunt his paternity before her admiring eyes.

Captain Small's face fell, on the contrary, when they told him of their plans. His bi-weekly visits to "Chatsworth"—he rationed himself to that number for fear of out-wearing his welcome—were marked with red letters in his greyly monochrome calendar. From the moment he opened his eyes in the morning those days were coloured with eager anticipation. He would sing the old tunes of the war with their scandalous words while he shaved or stumped round the garden. Long before the time for limping up to Tilton arrived he would be waiting, as smart as be damned, to go on parade. The prospect of three weeks without sight of Susan made his heart fall with dread as well as his face; their unbroken blankness invited the assaults and ghostly invasions which had made such havoc of his loneliness. Three whole weeks! God knew what might happen! Yet, while he feared the outcome, his generous spirit could only rejoice in his friends' excitement.

"Near Lesswardine?" he repeated. "No . . . never been there. Never been anywhere much outside Flanders. All I know of Blighty is this little spot and one or two camps and hospitals. But I seem to remember that name all the same . . . Yes, I've got it! A feller named Redlake was in dry dock with me at Thorpe Castle—no end of a posh sort of place, full of lords and ladies and whatnots—in nineteen-eighteen —and this feller Redlake came into a property near there. A bit of a high-stepper himself was old Redlake, not really my sort; and I'll bet he wouldn't remember yours truly in any case. You'll drop me a picture postcard, won't you? Just to show me everything's all right," he asked Susan pathetically. "And look after yourself, mind!" he added with real anxiety.

When they told George Lorimer he didn't even affect enthusiasm. In three weeks, at the present break-neck speed of decadence, almost anything might happen. He was only thankful that Susan hadn't asked him for money to finance their holiday, and so delighted that he immediately, impulsively, gave her a parting present of two pounds, which he had received that morning as the final dividend of a bankrupt customer who owed him fifty. That gift meant far more than its face value to poor George Lorimer. Mr. Bulgin, to whom such a sum was negligible, gave her nothing at all. His last visit to "Chatsworth" before Susan's departure coincided with one from Miss Maples, who was enchanted to meet him and reminded him of her mama's acquaintance with the Landseer poodle. She also alluded in a knowing and playful way to Susan's condition and the part she was destined to play in it; which made Mr. Bulgin shy, because even if he had been married, his instincts were still those of a bachelor, and that most disquieting side of matrimony had never, thank heaven, come his way. Miss Maples' presence made it unsuitable for him to kiss Susan good-bye, even in a fatherly way; and, oddly enough, he wasn't sorry it did; for though Susan did not appear physically altered by her present experience, Mr. Bulgin had never quite relished her in the rôle of an Annunziata and looked forward to the day when this natural, but unsavoury business should be forgotten. He was, in these matters, a creature of sensibility.

III

On the morning of the day on which they set out
for Shropshire Susan received a slight shock. It was
a letter from the Bromwich Furnishing Emporium, in
an envelope as plain as their vans, requesting her attention, in terms even plainer, to the matter of last month's
instalment, now three weeks overdue. This request,
though reasonable, filled her with indignation. In
these days she had so many important things to think
about that she had, naturally enough, overlooked their
first application, which had arrived, as by clockwork,
on the day when the payment was due, and the polite
reminder which followed it a week later. The tone of
the third request was peremptory. She couldn't believe that a gentlemanly person like Mr. Bellis could
have sanctioned it, and wasn't quite sure if she had
enough money in the bank at the moment to meet it.
If she had had a moment to spare she would certainly
have written to Mr. Bellis personally and pointed out
how rude his underlings had been. It might teach
them a lesson in manners, she decided, to leave the
matter where it was till they returned from their holidays. So she slipped the demand, along with the
others, into Captain Small's shell-case, which she had
found a convenient hiding-place for things that Dick
needn't be bothered with.

As it was, she had barely finished her packing when Dick hustled her off to the station in a hurry that made her irritable and ready to blame him for such evidences of bad management as a change at Mawne Road and others at Stourford and Kidderminster, and the fact that he had thoughtlessly forced her into a third-class smoker that reeked of stale tobacco, which he, of course, didn't notice.

Dick was in such high spirits that afternoon that not even her querulousness could touch him. So she subsided, not exactly sulky, but very dignified, into the corner diagonally opposite to him, by an open window which she longed to have closed but couldn't, because the compartment smelt so. She sat gazing, wistfully, at a series of photographs of Brinton-le-Sands on the carriage partition, regretting their funds had not allowed them to go there instead of to Lesswardine; and the thought of money renewed her indignation against Mr. Bellis's minions so acutely that she would have embroidered it for Dick's benefit if she hadn't known how punctilious he was about matters of that kind, and that the mere mention of it would certainly have precipitated a scene.

Indeed, as they crossed Severn above Bewdley, Dick underwent an odd metamorphosis. It was as though the passage of that boundary washed away from his mind all the heavy preoccupations of the last four months.

"After all, he's nothing but a schoolboy," she

mused, and remembered how, long ago at Brinton, he had glowed and been beautifully transfigured when he spoke of Shropshire. "It's all very well," she thought, "for him to become rejuvenated like that, and me sitting here just feeling as old as hell, with four dreary months of waiting in front of me! *The man scores always, every time*," she reflected, bitterly.

Again his naïve enthusiasm made her jealous by emphasizing another of the radical differences between them. The reason why he expanded and bloomed in this new land west of Severn was that his spiritual roots reached far and deep into ancestral soil. She knew that this country possessed him more completely than she had ever done; he was rapt in an alien passion that she could not share. Her spiritual roots, if they existed, had no such attachment. That was why she instinctively gravitated toward a suburban life among people as little devoted to any particular soil as herself. That was why, if she could realize an unspoken ambition, she would have liked to live in London and go to the Savoy, where Harry Levison had taken Muriel to see the New Year in. She hated and distrusted these mystical ties that pulled Dick away and made him happy apart from her.

Out of this atmosphere of self-imposed loneliness and distrust a new misgiving arose, a dread of the old lady at Lesswardine, with whom they were going to stay. That she would be "stuffy" and old-fashioned Susan had already taken for granted; her early experience with Edna Lorimer armed her against that. The exclusive solidarity of race and tradition which Aunt Judith would share with Dick would be far more difficult to deal with. She could see them engaged in eager conversations about things and people and places that meant nothing to her, in which she—who really had a right to the front of the stage—would only be included out of polite condescension. Every word that they spoke would be certain to "show her up" as—— well, what she was, a mere feather-brained suburban, without any of those solid qualities that made country-bred people so enviable and yet so dull. Once again she yearned for the easy, uncritical holiday-life of Brinton, where nobody knew or cared who you were or what you were like, and shoals of new people came and went every week. It was quite possible that Dick's aunt and she might dislike each other at sight. What fun that would be for everybody! Three long weeks of it! It would be easier to compose herself if Dick would only keep still.

But he couldn't. This Shropshire air had gone to his head. He was gay and flushed and excited, and talked continually. "That's the Forest of Wyre, Susie. It's big enough to get lost in. Do you see that blue smoke? I bet it's a charcoal-burner's. Neen Sollars! Don't you think these villages have topping names? Cleobury Mortimer's over there. There's a river runs through it that flows into the Teme. Whopping trout, but terribly bushed. I say, if we get to

Ludlow on time we may hear the carillon! We used to drive into Ludlow on market-days when I was a kid. There's a poem about Ludlow fair; I forget who wrote it. By Jove! Only smell the air! It blows right off Clee. Darling, what's the matter with you? I hope to goodness you're not ill."

"Of course I'm not ill." She smiled weakly. "Just a little bit tired. You see, all these names about which you get so excited mean nothing to me. Do you think we could manage a cup of tea somewhere? I'm simply dying for it."

"Oh, I'm sure we can get one when we change trains at Craven Arms."

"Another change? Really, Dick, what a ghastly journey! If we'd gone to Brinton we could have got a through-carriage, you know."

He stared at her. "Brinton? Good heavens, you're not comparing . . ."

"All I want is a quiet life," she said with a sigh.

"Well, you'll get that at Aunt Judith's all right," he told her cheerfully.

But they didn't get that cup of tea for which she was dying at Craven Arms, though Dick rushed up and down the platform and nearly missed the local train in his efforts to procure it.

As Susan approached Llandwlas her fatigue and dread of meeting Aunt Judith increased, while Dick, every moment, grew more and more excited. They were the only passengers to alight from the train. The station was no more than a grass-grown siding, a wind-swept platform, and a small, box-like building orna-mented with posters of Brinton, faded by sun and rain. When the train had puffed away round a curve in the line the place relapsed into the cold dream from which its arrival had roused it. It was wrapped, Susan thought, in such an intolerable silence that they seemed to have come to the very end of the world. Mr. Evans' pony-cart was waiting for them outside, as Miss Pennington had arranged. It was a tub-like jingle, as shabbily unkempt as the pony and Mr. Evans himself, and had obviously been kept in a fowl-house. Susan examined the seat with disgust; but Dick, apparently, failed to notice anything. He patted the pony's neck and chattered to Mr. Evans, who answered him in a sing-song, unintelligible dialect, then light-heartedly planked down the luggage on Susan's toes. But by this time she was so far reconciled to martyrdom that she didn't even complain.

"Have we got to go very far, Mr. Evans?" she asked angelically.

"The best part of five miles; 'tis an ugly road, and they'm Welsh miles hereabouts," Mr. Evans replied.

As they left the valley through which the railroad ran the country grew wilder. The surface of the road was stony-grey and worn with torrents. Hidden streams gurgled everywhere and small cups of hare-bells shimmered under the sky like pools of storm-water. There were no birds but frightened magpies

w

(Four for a boy! Susan thought) and redstarts that fluttered uneasily out of the lichened walls; and the air, in spite of the fragrance of briar and honeysuckle, had a cold mountain flavour. It seemed to droop downward to meet them from those bleak grey ridges of moorland that filled the sky whenever the pony-cart topped a rise.

For mile after mile they jogged on through empty lanes. Then, suddenly, they came on a group of bronzed workmen in corduroys, attacking with picks and crow-bars a boulder that blocked the road.

"It's them waterworks men," Mr. Evans explained. "They'm blasting a double track for the North Bromwich pipe-line. You have to keep your eyes skinned on this road when they fire their charges. By the look of it they'm finished for to-night."

A man with a red flag waved them on, and Mr. Evans touched up his pony. Dick gave the workman "good evening." Susan shivered and held her peace. She was cramped and stiff by the time that, steeply descending between high walls of hazel, they gazed down on to a level clearing—an emerald strip of common land edged by low buildings of white-washed stone and flecked, here and there, with the dazzling whiteness of geese.

"There you be, missus!" Mr. Evans proclaimed with enthusiasm. "There's Chapel Green for you, and there's the 'Parsonage' as us call it, and that'll be Miss Pennington looking out at the garden gate! I reckoned she'd keep her eyes skinned."

Miss Pennington did not resemble in the least any one of the many pictures of her which Susan had imagined during the last three weeks. Susan had never, oddly enough, conceived her as being like Dick. Yet here, if such things were possible, stood Dick's female counterpart. She was considerably older, of course—Judith Pennington must have been well over fifty—but her figure possessed the same tall, loose-limbed quality; her hair, though darker than his and by no means as unruly, showed no trace of grey; her eyes were as blue, or bluer, wide-set and candid; and her features, though undistinguished as Dick's in form, had another kind of distinction, the result of a simple, full, yet capable mode of living, and the serenity which only shows itself in a human face when its owner has reached the period when life as it is has been cheerfully accepted for better or for worse.

From the moment of their arrival Aunt Judith gave Susan an impression of happy, unhurried efficiency. Though she could never have had any more preten-sions to physical beauty than Dick, the lack of the quality appeared, in her case, unimportant. She was an aristocrat in her own highly specialized kind: a fine product of village life in the English countryside, at once cold and kindly, narrow and charitable, un-cultured and understanding, inelegant and refined, uncouth and completely unconscious of her own awk-wardness. Her experience of life or her breeding (or both of them) had given this plain, ill-dressed woman a kind of poise to which Susan, for all her prettiness and superficial sophistication, could never pretend to attain.

Though Aunt Judith, as she called her from the first, accepted her without question because she was Dick's wife, Susan couldn't help feeling subdued and rebelliously impressed by the implicit difference between them. There was nothing that emphasized this difference more than Dick's aunt's unemphatic speech. It had none of the fashionable inflexions which Susan had carefully imitated, at second-hand, from Muriel; there was even a hint of a West Midland burr in its "r"s and its liquid "l"s; yet the undecorated language Miss Pennington spoke was all of a piece like hand-woven homespun, and the quality of her voice itself had a low, level sweetness, unexcited always, yet capable of genuine emotion.

And her house was like the woman herself; cool, sweet-smelling and unpretentious—a house that in its unrestricted confusion of "styles" would have pained Mr. Bellis, yet so distinct in a style of its own as to make Susan's carefully-planned suites and colour schemes at "Chatsworth" look crude and shoddy. No one piece of furniture in it matched any other, though each might have been collected from a mid-Victorian parsonage, and none, of itself, was graceful or beautiful; yet so rich was the patina of use beneath which they were blended that their particular incongruities became merged in a congruous whole in which the most tactful addition would have struck a false note—unless, indeed, the accumulated influence of ages had reduced it to silence. The very clocks ticked on contentedly, as though they were aware and confident of their part in a well-tempered mechanism, or broke out into tinkling chimes that were like happy laughter.

It was this sense of continuity in Miss Pennington's house—although she herself had lived in it for less than four years—which made "Chatsworth" (even its Baronial features) seem like a hasty, ill-advised improvisation. Even if Miss Pennington was a newcomer, one felt that it must have been inhabited by people of her kind for numberless years and always have smelt just the same. The two badly-painted family portraits of black-frocked parsons with white neckerchiefs; the miniatures of low-necked ladies in oval frames; the trophies of wild life—moth-eaten fox-masks and otter-pads, the white owl with a mouse in its claws, the faded three-pound trout in its glazed aquarium; the hunting-crops and notched otter-staves and spliced greenheart fly-rods, the old racquets and croquet-mallets hanging in the hall—all these, no less than the needlework chair-backs and bead-work footstools and calf-bound volumes of sermons, proclaimed the uniform, obscurely contented life which Dick's ancestors, male and female, had been living for the last hundred years. If slow Pennington feet supporting the weight of big-boned Pennington bodies had not trodden smooth grooves in the slabs of the passage that cut clean through the house, giving vistas of the goose-green in front and black-barked damson-trees behind, those grooves had surely been worn by men and women of a similar race and of the same natural habits.

Dick's Aunt Judith was a countrywoman from her unfashionably-knotted hair to her thick-soled shoes. Those shoes were made for rough going, and she could out-walk most men of her age. It was nothing for her to wade waist-deep in the tail of a pool out otter-hunting. She played tennis, of the old-fashioned vicarage type, knowing nothing of the modern professional niceties of the game. She knew not only the appearance, but the call of every variety of bird in the district, and could cast a fly as well as Dick, if not better. And yet, to these hardier accomplishments, this bright-eyed, middle-aged woman, with her weather-beaten complexion and firm, clean, unmanicured hands, added many others specifically feminine. She was full of the traditional lore of household remedies, and though Dr. Hendrie, the local practitioner, often chaffed her, he knew Miss Pennington for his staunchest ally in any case of illness at Chapel Green. She ran the County Library and the Village Women's Institute and worked as hard among its members as a district nurse. Yet, in this full life, which every moment accused and convicted Susan of irresponsible idleness, there was always room for her consuming passion for flowers. The garden of the "Old Parsonage" was a symbol of love and piety. It seemed miraculous that so small a patch of earth could hold so many and such cherished inhabitants. It was her triumph to grow, by sheer instinct and garden-sense, shy plants that no others could persuade to flourish in that keen hill-air, for she had what gardeners call a "planting hand," and those square-nailed bony fingers of hers (so very like Dick's) became, when they handled a living plant, tactile organs of tender sensitiveness. It was almost as if the flowers with which she surrounded herself had some odd, green sense of the love she gave them and gave in return the best of their beauty and sweetness. Wherever one went in that house, in addition to its characteristic odour of age and cleanliness, one was conscious of the perfume of flowers living or embalmed in death; of lavendered presses and bowls of russet-leaved *pot-pourri;* of fresh roses, old-fashioned and scented, picked from the dew-wet borders; of climbing sweet-peas and jasmine and twining honeysuckle that clung to its walls and peered through its windows as though they knew they would find congenial company within.

So Susan felt as they entered the little spare bed-room, nearly filled by the four-poster bed, and a rich waft of honeysuckle moved through the window to meet her. The bed was of massive, turned mahogany (Dick was sure he had slept in it before) and the coarse linen sheets were as old as Aunt Judith herself. As

Susan lay on the patchwork coverlet, while Dick sniffed round the room like a terrier in search of familiar smells, she came to the conclusion that the part which she had imagined for herself to fit the Shropshire scene would have to be reconsidered; that no pose, indeed, would survive the quick scrutiny of Miss Pennington's innocent eyes.

"My clothes are all wrong," she told Dick regretfully.

"All wrong? What d'you mean? I thought you'd fitted yourself out with lots of things for the country."

"So I have. But I shan't dare to wear them. They wouldn't look right—to Aunt Judith, I mean."

"I'm sure she's never worried her head about clothes."

"I know. That's the point. And she'd see that I have. Well, it can't be helped. It's no good pretending. She'll just have to take me as I am, for your sake, Dick darling."

And that, precisely, was what Miss Pennington did. Those blue eyes, so like Dick's, but so much wiser, had penetrated at a glance even deeper than Susan imagined. "Very pretty," she had thought, "very vain, and quite inexperienced; an average product of Midland suburban life, so anxious to be ladylike that you can see she isn't a lady; but she's strong and possibly courageous, and, if they're happy, well, nothing else matters much. She'll feel awfully out of water here, so I must make things easy for her and not be critical. Dick thinks she's an angel from heaven, and it's right he should think so. I only hope to goodness she won't be bored. If she is, I can't help it."

There was something else that predisposed Judith Pennington in Susan's favour. In accepting the invitation to Chapel Green Dick had made no mention of his wife's condition. "She'll see that soon enough for herself," Susan had told him. Miss Pennington had seen it as soon as Susan got out of the pony-trap, and the sight had filled her with sudden warmth and pleasure. She was naturally blessed with a strong sense of family tradition—her whole house, indeed, was a shrine devoted to this kind of piety—and though the name that she bore had never been associated with any unusual distinction, it meant more to her than ever it had meant to Dick. The war had dealt roughly with the family; no living male Pennington, with the exception of Dick, had survived it. Though by nature robust and entirely free from morbidity, she had carefully bequeathed her small competence and the trivial family relics to this Pennington nephew, whom she had not even seen since his boyhood and with whom, till the unexpected letter arrived from "Chatsworth," she had entirely lost touch. When she saw Dick, on that first evening, she had flushed with pleasure. He was Pennington to his finger-tips, the image of her brother Jasper, who had been killed at St. Quentin. And now Susan . . . She was thankful that Susan and Dick weren't selfish modern young people who

refused to have children until it was too late. She
hoped—how she hoped!—that the baby would be a
boy. He should be named after his great-uncle Jasper
—there had always been a Jasper in the family, and
her cottage, soaked as it was in the Pennington tradition, should be a second home to him. If only for that
reason it was important that Susan should feel at her
ease.

She did feel at her ease, surprisingly, considering
how foreign to all her experience this life at Chapel
Green was. Aunt Judith was too natural to be formidable, and Susan, with her instinct for protective
mimicry, became natural too. Instead of trying to
adapt herself to this new sort of life she passively
surrendered herself to its powers of penetration. The
slow peace that saturated that minute and orderly
house, the sublimity of the green arc of moorland by
which it was girdled, the placid preoccupations of
Aunt Judith's own life, so crowded in spite of its
narrow compass, imposed themselves on her restlessness like a calm hand coolly laid on a burning forehead. Though this was a new kind of happiness, she
felt strangely happy—very largely because she made
no attempt to pursue it.

As for Dick—from the moment he entered the
house he had been supremely contented. Between him
and his aunt there was no need for explanations. Each
spoke an identical language, saw with the same eyes;
a whole body of experience—not only that of his child-

hood, but the inherited store that they had in common —made each accept and understand the other without reservations. Dick opened his heart to her on the subject of Susan and his hopes. She was the only person with whom he had felt able to discuss them, and her wisdom and cool commonsense swept every anxiety from his mind, for, spinster though she was, she had much experience of those matters and mothered, vicariously, every child in the village. Thus relieved and knowing that Susan was safe and happy in Aunt Judith's company, he re-lived the enchanted moments of boyhood, embarking, each day, on the recapture of past joys.

He would slip out of bed when Susan was still asleep under the patchwork counterpane and steal through the dewy meadows flushed with sorrel to stalk a rabbit before breakfast. On three days he rode away on Aunt Judith's bicycle with his grandfather's greenheart fly-rod tied to the frame, returning at dusk with baskets of pale-golden trout from the Teme, finger-marked like samlets and vividly spotted with coral. Men were laying the hay in the field behind the orchard (for a cold spring had backened the crop) and daylight came in with the sweet, singing sigh of the scythes. When the grass bleached in silvery swathes Dick gave them a hand with the cocking, for the sky threatened rain. There was a seat at the foot of the garden, from which Susan could see him as she sat at her sewing; and when he came back, with a

haymaker's appetite, for tea, his muscular forearms
were burnt to a deep brick-red and his palms were
blistered, but he only laughed when she wanted to put
cold cream on them. "I've no business to have such
soft hands," he said, "and it serves me right." That
night he slept heavily, drugged with labour, and,
most regrettably, snored; but next morning they were
all up for breakfast an hour earlier than usual, for the
otter-hounds were meeting at the Barbel Bridge.

Susan begged Aunt Judith to follow—she had sewing enough to keep her busy—but Miss Pennington
herself had business to do that day; on Saturdays she
always arranged the flowers in the altar-vases. They
walked down to the bridge at the moment when the
hound-van arrived. Hounds shook their ears and
rolled and scratched on the grass at the edge of the
road or sat upright, staring in front of them with
solemn eyes. The huntsman remembered Dick. They
shook hands, and he pointed out the progeny of
hounds whose names Dick remembered. Then the
master rolled up in an enormous old-fashioned tour-
ing car. He wore a cap and a coat of hunting pink, and
the back of his neck, between them, was of the same
fiery hue.

Susan noticed with pride how well Dick fitted into
the picture. He was hard and brawny, much bigger
than he ever looked in his dark city clothes. He moved
with long, easy strides among the thick-set men and
long-toothed women of the hunt. Susan supposed

they were "county" people, and immediately conceived a desire to wear a dark blue suit with red
facings and blue worsted stockings and brogued shoes,
and to drop her "g"s at the end of each present par-
ticiple. That would be even more distinguished, she
thought, than dancing at the "Savoy" with Harry
Levison: what was more, she could carry it off much
better than Muriel O'Brien with Dick at her side. "If
we only had enough money to live in the country!"
she thought.

The master cast off at the bridge. Susan stood on
the crown of it and watched them at work, crackling
through the alders and feathering over the greener
grass of a drain. A startled kingfisher streaked up-
stream like a blue electric flame. One great white
hound took the water and swam through the tail of
a pool to the farther side. He sniffed at an alder
stump, then threw back his head and spoke in a voice
that rang like a bell. "That's Spooner," Miss Pennington said. "He's an old hound; he knows." "Hi-
over, hi-over, hi-over!" the master was crying. "Wind
'im out . . . wind 'im out!" In an instant the draw
of the pool was churned to thunderous spray. Fifteen
couple, streaming as one with lifted heads above
water, took the scent as it moved down-stream and
crashed on a red-hot drag. They were running like
wild-fire now, and the hanging woods of the opposite
bank threw back an echo of music as though, in their
depths, another and a phantom pack were speaking.

The master was up to his middle crossing the stickle, with Dick behind him. On either bank the thick-set men and the long-toothed women were running for all they knew. Though she saw that the pace was too hot for her and though, thanks to Mr. Feilden, she disapproved of all blood-sports, some primitive instinct urged Susan to run, without thought, in the wake of that savage soul-maddening sound.

"Can't we follow a bit?" she begged; but Miss Pennington laughed and shook her head.

"You'd never catch up," she said, "and the going's too rough for you. Next year, perhaps . . ."

As they walked away from the bridge in silence they heard from a distance the quavering wail of a horn. Remote, sweet, melancholy, that thin note seemed to express a quintessence of summer life in those watery valleys to which Dick belonged.

He came back with a rousing appetite and soaked to the hips. After supper they sat and talked drowsily in the odour of old mahogany and jasmine and *potpourri*. Miss Pennington's lamp, which she trimmed every morning, gave too feeble a light for Susan to sew with comfort; so she sat in the great arm-chair that had belonged to Dick's grandmother and listened, with her work on her lap, to the quiet drone of his voice and Aunt Judith's (which resembled each other so oddly) as they spoke of old days and ways and the current gossip that apparently made existence at Chapel Green so various: how young George Malpas, the one who lived at "Wolfpits" and did time for manslaughter, had taken on the license of the "Buffalo" Inn after his mother's death and was scandalously encouraging the waterworks men to drink; how his wife had died and his daughter Gladys—such a lovely girl!—kept house for him, while Morgan, the boy, couldn't stand it and had gone to the mines in South Wales; how Jim Redlake, the rich young man who had come into "Trewern," had made sheep-farming pay, and what a nice woman his wife was—of course she was a clergyman's daughter and understood village people; how the new Lord Clun had been forced to sell his timber for death-duties, though the denuded coppices were, perhaps, more beautiful than ever with their sheeted bluebells and foxgloves and rosy willow-herb. Sometimes Aunt Judith would go to a cupboard and bring out dingy Pennington photographs of sporting parsons and mustachioed sub-alterns in obscure line-infantry regiments and old ladies with corkscrew curls and gay young ones with flounced skirts and bustles. Dick and she would pore eagerly for half an hour at a time over these yellowish images, and though Susan couldn't attempt to share their excitement, she began to feel herself part, through Dick, of this faded life. Her baby, when he was born, would have even more claim on it. They had decided to call him Jasper, as Aunt Judith suggested.

The one blot on this even, idyllic life was the

furious speed with which the brief weeks of holiday passed by. Night fell so softly, dawn came on such silent feet. One green morning of mizzling rain they woke to realize that the very next evening Dick should be back at Tilton.

"I can't bear to think of it," Susan told Aunt Judith at breakfast. "I've never been so happy anywhere in all my life."

Miss Pennington smiled. She rarely betrayed emotion. But that evening, when the gloom of parting hung over the lamplit room, she quietly suggested a plan that had been long in her mind. Since Susan was so well and contented at Chapel Green, why shouldn't she stay on for a week or two after Dick returned to North Bromwich? By this time she didn't need to be told that she would be welcome. "I'll look after her, Dick. Have no fear of that!" Aunt Judith promised.

At first Susan demurred. Dick was as helpless as a baby, she said, and couldn't possibly be trusted to look after himself. But later, when they talked it over in the great four-poster, they decided that for the baby's sake as well as for Susan's the opportunity was too good to be missed. She drove to the station in the pony-trap to see Dick off next morning. They talked bravely about anything in the world but their imminent parting, though Dick looked at her tenderly, anxiously all the time. On the empty platform they walked to and fro arm-in-arm unblushingly, as pretty a picture of a young married couple as one could wish to see. When the train bustled in, out of breath with the gradient and five minutes late, there was no time to spare for farewells. Dick kissed her blunderingly, leaning out of the carriage window. The engine whistled; the train gave a forward jolt and moved on. She saw him still waving at the window as it coiled round the curve of the line.

IV

Of course life at Chapel Green was not quite the same without him. It was the flux of his presence that had united her to Aunt Judith. Left alone to themselves, Susan found they had very little to talk about. Their spheres of life and of interest were so different; and with a woman of that kind it was no use pretending they weren't. When Dick had gone back to Tilton those evening hours which had passed like a flash on the stream of family talk began to drag dreadfully. Though Aunt Judith could see to sew or do anything else she wanted to in the feeble lamplight, Susan honestly couldn't. So she went to bed earlier and earlier, to the relief of both of them, thinking much of the past and even more of the future.

Dick wrote to her every day. His letters, she supposed, were love-letters, consisting of endearments and cautions and very little else. She answered them dutifully with detailed accounts of the way in which her days were spent and laments for his absence. There was really very little to tell him; for now that the excitements of his holiday excursions were over Miss Pennington had resumed the uneventful tenor of her life. She was busy enough, of course, catching up with neglected duties—with weeding and picking fruit and jam-making and visiting new-born babies and old-age pensioners; but none of these activities were very exciting to Susan. She would have liked to help in the house, and offered to do so; but the canons of house-keeping at Chapel Green were fixed with a standard of spinsterly precision that the slipshod improvisations which Susan had used at "Chatsworth" could not hope to satisfy. Aunt Judith was not ungrateful for her attempts to be useful, but she made it quite clear, by doing everything that Susan attempted over again, that the domestic life at "The Old Parsonage" was not for amateurs. She did this quite kindly—there was never a hint of patronage, much less of criticism, in anything she said—but her attitude, for all its kind-ness, was always old-maidish and (Susan thought) fussy.

By the end of a week Susan began to be homesick for "Chatsworth," where life was at once so much more complex and so much easier. Her vanity was hurt by the very tactfulness with which Miss Pen-nington took trouble to conceal the fact that all the affection and care that she gave her were not meant for Susan's self so much as for Dick's wife and the mother of Dick's child. "Apart from that," Susan told her-self, "I'm a woman of no importance in her eyes. It's always Pennington this and Pennington the other. The name's no better than Lorimer." There was a village called Pennington, Aunt Judith proudly in-formed her. In this state of sensitiveness she was always looking for slights. Wasn't it significant, for instance, that Aunt Judith never invited any of her friends to meet her—not even the Mrs. Redlake of whom she approved so strongly? "It wasn't as if she need be ashamed of me," Susan thought.

So she tried to assert her suppressed individuality by alluding, in a superior way, to her course at the university and showing how much she knew about modern literature. Miss Pennington, oddly enough, was not suitably impressed. She admitted frankly that she knew nothing whatever about books, but implied that the less one did know about them—particularly modern ones—the better. Since the display of erudi-tion had failed to increase her prestige, Susan decided to make herself loved for herself alone by displaying a sweetness of disposition and old-fashioned feminine inanity such as never existed outside the novels of Dickens. This worked better, not because, for one moment, Aunt Judith admired or believed in it, but because this particular pose left her free to pursue her own life and made no demands on her powers of polite conversation.

As for Susan, although it paid to be thought a fool,

this passive rôle bored her, almost literally, to tears. There was nothing left for her to do at Chapel Green but picking flowers in the garden and arranging them in bowls and vases. In this the "flare" which had staggered Mr. Bellis came to her aid. Aunt Judith loved all flowers so passionately that Susan's unconventional ideas of arrangement did not shock her, and Susan herself found a kind of creative pleasure in new combinations of colour that caught her fancy. Having exhausted the resources of the garden she went farther afield in search of them. In the still cool evening, when Aunt Judith had ridden off on her bicycle to visit her pensioners, it was pleasant to hear the garden latch click behind her, to cross the wide sweep of the green, where the geese and "gullies" were grazing and yellow ducklings dabbled among king-cups and cresses, to explore the labyrinth of lanes between Chapel Green and Llandwlas. Wherever the hazel hedges retreated the sward was set with white clover or plumed with heads of cow-parsley; the may and wild roses were over, but the midsummer pomps of the elders (or ellern trees, as Aunt Judith called them) were about to begin, and every lane was drenched with honey-sweet woodbine.

One sultry evening, heavy with the threat of thunder, Susan found herself wandering farther than usual in the direction of Llandwlas. Though the sun shone fiercely, tattered clouds moved up from the south in a windless sky, and a rumble like distant gunfire warned her that the storm was nearing. As she stood undecided for a moment she suddenly remembered a colony of foxgloves in bud to which Dick had called her attention during their drive to the station. That was nearly a fortnight ago; by this time their solemn spires should be belled with purple. "I could get a whole armful of them," she thought, "for the drawing-room fireplace. They'd be lovely, and it won't take long. If I climb this path I shall strike the Llandwlas road within a few yards of them."

Another rumble of thunder quickened her steps. The slope was steep; she breathed hard as she gained the top of it. Yes, there was the stile, and beyond it the rain-scoured highway. She remembered this corner quite well; the foxgloves grew just beyond it on the further side. Still panting, she climbed the stile and lowered herself gently to the road. As her feet touched the earth the clear sky seemed to crack overhead and a fragment of rock hummed past within a hand's breadth of her face. Her mind framed a quick question: "Thunder?" No, not thunder. It was blasting. She had blundered into the zone of fire between the red flags. In an instant her legs started running, she couldn't tell why. She didn't know where she was going; only that she had to run. Another shot crashed on her right. A shrapnel-fire of loose earth and pebbles raked her; a splinter of rock cut her cheek. She put up her hands to her bleeding face to protect her eyes and ran on blindly while another crash came and a boulder of half a ton's weight struck the road behind her. By this time she was no longer a sentient creature. Like a terrified animal she fled across the face of the barrage, while the smoking hillside was shattered and convulsed by charge after charge like the cone of a breaking volcano. A fragment of rock struck her leg below the right knee. She span round like a shot rabbit, then fell to the ground and lay, face downward, unconscious.

When she opened her eyes a ring of gigantic, solemn-faced men were standing round her; a yellowish reek of explosive still hung in the air. One stooped, slipped his arm under her shoulders and knees and lifted her bodily. She stared at him wildly for a moment, then closed her eyes, vaguely conscious of the sweaty smell of his corduroy waistcoat. As they laid her down on the grass at the side of the road she heard them talking in slow undertones:

"It bain't no fault of yourn, Charley, nor yourn, George. The flags was up."

"Ay, 'er mun 'ave scrobbled through the glat unbeknownst; it bain't no fault of George's; they conna chastise 'im of doing it."

"Poor mossel, too! Her anna half bloodied 'er face, and 'er dress all dagged!"

"I wouldn't have 'ad this 'appen, not if it was ever so."

"Some stranger, I reckon; I doubt this bain't 'er native or else she'd 'a knowed."

"Look, Joe, 'er's a'battin' of 'er eyes, 'er's a'comin' round."

"Shut yer face, yer blob-mouthed fussock. Keep clear. Let 'er breathe . . ."

"Look out, boys!"

She heard the squeak of a motor-car's brakes. Then another voice spoke. It was confident and cultivated: "What's the trouble, Condover? An accident?"

"Ay, that's it, Mr. Redlake."

"Why, she may be Miss Pennington's niece. Just give me a hand, and we'll lift her into the car. If you had the flags properly posted, it's not your fault. Just bad luck! Steady now! That'll do. I'll take her on chance to Miss Pennington's first. She's as good as the Cottage Hospital."

The self-starter whirred harshly. The car slid gently down hill.

v

Dick Pennington hated going back to his work in North Bromwich, but, far more than that, he hated leaving Susan behind. A year ago he would have considered it rather fun to "camp out" alone at "Chatsworth." It was no fun at all without Susan. Much as he knew he loved her, he could never have believed that her absence would make such a difference as this. It wasn't domestic comfort that he missed—during the

last month or two the standard of Susan's housekeep-
ing had steadily declined: nor was it their marital relations—those, naturally, had been greatly modified; it
was, rather, her mere existence as an integral part of
his habit of living, and the loss of her, magnified out
of all proportion with reality, gaped like that which
is left in the jaw by a tooth's extraction. Though in
time, he supposed he would get used to it, the very
house seemed so oddly empty that he couldn't bring
himself to sit in it. Each dispirited room struck chill
to his heart when he entered it, and the black Baronial
chamber had more than ever a funerary air.

To escape from himself he tried to pick up the
threads of his bachelor life at Winsworth and to
identify it with that of his office friends. He played
tennis with them in the parks; went to row on the
Avon at Evesham; even joined in a jolly music-hall
party with two of them and three girls. Yet in all
these diversions he was conscious of a certain detachment; he could never again look on life with care-free
eyes, and whenever his thoughts were left to themselves they returned to Shropshire and Susan. He was
happier, on the whole, he decided, at "Chatsworth,"
where at least some pathetic wraiths of her spirit clung
to a silk-padded work-basket, a note she had scribbled
to remind herself where she had hidden the keys, an
odd glove dropped in the hurry of their departure,
and the half-worn night-dress he discovered under her
pillow. When he shaved in the morning his ears were

strained for the sound of the postman's knock. He opened her letters with fingers that trembled with eagerness and anxiety. When she wrote that the weather was fine and that she was enjoying herself, he smiled and the day was lightened. He was a fool, he told himself, to be so ridiculously anxious. Miss Maples, whom, though he disliked her, he had visited several times since his return, assured him that everything was bound to turn out all right.

There was nothing like physical labour, people said, to settle one's thoughts when one happened to be at a loose end; so, when he came home, he worked in the garden as long as it was light. The asters they had sown in the spring were coming into bloom and the gladiolus bulbs he had bought at Woolworth's looked surprisingly good for the money. It would be an even greater surprise for Susan to find the rockery an accomplished fact when she came home. Once more he consulted Inspector Frome on the subject.

"You see," he explained, "we've been away for three weeks in Shropshire, and my wife is still there."

"Oh, that's it, is it?" the inspector replied, after his statutory three minutes' pause. "There was a man up the road last week enquiring after you," he said. "So you've left her behind?"

He stared so fixedly with his dull blue eyes that Dick felt he was being suspected of having done away with her. His urgent desire to get on with the rockery became suspect, too. What could be easier than to bury the body under a cart-load of stones? The more innocently he explained his motives the more deeply he seemed to involve himself. The sudden desire to launch out on a rockery at all suggested embezzlement.

"Of course, Mr. Pennington, if money's no object" —the inspector followed these words with a significant pause—"you can go in for stone. What's much cheaper is to get a nice load of slag from the Wednesford blast furnaces—that's the place where Garside was working on the date of the murder. I could give you a letter to one of the chaps in the office. I'm pretty well known over there," he added, "as you can imagine. When will Mrs. Pennington be back, did you say?" he asked suddenly, with another fixed stare.

"Well, to tell you the truth, I can't be quite sure," Dick guiltily admitted.

"In Shropshire, I think you said?"

"Well, it's really in Radnorshire. My aunt's house is just over the border."

"Oh, your aunt," said the inspector. "I don't think you mentioned her before. These county boundaries make a lot of difference in our line of work. In Garside's case, now . . ."

"Oh, by the way," Dick broke in, "your speaking of Garside reminds me. My wife was most terribly upset by that bit of rope you showed her."

"Budge Garside deserved the rope if ever a man did," the inspector said sternly.

"Yes, I know," Dick agreed. "All the same, I

should be most awfully grateful if you wouldn't mention it again when she happens to be present—about my name-sake, you know. You see, she's . . . you've probably noticed it . . . and that makes her nervous. You don't mind my mentioning it, do you?"

The inspector didn't. Indeed, when Dick started to clear the site for the rockery, he stole up in his carpet slippers and watched the work with approval, though he enquired, as usual, for the precise date of Susan's arrival, and Dick couldn't help feeling his interest was faintly professional.

That same evening Captain Small limped up hopefully to the front door of "Chatsworth." During the three weeks of Susan's absence he had made heavy weather, and once, when he visited North Bromwich to draw his pension, had returned with three sheets in the wind. Dick saw Captain Small's face fall when he learned that Susan had not come back with him, and felt, for one moment, a sharp twinge of jealousy; but the very frankness with which Captain Small confessed his interest in Susan disarmed him and made him feel mean; so he asked him to stay for a snack of pot-luck and a smoke, and they sat on far into the night (there was no inducement now for him to go to bed) simply talking about Susan—how beautiful and brilliant she was, what breeding and taste she displayed (only look at the dining-room, my boy!) and how thankful Dick ought to be to have found such a wife. They became increasingly confidential.

"You might get a shock, old chap, if I told you what your missus means to me."

Dick shook his head solemnly. "No, I quite understand, old fellow."

"A guiding star—that's the only word for it!" Captain Small declared.

They drank Susan's health in a night-cap. (Well, it's time I pushed off, old chap!) After which Captain Small showed no further inclination to push off at all. Having negligently possessed himself of the decanter he went over the gamut of Susan's perfections again and again, till suddenly catching sight of the clock, which was pointing, as usual, to half-past two, he put his foot down and refused to let Dick keep him up any longer.

"I don't want to break up the party, old fellow," he said, affectionately clinging to the garden gate-post, "but late hours are extremely bad for the nerves at my age. My old shell-shock, you know. Well, I may be the least bit lit—we're all of us human—but oiled or sober, Pennington my boy, I can tell you this. She's a woman in a million—that under-states it—ten million! There's nobody like her. *You* don't deserve her. *I* don't deserve her. Nobody living deserves her. She's an angel on earth. She's a bloody miracle, my boy, and that's the truth! Where's my blasted hat got to?"

It was on his head, Dick told him. "Well, that shows you, doesn't it?" Captain Small remarked enigmatically. Dick heard him go, singing somewhat jerkily, down Ada Road. Miss Maples heard him, too. She thought it was Dick rollicking home from a night in town, and thanked heaven that, though she had once been practically engaged, she had never run the risk of marrying a man who drank. Dick went to his lonely bed feeling more contented. To talk about Susan was the next best thing to having her with him, and half a decanter of whisky was a small price to pay for the privilege. If Susan was a miracle, Small was a damned stout fellow. His attitude toward her had shown not only unusual perception, but the greatest delicacy.

As Dick rarely drank whisky his head ached next morning, and his feelings for Captain Small were less enthusiastic than they had been overnight. The post brought no letter from Susan. It was Saturday, which meant he would have to go without news of her for two more days. It was thoughtless of her not to have realized how anxious that made him. As he left "Chatsworth," later than usual, Miss Maples, who was sweeping her front-door steps, returned his good morning with the stoniest disapproval. "And what the hell's the matter with you?" Dick said to himself. Inspector Frome, in uniform, sat beside him on the top of the bus. "No news of your wife yet, I suppose?" he asked significantly, Dick thought. At the Wolverbury by-pass the bus skidded on wet tar, avoiding a collision by inches, and the subsequent explanations made him five minutes late at the office.

An extraordinary atmosphere of gloom hung over it that morning. In answer to a hushed enquiry he gathered that the head of the firm had already been "off the deep end." That wasn't unusual in these days. The disruption of China and the Indian boycott had played havoc with the export trade. At the end of a crushed and silent morning the senior clerk, who was generally supposed to be booked for a partnership, came up to Dick's desk and told him that the "old man" wanted a word with him in the board-room.

"Just like my darned luck," Dick thought, "that he should happen to turn up early on the only morning I've been late in the last five months!"

As he entered the presence—he had only set foot in that room once before—the "old man" was struggling, red in the face, with a badly blocked pipe.

"Oh, it's you, is it, Pennington?" he grunted, going on with the operation.

"Mr. Cash said you wanted me, sir."

"Yes, I do . . . or rather. . . . Well, to put it quite plainly, Pennington, we've been thinking for some time past of. . . . Oh, damn this pipe! Miss Mellows, do you happen to have such a thing as a hairpin?"

The secretary confessed she had only an invisible one.

"What's the good of it if it's invisible?" the "old man" snapped. "Oh, that's what you call invisible, is it?" he said, relenting. "H'm, that's better!" He blew through the pipe. "Let's see. . . . What was I saying? Oh, the staff reduction, of course. Yes, we've just decided to cut down our overhead, Pennington. Nothing against you personally, mind. As a matter of fact, you're exactly the sort of fellow we like to employ, and when times get better—as I hope to God they will when we've pushed out this Labour Government—I shall only be too glad to take you on again. You'll agree that it's fairer all round not to show any favouritism. It's just your bad luck that in the branch where we have to reduce, you've been with us less time than the others. You're entitled to a week's notice, as you know; but as jobs are scarce and you'll probably have a good bit of trouble in finding one, you can clear off to-day if you like and start looking round right away. We shall give you a month's salary, too, just to show . . . well, you know what I mean. Will you make out Mr. Pennington's cheque, Miss Mellows? I've just time to sign it. Though I'm afraid you can't cash it till Monday, Pennington," he added, with a smile.

With trembling lips Dick tried to return that smile. He wished he could have spoken; but he knew that above this court there was no appeal. While Miss Mellows made out the cheque the "old man" refilled his pipe. He felt sorry to see Dick's disconsolate face, his moist hands clasped together.

"Been playing any cricket this summer, Pennington?" he asked encouragingly. "Got your colours at Brunstone, didn't you?"

"Only second eleven, sir. Footer's really my game," Dick answered tremulously. He grasped at the chance of an indirect appeal. "You see, sir," he went on hurriedly (for Miss Mellows was blotting the cheque), "I've had to give up games, practically. I got married this time last year, sir, and my wife's . . ." He glanced shyly at Miss Mellows.

"H'm, a family, what? Quick work! Well, well, my dear Pennington, if you will go in for these luxuries . . ."

"Damned young idiot!" he thought, as he glanced at the figure of Dick's cheque and signed it. "I'm afraid this won't go very far. Well, that's his christening." He said: "Here you are, Pennington. I think this is correct. Good-bye and good luck to you! Keep in touch with Miss Mellows. If anything turns up. . . . Well, of course, you can leave your address."

Miss Mellows nodded and smirked, the "old man" smiled and held out his hand. Dick's, cold and perspiring, grasped it. "Good-bye, sir, and thank you," he said.

Then he stiffened his shoulders and went out without speaking to anybody. Although for many months he had been aware of the precariousness of his position, this disaster took him by surprise. As he left the office the clock in the Art Gallery tower struck one, and the main streets of the city, which, during the last four hours, had been given over to the slow-moving trickle of Saturday morning shoppers, became turbulent as rivers suddenly in flood. From the work-benches of the jewellers' quarters, from the office-desks of Sackville Row, from the counters of banks and department stores and shops and warehouses, human beings of both sexes and every condition of life gushing forth filled each alley and by-way with the turmoil and density of hill-streams feeding a spate. It was the moment at which the mighty heart of North Bromwich, whose pulsations gave life to the Midland industrial organism, achieved its daily systole; the moment in which the half million corpuscles of its blood-stream were forced outward to enrich the last capillaries of suburb and village with the fruits of seven days' toil; a moment of relief and release from the pressure of labour. The flood that caught up Dick Pennington and swept him along had a happy movement. He was jostled by thread-bare clerks with rolled umbrellas and well-fed business men with hot-house blooms in their button-holes; by pallid mechanics in dungarees carrying bags of tools; by pink-legged shop-girls and office-girls hurriedly powdering their noses; by newsboys, bawl-ing the one o'clock sporting special; by brisk young fellows like himself in plus-fours with racquets in presses and golf-bags slung over their shoulders; by stiff-kneed cleaners and charwomen wrapped in black shawls hobbling back to their slums; by wayward dogs, and bewildered children clutching balloons. As it

Y

eddied and swirled through the canalized streets toward the sluices of railway-stations and bus and tram
terminuses that would give it vent, the faces that
bobbed up from its surface all seemed to Dick to be
wearing a holiday air; the eyes that momentarily met
his without recognition were full of eager purpose. In
all that anonymous multitude only he was dazed and
purposeless, swept on with as little volition as a floating straw.

In the set of the current toward the Western Station
he found himself checked by a traffic block in Sackville
Row, at the moment when Harry Levison was slamming the door of his yellow Bentley, and the sight of
that confident, handsome face, the first he had recognized, recalled him from his confusion and brought
him suddenly to earth.

"Why on earth am I wandering here?" he asked
himself. "I'm out of a job. I ought to be doing something about it at once, before Susan comes home."

On a Saturday afternoon, that was easier said than
done; but the urgent need of sharing his trouble with
somebody sympathetic made him turn against the
current and struggle for a place in the queue that stood
waiting for the Halesby bus. Two possible confidants
came to his mind: Mr. Bulgin, who had shown such a
kindly interest in his business career, and George
Lorimer. Of the two he inclined to George Lorimer,
if only because he was so much nearer to Susan. So,
neglecting his lunch—the idea of food revolted him—

he went straight past the Tilton cross-roads and through to Halesby, where he knocked at the house in Great Cornbow.

Mrs. Lorimer opened the door to him. "Oh, it's you, Mr. Pennington?" she said. "It's not often we're honoured like this. Nothing wrong with Susan, I hope?"

Nothing wrong with Susan, thank heaven, he repeated. He had heard from her yesterday, he said. He'd just thought he'd pop in for a chat with Uncle George.

"Well, you might have known better than expect to catch him here on a Saturday," Mrs. Lorimer scornfully replied. "He takes his lunch with him. If he's not at the office you'll probably find him fishing. I suppose you've had dinner?" she asked, with a reluctant gesture of hospitality.

"Oh, I'm quite all right, thank you," Dick said.

"Well, you might just catch him at the Dingle," she answered, obviously relieved.

It looked hardly a suitable refuge from trouble, Dick thought, as he hammered at the great wooden doors of the warehouse yard and stared up at the broken windows in search of any token of life. The sudden materialization of George Lorimer had the effect of an apparition. He looked shabbier than ever, and his clothes were smothered with crumbs and rust, for he had been eating his lunch and counting nail-rods. For the first time in his life he had done this work single-handed. A fortnight before he had been forced to dispense with his clerk, and that morning, after a painful scene, he had sacked Mr. Pound, the salesman. When he heard and recognized Dick's voice alarm banished all other emotion.

"Nothing wrong with Susan?" he gasped.

"No, no," Dick told him, "I only want to have a talk with you."

"Come in, Dick. I'm just having a snack." He led the way up a tottering staircase that smelt of straw and wrought-iron to the blear-windowed office, where his bread and cheese were laid out on an open ledger. "Well, what is it?" he asked, with a sigh of apprehension.

"I want your help, Uncle George."

"My help?" George Lorimer went red. That meant money, he supposed. If Dick Pennington only knew!

With enormous relief to his feelings Dick blurted out the whole story. As he spoke, George Lorimer munched and wagged his head slowly in utter hopelessness.

"Of course," Dick explained, "it's particularly awkward just now. There's nothing I'm not prepared to do short of begging," he said. "I suppose"—the idea had just entered his head—"I suppose I couldn't give you a hand with the books or anything?"

George Lorimer sighed again. "You see, as a matter of fact, our business is just a bit slack at the moment.

I've been cutting down staff myself. The clerk I employed wasn't any too satisfactory, so I decided to dispense with him, and Mr. Pound and I parted this morning, I'm sorry to say. We had a slight difference of opinion on policy," he explained, rather grandly, "and, to tell you the truth, Dick, I'm running the show single-handed."

"Then, surely," Dick ardently exclaimed, "that gives me a chance? The books won't fill my time; I could do a bit of travelling as well."

Uncle George shook his head. "It's entirely a question of expense. I had intended to carry on by myself till times improved. The clerk, of whom I spoke just now, wasn't exactly a clerk. Rather more like an office-boy, really. He only had a guinea a week."

"Well, I'll take that gladly if you'll give me the chance," Dick pleaded. "I've a cheque for twelve pounds and there's Susan's last quarter to come in. It was due on the twenty-fifth, wasn't it?" he went on eagerly.

George Lorimer blushed. "Dear, dear, it had slipped my memory."

"Oh, that's quite all right," Dick continued enthusiastically. "We've not spent it, anyway, so we're thirty-seven pounds to the good—call it forty. I think we can carry on for a bit with that; and of course, if I prove I'm worth more than a guinea a week, you'll raise my screw, won't you?"

George Lorimer hesitated; but Dick didn't wait for an answer. His crushed spirits soared.

"I can start to-morrow," he said. "Never mind about Sunday. I'll have a look at the books right away." ("Oh, will you!" George thought.) "Did Pound draw a commission on orders? I'll take half what he had. I can cover five times as much ground as he did on my motor-bicycle. If we've got the right stuff, Uncle George, I bet you I'll sell it!"

George Lorimer smiled timidly. "We needn't be in a hurry."

"*I*'ve got to be in a hurry," Dick firmly maintained.

"Well, I'll think it over," George said, "between now and Monday." He brushed the crumbs from the ledger and began to assemble his fishing-tackle. He felt a dogged desire to escape from this persistent young man; but he knew, all the same, that he couldn't afford to give him a job.

As for Dick, he returned to "Chatsworth" in the highest of spirits. He was master, once more, of the fate that had threatened to crush him. In his absence the cart-load of slag for the rockery had arrived from Wednesford and had been dumped on the garden path. If he had known what was going to happen he wouldn't have been so extravagant as to order it; but now it was there he supposed he might just as well deal with it. He moved the heap laboriously, piece by piece, to the site he had chosen for the rockery; and this mountainous labour accorded with the height to which his spirits had leapt after their morning abasement. Inspector Frome poked his head over the fence. "*You* look pleased with yourself," he said.

Dick laughed. "I *am* pleased," he said. "I've been sacked and made pretty well sure of a new job since I saw you last. The two together took under three hours. D'you call that good going?"

"Not so bad. That chap who was asking for you when you were away has been round again," the inspector reported.

"If he wanted to see me as badly as that, he might have waited."

"Well, he said he'd look in again to-night or to-morrow. I told him he'd be sure to find you."

Dick heaved and dug at the rockery till half-past seven. By that time he felt hot, tired and ravenous, which was natural enough, seeing that he had eaten nothing since breakfast and sweated for three hours on end. So he took a cold bath, fried a huge dish of eggs and bacon over the gas-ring, and fell to with a splendid appetite. When he ate his meals without Susan they never lasted more than five minutes, and by eight o'clock he had finished. Washing-up was the most unpleasant part of this grass-widower's life, revealing the intense antagonism of bacon-fat and cold water. In the middle of the noisome process he was startled by a sudden knock at the door. He abandoned the greasy plates and went to answer it. "It's probably," he thought, "that chap who was asking for me. I wonder

who the devil he is and what he wants." He saw only
a red bicycle propped against the fence, until a small
boy in uniform dodged round from the back of the
house.

"It's a telegram, sir," he announced, unnecessarily.

Dick opened the envelope quickly. "She's remembered," he thought, "that I can't get a letter till
Monday. How like her extravagance!"

He read:

"COME AT ONCE DON'T WORRY. AUNT JUDITH."

"Any answer, sir?" the boy asked briskly.

Dick Pennington didn't hear him. He was already
fumbling with the key in the door of the garage. In
its gloomy interior, draped with the folds of tarpaulin
that had once sheltered the Baronial table, stood his
motor-bicycle. It was smothered in dust and grease;
the tyres were inflated. He had taken out no licence
this year, but fear of the law did not trouble him. He
emptied a can, which possibly held petrol, into the
tank and flooded the carburettor. For a wonder, the
capricious engine fired after a single kick; it roared
like an aeroplane, filling the garage with smoke. Then,
just as he had come from the scullery, without hat or
coat, Dick straddled the seat and the unlicensed
machine went screaming westward, with the drone of
a high-velocity shell, toward Chapel Green.

VI

That evening Miss Maples lost her prospective job at "Chatsworth." That premature baptism of fire had been too much for Guy, or Jasper, or whatever his name was. He was born dead, just after midnight. Dr. Hendrie spoke guardedly, but said things might have been worse. "It's my nephew who'll feel it most," Miss Pennington told him, with unwonted tears in her eyes.

CHAPTER IX

MR. BULGIN GETS BUSY

I

It was a pale, thin, chastened Susan who returned to "Chatsworth" three weeks later. Her features were sharpened and the lines of her mouth and chin had grown harder. It was the difference between a model in clay and a sculpture in marble, and this new severity gave her eyes a hungry look. Dick met her early in the afternoon at North Bromwich. It was clever of him, she thought, to have managed to get away from the office so early. From the first moment of meeting, his eyes devoured her; for he saw she was changed, though he couldn't exactly think how. Going home on the bus he plied her with anxious enquiries.

"No, I'm perfectly well," she told him. "Of course you can't go through a horrible business like that without showing some signs of it. Does the scar on my cheek look too dreadful?"

He protested that he hadn't noticed it. "You'll always be lovely to me," he told her passionately. "Yes, that's all very well," Susan thought. "Notices nothing." She, herself, had been somewhat shocked by his appearance on the station platform. Her seven weeks' absence at Chapel Green compelled her to examine him with a mind detached and coldly objective eyes. Striding out in his coarse-textured tweeds with a fishing-rod or an otter-hunting staff, Dick had satisfied her sense of fitness to his surroundings. Here, in urban North Bromwich, his dark office clothes diminished him. In the emotion of meeting her he had cut his chin that morning. The distress of the last three weeks made him look as though he had been through the mill; and the tremulous cheerfulness and rapture that he showed when he met her seemed less romantic than pathetic. As he lifted her suitcase and lugged it up the steps to the station entrance he looked such an ordinary young man, undistinguished and undistinguishable from scores of others who thronged the noisy booking-hall and the street outside. She couldn't identify him with the gay lover of Brinton or the eager young husband of "Chatsworth." "You can't make a silk purse out of a sow's ear," she thought. And in this case, whatever it was made of, the purse held so little.

Even "Chatsworth" itself had suffered a subtle change. It was no longer the compact and smart little suburban residence after which, only nine months before, her soul had lusted. She saw it now as it was: a raw, cheap, jerry-built bungalow, as typical of Mr. Duke's taste as all its neighbours, without any of the mellow shabbiness that gave the "Old Parsonage" its distinction, or the unimaginable refinements of Trewern, the home of the man who had picked her up in his car, to which glimpse of heaven she had been admitted for tea, in the last week of convalescence.

On the left of the garden path she observed a barren erection in the shape of a miniature barrow or an enormous grave-mound.

"Oh, what *have* you been doing?" she cried.

It was his rockery, Dick told her proudly. At the moment, he confessed, it did look rather bare; but next spring, when the bulbs and the arabis and aubrietia came out . . .

"It looks just like a cake with dirt almonds stuck over it," she said. "What horrible, dead-looking stone . . . !"

It was slag, he told her. Real stone was frightfully expensive. Inspector Frome had suggested it.

"That awful man?" Susan cried. "How could you expect a creature like him to have any taste? If you'd only waited until I came home, Dick darling! It's so huge and solid! I suppose you can't move it now? Oh, dear, dear, how dreadful!"

He had wanted, Dick explained, to give her a surprise. Inside the house there were other surprises awaiting her. With the best of intentions, Dick's standards of domestic cleanliness were not hers. Dust lay thickly everywhere; the whole place reeked of tobacco; and the kitchen sink had not been properly cleaned. Her heart fell; yet these superficial blemishes were trifling compared with the deeper dissatisfaction that filled it when she surveyed the living-room of which she had once been so proud. It was all wrong, irredeemably wrong, from the Kidderminster carpet and the bright-figured chintzes and cretonnes she had chosen to Mr. Bellis's *Louie Cans* chairs. In comparison with the shabby Victorian furniture of Chapel Green, it looked as shoddy as a factory-girl prinked up in her bank-holiday best beside the *grande dame* of an impoverished county family. "If only," she thought, "we hadn't been in such a hurry to furnish!" As for the Baronial suite, she didn't even dare to set eyes on it.

These vain regrets haunted her as she unpacked her bag in the bedroom and changed to rid herself of the dirt of the train. Dick hovered round her, full of tremulous affection. He kissed her again and again, he was always touching her, and she submitted to these demonstrations with the show of enthusiasm that was due to him.

"I can't believe that it's really you," he said.

She smiled; but she wasn't quite sure herself that his doubts weren't justified. The Susan who had returned to "Chatsworth" was certainly different in some odd way from the girl who had left it. She supposed that everything was bound to feel strange at first; and when they sat down in the kitchen to the cold meal which he had so lovingly and clumsily prepared for her, she did her best to recapture the ancient air of adventurous happiness, and felt terribly sorry for Dick as well as for herself.

After dinner, when they moved into the living-room, its deficiencies smote her again.

"Dick darling, I really must change those curtains," she said. "I can't imagine how we ever chose them. Do you think we can afford it?"

The question gave him the opportunity for confession which he had despaired of finding. It was a shame to tell her the shattering truth on their very first evening together; yet, sooner or later, he knew, it would have to be broken to her.

"Heaven knows when we shall be able to afford anything, Susie," he said. "We've struck a bad patch. I didn't tell you before . . . well, for obvious reasons."

"A bad patch? What d'you mean, Dick?"

"They've been cutting down staff at the office. I'm out of a job. Never mind, we shall soon pull round again; but it's terribly difficult in these days to get into another. It just means . . ."

"Dick, how *could* they do that? Did you tell them you were married?"

"Well, I did. But that makes no difference to them, you know. It's simply bad luck!"

Her face hardened. "You ought to have told me. I could have come home earlier. Well, what have you done about it?"

"I've done all that I can. First of all I saw Uncle

George. I said that I'd take on his clerking and travelling as well."

"And wouldn't he let you? How mean of him!"

"I don't think he could. I imagine his business must
be in a pretty bad way. He's sacked Pound and his
clerk and is carrying on by himself."

"I must see him at once. That's all nonsense. He
never spends anything. It's Aunt Edna who's made
him refuse. Just wait till I've talked to him!"

"No, Susie, I don't think she's to blame. I believe
he's in a tight corner. I had to remind him twice about
your money for last quarter."

"Next year, thank heaven, we shan't have to wait:
I shall have my capital."

She sat silent, with puzzled brows. She still found it
difficult to realize how bad things were. "But surely,"
she said at last, "there are dozens of other places?"

"Yes, and hundreds of chaps better qualified than
me to fill them."

"Dick, you sound so helpless. If you'd only told
me," she repeated, "I'm sure we could have found
some opening by now."

"There was a job at Magnus and Levison's . . ."

"Well, that sounds splendid. Muriel knows Harry
Levison. We might ask her to speak for you."

His face reddened. "That sort of introduction
wouldn't appeal to me. As a matter of fact, I went
to their office this morning. Mr. Magnus was busy and
I saw young Levison himself. I dislike him intensely."

"And showed it, of course! We can't afford to dislike people. I suppose you were too shy to remind him of Brinton?"

"Oh, no; I reminded him. He said he remembered me, and asked after you, and promised to let me know later: but he was far too polite to mean anything; I could see there was nothing doing."

"How like you!" she cried. "You take everything lying down. I'm sure you never opened your mouth. If you'd only taken me with you, I could have explained . . ."

"You don't understand, darling. Jobs don't go by favour in these days. It's a matter of business. If you haven't got what they want they just turn you down. I know. I've tried dozens of places."

"Have you tried Mr. Bulgin?"

"No, I couldn't. He was away in South Wales at those big new works."

"Then why didn't you write to him? You ought to have written at once. Oh, Dick, how foolish you've been! Such a waste of time. Of course, Uncle George sent the cheque as soon as you asked for it, didn't he?"

"Yes. He sent it last week. But by the end of the month there won't be much left of it."

"What do you mean?"

It would be better for both of them, he supposed, if she knew the whole truth.

"I've had trouble about the furniture, Susie. A man came to see me three weeks ago. He'd called here before when we were away and again on that night when I rushed off to Chapel Green. I'm glad you weren't here. I can tell you, I jolly near kicked him out of the garden gate!"

"Why, what did he say?" Susan nervously enquired. She stole a swift glance at Captain Small's shell-case. The fact that it was as dusty as everything else on the mantelpiece reassured her.

"What didn't he say? He was shouting so loudly that old Mamma Maples must have heard. He said we were two months overdue and he must have ten pounds on the spot. Of course, I told him you'd probably overlooked it, what with one thing or another. But he wouldn't have that; he swore that they'd posted us three reminders already. When I told him we hadn't had them he turned quite nasty—practically called me a liar and threatened to sell up the house. *You* never had any letter, did you, Susie?"

"Of course not, darling," Susan answered indignantly.

"Well, that's what I told him; but he said he was fed up with excuses and that was an old story."

"I hope you said Mr. Bellis was a friend of ours?"

"Most certainly I did. He'd the cheek to ask who the devil Mr. Bellis was. When I told him Mr. Bellis was one of the heads of his own firm he laughed in my face. He said he didn't want any arguments or explanations. All he wanted was money, and if I didn't pay on the nail he'd send a van next day to cart off

z

the stuff they'd supplied."

"And a jolly good job if he had!" Susan thought.
She said: "What disgusting people! If I'd known they
were going to behave like this we'd never have gone to
them. Such lies, too! I shall go straight into town and
see Mr. Bellis to-morrow. As for money. . . . It
would do them no harm to be kept waiting a bit."

"That's all very well, Susie. But even if the letters
did go astray, we owed it. I was bound to pay him.
And the devil of it is there's another instalment due in
ten days, to say nothing of the rent on quarter-day, and
I'm damned if I know where that's coming from! I
can't bear to think of your coming home to a mess-up
like this, on the top of the other thing."

He knelt beside her and took her in his arms. She
compelled herself to make some response to this
pathetic embrace, though it failed to move her. As she
stroked his rough hair with a mechanical listlessness,
she reproached herself for her own odd lack of
emotion. She was conscious in that moment of reunion, which should have been so moving to both of
them, of the cold and critical detachment she had felt
on the station platform. The fingers that stroked his
hair belonged to somebody quite different from the
romantic, palpitating girl who had fallen in love at
Brinton or the glowing bride who had come to "Chatsworth" less than a year before. "A year ago," she told
herself, "I couldn't have lied to him about those
letters; a year ago I should have trembled when he

took me in his arms and kissed me like this. The things
that used to matter don't matter any more. Either he,
or I, or both of us, have changed in some way," she
thought, as her fingers continued to stroke his hair. "I
have no more feeling left in me; I'm as hard as steel;
and the things I used to feel are just as unreal now as
if I'd dreamt them. I can't help it. I suppose it
means I'm no longer in love with him. How dreadful!" She slipped her hand into his, and his fingers
tightened; she was not so much holding on to him as
to the idea of him that had vanished. He was speaking: "Nothing really matters, does it? as long as we
have each other?"

The words mocked her thoughts. It would be cruel
to tell him the truth. Even if she didn't love him she
was sorry for him—and even more sorry for herself.
The new situation, unfortunate as it was for both of
them, held elements of tragic drama in which she must
play a heroine's part.

"No," she murmured tenderly, "of course that is
all that really matters, you poor dear."

This artistic achievement, to which he responded so
eagerly, so happily and in such perfect faith, gave her
a sense of dramatic satisfaction so closely resembling
the emotions to which she believed herself to be dead
that she almost wondered if her change of heart wasn't
really a mood, the result of her physical weakness and
the fatigue of the cross-country journey—if she wasn't
still, after all, a little in love with him. That problem

was emotionally interesting in any case, and time would solve it. The immediate question of ways and means which Dick, reinstated provisionally, had signally failed to deal with, was far more pressing. So, discarding the secret rôle of a disillusioned wife, she assumed that of a practical and resourceful woman of the world, somewhat hardened by fate's ill-usage in the matter of sickness, but determined to apply that hardness, so bitterly acquired, for better or worse, for richer or poorer, in her own and her husband's defence. Releasing herself from Dick's arms with a wise and tender determination, she kissed him maternally and sat down at the dusty writing-desk.

"What are you doing?" he asked. "There's plenty of time to write to Aunt Judith to-morrow."

She laughed. "I'm not writing to her. I'm doing what you ought to have done long ago. We've got to get out of this mess, my child, as soon as possible. I'm writing to Mr. Bulgin."

II

Two days later Mr. Bulgin returned from South Wales to Halesby. He had spent a whole fortnight in superintending the erection of the most modern machinery in the works that were to handle the heavier part of his output and the treatment of raw materials. This plant had been carried by sea to Newport from Hamburg and Philadelphia; for Mr. Bulgin, though an ardent protectionist in the matter of tubes, was, for the moment, an equally ardent Free-trader with regard to the machinery that made them. He liked having it both ways, and generally succeeded in doing so.

He was satisfied, moreover, by the impression he had created in Monmouthshire, where he had been welcomed as the immediate saviour of a district lost in the abyss of industrial depression. As a bluff man of deeds rather than words, bustling in from the North like a stringent wind, he had given—reluctantly, for he hated publicity—a number of interviews to the South Welsh papers in which he poured kindly scorn on the stagnant methods of the local tin-plate industry, talked big about mass-production and rationalization, and preached Henry Ford's doctrine of short hours and high wages with a confidence that stamped him at once as a public benefactor and assured him a supply of the best class of labour as soon as the new works were opened. These, for all their magnitude, he hinted darkly, must only be regarded as a beginning; he had plans, mature but secret, for development and expansion. Yet, even as they stood, the new works would have an enormous effect on the district, not only by giving highly-paid jobs to a couple of thousand Welshmen, but by burning Welsh coal and crowding Welsh docks with incoming freights of raw material and outgoing manufactures.

The humility with which the press and the people who read it deferred to his dogmatic pronouncements was flattering to that sense of strength which, during the years of his rise to industrial power, had become his besetting weakness. At home, in Halesby, he was always shy to "show off" for fear of exciting the ridicule of those who had known him before the war as "Young Johnny Bulgin." Returning from South Wales, intoxicated by flatteries, self-conscious and rather lonely, he was immediately delighted by two incidents, trivial in themselves, that gave him an opportunity of exercising the power on which he prided himself.

The first was a request for an interview from Mr. Pound, George Lorimer's ex-salesman. During his absence, engrossed in larger affairs, Mr. Bulgin had almost forgotten the existence of the new British Nail Company, and his capricious desire to juggle George Lorimer out of the Dingle site. Now, just as a fisherman returning from struggles with sword-fish and tarpon can while away idle hours trapping minnows for bait, he found amusement and relaxation in dealing with Mr. Pound. Mr. Pound, after waiting over three hours on the door-mat, was finally admitted.

"I seem to have heard your name before," Mr. Bulgin said distantly.

"Your father knew me quite well, sir. I've been traveller for Lorimer and Sons for more than twenty-five years," Mr. Pound said, nervously tugging at his wisp of grey beard.

"Then what can you want with *me*, Mr. Pound?"

Mr. Bulgin smoothly enquired.

"What I want is a job, sir. Mr. George and me unfortunately don't see eye to eye, so I'm sorry to say I'm leaving him."

"Leaving?"

"Well, left, then."

"The sinking ship!" Mr. Bulgin thought. "What a mangy grey rat!"

"I understand," Mr. Pound continued, "that you hold the controlling interest in New British Nails. Well, what I don't know about the nail trade, modestly speaking, is not worth knowing. I reckon I've sold more nails in the Midlands area than any man living. You ask your partners; they'll tell you."

"Then why have Lorimers let you leave them?" Mr. Bulgin asked innocently.

"Because—now I'm speaking straight, sir, in confidence like—because Lorimers is bust. I give them six months at the outside to put up the shutters."

Mr. Bulgin was shocked. "That's bad news, Pound: very sad news! He's an old friend of mine, is George Lorimer."

"Bad or good, it's a fact," Mr. Pound replied, with bitterness. "Mr. Lorimer may be a friend of yours, but he's no friend of mine. He's treated me shameful. After twenty-five years, with his father an' all, and never as much as thank you! If Lorimer goes under— as he will, mind—he's himself to thank for it. Now look here, Mr. Bulgin, you and me aren't fools, we're business men. I carry what's left of the Lorimer connection here in my waistcoat pocket. It's yours, if you like to pay for it. I don't want a salary. I'll do the whole job on commission. I'm not a young man, but if I bust a blood-vessel I'll promise that you get the lot! Now that's straight!"

Mr. Bulgin smiled. The word seemed not quite appropriate. A decidedly ugly rat, he thought, as Pound in his lust for revenge twitched his tremulous lips, revealing, beneath the grey fringe of moustache, an isolated pair of long yellow canine fangs. Decidedly ugly, but useful. . . .

"I make it a rule, Mr. Pound," he replied, with disinterested calm, "to take nobody on to our pay-list without a reference; so, before I consider your application, I shall write to Mr. Lorimer about you."

"If you believe what *he* tells you . . ." Mr. Pound broke in. "Well, go on. Do it!"

"You can call again in three days' time," Mr. Bulgin said finally. He had never, from the first, the faintest intention of employing George Lorimer's salesman; the man was too old and his mood at the moment too nasty to be reliable; but the opportunity of sending a formal request for his character to George was far too amusing to be missed. He laughed in his heart as he dictated it, thinking how George would go red and fussed and bounce about the dusty office at the Dingle when he received it. "So poor old George Lorimer's bust," he thought triumphantly. "Well, he's given me a better run for my money than I ever expected."

Within a few moments of Pound's departure, among the private correspondence which he had laid aside till business was dealt with, he found Susan's ardent, exclamatory letter about Dick's misfortunes; and this, too, ministered pleasantly to his sense of power. It did more than that. It gave him a twinge of excitement. Now that the main obstacle to his paternal interest (which had never included that of a grandfather) had been violently removed, he had every reason to hope for an early resumption of their former charming relationship. Though her Annunciation-pose embarrassed him and made him shy away from her, the image of Susan had never ceased to haunt him. Even in Newport and Cardiff, where a number of attractive women had made themselves pleasant to him as the man of the moment, his mind had often returned to the Susan he had known before that unfortunate complication. He felt tired and irked by the exacting world of big business; a man who had achieved so much in so short a time had a right to some snug little relaxation. The fact that her silly young fool of a husband had "let her down" by losing his job might have taught her to appreciate the society of an admitted paragon of success like himself more keenly than ever. If he gave Dick a job—and that was a simple matter—he would be able to assert a confident claim on Susan's gratitude, and become by gradual degrees a little less strictly fatherly. Generosity, like everything else, had its market value. As a business man he would use it shrewdly and strictly according to results. "Beggars can't be choosers," he reflected. "A little on account, to begin with, but not too much . . ."

It would be wiser, for instance, not to help the Penningtons in a hurry. "To-morrow will do," he thought; but when the day's work was over, the desire to see Susan restored to her former state grew stronger and stronger. Once more the old restlessness seized him, and with it that old, exultant illusion of youth within grasp. It was with a sensation of reckless bravado that he ordered the chauffeur to drive him to Ada Road, though the spice of adventure was slightly diluted by the prospect of Dick's being present.

Half-way up the hill on the way to Tilton he overtook Miss Maples, and snatching at the chance of inside information, offered her a lift. If he was going to see as much as he hoped to see of Susan, it would be wise to check gossip by becoming friendly with "Welbeck." Miss Maples was fluttered. "Mamma *will* be pleased!" she thought.

"I'm just popping in to see that poor little Pennington girl," Mr. Bulgin told her. "Rough luck her losing her baby, wasn't it?"

"Rough luck!" Miss Maples snorted. "Some people have no sense of duty in these days, Mr. Bulgin."

"I suppose it's knocked her about a good bit?" Mr. Bulgin suggested.

"She never looked better in her life than when I

saw her this morning" ("H'm, that's good," Mr.
Bulgin thought), "though I must say if *I* were in her
shoes I should hesitate to show my face."

"Come, come, Miss Maples," Mr. Bulgin smiled.
"Accidents will happen."

"Oh, I don't mean *that*," Miss Maples said archly.
"It's the furniture, I mean."

"The furniture?"

"Well, really, I hardly like to mention it. It's none
of my business. But if you live opposite you can't help
noticing, can you?—*or* hearing what's said."

"No, you couldn't," Mr. Bulgin agreed, though still
considerably mystified.

"The man was round making enquiries no less than
three times while they were away on their holidays.
And the fourth time, Mr. Bulgin, when he found this
young Pennington in, they had it out, as you might say,
on the front garden path. I heard him—with these
ears, Mr. Bulgin!—actually threaten to send a van
and take the whole lot away. Such a thing has never
happened before in Ada Road. I felt quite ashamed,
and so did mamma when I told her. She couldn't get
over it for days. She's so innocent, you know, it hurts
her to think of people like that living near. Not that
I have anything against them," Miss Maples added
charitably.

Mr. Bulgin whistled silently. "So *that's* it, is it?"
he thought. "I shall have to go easier than ever." Yet
even as these counsels of prudence rose in his mind he

couldn't forget that the more urgent the distress the greater was the opportunity. Having deposited Miss Maples at "Welbeck" and reluctantly postponed the privilege of a chat with mamma, Mr. Bulgin skirted the rockery and knocked at the door of "Chatsworth."

A sound of hard breathing and spade-work in the back garden raised his hopes of finding Susan alone in the house—very reasonably, in fact, for she had set Dick digging on purpose and had been waiting, all dressed up, for Mr. Bulgin's arrival since five o'clock.

"I knew you would come," she said quietly, with a confident smile, withdrawing herself a little, but not too much, from his customary embrace. Her lowered voice gave him a pleasant sensation of intimacy, and as she led the way to the living-room, where tea was laid for two, Mr. Bulgin was thankful to confirm Miss Maples' report that she looked none the worse. In the dusk of the hall, her allurement surpassed his memory of it. If her features and shape were firmer, her attitude towards him less impulsive, if she had lost, in a word, her old affectation of girlish innocence, the three months which had elapsed since last they met had surprisingly lessened the gap between his age and hers. They were meeting this evening, it seemed, on more equal terms. She was on the defensive with him; and the fact that she deemed this attitude necessary was in itself a compliment.

Susan gave him his tea in silence and always at a

distance which suited her make-up. Her manner, at once formal and familiar, exactly accorded with Mr. Bulgin's mood; repose was a quality that the tired business man found particularly grateful in women. Though she spoke of her stay in Shropshire, she alluded neither to her accident nor to the subject of her letter. Her reticence compelled Mr. Bulgin to broach it for himself.

"What's all this you wrote about Dick having lost his job?" he enquired at last.

"Only just what I told you. It's hard lines, isn't it?" she answered demurely.

"There are plenty of jobs going begging for men who are worth employing. What have you done about it? If you think my advice is worth having . . ."

That wasn't at all what she wanted. "And he knows that quite well," she thought; "but I mustn't appear to be too eager at first."

"Dick's done everything possible," she said. "He's tried Magnus and Levison's this morning."

"That's a good idea. I could put in a word with old Magnus," Mr. Bulgin suggested.

"I'm afraid that's no good," she told him. "The job isn't vacant any longer. First of all he tried Uncle George."

Mr. Bulgin's eyes brightened. An amusing idea had struck him.

"Well, surely old George can do something?"

"I'm afraid he can't I'm certain he would if he

could. He's been cutting down staff like everyone else. He's even got rid of Pound."

"Got rid of Pound? You don't say so!" Mr. Bulgin exclaimed. "Well, well, that sounds bad. Why, Pound must have been with Lorimers for twenty-five years! If he's got rid of Pound doesn't that make an opening for Dick?"

Susan shook her head. "Uncle George says he can't afford it. As a matter of fact, when I wrote you that letter I was wondering . . . I hate to ask favours— particularly of an old friend like yourself . . ." She paused, giving Mr. Bulgin the opportunity to play the game. But he wouldn't; though he leant forward and patted her hand his heavy face was a mask; so she had to go on: "Do you think you could possibly find Dick some temporary billet—just to tide over the awkward patch? He's keen to do anything and content with the tiniest salary."

Mr. Bulgin knitted his brows in profound meditation, prolonging the pleasure of keeping this desirable creature hanging on his words. Then he sighed. "Well, Susie, there's only one job I can possibly think of, and that's rather a ticklish matter, seeing who you are."

"He'll take it, whatever it is. I can promise you that."

Mr. Bulgin smiled slowly. "You'll see what I mean when I tell you. The job I'm speaking about is travelling for a company of mine called New British Nails.

The salary naturally won't be much for a beginner, thirty-five bob a week is the most we can offer; but if he makes good, mind . . . However, that's not the point," he went on. "My position is this. The New British Nail Company competes directly with your uncle, and if Dick came on to our staff old George might take exception."

"I'm sure he would understand," Susan said. "There's nothing personal. It's a friendly rivalry, isn't it?"

"Oh, perfectly friendly. In fact we asked your uncle to come in with us. He refused, unwisely, I think."

"And there's no other job you can give Dick? Couldn't you move someone else into this one and put Dick in his place?"

"I'm afraid not. We don't like changes. It's this or nothing."

"Then he'll take it," said Susan emphatically. "You've lifted such a weight from my mind. I knew you would when I wrote. I only wish to heaven I knew how to thank you."

There was no need, Mr. Bulgin said, to think about that. It was reward enough for him to find her looking so well and pretty after that trying time. "Send Dick down to the office to-morrow," he said, "and we'll fix up everything. And don't trouble your head about the future. Old friends are the best friends. Remember, I'm going to stand by you," he added, affectionately slipping his arm round her waist.

When they said good-bye in the hall he received a reward more tangible. Instead of presenting her cheek as usual, Susan astonished him by putting up her face in a way that appeared to offer her lips. She did this deliberately, coldly. It was just like putting a stamp on a legal document. Mr. Bulgin, on the other hand, was innocently transported by this spontaneity. That, according to one of his engineers who had been in New York superintending the shipping of the plant, was what girls did in America. A very commendable custom, Mr. Bulgin thought, and, in this case, dirt cheap at thirty-five shillings a week. "But she wouldn't have acted like that," he told himself, "three months ago. She's different from what she was. Now I wonder what's happened."

When Dick burst in hot from his garden he found Susan sitting alone in the dusk. She looked smooth, hard and elegant, and her cheeks were bright with a high colour that was partly her own.

"Why, Susie, how quiet you've been. I thought you'd gone out," he said. "I say, d'you know I've lifted all those potatoes? By Jove, I could do with some tea! You don't say you've finished without me?"

"The kettle's boiling; you can get it yourself," she told him. "By the way," she added casually, "I've got you a job."

III

If George Lorimer jumped at the pinprick of Mr. Bulgin's maliciously-phrased request for Pound's "character," he was wounded deeply when he heard that Dick Pennington had been taken on by New British Nails. Mr. Bulgin had made certain that his neat little joke should be widely appreciated by instructing his other travellers to spread it wherever they went. George Lorimer didn't mind ridicule—heaven knew he was used to it!—but he did think he might have been warned. Though Dick wasn't bound to consider his feelings, he would certainly have expected Susan to show more delicacy. It was Dick's delicacy, in point of fact, that nearly queered her pitch.

"I feel a bit rotten about this job," he told her. "To go in with the other side . . . well, it's hardly cricket."

"It's not cricket; it's business," she answered ruthlessly. "You gave Uncle George the first chance and he didn't take it."

"He couldn't, you know."

"Well, that isn't *our* fault, is it? If you want me to starve . . ."

When she put it like that there was nothing more to be said; and George Lorimer, visiting "Chatsworth," avoided the subject. His position was far too grave for him to worry his head over matters of punctilio

AA

and sentiment. He knew, by this time, that he was beaten; a few more rounds would finish it; and Dick Pennington's fist, from what he knew of him, was hardly likely to deal the knock-out blow. With a loyalty that was part of his amiable nature he carefully refrained from mentioning his grievance to Aunt Edna and continued to visit "Chatsworth" as though nothing unusual had happened. A sad little figure, for all his plump rosiness. He drifted in and out of the house like a restless ghost. His affection for Susan was his only solace in those days; but even he couldn't help noticing that Susan was changed in some way.

Captain Small also noticed the difference without understanding it. He had the instinct of a dog for scenting a change of emotional atmosphere in a house to which it is attached, and Susan's new attitude—toward life rather than toward himself—bewildered his small and faithful brain. Superficially Susan looked well enough; her beauty, if somewhat harder and more mature, was as compelling as ever; she was gay, she was kind; yet her kindness and gaiety were tinctured with impatience and ruthlessness—even at times with a hint of scorn. There were moments at "Chatsworth" in which the spirit of the house became suddenly charged and threatening, like a bright day menaced with thunder; when a gloom and silence descending made him feel that he wanted to bolt yelping into the open air, with his tail between his legs.

At such times he felt almost more sorry for Dick

than for Susan—her manner repelled compassion—
though he knew that this vague disquietude emanated
from her. He supposed, in a vague and masculine way,
that she was still fretting over the loss of her baby, and
felt awed and reverent in face of this secret sorrow.
This explanation of her mood would have given Susan
a moment of wry amusement, though it is probable
that Captain Small was far nearer the truth than she
suspected: that the change in her nature may well have
been due to fatigue, combined with disturbances in the
balance of internal secretions. She knew nothing about
those mysterious agents of destiny. She only knew that
there was something wrong with her world; that she
saw familiar people and objects with an odd apartness;
that the hues and delights of life had lost their sharp-
ness and savour; that the things she had once found
exciting now bored her, and that these unfortunately
included the society of Captain Small. "If he sees
that I am bored with him," she thought, "I'm terribly
sorry. But it just can't be helped."

In this listless state she found welcome stimulation
from the increasingly frequent visits of Mr. Bulgin.
For him Dick's employment at the works had simpli-
fied matters. He now knew the hours at which Dick
would be absent on his rounds or working overtime, and
no longer made any pretence of desiring to meet him.
It gave him an odd thrill to know that the woman who
had rejected his proposal was now as completely in his
power as her uncle, George Lorimer. He didn't abuse

that power, as he had done in George Lorimer's case, because he was admittedly, genuinely, foolishly in love with her.

Susan's kiss in the hall at "Chatsworth" had kindled a conflagration which crackled like wildfire through Mr. Bulgin's autumnal tinder. That his love-making didn't immediately take a more violent and practical form was less due to scruples of honour than to those habitually slow processes of mind that had proved themselves so sure in his business. To come to the point without due preparation was not part of his game. No more, though she recognized the danger, was it part of Susan's.

It was the risk of the situation, after all, that made it exciting and entertaining. She knew just where she stood, and played her cards with as much interest and as little emotion as one feels in a game of two-handed Patience. She knew that there was little likelihood of her ever falling in love with Mr. Bulgin, and even less of her yielding to him out of pity, caprice, or sheer convenience; but even an elderly admirer was better than none, and in the task of dealing with his leisurely tactics she acquired a certain tactical virtuosity of her own that gave her intense satisfaction and provoked the reluctant admiration of Mr. Bulgin. Susan Pennington was not, like George Lorimer, a "sitting bird." Not one of his business rivals was more adept than she at driving a bargain.

The small change of flattery, though she pocketed it

gratefully, had no purchasing power. She was, he re-marked, quite appropriately, as hard as nails. Her response to his more material benefits was calculated to the last farthing, and Mr. Bulgin, as a man of affairs, felt entirely at home in this adaptation of business methods to the tender passion. He was more able than most men to appreciate her commercial shrewd-ness, and even, for his own entertainment, encouraged her to display it at his expense. For he knew, well enough, that he held the best cards in his hand. At a pinch he could give Dick Pennington notice any day. It was just to remind her of this that he kept him on so small a salary.

In the meantime, between Mr. Bulgin's visits, life at "Chatsworth" seemed duller than ever. When the demands of the Bromwich Furnishing Emporium and Mr. Duke had been met there was nothing between them and starvation but Dick's weekly wage, which disappeared as soon as he brought it home on Satur-days. Susan had to abandon those "shopping" trips to North Bromwich that had been her principal recrea-tion in more prosperous times. Her "shopping" trips had not involved any great expenditure. They had consisted largely of gazing at clothes in the windows of the great women's stores and enquiring the prices of garments that she had no intention of buying, of enjoying an expensive tea at Battye's or a stall at the "pictures," and of returning to Tilton, flushed and triumphant, with a card of safety-pins or a skein of stocking-silk in a minute brown-paper packet. They involved, however, a certain invisible lapse of coin, and in these days she found it hard to scrape together enough for the bus-fare alone. The cheque-book, which only a year ago had tempted her to indulge each darling extravagance, was now of no greater use than a cancelled passport. She yearned for the noisy petrol-fouled streets of North Bromwich and the jostling crowds among which she felt so completely at home. If she had known that fate was going to use them so scurvily she would never have left Winsworth.

Thus immobilized, she was forced to fall back on the resources of Tilton. These were meagre enough in all conscience. The village Cinema Palace, as it was called, only opened at six o'clock on alternate nights, and the films it "featured" were generally worn and at least a year out of date. There was, however, a newly-opened chain drug-store with a lending-library attached to it; and since her visit to Chapel Green had destroyed her interest in "Chatsworth" as a vocation, she became an addict to the particular kind of literary drug it provided.

She read, on an average, at least one novel a day, and chose them on the advice of the "young lady" who had charge of the library, whose tastes, most fortunately, coincided with her own. There were "serious" novels one *must* read because they were "being read." There were modern memoirs of unthroned minor royalties and ladies of fashion, which showed one how human titled people were, revealing a world in which the same figures cropped up so often that Susan (and the library young lady) ended by knowing them by the Christian names with which they were invariably described. There were strong rustic novels about the "good red earth," with purple patches of landscape as a background for rude figures that might well have peopled a Freudian plumber's nightmares. There were "daring" novels that poured unceasingly, with seasonal variations, from the London publishers' vans.

A large number were written by women who should have been men and young men who were really women; but, homo- or hetero-sexual, their main pre-occupation was sexual promiscuity in one form or another. Polite living on paper, it seemed, consisted of nothing else; and Susan, baptized by total immersion in this stream every day for hours at a time, began to wonder if there wasn't something the matter with her. By these literary standards she seemed to have missed the whole point of life. Her reading convinced her that she knew nothing whatever about it, which was rather humiliating for one who had always thought of herself as a rebel. She had certainly never known the ecstasy of a "splendid sin" (there was a certain monotony in the sins that achieved this quali-fication), and as for poor Dick . . . !

It became apparent that both of them lived on a lower emotional plane than that of the average novel's

heroes and heroines, and though she herself was undoubtedly teeming with passionate possibilities, it
seemed extremely probable that Dick's were already
exhausted. Comparing him, physically and spiritually,
with the adventurous males of fiction, she was forced
to confess that she found him dull. His love—for he
was still quite obviously in love with her, poor dear!—
had so little variety. He took everything—including
her acquiescence—for granted. He had reached a
point at which finesse seemed to him no longer necessary—as witness certain lapses from personal delicacy
in private. In view of the unqualified intimacy of their
married life it might well be illogical to object to
these little lapses. But, logically or no, she did object
to them. Like so many other things about him, they
were destructive of Glamour.

Yes, Glamour . . . That was the word for what
she had missed when he met her at the station on her
return from Shropshire. In novels the decay of
Glamour, half-way through the story, was never fatal
to a heroine's happiness. It was always the harbinger,
indeed, of a new emotional efflorescence. In life, on
the other hand, and particularly in Tilton, it had no
such significance. Splendid sins never wandered into
the blind alley of Ada Road!

This new restlessness tormented her most in the
hours that she spent, for want of any other diversion,
in front of her mirror. Dick's eyes never rested on her
tangible form with such satisfaction as did her own on

its reflection. Her little mishap had done nothing to spoil her figure. Her throat and shoulders were as supple and smoothly moulded as before. Her face, though paler and harder—both with good reason— was still young and vivid; the scar left by the stone-cut was hardly visible now; she had beautiful teeth and lips, and hair and eyes that clamoured for admiration. All wasted. . . . ! Except in the case of Mr. Bulgin (who fell further beneath heroic standards than Dick) and of Captain Small, who, of course, didn't even count. Though she never seriously entertained the thought of being unfaithful to Dick (it was his nature, not his fault, that he happened to be blind) she wished—how she wished!—she could be in love with somebody.

As for Dick, it was part of the irony that so deeply affected her that he should be entirely unconscious of the thoughts that filled his wife's idle fiction-ridden brain. Susan was perfectly justified in saying that he took her for granted; but what he took for granted in her was not only the beauty of which he was so proud, but her honesty, her innocence, her modesty, her loyalty, her erudition (a great reader, my wife!) and her superior intelligence. It was this last, together with sheer rightness of instinct, that had solved within forty-eight hours the problem of unemployment that had baffled him for a fortnight. She had made Mr. Bulgin recognize those sterling qualities which had escaped the notice of all the other employers he had

approached. He owed her his job, and he owed it to
her to make good in it. He accepted the miserable
salary which Bulgin offered without complaining, as
that of an industrial esquire set to the trial of winning
his spurs. He put all his weight into the work. No
hours were too long for his pertinacious enthusiasm.
When he came home at night after journeys that
covered the uttermost limits of the district he would
fall asleep in his chair by the fire, happily conscious
of the presence of Susan, who sat reading on the
opposite side of it. He was often so tired that her going
to bed didn't rouse him. When he woke with a start
in the cold small hours—they had to be careful about
coal—he would find that her chair was empty, and
undress in the dark Sanitation and steal into the bedroom bare-footed for fear of waking her. Her languor
and lack of interest troubled him less than they might
have done, because now his hours of work were so
long and autumn afternoons so short that he scarcely
saw her by daylight, except when he carried her breakfast in on a tray. Of course she was still an invalid
and must be treated as such. Dr. Martock had said
that it might take some months to build her up again.

In this period of probation what mattered most was
that he should make himself indispensable to the New
British Nail Company and succeed in getting a rise of
salary before the winter set in, with its greater expenses for light and firing. He believed he had
achieved this object. If he hadn't it certainly wasn't

for the want of trying. His open manner and honest belief in the wares he sold made him popular as a salesman. The chief of the sales department had congratulated him more than once on his order-book. The benevolent Mr. Bulgin himself was bound, sooner or later, to hear of it.

One morning in late September—the date was significant, for it was on that day that the quarter's rent was due and, almost to his surprise, he had found himself able to pay it—Dick received a summons to await Mr. Bulgin's pleasure in the main office building before setting out on his round. He was so excited by the prospect that his first impulse was to send a message to Susan through Miss Maples, who had recently installed a telephone at "Welbeck." Miss Maples' manner, unfortunately, had become somewhat frosty since she had been done out of her baby, for babies were scarce that year. It would be wiser on the whole, he decided, to wait till the interview was over.

Mr. Bulgin had been slightly dissatisfied lately with the progress of affairs at "Chatsworth." However much he may admire an opponent's skill, no game is much fun to a player who always loses; and much as he appreciated Susan's business dexterity, her complete disregard of rules was beginning to tire him. She had bluffed long enough. It was high time for both of them to put their cards on the table. He had decided, in short, to give Susan Pennington a lesson that would not only demonstrate his power, but possibly pave the way for a better understanding.

Though he felt rather sore, Mr. Bulgin received Dick effusively.

"Take a seat, my boy, and make yourself comfortable," he said. "How's the wife getting on? I've been looking over the sales-manager's reports on your work, and I don't mind telling you—though it's against our rules to do so—that you've made a very good start. You've the makings of a first-rate salesman in you, my boy."

Dick glowed. "By Jove, he's going to offer me a rise," he thought.

"Now it seems to me," Mr. Bulgin continued paternally, "that this travelling job hardly gives you the scope to which you're entitled. The wrought-iron nail trade, as you know, is a decaying industry, and I think it would be better for all of us if you turned your attention elsewhere."

Dick blanched. "No, he's going to sack me. I wish he'd get on with it. Thank heaven I didn't telephone!"

"And so," Mr. Bulgin went on, "I've decided to transfer you to another branch of the business. I want you to learn all there is to be learned about tubes, right through, from the raw material to the finished article. Now you may or you may not know that the tube-making industry, as far as we are concerned, is on the eve of striking developments. The plant we've erected in South Wales is quite unique in this country. A fellow who gets his experience in our new works from the very beginning has a good three years' start on one who goes for it elsewhere. So that's my idea. I'm going to send you down there to-morrow with one of our engineers, and if you don't make the best of your chances, well, that'll be your fault, not mine. There's a through train to Newport leaves North Bromwich at two-thirty. That'll give you fair time to pack up your things for the journey."

Dick was staggered. His first duty, after all, was to thank Mr. Bulgin. He did so.

"Not at all, not at all," Mr. Bulgin smiled. "It's six for you and half a dozen for myself," he said—which was hardly correct arithmetically.

"I suppose, sir, this means we shall have to give up 'Chatsworth?' " Dick asked.

"Oh, no no. Give up 'Chatsworth'! Of course not. This is merely a temporary arrangement. As I've said, I'm sending you there to learn about tubes. You're to have what some people call an intensive training. When you've seen how the new rolling-mills and hydraulic presses work and picked up a general idea of the latest methods I shall bring you back here and put you through the finishing shops. You won't be away for more than three months at the outside."

Dick pondered. "You see, sir, I have to think about everything. It's expensive living in lodgings, and on my present salary . . ."

"Don't worry about that," Mr. Bulgin broke in magnificently. "I've been through it myself. You can't teach me anything. From to-morrow we raise your screw to two pounds ten."

Dick made rapid calculations. "That's very generous," he said. "But counting in Susan as well, it will be a bit tight."

"Counting Susan as well? My dear Pennington, what are you dreaming of? You'll be up to your eyes in work from dawn to sunset. You're a man; you can rough it of course; but a woman is different. You can't plank down a girl like Susan alone in a Welsh mining village," he continued indignantly, "without a soul who speaks her own language within ten miles! It isn't as if Pandypool were a health resort either. In her present state it would be no better than a crime to take her there."

"She'll want to come with me, you know," Dick told him anxiously. "Except for that month in Shropshire we've never been separated."

Mr. Bulgin smiled wisely. "Now listen to me, young man. It may strike you as heartless, but, mind you, I'm speaking the truth when I tell you that being too much together's a great mistake. Oh yes, you may smile; but I've seen it again and again. What's three months, after all? I'll try to slip up this evening and make Susan see sense. Don't you worry about Susan, my boy. I'll look after *her*," Mr. Bulgin chuckled.

IV

It was, of course, Dick told himself, a marvellous opportunity, the beginning of a career that might lead to incalculable pinnacles of success; but, for all his excitement, the prospect of leaving Susan subdued him. He would have to break the news to her that evening somehow or other. As luck would have it he found Captain Small at "Chatsworth," and the presence of a friendly third person made this task easier. Susan took his announcement with a composure that might have shocked him if he hadn't attributed it to her courage and self-restraint.

"Why, how wonderful! It might mean almost anything, Dick," she told him bravely.

(She had, secretly, a shrewd idea of what it did mean.)

"Yes, by Jove, old man," Captain Small enthusiastically agreed. "Upon my soul it looks to me like the chance of a lifetime. Only wish I was younger and had it myself and the brains to tackle it with! You'll be a director of Bulgins' before you've finished. That old chap's got his eye on you; you take my word for it!"

"Yes, I know. That's all very well," Dick answered ruefully. "It would be quite different if Susie were coming with me. But three months is a deuce of a long time."

He kissed her tenderly. She smiled: "Why, Dick, darling, it'll be over in no time."

"But I can't bear leaving you alone, Susie."

"Your career comes first, Dick."

"Such splendid courage, such sublime unselfishness! What a marvel she is," Dick thought, "and how lucky I am!"

"Mrs. Pennington's right, old man," Captain Small declared with sagacity. "It's astonishing how time slips by. Why, the Armistice seems like yesterday, and it was nearly twelve years ago. Don't you worry your head, old fellow. I'll look after *her*." He hoisted himself up from his chair and tactfully withdrew. "If this is old Dick's last night," he said, "you two are best left to yourselves; you'll have lashings of things to talk about. No, don't move, old man," he protested, "I can find my way out. And don't you forget, your missus is perfectly safe while Joe Small's on the map."

As Small limped away Dick relapsed into the state of misery from which their excited talk had temporarily rescued him. He knew how wretched and disorientated he had felt when Susan was away for three weeks; the thought of three months without her was devastating. Not merely for his own sake. A man, after all, had his work to distract his mind. He was prepared to make the best of this job and "pig it" cheerfully in lodgings at Pandypool; but for Susan this new separation would not only be longer, but much more difficult than the other. At Chapel Green she had had the advantage of Aunt Judith's care and society; alone at "Chatsworth" for three long months she would hardly have a soul to talk to. It was a pity, he thought, that she had taken such a dislike to Miss Maples and had not made friends with the other women in Ada Road. This loneliness was one of the penalties that must be paid for the privilege of an ideal marriage like theirs, in which each was so utterly dependent on the other's company. When he imagined Susan taking her solitary meals and sitting alone through the long winter evenings, so brave and small and pathetic in the half-empty house, he could hardly bear it.

In the meantime he could only aspire to emulate her courage, to be cheerful and to make the most of the few poignant hours that remained. He shadowed her everywhere that evening like an anxious ghost; wherever she went he was near her, touching her, kissing her; and Susan, who thought she had passed beyond all feeling, was strangely moved by an anxiety which she knew was more for her than for himself; so that now, when she looked at Dick, her mind underwent a quick revulsion in his favour. He was no longer merely the underpaid, overworked, shabby suburban husband. The emotion of parting stripped away from him those trappings of sordid circumstance, and beneath them she rediscovered a Dick whom she had almost forgotten, the lover in whose arms she had

BB

trembled long ago at Brinton.

It was oddly exciting to find herself moved so profoundly. As she yielded herself to this astonishing mood, remorse for the ungenerous, unspoken thoughts of the last few months reinforced its poignancy. The swing of the pendulum in the opposite direction gave to the very aspects which she had despised and resented in him a new significance; his slowness became dignified as patience, his clumsiness as strength, his lack of understanding as simplicity, his apparent neglect of her charms as a subtle expression of faith—all qualities to which she herself had no pretensions. After all, she had never known anyone who was so radically sound and reliable and, yes, so good.

When supper was finished they sat together on Mr. Bellis's Chesterfield, hand in hand, Susan's head on his shoulder and her cheek against his. They stayed there in silence, and the silence, for Susan, was not invaded that evening by restless and vague aspirations or discontents, but possessed by a calm satisfaction of spirit proceeding, as in the old, careless days, from Dick's physical nearness. Although she hated the thought of his leaving her and the hours were the last they would spend together, those moments were flooded with a rich content resembling that of an evening in early autumn when birds sing timidly and the still air seems drenched with gold. Yet later, when the whitening embers warned them that it was time for bed, the influence that enveloped them was nearer to spring than to autumn. A quicker fire awoke in their eyes and kindled their blood. When she fell asleep that night it seemed, after all, that Glamour had not utterly fled.

Next morning they talked, like lovers, of trivial things, each desiring to convince the other that their parting was a small thing compared with the benefits that might spring from it. They walked arm-in-arm round the garden and over the field. Dew whitened the grass and frosted the gossamers like rime. Dick pushed through the sharp-spurred brambles and picked her blackberries and stole quick kisses from cool, empurpled lips. Though the sky was pale and cold, though the hedges were plumed with clematis and bright with the coralline berries of hips and haws, Susan's heart still dwelt under a strange illusion of spring. It was still possessed by mingled hope and gratitude when she waved good-bye to Dick at the Tilton cross-roads and returned in meditative slowness to Ada Road. As she re-entered "Chatsworth" and briskly set about the household tasks she had neglected, for his sake, that morning, her thoughts followed Dick on his journey into North Bromwich with unusual tenderness. She felt humble, confident, and, oddly enough, extremely virtuous.

At that moment Mr. Bulgin, in his office, had none of those feelings. As he glanced at the clock which the Midland Metallurgical Association had presented to him as a memento of his presidency, he reflected

that Dick Pennington's train had just left North
Bromwich for South Wales. Though the fact that
that foolish young man was now well out of his way
gave him pride in his own astuteness, he felt neither
confident nor virtuous. He continued to glance at the
clock all afternoon, and found it difficult to concentrate on important matters of business. The job he
was about to tackle demanded greater delicacy than any
commercial enterprise. As the clock struck five he
scandalized his typist by abruptly abandoning a half-
written letter, dismissed her, washed his hands, put a
dab of lavender-water on a clean pocket-handkerchief,
and ordered the car round at once to drive him to
"Chatsworth."

On his way up the hill that day he felt far more
nervous than he had been, for example, on the day
of his wedding. Though his heart, as he told himself,
was still that of a boy, his face and figure, revealed in
a mirror which he furtively extracted from a pocket
in the car, looked more definitely mature than usual.
His mind was all caution. It was this that made him
direct his chauffeur to stop first at the gate of "Welbeck" and to cover his movements by frankly explaining them to old Mrs. Maples.

"While I'm up here," he told her, when he had
listened politely to her reminiscences for half an hour,
"I think I might just as well step over and have a
word with that young Mrs. Pennington. Her uncle,
George Lorimer, you know, is one of my oldest

friends, and I'm interested in her husband, too. As a matter of fact I've just packed him off to our new works in Wales to learn the business, and I expect Mrs. Pennington will be feeling a bit lonely and down in the mouth."

Mr. Bulgin's heart thudded like the old-fashioned water-hammers of his childhood when he knocked at the door of "Chatsworth"; but from the moment that Susan opened it he knew by instinct that nothing was going to work out according to plan. It was not that he found her less lovely or less desirable than he had imagined. She was, on the contrary, physically trans-figured by the afterglow of last night's renewal of passion. Her face was softened and tender with a gentle moonlight radiance. She looked frail and wraithlike in the dusk, and as a wraith intangible. In place of the hard and calculating opponent with whom he had prepared himself to match his skill in driving a final bargain, he found himself faced by a dis-embodied spirit, insensitive to his methods and as elusive of capture as a luminous will-o'-the-wisp. It would be futile, he knew, to attempt to go floundering after her; even if he caught her there was nothing on which his clumsy hands could close. There was none of the arch vivacity to which he was accustomed. She made no attempt to flirt with him. Serenely, dis-tantly wrapped in an impenetrable dream, she spoke seldom, and, when she did speak, mostly of Dick and of Mr. Bulgin's kindness in letting him enter the more important branch of the business.

"What's this new game?" Mr. Bulgin asked himself impatiently. "Is she trying to make me jealous at this time of the day by pretending to be in love with him?"

Whatever her purpose might be, the result was the same. That evening she was as unapproachable as any flame-girdled Brünnehilde, and Mr. Bulgin, though physically equipped for the part of a *Helden-tenor,* was, temperamentally, no Siegfried.

By the end of a week of this nonsense his bewilderment gave way to a smarting conviction that Susan was making a fool of him. If only for the sake of his self-respect he would have to assert himself and teach her a lesson. He drove up to "Chatsworth" determined to call her bluff, for he declined to believe that her attitude was anything else. If he trembled as he knocked at the door that evening it was not so much with passion as with righteous indignation. It filled him with anger to find her at the same old game; she was full of an enthusiastic letter which she had received from Dick by the morning's post, and even insisted on reading him extracts from it, with coy suppressions of the endearments with which it was sprinkled. He sat glowering at her, chewing the cud of resentment, with the spindly tea-table between them. There were moments in which he felt like kicking the whole lot to smithereens.

"Isn't that splendid?" she cried, when she had

finished her reading. "He's so keen about everything!"

Mr. Bulgin did not answer. He pushed back his chair and rose to his feet. The blood was in his head. He stood there, heavily impending, like a bull that snorts and lashes its tail, and when, at last, he spoke, his voice had an ugly snarl in it.

"Look here, Susie," he said, "I'm just about fed up with this."

She gazed at him innocently, with the smile checked on her lips.

"With . . . What do you mean?" she asked.

"You know perfectly well what I mean. You're making a fool of me. And I've had enough. Understand?"

"I don't even know what you're talking about," she said with a nervous laugh.

That laugh incensed Mr. Bulgin beyond the limits of control. "You know what I'm talking about as well as I do," he went on harshly. "About you and me!"

"Mr. Bulgin!"

"Oh, cut that out. Let's get down to business. Do you think that I want to hear all this damned blither of Pennington's? You needn't pretend you don't know why I sent him to Pandypool. You're too fond of play-acting; that's what's the matter with you. I've no use for that stuff. I know what I want, and I'm going to have what I've paid for. No nonsense! See?"

"Mr. Bulgin . . . you must be mad!"

"Ay, that's it," Mr. Bulgin panted. He lurched heavily toward her; his clumsy foot caught in the leg of the folding tea-table and brought the tray down with a crash of broken crockery. This violence suited his temper. Mr. Bulgin laughed loudly. "That's all right," he cried, "I'll buy you some more. Leave those damned things alone, lass."

Susan was down on her knees collecting the shattered fragments. Mr. Bulgin stooped and picked her up bodily in his arms. There was no pretence of the paternal in his attitude now. He was a strong man taking violent possession of what had been unreasonably denied him. Let her struggle! He'd teach her!

She did not struggle at all. "Ah, so that's what you wanted, is it?" he thought triumphantly. He covered her face and neck with voracious kisses, his blunt hands had their way with her; yet, in the midst of this rapturous loosening of such long repressions, a vague disquietude seized him. Neither response nor resistance. . . . This was not as it should be, nor in the least as he had imagined it. He might just as well have been crushing a corpse in his arms. The passionate wind that had swept him dropped and left him with flapping canvas. He released her and stepped back, breathing heavily, like a bull that stands puzzled over the body of a man feigning death.

"What's up with you, Susie?" he panted. "I've not hurt you, I hope?"

Susan stood exactly where he had left her. Her coolness made a strange contrast with his hot confusion. She was pale, and her eyes were enormous, though not with fright. She spoke not a word, but began methodically to rearrange the neck of her torn blouse and comb back her hair with her fingers. This silence was as disconcerting as her former passivity.

"I've not hurt you, I hope," Mr. Bulgin lamely repeated. "You must make allowances when a man feels as strongly as I do and has been kept waiting so long."

Susan stooped once again to pick up the broken crockery. Her action irritated him.

"Leave that stuff where it is," he said angrily. "Come here and sit down and be friendly."

He caught at her arm. She turned and faced him calmly.

"I think you had better go," was all she said; then she turned away again.

"Better go? I like that!" was all Mr. Bulgin could say. He stumped round the little room to let off steam and try to recover his self-possession and dignity; the first was relatively easy, but the second impossible. Indignation or violence, evidently, wouldn't help him. He sat down heavily on the sofa and addressed her in the friendly tones he would have used to a child or a dog.

"So I've frightened you, have I, Susie?" he said with a chuckle. "Well, I'm sorry for that. No offence.

My feelings must have got the better of me. I wouldn't harm a hair of your head. Come on, be sensible!"

Susan picked up the tray of fragments and carried it into the kitchen without even looking at him. Mr. Bulgin, puzzled, but still optimistic, awaited her return. Women were curious creatures; he knew much less about them than he might have done; but he had a strong feeling that, in the end, they invariably came to heel. "She's saving her face, that's all," he reassured himself.

Two minutes passed, and still she did not return. "She's sulking," he thought. "I suppose she expects me to follow and eat humble pie and make it up with her. Well, well, let her have her own way," he reflected charitably. He got up and called her name, then followed her into the kitchen. It was dark and smelt faintly of washing-up; but she was not there. A new idea seized him, an idea that made his blood tingle. He opened the bedroom door and switched on the light. That, also, was empty. The door of the bathroom stood wide. Inside it the cistern dripped dolefully. As a last resource he approached the Baronial dining-room. Susan was standing there in the window as still as a statue.

"Why, here you are," he said friendlily. "What's up with you, lass? Why won't you speak to me?"

At last she did speak. "I've told you already," she said; "you'd better go."

"And is *that* all you've got to say?"

She nodded her head.

"I suppose you know what this means?" Mr. Bulgin said hotly.

As she did not answer, he thought it as well to explain. "You realize you've led me on. You can't deny that, now! Remember you're not the only one who can give the sack!" he went on threateningly. "I can fire young Pennington at five minutes' notice and chuck him back on the streets where he was when you got round me. He can go there and join that other damned fool, your uncle. You think what you're doing! You don't know which side your bread's buttered on; that's the trouble with you. If I go now, I go for good. Understand that plainly!"

Susan threw out her hands in a gesture of despair. "I do understand," she said.

"Oh, you *do* understand," Mr. Bulgin repeated bitterly. "Well, in that case I'm off. If you think you can whistle me round again you're badly mistaken. I'm not that sort. I may be made a fool of once, but once is enough. Got that clear?"

Once again Susan answered nothing. Mr. Bulgin turned and went blundering down the passage. He was nearly beside himself now with rage and humiliation. If he hadn't been younger than his arteries he might easily have burst one, and his sense of frustration and wounded dignity was not diminished when he heard the key turned in the door that he had slammed behind him.

CHAPTER X

GRAND MIDLAND

I

At the moment when she locked the front door behind Mr. Bulgin's back a consciousness of victorious virtue filled Susan's mind. A few hours later, as the wave of excitement gradually subsided, she began to question the rightness of the method with which she had defended what books called her "honour." Might she not, for example, have given back violence for violence? Young women in old-fashioned novels frequently smacked men's faces. That proceeding, however, smacked of vulgarity, and if she prided herself on anything it was on being "refined." Supposing, again, she had dealt with the situation humorously. Her reading of recent fiction would have enabled her to carry this off quite well; but humour—particularly in matters of that kind—was not in Mr. Bulgin's style, and it was doubtful if he would have been able to keep up his end in a smart modern dialogue. She might even, now that she had time to think of it, have treated his infamous advances with a sad, wise, seriousness, paying due respect to the overwhelming power of the passion that had risen to wreck their charming platonic relationship, and persuading Mr. Bulgin's better self to continue being a brother (or father) to her. That course, she decided, would have wounded his pride less deeply. By a judicious mingling of shocked astonishment and kindness she might have dangled the carrot before the donkey's nose indefinitely, instead of awakening that desire for revenge which was the natural consequence of her contemptuous silence.

The trouble with this plan was that she hadn't really been shocked in the least. On the contrary, she had been thrilled beyond measure by this practical proof of the power of her physical attractions, about which, of late, she had felt a little in doubt. That Mr. Bulgin, though no Adonis, should for her sake have broken through a fifty years' growth of convention and smashed china like any mad bull, was an obvious, if not exactly a delicate, compliment. What wasn't a compliment was the fact that he had apparently taken it for granted that she would succumb to such summary treatment. It was this that had wounded her pride and, unfortunately, made her wound his.

That lonely evening she would have given anything to have been able to tell the whole story to an audience which would appreciate the creditable part she had played in it. At the moment she could think of nobody but Captain Small; but knowing Captain Small as she did, she shrank from telling him; he might feel it his military duty to thrash Mr. Bulgin and create a public scandal. It was a pity, she thought, that, through no fault of her own, she had estranged Miss Maples; though, on second thoughts, it seemed probable that Miss Maples would have taken Mr. Bulgin's side and laid all the blame upon her. At last, out of the sheer necessity of expressing herself, she decided to write to Dick.

It was a very long letter; it took her three hours to write and made excellent reading. It drew, to begin with, a touching picture of the desolation of "Chatsworth" without him—of that huge empty house with all its pitiful reminders of past happiness; of herself, diminished in scale to give the right value, living innocently engrossed in the domestic tasks that she loved— (*I was darning a pair of your socks, darling*)—and thinking, with innocent, serene expectancy, of nothing but him: a Penelope for constancy, a Lucrece for placid devotion. Then, enter suddenly, unexpectedly, Mr. Bulgin. (*I thought he was going to tell me good news of you, Dick!*) Mr. Bulgin's physical scale was naturally exaggerated to a degree that would have flattered him; but the finesse with which he handled the scene was Susan's, with an acknowledged debt to Scarpia in *Tosca.* Nothing so crude as the actual assault was permitted to appear; it would be impolitic to dwell on physical details that showed her, even for a moment, in Mr. Bulgin's power: far better depict Mr. Bulgin as an evil, sinister figure, presenting cynically—(*I felt myself going pale, Dick*)—the horns of his dastardly dilemma: Dick's job or her virtue. By the device of preserving an appropriate distance—(*I was careful, of course, to keep the sofa between me and him*)—she was able to achieve a page of impassioned dialogue that, when she re-read it, sounded rather too oratorical —(*but of course I can't possibly remember it word for word*)—culminating in an exit of muttered threats from Mr. Bulgin, completely cowed, though still venomous, and a curtain of virtue, transfigured, tried, but triumphant, for the leading lady. (*As I heard him go muttering down the path I turned the key in the lock. Then I went and sat down on the sofa, where you always sit, darling, and cried like a child.*)

The turning of the front-door key was the only strictly veracious incident in Susan's letter; but her imagination became so active in dramatizing herself on paper that, by the time she had finished, she believed every word she had written to be true. If she hadn't actually behaved or spoken in the way she described it was only because she had been unfairly deprived of the opportunity of thorough rehearsal. The more often she read through her letter the more fully convinced she became of the fineness of her own behaviour. She perused it three times, and felt much more interesting for doing so. Then she tore it to pieces; for, as she prudently reflected, if Dick read it he would be certain to rush home to Tilton in a fury, and there was always the possibility that Mr. Bulgin might feel so ashamed as to shrink from putting his threat of dismissing Dick into action. A few days would show which way the cat was going to jump. Of course if Dick *did* get the sack, she could easily explain the reason, having improved on her story in the interval. Or perhaps it might be even wiser not to explain it at all.

For a week, with each post, she expected to hear the worst. Dick wrote to her every day before breakfast and when he came home to his "digs" at night. He even wrote in his dinner-hour at the works, as was proved by the smudges of coal-dust and oil on the envelopes. Dick had never, he confessed, been "much of a hand" at writing; the endearments with which his pages were sprinkled were so banal and unvaried that Susan ended by taking them for read. He wrote of his work, however, with a certain passion. His brain had always concealed a thwarted mechanical bent, and a first-hand acquaintance with Mr. Bulgin's monstrous new plant made him write almost lyrically of things such as cams and valves and eccentrics. This technical jargon bored Susan and made her vaguely jealous. "He's far more excited," she thought, "about his rotten old machines than he's ever been about *me*."

The main satisfaction these letters gave her arose from a secret sense of dramatic irony. Dick continued to insist on his gratitude to Mr. Bulgin for the wonderful chance he had given him. *If you ever see him,* he wrote, *I hope you'll let him know how keen I am, and how much I appreciate everything.* "If I ever see *him!*" Susan thought, with supreme satisfaction. "If only Dick knew!"

Yet a week went by, and then another week, and still the blow did not fall. Mr. Bulgin, it seemed, had decided to hold his hand. This puzzled Susan. She could only explain the abstention in a manner flattering to herself. Was it possible, she wondered, that his passion was sufficiently strong to have made him swallow her insults—that the white flame of her fidelity had melted away the dross in his nature and left nothing but the heart of gold to which Dick's letters frequently alluded? "I expect," she thought, "he's waiting till he can pluck up courage to come here and apologize." It was fortunate that Mr. Bulgin's diffidence gave her time to practise the manner in which she would receive that apology and, finally, forgive him.

But her preparations were wasted. Mr. Bulgin neither gave Dick the sack nor came in a white sheet to "Chatsworth." After taking much thought he had formed a new theory of the situation. There were only two ways of explaining Susan's rejection of his advances: the first (and this, from what he had recently observed, seemed improbable) was that she still loved her husband; the second, and more likely, suggested that she was in love with some other young man. In either alternative he stood to gain by keeping Dick Pennington at Pandypool for the present. If she had a lover, a casual hint dropped to his new friend Miss Maples to keep an eye open for visitors would soon provide him with evidence sufficient to destroy Susan's pretences of faithfulness and put her in his power. If she was still in love with her husband, this prolonged separation would mortify her; she would learn, incidentally, that life on a subsistence salary unaugmented by the generosities of a faithful admirer was no bed of roses. In either event, it pleased him to think, he had secured the whip-hand and could continue to keep it at an extremely moderate cost.

It gave Susan a triumphant thrill of expectancy when, one afternoon, she saw Mr. Bulgin's Rolls draw up at the gate of "Welbeck"; but the scene for which she instantly prepared herself did not take place. After exchanging compliments with Miss Maples' mamma, Mr. Bulgin addressed himself to the virgin herself.

"I want you to do me a favour, Miss Maples," he said. "It's about those young Penningtons. I think I told you before, I'm interested in them."

"Most generously interested," Miss Maples agreed. "I only trust they'll prove worthy of your interest," she added gloomily.

"Well, the young man's all right; we needn't worry about *him*," Mr. Bulgin said generously. "But the wife . . ." He hesitated. Miss Maples wagged her head understandingly. "Ah, I see that you have the same fears as myself," Mr. Bulgin went on. "A trifle inclined to be gay? Is that what you mean? Well, to tell you the truth I'm sorry to confess that's exactly my feeling. A young woman of her sort, not bad-looking—though of course that's a matter of taste —is bound to attract admirers when her husband's away. Now I don't want that poor young man's life to be wrecked by anything of that kind, so I thought I'd just ask you to keep a friendly eye on her. Fore-warned is forearmed, don't forget; and if you notice anything out of the ordinary I shall take it as a per-sonal favour if you'll drop me the hint. In that case I might feel it my duty to bring young Pennington home again. Just a word on the 'phone will be ample. I'm sure I can count on you."

Mr. Bulgin's visit left a deep impression on "Wel-beck." "There are not many employers," Mrs. Maples proudly maintained, "who take such a personal interest in their employees in these days. It's quite like old times and in the Bulgin tradition. John Bulgin is his father's son, and a really good man."

Miss Maples agreed. Mr. Bulgin's commission gave her a new object in life. Her flagging interest in what "went on" at "Chatsworth" kept her glued to the window long after she had put her mamma to bed, yet the only fish that swam into her net was poor Cap-tain Small. She reported his visits dutifully; but though Mr. Bulgin congratulated her on her watch-fulness the catch disappointed him. The way in which

Susan and Dick together had spoken of Small convinced him that here, at least, he had no grounds for suspicion. Fate was working against him in another way that he had not expected. The engineer's reports from South Wales informed him that Dick Pennington was showing intelligence as well as enthusiasm, and already proving a useful member of his staff, with a particular talent for handling the human material of labour. In a way he was disappointed; he much preferred to look upon Dick as a fool; in another it pleased him to think that he was getting unexpected value for money.

As for Susan, the lonely hand-to-mouth existence at "Chatsworth," its dull tenor not even enlivened by the excitement of Mr. Bulgin's visits—to say nothing of his presents—was pretty awful. George Lorimer, fathoms deep in his own embarrassments, hardly ever approached her; on the occasion of his last visit he had only just managed to escape without bursting into tears. Captain Small came to see her, of course, as Miss Maples reported; but if only Miss Maples had known how Captain Small bored Susan now—with his military cheerfulness, his out-of-date catchwords, and the air of dog-like devotion with which he hung round her—she would not even have troubled to send Mr. Bulgin her report.

With every week that went by Dick seemed somehow more distant. Susan no longer listened for the postman's knock with eagerness. She received Dick's letters perfunctorily. Their stereotyped endearments grew staler, their technical details of engineering more wearisome. Even that sudden and brief re-blooming of passion which had marked their night of parting became unreal in retrospect. It was the continuing illusion left by that odd experience that had armed her against Mr. Bulgin. "Supposing," she thought sometimes, "I had let Mr. Bulgin make love to me?" By no stretch of imagination could she see herself doing that. "But supposing," she asked herself again, "it had not been Mr. Bulgin, but somebody young and good-looking by whom I was really attracted?"

In that shape she found the question far more difficult to answer with confidence, though the lines on which it might have been answered were suggested by many of the library novels through which, vicariously, she enjoyed the richer emotional experience denied to her in real life. The grey days grew so short and the evenings so long that she found herself reading as many as ten a week. There was no more temptation to go for long walks alone; for October fell wet, and the view from their bedroom window was so obscured by fuliginous fog that the beckoning hills were rarely visible.

There were other, and even stronger reasons for staying indoors. From motives of economy she had reluctantly let her hair grow, and looked a "sight"; in addition to this, the autumn fashions decreed that skirts be worn longer. This command gave her real

distress. To buy new clothes while the monthly instalment on the furniture remained unpaid was out of
the question; and the hems of the skirts she possessed
had been made with such economy of material that
there was none to let down. As a woman who prided
herself on being up-to-date, Susan couldn't possibly
appear with visible knees. It was true that, except in
Tilton, they wouldn't matter so much; but, wherever
she went, Ada Road would have the privilege of seeing them first. This grave disability preyed on her
mind so hungrily that she wrote an impulsive,
querulous letter to Dick, begging him to let her sell
the furniture for what it would fetch and join him in
Pandypool.

His reply was typically cautious. *We can't sell anything,* he wrote, *unless everything's paid for. Of
course I should die with joy at having you here, but
the future seems so uncertain. It sometimes looks as
if they might give me a permanent job here, but they
refuse when I ask them to say anything definite, and
I simply daren't face the risk and expense of getting
you down here . . .* "The risk!" she reflected bitterly
as she read. "How like him that is! If he really
wanted me to come, he wouldn't consider it! What
about the risk of leaving me here?" *You ought to
have money in hand,* he went on to remind her, *Uncle
George's quarterly payment was due at the end of last
month. I suppose you've put it in the bank? I could
do with a couple of pounds for myself, by the way.*

"What a fool I am!" she thought. It showed how dull her mind was becoming that this reminder should have been necessary. She wrote a sharp little note to George Lorimer demanding her due. By return he sent her three five-pound notes and profuse apologies. The remainder should follow, he promised, within a few days, when the interest-vouchers arrived.

The possession of a sum which, in those days, seemed so enormous, completely turned Susan's head. She set out at once for North Bromwich; had her hair cut and permanently waved; bought a reach-me-down coat and a tailor-made costume of fashionable colour and cut, together with a variety of materials with which to remodel the black lace dress; lunched greedily at Battye's, damning expense, and went on to the *Futurist*, which she entered at the moment when her particular idol, Miss Greta Garbo, lay locked in the arms of a Cosmopolitan Adventurer, who obviously knew a great deal more about making love than Dick.

It was with a peculiarly thrilling sensation of having regained, after long months of exile, her spiritual home, that Susan inhaled the mingled odours of cigarette-smoke, atomized jasmine, and the Great Middle Class. The mere feeling of the plush that covered the arms of her *fauteuil* aroused delicious memories. When the Wurlitzer organ ascended from the pit in which, like some monstrous beast, it had been confined, and rainbow spot-lights played on the well-oiled head of its diminutive keeper; when the bourdon groaned and the vox-humana quivered with a super-human, a sheerly angelic intensity, she recognized this for the veritable music of the stars.

On this occasion passion "bloomed like a sinister orchid," not in Java, but in Alaska (or the nearest approach to it that could be contrived in Hollywood); but the fall of temperature made no difference to its florescence or its frustrated fruition; it bloomed just the same—which seemed to prove that climate had nothing to do with it—and the thunderstorm which had ruined Miss Garbo's Parisian creation in Java pursued that unfortunate young woman with equal malevolence and a similar organ-accompaniment to the frozen North. Once more, on the very brink of sinning magnificently, that wan beauty's virtue was saved by a Clean Young American Husband; once more the dastardly (but so handsome!) Cosmopolitan was foiled and gave startling evidence of his "better self." When the lights flashed out again Susan gave a sigh of relief and extreme contentment. If only she lived in Alaska (or Java) and not in Tilton!

That life in North Bromwich could be adventurous was proved, a moment later, by the young man who sat beside her proffering his cigarette-case. While the lights were down Susan had wondered what this shadowy neighbour looked like; but the sudden illumination had revealed him as a meaner version of Dick —not remotely resembling either the Cosmopolitan Adventurer or the Clean Young American Husband who were competing, at the moment, for her imagination's approval. She declined the cigarette he offered with what she herself thought of as "*hauteur*"; then, as soon as the darkness of the next film concealed her short skirt, moved on to the other end of the row.

As she sat there, mildly fluttered and pluming herself on the correctness of her reaction to this mild provocation, she became aware of a voice most appropriate to these surroundings. There was no mistaking that honeyed, languid, richly sensuous drawl. She knew at once that its owner was Muriel O'Brien, and sat listening, close in her seat, like a hare in its form. Muriel must have been deeply engrossed in her companion not to have noticed her approach; and Susan thanked heaven that she was, for the deficiencies of the short skirt would not have escaped her. She leant forward in her seat to hide it, always listening, though Muriel's low voice was so confidential that, near as she was, Susan could only catch a word here and there. Muriel's companion chuckled a good deal—she had the gift of exploiting her naïveté for male entertainment—and spoke mainly in monosyllables; but his voice was pleasant, musical, and that of an educated man. In the back of her mind she guessed it was Harry Levison.

The comic animal whose misadventure now occupied the screen was of far less interest to her than the couple behind, and she found herself wondering what Harry Levison was really like. Superficially, indeed, he closely resembled the Cosmopolitan Adventurer of the last picture. As a lover, no doubt, he would be equally alluring and dangerous. She began to feel faintly envious of Muriel. What fun to be taken to the pictures by a man of that type, so well dressed, so physically sleek, so smoothly mannered, so humorously alert to adjust himself to feminine whims and so richly equipped with the means to gratify them! As Muriel had often told her, Harry Levison understood women, and that made things so easy. If Dick lived to be a hundred he would never understand the least thing about them. He was solidly, bluntly male in body and mind; and solidity, at that moment, was a quality by which she was bored.

Not only in men, but in women—particularly in herself. During the last eighteen months she had submitted, with conscientious difficulty, to Dick's austere standards: and where had it brought her? To the meagre suburban isolation of Tilton, in a skirt quite five inches too short; to a life in which her emotions languished like a sick pot-plant; to an existence so subdued and devoid of incident that a lonely visit to the pictures like this marked a red-letter day! If she had been less conscientious, more selfish, she might have had a good time, like Muriel; and nobody, as far as she could see, would have been any the worse for it.

Muriel, certainly, wasn't. As Susan sat there, solemn and envious, while the audience roared at the comic animal's pranks, her liking for Muriel's easy company, which she had repressed for Dick's sake, reasserted itself. Muriel might be idle and mercenary, unscrupulous and sensual, but what good company she was, and what fun they had had together! There was nobody like Muriel for getting rid of the blues. No qualms of conscience shadowed those limpid eyes; no predicament was so grave but a careless laugh could evade it. And the proof of the pudding was in the eating. Muriel O'Brien enjoyed herself, while she, Susan Pennington, didn't.

"And I've only myself to blame," she told herself —rather rashly, for a moment later she realized that the real culprit was Dick. It was Dick who had condemned her to imprisonment for life at "Chatsworth" by rushing her into marriage before she knew what she was doing, by compelling her to languish alone as an unpaid caretaker, by stupidly losing his job and forcing her to hide her shame in a skirt five inches too short, by jealously separating her from her oldest and best friend, Muriel! Marriage gave him sufficient rights already, she reflected bitterly; he might surely have left her that of choosing her friends. It was unreasonable to allow him to exercise it after six weeks' absence at a distance of over a hundred miles. "What's more, I won't stand it, and that's that!" she told herself angrily. "In a few days' time, when I've got my new coat and skirt, I shall get in touch with her. If I slip away quietly now she probably won't see me."

As she rose to do so, the lights flared out. She was

caught half facing Muriel, who instantly recognized her and showed not the least surprise.

"Hello, Susan!" she drawled in that smooth Irish voice of hers, the equivalent in sound of her soft marsh-mallow complexion, of the heavy sweet scent that she used, of her radical lazy good-nature. "How are you, my dear, and what are you doing here? I haven't seen you for years. I thought you were married or buried or something."

She laughed. "I've been both. It's funny we should meet like this. I've been thinking so much of you lately."

As she spoke Susan scrutinized Muriel's escort, and Muriel, in return, examined her unfashionable clothes. The escort was not, after all, Harry Levison nor anything like him. He was a shortish, bald-headed young man, with enormous arched eyebrows and the shape of face that positively demanded a tarboosh. Beneath his heavy blue jowl Susan saw a single pear-shaped pearl tie-pin that must surely be valuable because of the little gold safety chain with which it was caught. From the flicker of faint disdain that haunted Muriel's eyes Susan knew that, in spite of the low-voiced intimacies she had half overheard, her friend was bored with him. And Muriel, having noted with satisfaction the deficiency of Susan's skirt and her last year's hat, felt so secure from competition that she introduced him.

"Mr. Morris—Miss Lorimer. I'm sorry, Susan. How pricelessly stupid of me! I've entirely forgotten his name. Mrs. . . . What is it? Help me!"

"Mrs. Pennington."

"Yes, Pennington. Of course! I've no memory, you know. Never had," she confessed, with a brilliant smile designed to suggest to Mr. Morris an exquisite feminine helplessness. "You ought to know Susan, Mr. Morris. She's my oldest and dearest friend."

Mr. Morris seemed enchanted, or had to pretend that he was. Susan recognized Muriel's old game of securing a foil for her blondness and (in this case) her fashionable clothes. The first didn't matter, for she found Mr. Morris unattractive and Muriel was welcome to him; but in spite of her pleasure in re-discovering her friend, she resented the second. So, when Muriel generously invited her to take tea at the Grand Midland at Mr. Morris's expense, she excused herself. "I was just going home," she explained.

"Oh, go on, don't be silly, darling!" Muriel pressed her.

"Some other afternoon, perhaps?" Mr. Morris said melodiously, clinching her refusal.

"But I'm longing to have a talk with you, Muriel, after all this time," Susan said.

"Well, my dear, I shan't fly away. I haven't grown wings yet. What about lunch to-morrow? Oh dear— I'd forgotten. I'm lunching with you, aren't I, Nosey? at the Midland."

"If Mrs. Pennington would care to join us . . ." Mr. Morris said, with obvious reluctance.

"Of course! Why, that's splendid! We're lunching in the grill-room, aren't we?"

Mr. Morris sighed heavily, consenting. No cheap *tables d'hôte* for her! He hoped Susan's tastes weren't quite as expensive as Muriel's.

"At the grill-room, then. One o'clock sharp," Miss O'Brien confirmed. "Don't be late. I always send Nosey back to the office at three. He has to make pots of money, don't you, darling?"

Mr. Morris laughed sardonically. If he were to continue the enjoyment of his present company it was only too true.

II

At eight-thirty on the following morning, having finished his breakfast, Harry Levison briskly climbed the great staircase at Mawne Hall and made his way to his uncle's bedroom. He tapped at the door—the relations of the Magnus family were always formal— and waited until Mr. Magnus's irritated voice called "Come in!"

At the moment Solomon Magnus had every reason for feeling irritable. Two days before, his wife had compelled him to undergo another medical inspection. The physician whom he had consulted had been even more vague and non-committal that the last. He had admitted there was "reason for alarm," but wouldn't say why.

"If I were in your shoes," he had said, "I should go straight to Nauheim."

"You can cut out the shoes," Mr. Magnus had replied, somewhat testily. "They're *my* business. Yours is my heart."

The doctor had smiled. "Very well then. Your heart needs a rest."

"In a *wagon-lit?* Many thanks! Can't I rest it at home?"

"The fact that you shrink from a journey shows that it needs one. If you won't try Nauheim, go to bed for a week. Then I'll come out to Mawne and see you again."

"At ten guineas a time," Mr. Magnus thought. "Not if I know it!"

He asked: "Couldn't you give me something to whip this heart up a bit?"

"Yes, I could; but I'm not going to. What you need is a curb, not a whip. Of course, if you want a short life and a merry one . . ."

Mr. Magnus laughed shortly: "A merry one? Young man, I'm a stockbroker. Do you read the papers? Have you heard anything about Wall Street lately?"

The doctor was obdurate. "You've asked me for my advice" ("Yes, *and* paid for it through the nose," Mr. Magnus thought); "you can take it or leave it. I repeat: go to bed for a week."

Rebellious, but awed none the less, Mr. Magnus

submitted. Harry Levison discovered him grotesquely clothed in his white cotton night-shirt with a Jaeger bonnet on his head and a Shetland shawl draped round his shoulders; on his knees the *Financial Times*, at his left hand a telephone. Mr. Magnus had already been awake and fretting for over four hours, making notes of questions and instructions to give to his nephew. He breathed heavily and puffed out his lips as he spoke, but his mind was as hard and clear as a Kimberley diamond. Harry Levison, sitting at his side in an attitude that did no violence to the knife-edged crease of his trousers, took shorthand notes with a pencil in a platinum case. His brain, he knew, was as clear as his uncle's, though much less cautious. When he spoke it was with the swiftness and penetration of lightning. Mr. Magnus generally approved.

"He moves faster than I do. No half measures about this young man! When I'm gone," he reflected —for the doctor's warning still lurked in the back of his mind—"in six years he'll be either a millionaire or a spectacular bankrupt. His only danger is women— just like his poor father. What he needs," Mr. Magnus thought, "is a sobering influence. Leonora will give him that as well as more money to play with; and old father Marx will see that nothing goes wrong. In a case like this there's no point in a long engagement. The sooner they're married the better."

"Is that all?" Harry asked, recalling his vagrant mind.

"Yes, that's all for the moment. You'll 'phone me at midday, of course?"

"If there's anything important." (Why the devil couldn't he trust him?)

"No, ring me up, anyway. I shall want to know about Courtaulds."

"All right. I'll be off."

"Just one moment, Harry." Levison paused at the door impatiently. "Any news of Leonora?"

"I had a letter this morning. Nothing startling. There never is in Frankfort."

"I wish you'd get that job settled, Harry. If anything happened . . ."

"Nothing's going to happen. You're all right. If you'd only take the cure at Nauheim as that fellow suggested . . ."

"Well, that's what I've been thinking. If I consented to go to Nauheim we might kill two birds with one stone. I should like to see you married in the *Haupt-synagoge*, the same as your aunt and myself. It's one of the most costly buildings in Frankfort," he added, "and I know the chief rabbi. What's more, a stylish wedding would make a good impression in family circles and might lead to something."

Harry's eyes narrowed quickly. The idea of those family circles made him wince. Solly Magnus's old-fashioned Jewish loyalties meant nothing to him but an incubus. He preferred to consider himself a typical, smart young Englishman, which was why he invariably wore an Old Harrovian tie. If anything *did* happen, as his uncle euphemistically put it, he would probably sell his share in the business, change his name by deed-poll, and make a new start—though Leonora and the whole brood of Marxes would probably have something to say about that! As for marrying—the match was, financially, of course, too good to be sniffed at, and Leonora, a sort of third cousin, not so obviously Jewish as she might have been. When the time came, he might do far worse. But the time had not come. There were lots of money to be made and fun to be had in the meantime. Their engagement, being a Jewish engagement, was as binding as Gentile matrimony.

"There's no earthly hurry for that," he said firmly. "If you did go to Nauheim I oughtn't to leave the office. You can't trust the beggars not to do something stupid, and you know that as well as I do."

Mr. Magnus sighed and was silent. It was only too true. As a matter of fact, he didn't trust even Harry in ticklish matters of judgment. That was where Leonora came in. If Harry once settled down with a wife and a family. . . . But Harry, more credit to him, was eager to be off to business.

"All right. We'll talk of that later," Mr. Magnus said. "Don't forget to telephone at twelve, and if anything else turns up . . ."

"Suspicious old devil!" Harry thought as he drove into town. He looked forward to the chance of running the show on his own. He liked making swift decisions in which risks were involved and handling, on paper, big sums of money—not so much for its own sake, as Solomon Magnus did, as for the power it represented and what it could buy. He enjoyed the prestige of advising important clients, men of substance in the mercantile and industrial world of the Midlands, whose blunt ways contrasted so awkwardly with his easy Harrovian manners. He liked showing off to the office staff, particularly the women. He liked ringing bells, consulting card-indexes, speaking through to Paris or Berlin, at once testing and exhibiting, like a trained engineer, the power, flexibility and economy of his business machine. He enjoyed the whole adventurous atmosphere of the stock exchange because it was modern and swift and glittering and invited boldness; because, when he was in it, he experienced the same illusion of strength and sniffed the same spice of danger as when he "stepped on the gas" of the yellow Bentley and went screaming along at a speed at which a skid or burst tyre spelt death. He enjoyed, again, the precarious social position he had acquired in North Bromwich; his skill as a tennis-player; his Savile Row clothes; little things like his wafer-thin watch and his platinum pencil-case; calling Page, the head waiter at the Grand Midland, by his Christian name; ordering wines by their number without consulting the wine-list, and illegibly signing chits without looking at the bill.

That morning, with his uncle in dock, his zest and energy had full scope. When, at twelve precisely, he rang up Mawne Hall, he had covered more ground in three hours than Solomon would compass in twelve. At one, brimming over with conscious achievement and as smart as a brand-new piece of Brummagem pinchbeck, he entered the Grand Midland grill-room and took his seat, alone, at the table which was daily reserved for him. He ordered two grilled cutlets, a heart of lettuce, and a light dry Moselle, and sat back in his chair to see if any of his clients were lunching.

There were several, to whom he nodded casually or effusively according to the size of their accounts. He saw also, in the distance, the bald head and bristling eyebrows of his friend Mr. Morris. (It was sad, Harry thought: you could guess the poor fellow's race if you saw nothing else.) Mr. Morris had a lady on either side of him. One was Muriel O'Brien: Harry Levison knew all about *her*. If he hadn't, she wouldn't have been lunching with Mr. Morris; though Muriel and he were still quite good friends, their relationship having ended on terms satisfactory to both of them.

Mr. Morris's second guest, on the other hand, was unknown to Harry, and therefore excited his curiosity. She was young. Not too young. Her face had an air of experience. It was pale and clear-cut, and showed a demure excitement that promised an odd mixture of worldliness and innocence. She was dressed with severe and admirable taste. The austerity of her tailor-made suit and impudent hat made as welcome a contrast with Muriel's incurable flamboyance as did the darker tinge of her skin with Muriel's blondness, which, characteristically, had already begun to "go off."

Miss O'Brien's interest was by no means absorbed in her host. She had seen Harry Levison enter the room, and when Mr. Morris's opaque brown eyes were turned toward Susan, she winked at Harry and pulled a wry face which suggested that she was bored and wished he would join them. Harry smiled to himself. Her vulgarities still amused him. But it wasn't for Muriel's sake that when he had finished his small, well-chosen meal he moved to their table.

Muriel introduced Susan, who blushed delightfully. "As a matter of fact, Mr. Levison, we've met before," she told him.

"Impossible! I couldn't have forgotten you."

"Last year, at Brinton," she reminded him.

"Of course. But I should never have known you. You're quite different; you look so much . . ."

"Older? That's the result of marriage, I suppose. My husband called on you to ask for a job some weeks ago. His name is Pennington. You didn't give him one."

"How stupid of me! Why, of course, we must look into this."

"Too late, I'm afraid. He's found one down in South Wales."

"And left you behind? I say, isn't that rather dangerous?"

"That depends . . ." Susan answered slowly, with downcast eyes.

"On what?" he persisted.

"On me," she said, with a smile.

They were getting on now, Susan thought, like a house on fire. Muriel left them to it; commercial honesty compelled her to give Mr. Morris at least the value of his lunch. Harry Levison found Susan's provocative shyness enchanting. She was so neat, so quick-humoured, so frank, so completely composed. That composure, the result of her confidence in her new suit, simultaneously invited and challenged his virtuosity as a professional charmer. There was always a hint of devilry lurking behind it. Was she really as innocent, as guarded as she appeared to be? It was up to him to find out.

As for Susan, there was little about Harry Levison that her downward glances missed. She had never seen him at such close quarters before, and proximity confirmed the romantic idea of him which she had cherished on such slender grounds. He was older than she had imagined, but that was all to the good; she was no longer a schoolgirl herself, and a certain hardness distinguished him from the movie heroes whom, physically, he so closely resembled. That air of polished costliness which emanated from his clothes and his person was superficial; it concealed the silken power and efficiency of a Rolls-Royce engine which, for all its elegance, could give away handicap to any mass-production machine (poor Dick, for example) over roads rough or smooth. Though he kept a tight grip on the realities of life, he could see the fun of it; in his quick sense of humour she found a match for her own; he picked up every sly point she made with infallible adroitness. And that, too, was a welcome change from human relationships in which every little joke that she made had to be explained.

There were other things that did not have to be explained. Though his bold eyes—(they were blue, she noticed, not brown and opaque like Mr. Morris's) —never left her in any doubt as to his being completely male, he showed delicacy of perception in matters so completely feminine as her clothes and her new hat, on which he complimented her. This acuteness had its disadvantages; it made her aware, for instance, that her shoes were not in keeping with the rest of her new toilet; but his admiration of her taste, in which his enthusiasm vied with Mr. Bellis's, warmed her pride by assuring her that, on him at least, her niceties were not wasted.

By the end of the elaborate lunch that Muriel screwed out of Mr. Morris, Susan had discovered, in short, an opponent worthy of her steel. Here were none of the brutal bludgeonings of Mr. Bulgin or the hearty single-stick play of Captain Small, but a chivalrous and elegant flicker of slender rapiers— their fine points well buttoned, to be sure, with her caution and his forbearance, but none the less sharply pointed. All through this long duel she was aware that a single turn of his sinewy wrist could have disarmed her; but he was, as she decided, too much of a gentleman for that. And what could have been more gallant and tender than the way in which—when Muriel broke up the party at three to return Mr. Morris's regrettable nose to the grindstone—he helped Susan on with her coat, just pressing her shoulders for a moment when the action was completed and never, thank heaven! glancing at the cheap label inside! "I might almost have been a queen," she thought to herself.

"Are you in such an uncomfortable hurry?" he asked her persuasively.

She sighed and smiled faintly. "Yes, I'm afraid so. I ought to go back to Tilton."

"Don't you find it frightfully lonely out there all alone?"

"Just a bit. But time passes quickly. I read quite a lot."

"And we've never talked about books! That's too bad! Another thing in common! Shall I ever get to the end of you?"

"I think, on the whole, you'd better not try. It might come unexpectedly."

"That's sheer modesty on your part." (They were walking together over the wide spread of Turkey carpet that led to the entrance. Susan felt, with pride, that the eyes of the great world were on her.) "Look here, Mrs. Pennington," he went on. "I feel that you're just going to fade away, as you did at Brinton, and I simply can't bear it. Will you give me your telephone number? May I ring you up some day?"

The nearest telephone was at "Welbeck," and the thought of Miss Maples's curiosity frightened her.

"We're not on the telephone. You see how old-fashioned I am. It's not my fault. My husband won't have it."

"Your address, then? I'll send you a wire."

Susan hesitated. For the first time in her life the ludicrousness of the word "Chatsworth" struck her. "Ada Road" was bad enough; but she told him that that would find her.

"You and I have so much to talk about," he told her. "We might lunch at this place. Or, if you like, we could dine and dance afterwards. I'm sure you dance beautifully."

"You're so sure about everything, aren't you?"

"I'm quite sure about one thing."

The page-boy saluted him as he spun the revolving glass doors. Harry Levison swept off his hat to her. "*Au revoir*," he said tenderly.

"*Au revoir.*"

As she walked along Sackville Row toward the Tilton bus terminus her head was unsteadied by an odd exhilaration.

"Yes, everything was perfect," she told herself, "except my shoes."

Instead of catching the three-thirty bus she turned

down the High Street and broke into the last of George Lorimer's five-pound notes to buy a new pair of black lizard-skin walking-shoes, which would go with everything, and some silver dancing-slippers to set off the black lace.

III

If she were going to dine and dance with this glass of fashion she ought really to have had a new evening frock as well. That was out of the question. Even now, thanks to that inevitable burst of extravagance on footwear, she had not enough left of George Lorimer's fifteen pounds to pay the instalment due to the Furnishing Emporium. She scribbled a brusque note to George, demanding the balance with many under-linings, and settled down, with the length of tulle she had bought, to re-fashion the black lace.

"After all, it's a Chanel," she thought.

Yet, though she worked so hard that she had the dress ready to wear on the following night, a whole week passed without further news of Harry Levison. The only telegraph-boy who cycled along Ada Road left his telegram at "Welbeck," giving Susan a moment of alarm, in case he had made a mistake; but she saw Miss Maples open the envelope and nod and smile, so it evidently belonged to her. Nobody else came near "Chatsworth" that week except the milkman, the

grocer's vanman and the postman, with Dick's daily
letter. She hardly took the trouble to read Dick's
letters now; she knew what was written inside before
she opened them, so why on earth should she? Captain
Small stumped up one afternoon very much out of
breath. When she heard his step on the path she shut
herself in the bedroom and lay low while she heard
his knock echo through the apparently empty house.
There was nobody she wanted to see less than Captain
Small in those days. She only wanted to see Harry
Levison, and he had forgotten her!

Harry Levison had not forgotten; but life at
Mawne Hall was becoming extremely complicated.
Mr. Magnus's temper had not been improved by
enforced abstention from business. Under the illusion
that he was still in control of the office, he exacted
from Harry a precise account of all that had happened
each day and kept him chained to his side. Mr.
Magnus lay heaving in bed like a sick Polar bear; he
grunted and growled and snapped at all who came
near him; he rang up the office in Sackville Row every
hour and delayed important decisions. In the interval
he brooded much on the subject of Harry's marriage;
the idea of a visit to Frankfort *en route* to Nauheim
was becoming a fixed idea—which was very provoking,
since Harry's ideas of marriage had become, since his
meeting with Susan, much more fluid.

It was only when, flatly defying the doctor's orders
and reducing his wife to tears, Mr. Magnus suddenly

heaved himself out of bed, waddled forth from his prison, lit a long Corona, and appeared, like some escaped monster, in Sackville Row, that Harry had time to send Mrs. Pennington her wire—an invitation to dine with him that evening at the Grand Midland French Restaurant.

The message was in the grand style, consisting of no less than eighteen words. *Longing to see you,* it said. Susan read it again and again; she could not bear to destroy it; so she concealed it, along with her other secrets, in Captain Small's shell-case. Though the appointment was for seven o'clock, she began dressing at four. Grey daylight was hardly flattering to her evening dress; the tulle with which she had re-modelled it was of a different black from that of Madame Allbright's original. That couldn't be helped. What was infinitely more embarrassing was the fact that she hadn't an evening wrap to go with it—nothing better, indeed, than the cloth coat she had worn at the luncheon-party. She almost cried with vexation when she thought of its incongruity. If George Lorimer had only sent her the balance of her quarterly income she could have bought something suitable in time. There was something exceedingly queer about Uncle George's behaviour in these days. He hadn't sent it, nor even deigned to answer her brusque little note.

The only way out of the difficulty that she could see was for her to arrive at the hotel some time before the appointment, to conceal the offending garment in the cloak-room, and await Harry's arrival in the lounge. She achieved this plan in the end, though not without acute self-consciousness. The presence of a lonely lady, so extremely décolletée, in the lounge attracted the attention of a number of men who stared at her. It came as an enormous relief when she saw Harry Levison enter. He was beautifully dressed, with a large black butterfly tie, a white waistcoat with diamond-set onyx buttons, and pearl studs in his shirt-front, each bigger than the tie-pin affected by Mr. Morris, and his plastered hair was as sleek and dark as his onyx buttons. When he saw her he smiled the sad and beautiful smile that is seen upon Jewish lips. "At last!" he said, as he took her hand and kissed it (Fancy Dick kissing anyone's hand!) like a foreign nobleman.

"Is it really you?" he whispered. "You're so lovely to-night, Susan." (Was it possible that he had found out her Christian name from Muriel?) "And so smart! I'm sure I have seen that frock somewhere before."

It seemed wonderful that a man should remember a detail of that kind. Yes, he understood women.

"How clever of you!" she replied. "That's just why I put it on. I was wearing this frock when we met first of all at Brinton."

"That was sweet of you, Susan. It's perfectly up to date."

"It's a little Chanel," she told him modestly. "It came over from Paris by air."

"Ah, the great Gabrielle? There's nobody like her for neat little figures like yours. She's little herself. I saw her once at Le Touquet."

Susan didn't quite know what this meant, but was saved from the shame of confession by his offering her his arm with a gesture of formal respect.

"What about dinner?" he said. "Let's have our cocktails at table."

The "side-cars" which he ordered were the first she had ever tasted, and so were the oysters. She gulped these down bravely, but they nearly made her sick. "One has to suffer to be wicked," she told herself. The champagne, however, proved insidiously pleasant. Its golden hue seemed to permeate all their surroundings; its stimulation emboldened her to examine her companion more closely. She noticed particularly his hands. They were not spatulate, like Mr. Bulgin's, nor tremulous like Captain Small's, but beautifully formed and sensitive, strong and capable. It seemed a pity that he spoilt this impression by wearing that diamond ring. She asked him why he did.

"Well, *you* wear one, don't you?" he said.

"Yes, but mine's a wedding-ring."

"Well, mine's an engagement-ring."

"Is that serious?"

"Terribly serious. Just as serious as yours," he told her.

On the whole she was glad. It put them on an equal footing. If anything happened—(she used Solomon

Magnus's phrase in a different sense)—though of course nothing *would*, the loyalties endangered would not lie only on her side. Those words "Just as serious as yours" were designedly equivocal. To cover her embarrassment she continued to question him, and he gave her a joking description of Leonora and the family circle in Frankfort.

"You don't sound as if you were in love with her," she said, reproachfully.

He laughed: "In love? My dear child, I'm going to *marry* her."

"Well, surely," she began, with elder-sisterly gravity; but he only laughed again and filled her glass. "Let's talk about something more pleasant, Susan," he rallied her. "I believe in having a good time as long as I can."

But that didn't mean, as she half expected it would, that he began to make love to her. He amused her, instead, with ironical, witty descriptions of the other diners, including Sir Joseph Astill, a pasty young man who had just succeeded to his uncle's baronetcy, and several of the men who had stared at her in the lounge and turned out to be local celebrities. Some had even been knighted. Harry knew them all, he said, modestly, and nodded familiarly to most of them. Susan had no idea that the Grand Midland was such a Haunt of the Aristocracy.

When dinner was over they proceeded to dance in the room that was called the Grand Salon. The first steps were rather an ordeal, for her head was still spinning with wine, and she was well aware of her own deficiencies as a dancer. She need not have been frightened; Harry Levison danced well enough for both of them; his adroitness swiftly concealed her own lack of skill. She thought the music thrilling. He agreed. Every bit as good as the Savoy, he told her. Though the floor, at that time of evening, was nearly empty, the musicians played as though they enjoyed every note, and their leader became so excited by his barbaric rhythms that he swayed, jumped and contorted his face like a man possessed. Harry Levison's virtuosity made everything easy; it inspired her. She found herself floating round and round, unconscious of her steps, in a golden haze that seemed, somehow, not of this earth. When he began to teach her new steps she fell to them at once. They might have been dancing together, she thought, ever since they were born. There seemed no reason why they should not go on dancing together until they died. And the most surprising thing about this man was his delicacy. He was so impersonal. She could surrender herself to his arms without reservation, even without caution. Their experience was not sensual, but purely æsthetic, and beautifully innocent.

Only one incident marred that miraculous evening, bringing her back to the world from which she had momentarily escaped. It came unexpectedly when the band played *A Room with a View*. The first notes of that tune, the *leit-motiv* of her romance at Brinton, awoke in her brain the answer of a sinister vibration. Her mind was snatched suddenly away from the brilliance of the Grand Midland and her immaculate partner to the sordid room which Dick rented in Pandypool and Dick sleeping inside it. She felt guilty —unreasonably she told herself, but none the less, guilty.

Harry Levison laid his hand on her waist. "Won't you dance this?" he said.

"I feel rather tired," she told him. "It must be getting quite late."

"Well, just as you like," he said gaily. "It's an old song, anyway."

The words seemed to carry a subtle symbolical meaning.

"I'll wait for you in the hall while you get your wraps," he went on. "The car's parked outside."

Susan's feeling of guilt was quickly submerged by another immediate concern. Her tweed coat! Whatever happened he must not see it.

"I can find my way home quite easily," she protested. "I won't keep you. Let's just say good night."

He showed her his wafer-thin watch. "My dear child, the last bus left an hour ago. Get your wraps, and don't be ridiculous. Of course I shall drive you."

As she stepped into the Bentley she made explanatory apologies.

EE

"The nights are getting so cold now. This tweed coat is nice and warm."

"It's a charming coat, anyway." He approved without looking. "You have very good taste, Susan. That's one of the things that I like about you. Of course, there are others. . . ."

She was glad when he left it at that. That haunting tune was still in her mind. The six-litre engine roared, but could not drown it; the lamps of the Halesby road flashed past in a continuous ribbon of light. He slowed down for the Tilton cross-roads.

"Thanks so much, you can drop me here," she said anxiously.

"What nonsense! Of course I'm going to see you home."

The surface of Ada Road, she told him, was awful.

"My old bus won't mind it," he said. "Now which is your house?"

"The last on the left."

They pulled up at the gate of "Chatsworth." Susan found her latch-key and held out her hand again.

"No, I'm going to see you in safely."

She hesitated and held her ground.

He laughed softly. "You're not afraid of me, Susan?"

"Of course not."

She switched on the light in the little living-room. Harry Levison's presence made it look mean and dingy. He peered at the photographs of sporting groups on the wall. "Which is your husband?" he asked.

She showed him. "Do you think he's good-looking?"

"Well, really . . . !" he said, with a laugh, a little contemptuously. "So he was at Brunstone, was he? Not a bad school." He turned of a sudden and held out his hand.

"*Au revoir*," he said. "You've given me a lovely evening. We get on rather well, don't you think so? What about—let me see—next Thursday; same time, same place?"

"I should simply love it."

"Splendid! Then that's a fixture."

He went. Like a perfect lamb. . . . And this time he didn't even kiss her hand, which showed, of course, what a thorough gentleman he was. As she sat there, her mind swirling with the back-wash of all the evening's emotions, Susan's wandering eyes fell on the clock in the middle of the top book-shelf. The hands pointed to half-past two, as they had always done. That night the obstinate time-piece seemed to Susan an appropriate symbol of her life at "Chatsworth."

She went to bed wearily and fell asleep almost at once. On the opposite side of the road, at "Welbeck," Miss Maples lay wide awake. She had been roused by the sudden roar of the Bentley starting, and had staggered to the window, still half asleep, to see what was happening. Just too late—for the Bentley's acceleration was excellent, and by the time she reached her window it was out of sight. A light still shone, however, through the blinds of the "Chatsworth" living-room, and she had the satisfaction of feeling that the process of ruin foreshadowed by Mr. Bulgin had already begun. She would give him the news as soon as he reached his office next morning.

IV

From that moment there began, for Susan, a period of sheer enchantment. Neither the dank Midland autumn nor the dullness of "Chatsworth" weighed on her spirits now. She lived in an airy world of her own, unhampered by circumstances, a high world, irradiated by the warmth and light of this new, unexpected friendship. That it was friendship and nothing more (on his side, at least) she was able to assure herself proudly, again and again. Yet, even as friendship, it gave far more than the relationship suggested by that common word. It was not merely an equal communion of tastes and thoughts and pleasures. It was romantic in the highest degree, implying, on her part, a continuous effort to please through the refinements of her physical beauty and her alert adaptability of mind, and on his, in return, the tribute of unbounded admiration, sedulous tenderness, complete understanding, and—what was more important to her

—perpetual, delicate flattery.

Harry's flattery was not, perhaps, so delicate as she imagined. In any case, it was so skilfully adapted to its object as to be convincing. What could have been subtler, for instance, than the telegram which she received on the morning following their dinner-party: *Can't possibly wait till Thursday. Can't you come tonight? Am terribly lonely. Shall be waiting at eight same place and quite understand if you can't.* Its humility touched her. There was no reason in the world—save, perhaps, that unfortunate tweed coat— why either of them should be deprived of a pleasure so innocent. As luck would have it, George Lorimer's balance of ten pounds turned up by the afternoon's post; so she hurried into "town" and secured, in the nick of time, an evening wrap of silver tissue which had been marked down in the sales and, carelessly, not marked up again. It was a cloak, the assistant asserted, in which one could "go anywhere."

The atmosphere of that evening was not so high-pitched as that of the night before. Bereft of the wariness and excitement of a first encounter, discarding the elaborate preliminary compliments of foil-play, they settled down into an idle, intimate companionship in which each was concerned with probing the inner nature of the other in search of differences and thrilling resemblances. The process proved easy and natural beyond belief. No other person, in all her life, had shown such appreciation of those mysteries of her personality which she herself found so interesting. His frankness in revealing his own temperamental deficiencies challenged an equal candour on her part. They talked about marriage in a detached, impersonal way (though, somehow or other, the names of Leonora and Dick cropped up now and then, to be swiftly suppressed), and Susan was astounded to find not only how nearly their points of view coincided, but how eminently sane and modern they both were.

"I make no pretensions to be anything more than human," he admitted candidly. "I'm afraid I've no morals to speak of."

Though she couldn't go quite as far as that—it would hardly be prudent—she confessed that traditional morality didn't impress her. "All those things," she said, fortunately remembering a phrase she had read somewhere, "are with me a matter of taste. I just happen to be . . . fastidious."

"One sees that at a glance," he assured her. "My own rule's quite simple. I call anything immoral that inflicts unnecessary pain on other people. After that nothing matters much. Take ourselves, for instance. Some people might think it odd for you and me to be sitting here this evening. But what harm does it do?"

There, at least, she could agree with him. It was astonishing to find in a creature so superficially brilliant such profundity of thought. This reminded her that he probably didn't realize how well-read she was; so, remembering his hint of the evening before, she talked about books in the hope of finding another identity of taste. This subject was rather less fertile than that of human relationships.

"I'm sorry to say I have practically no time for reading," he told her. "When I do read it's generally French, for the sake of the language. It's useful in business. I suppose you read heaps of French novels?"

"Not often," she confessed. "Of course I *could* if I wanted to. I can read newspapers easily."

"I'll remember to send you some. You may find them amusing. You mustn't blame me if you're shocked."

"No, no. I'm unshockable."

That evening they drove home earlier. As he dropped Susan at "Chatsworth," Miss Maples was satisfied by the vision of a huge yellow car and a young man in evening dress. Though, this time, Susan showed her confidence in Harry by inviting him to come in, she was relieved when he didn't. The very air of "Chatsworth" destroyed illusion.

"I'm going away for the week-end to-morrow," he said. "Don't forget me completely, Susan," he added pleadingly.

Even if she had wanted to forget him she couldn't have done so; for next morning, as if to keep him in mind, the books which he had promised arrived by special messenger. There were five of them: *Madame Bovary*, Maupassant's *Une Vie*, *Nana*, *La Garçonne*, and a novel by Maurice Dekobra about a noble British lady who elected for some strange reason to "go wrong" amid the discomforts, the grime, and the composite odour of international humanity, steam-heating and disinfectants that can only be found at great cost in a Grand European Express.

Susan had been rather rash when she boasted that she could read French, but the danger of being compelled to confess her ignorance induced her to try. During an intense week-end, with occasional references to a dictionary, she managed to extract the gist of *Une Vie* and *Bovary*, and felt, as a consequence extremely daring and cultured. If these volumes were designed by their authors to suggest a moral, they signally failed. On the contrary, she found herself thrilled and intoxicated by their realistic presentation of illicit love, which her imperfect mastery of the language invested with a peculiar glamour. It was evident that they managed those things better in France, and the luscious zest with which these Latin heroines abandoned their virtue seemed a fair reward for the melodramatic fates by which they were overtaken. It did not surprise her that English girls married foreigners. Was it this spice of the exotic, she wondered, that attracted her to Harry Levison?

For he did attract her, she confessed. In spite of his unfortunate association with Muriel she had always pictured him as a lover—though, of course, not necessarily of herself. She lay on the sofa brooding all through that week-end, her mind haunted by voluptuous images and romantic conjectures.

On Tuesday they dined and danced at the Grand Midland as he had arranged. He looked pale—she had almost said "dissipated"—and was more than usually silent. When she asked him where he had been and what he had been doing, he was uncommunicative. His evasions provoked her.

"Why, Susan," he taunted her at last, "I do believe you're jealous."

"How can you say that?" she replied indignantly. "As if anything you did could have any effect on me!"

He laughed. When they parted that evening she was still on her dignity, a pose that afforded him amusement, but didn't prevent his proposing a motor-drive on the following day. Mr. Magnus, in spite of the doctor's injunctions, had resumed his routine, and Harry, with luck, could slip away from the office in the middle of the morning.

He arrived at "Chatsworth," in fact, soon after eleven, and Miss Maples had a rare opportunity of studying him and taking the number of the Bentley. It was a brilliant October morning with a touch of frost in the air and a bright sky that promised at least five hours of daylight. Susan had never felt quite so grand as she did that day, alone with this handsome young man in a magnificent car which (he mentioned it casually) had cost more than two thousand pounds and was capable of moving twice as fact as an express train. This method of travel was very different from sitting on the pillion of Dick's motor-bicycle. As she leant back superbly in the low bucket-seat and the wind of their speed roared by, her exhilarated mind had only one regret: she ought really to have had a fur coat, or at least a fur boa, to "go with" this opulent vehicle—quite apart from the fact that the shoddy cloth of her new tweed coat let through every draught. The only fur she possessed was the strip of dyed rabbit on last year's bottle-green coat. Still, freezing as she was, she would not have exchanged her lot for any other. Harry's driving was rash and impetuous; the great car screamed through the brilliant autumnal world like a yellow meteor; there were moments in which he brought Susan's heart into her mouth, but she didn't care. Supposing they crashed, such an end would be only in keeping with the ecstatic speed and liberty of their wild career. In every sense of the words, this was "living dangerously."

Whirling homeward at dusk through the lanes on the outskirts of Tilton they had a close shave. As they swerved round a corner the off wing brushed the sleeve of a man in a khaki trench-coat. Captain Small had never been nearer to death in the trenches than he was at that moment. Harry jammed on the brakes, and the Bentley skidded away from their victim. He would have stopped to apologize; but Susan, who knew it was Captain Small, implored him to drive on. Even then she couldn't be certain that Small hadn't recognized her—as, indeed, he had—and the prospect of making explanations filled her with what she repeatedly told herself was an unreasonable dread. When they sat down to tea at "Chatsworth" she confessed her alarm. Harry only laughed.

"Anyone would think you'd a guilty conscience. Why shouldn't he know it was you?"

"People talk so," she told him.

"Well, let them! What harm have we done?"

"He's a great friend of Dick's. I suppose it's all right," she said weakly.

"If your husband's as jealous as that he shouldn't leave you alone. Is there any reason why you should behave as if this were a nunnery?" He took her hand tenderly. "Why, my child, you're as cold as ice! Why didn't you tell me? It was thoughtless of me to let you come out at this time of year without your furs."

"Furs, indeed!" she replied. "That just shows how observant you are. If I had a fur coat I'd have worn it."

"Well, the sooner you get one the better. I know a man named Rosenthal, one of our clients. If I gave you a letter he'd let you have one at wholesale price. Don't forget to remind me."

"I've no money to spend on things like that," she said bitterly.

"You could easily make some."

"What do you mean?" she asked quickly.

"The simplest thing in the world. I can buy you some shares."

"I've no money, I tell you. You don't understand."

"My sweet child, I understand perfectly. There's no money required. You're a trustworthy person, aren't you? Well, we recognize that—as a firm, I mean—and give you the usual month's credit. You order me to buy certain shares, which I shall select. They go up—you can trust me for that—and at the end of the month you sell and collect your balance. I'll arrange for Rosenthal to give you credit as well. Now, d'you see what I mean?"

Susan shook her head slowly. "No. I couldn't do that," she said. "You see . . . well, it's difficult to say exactly what I mean. I loathe money, anyway; and the thought of anything like that between you and me. . . . It would just spoil everything."

"It's an ordinary business transaction . . ."

"That makes no difference. We're such wonderful friends, Harry."

"Well, have your own way and go on freezing, you silly little thing!"

"You understand, don't you?"

"No, I don't. I think you're ridiculous. However . . ."

"Won't you leave me a little pride?"

He laughed. "Yes, a little. Within reason."

When he had gone (Miss Maples made a note of the exact hour and minute) Susan wondered whether her instinctive scruples hadn't been, as he suggested, ridiculous. Was there any difference, after all, between

accepting Mr. Bulgin's expensive presents and profit-
ing by Harry's advice? Wasn't the second, in point
of fact, more strictly honourable than the first? To
fall in with Harry's proposal—an "ordinary business
transaction"—seemed reasonable enough as long as
they weren't in love with each other. Was it possible
that this appalling condition might have explained her
instinctive dislike of a business relationship? Fantastic!
From the moment they met, their friendship, the most
engrossing in her life, had been ideally, dispassionately
platonic. He had kissed her hand once, and to-night,
just once, he had touched it. He was engaged, and she
married. No hint of "that sort of thing" had passed
between them. Why, then, had she felt guiltily scared
by her encounter with Captain Small? Disentangling
these contradictory motives she sat crouched in front
of the fire. Her body was still chilled to the bone, and
the thought of Mr. Rosenthal's fur coat, at cost price,
became acutely alluring.

Next morning she had more cause than ever to
regret the rigid line she had taken. Fate knocked at
the door with an unusually peremptory demand from
the Bromwich Furnishing Emporium which she could
not meet. So, dressing in her complete new outfit (she
had half promised Harry to drop in to the Grand Midland for tea), she determined to try its effect upon Mr.
Bellis.

It was with an odd sense of being a *revenante* from
another world that she entered the shop which, for one

ecstatic week of her life, had seemed such a temple of
taste and elegance, and inhaled once again the odour
of French polish, unseasoned wood and new up-
holstery. In her present disillusioned mood and the
throttled light of the October day it looked cheap and
dingy; but the salesman who welcomed her as a prospective customer was as suave and gentlemanly and as
faultlessly dressed as Mr. Bellis himself.

She enquired for her friend by name. The new
salesman looked blank.

"Mr. Bellis? You must be mistaken. I've never
heard of him."

"I think you're quite wrong," Susan told him, with
dignity. "I understood he was someone high up in the
firm."

"Bellis? Bellis? Why, now that I come to think
of it that was the name of a man we employed temporarily just over a year ago. I believe you're quite
right, madam. Is there anything I can do for you?
We've been making a lot of startling reductions
lately," he said seductively. "A lady of taste like
yourself couldn't help being struck with them."

Susan told him her business. The salesman's smile
faded immediately; his bland manner hardened; his
attitude was no longer respectful.

"That is outside my province, I'm afraid. If you
care to step round to the office . . ."

She stepped round to the office. A shabby stout man
in spectacles received her gruffly and turned over files.

"H'm . . . Pennington . . . yes," he said darkly, and took off his spectacles. The office was dingy and cobwebbed; the man himself, she thought, resembled a fat black spider. "Have you brought the money?" he asked sharply.

"I came to ask you . . ."

"It's no good asking *me* anything. *I* can't accommodate you. If you want to know, Mrs. Pennington, I think the firm's behaved handsomely. We have to pay our creditors honestly like anyone else, and your account, I may tell you, has given us a lot of trouble. A firm like us has to put down its foot occasionally or people would take us for fools; and it's just about time we put down our foot in your case. I'll give you a week to pay in. To-day's Thursday. Unless I hear in the meantime we shall send round the van next Friday. I'm not here to argue, Mrs. Pennington. I've no more to say about it. We act fair, and naturally we expect our clients to do likewise. Good afternoon."

As she left the shop the gentleman who had received her did not even trouble to open the door for her. The contrast between this behaviour and the smiling farewells of Mr. Bellis cut her to the heart. If only she had money, how she would make him grovel!

She met Harry Levison two hours later in the Grand Midland lounge. He was half an hour late for their appointment: Mr. Magnus's temper that day had been unusually exacting. He had looked forward to Susan's chatter as a pleasant relief. The game he was playing with her had reached an amusing stage. He found her, on the contrary, mute and melancholy and anything but good company. He could not imagine what had so crushed and diminished this usually lively creature.

"What's wrong with you, Susie?" he asked her at last. "What have I done? Be a sport and tell me."

"Oh, it's nothing to do with you, Harry dear. I'm just feeling blue."

"Husband?"

"What an idea! Of course not."

"Ah, money then. Is that it?" He pressed her till at last she admitted it. "Well, my dear child, that's nothing to worry about. I'll lend you whatever you want."

"No, I couldn't do that. Not with you. It would spoil . . . oh, everything."

"Is that all our . . . friendship's worth? Don't be foolish, Susie! I'll write you a cheque. How much is it? Will twenty-five do to go on with?"

She shook her head obstinately.

"Well, my child, if that doesn't suit you, why not do what I suggested last night—just a little flutter? I'll take care that the risk isn't great. As a matter of fact, you're practically the only woman I know who never asks me for stock-exchange tips. It's the usual thing."

"I'm terribly dense about things of that kind," she said. "What would I have to do?"

He laughed. "Just trust *me*. You instruct me to

buy you a thousand Bwana M' Kubwas, called Bwanas for short. That's a five-shilling share which stands, at the moment, at twenty-nine shillings, and is worth, in my humble opinion, considerably more. Well, to-morrow or the next day, or next week, your Bwanas go up to thirty. You instruct me to sell; I do so; and you take your margin; fifty pounds minus brokerage, etc.—but that needn't trouble you."

"But, Harry, I've no money of my own till I'm twenty-one. A thousand times thirty shillings is fifteen hundred . . ."

"Good arithmetic! Go up one! What's more, it seems you're a minor. We're on dangerous ground. I'm not sure if you're competent to pledge your husband's credit," he teased her.

"Would Dick have to know?" she asked anxiously.

"Good God, no!"

"But if they went down?"

"I shall hold them until they go up."

"I must have the money by next Thursday."

"I'm prepared to guarantee you'll have it by the end of the week."

"It all sounds so easy."

"It is, when you know," he told her. "Now wake up and smile. I can't bear to see you depressed. I'll buy your Bwanas to-morrow and let you know when I've sold them. By the way," he went on. "Will you keep Tuesday evening free? It's my birthday, Susie, my very last bachelor birthday! I thought of having

FF

dinner here—a small party, just eight or ten of us—
and then going on to a show or possibly dancing. Will
you honour me with your company—and wear the
black lace?"

"I can't wear anything else," she told him. "It's
all I've got."

"What a shame! You poor darling! Anyway, you
look lovely in it."

Next morning, for the first time in her life, she
scanned the financial columns of the *Daily Mail*. She
discovered *Bwana M'K's* among the Rhodesian
Mining shares. They were quoted at less than Harry
had suggested, at twenty-seven and ninepence. The
fall seemed sinister. It was all she could do to restrain
herself from sending a wire with instructions not to
buy. In the evening she walked up to Tilton cross-
roads and bought an *Evening Courier*. The shares
stood at twenty-nine shillings. A thousand times one
and threepence, her spinning head told her, was over
sixty-two pounds. If he held on a little longer. . . .
How thrilling life was!

The morning post brought her two letters. One
was from Dick, but the other, which she opened first,
was from Harry Levison, and enclosed, without any
comment, a cheque for thirty-three pounds. Considering what she had read in the *Evening Courier* the sum
seemed much too small. "If he'd only waited!" she
thought.

The sum, however, was enough and more than

enough to solve her present difficulties. She dressed hurriedly, paid it into her banking account, wrote a cheque for the Bromwich Emporium, and drew the remainder in cash. Thus furnished she caught the next cityward bus from the Tilton cross-roads and returned to "Chatsworth" triumphantly after one of the most exciting mornings of her life with a new silver evening frock (to match the dancing-shoes) in a parcel that also contained three pairs of silver-grey stockings (it saved a shilling to buy three) and the flimsy tweed coat. She was wearing, instead of this, a sweet little fur coat in nutria, a genuine model, for which, according to Mr. Rosenthal, the furriers in High Street would have charged her at least ten pounds more than she paid for it.

Miss Maples saw the fur coat and made an indignant note of it; but Susan was far too entranced to notice Miss Maples. She ate an enormous lunch—the cold air made her hungry—then virtuously wrote an affectionate letter to Dick, in which the name of Mr. Levison did not appear. After all, why should it?

CHAPTER XI

MR. MAGNUS PAYS

I

THE new silver evening frock was a perfect dream. Even if it had been marked down in the sales, it was sufficiently up-to-date to be the "living image" of one that was advertised for sale (*beige, nigger, havana, coral, lettuce, pigeon's breast, and other fashionable shades*) on the front page of the *Daily Mail* that morning. Its only defects were a complicated system of lining and shoulder-straps which made it extremely difficult to get into single-handed, and a row of press-studs and hooks-and-eyes at the back that only a contortionist could fasten when once it was on. These obstacles, however, had implications of grandeur: the frock had been obviously designed for the class of wearer who kept a maid. As Susan squirmed in the grip of its lining and struggled with the fastenings at the back she wished she had remained sufficiently friendly with Miss Maples to ask for her aid; but of late, for some unknown reason, the disapproval of "Welbeck" had hardened into sheer hostility. Susan regretted that Miss Maples missed seeing her as she set out that evening, so emphatically did the silvery ensemble beneath the new evening-wrap and the nutria coat proclaim the gulf that separated the sordid narrowness of "Welbeck" from the elegance of "Chatsworth." Quite unnecessarily. Miss Maples missed nothing, and what she saw impressed her not with envy, but with a bitter, unhallowed relish.

As for Susan, the consciousness of being dressed, for once, beyond criticism elated her. It was with acute satisfaction that she took stock of her dowdy fellow-passengers on the Tilton bus. They must surely wonder, she thought, who this rare visitant from the fashionable world might be. An even richer emotion thrilled her as she passed, with delicate high-heeled steps, along the pavement of Sackville Row toward the Grand Midland. The hotel's august portal no longer intimidated her; she had no self-consciousness now when she entered the brilliantly-lighted lounge. The page-boy who swung the revolving door chirped "Good evening, miss." The be-medalled porter in his lodge had a friendly smile for her as one of the accepted denizens of his exalted realm. She belonged there. She no longer had to enquire her way to the Ladies' Room, whose vague odours, resembling those of a hair-dressing saloon, had become as familiar to her nostrils as those of "Chatsworth."

When she emerged from her last tittivations Harry's other guests were already assembling at the

cocktail-bar. There were six of them, all unknown to
her save Muriel and Mr. Morris, and the sight of the
party gave her a shock, for one of the women was
wearing a silver dress identical with her own. This
lady glared at her savagely and Susan glared back. It
wasn't anybody's fault; it was rotten hard luck on both
of them, and the awkwardness of the situation was
fortunately lost in the flush of pleasure that swept
over her when she found herself meeting Sir Joseph
and Lady Astill and a Mr. Hingston, who must surely
be connected with the Wolverbury family. It was the
first time that Susan had ever met a man of title, and
though this one owed his to his father's success in the
adulteration of malt-liquors, and looked like it, she
couldn't help feeling that life was richer for the
experience.

When once they had been introduced, Sir Joseph
became dumb; but whether his silence was due to the
sublime unconcern of a born aristocrat or to the
stupor induced by his third cocktail, Susan could not
decide; and even if Sir Joseph had been trying to
entertain her she would hardly have heard him, so
greedily was her attention fastened on the woman who
had already stolen her dress and appeared, at the
moment, to be stealing Harry as well.

Miss Egerton, her rival—for that was how Susan
thought of her—was a hungry blonde, a little older
and taller and much more made-up than herself, with
swinging diamond ear-rings. She had a hard, husky

voice, which rose piercingly above the chatter of the group that surrounded her, and she spoke to Harry in a confident, proprietary tone, with sly smiles and allusions by which the poor simple soul appeared to be flattered. When Miss Egerton lowered her voice for a moment and leaned towards Harry so intimately that her ear-rings brushed his cheek, Susan found her face burning; she felt sure they were talking about her. Harry laughed uneasily, reproving Miss Egerton for what she had said; but the coolness with which, a moment later, that arrogant blue gaze contemptuously swept Susan from head to foot made her more self-conscious and hurt and instinctively hostile than ever.

"Who *is* that lady?" she asked the baronet softly.

"Teddy Egerton?" Sir Joseph replied, with a leer. "If you asked me *what* she was, I could tell you far more easily. She's a great friend of Levison's—oh, yes, a *very* great friend. As a matter of fact, I imagined that business was over. Apparently it isn't," he added, with a throaty chuckle.

"She was introduced as *Miss* Egerton," Susan persisted. "But I see she's wearing a wedding-ring."

The baronet winked. "I don't think a ring would make very much difference in her case," he whispered thickly. "We all know our Teddy. Surprisin' how she keeps her looks!"

As they passed in to dinner—Harry had taken a private room—Susan's hatred and distrust of the blue-eyed vampire increased. Apart from his first words of greeting, Harry had not spoken to Susan. Miss Egerton had taken such confident possession that he could not escape. She was clinging to his arm, with her long, white, red-taloned fingers, so tightly that he couldn't shake her off without being rude to her; and the worst of it was that the dance-frock of silver tissue suited her hungry, slender, pale figure far better than Susan's. At the long table, smothered in pink carnations, another check awaited her. Lady Astill, naturally, had been placed at Harry's right hand. Susan herself, as a married woman, had expected to sit on his left; but that precedence was promptly usurped by the so-called Miss Egerton, who beckoned the willing Sir Joseph to her other side, and Susan found herself sitting between the dour Mr. Hingston —who had forgotten her existence and devoted himself exclusively to Lady Astill—and Mr. Morris, who was too much intimidated by Muriel to speak to anybody else.

Thus isolated she sat frozen through the elaborate dinner; while Mr. Hingston talked racing (she gathered) with his left-hand neighbour; while Mr. Morris steadily and noisily enjoyed his food; while Muriel giggled and crooned in Sir Joseph's dull ears; while Harry submitted, willingly it seemed, to the feline clutches and blandishments of the carnivorous Egerton. As far as the rest of them were concerned, she might just as well have remained at Tilton. No one spoke to her; no one even looked at her except Harry's partner, who occasionally shot a blue glance of mischievous scorn in her direction. For Harry himself she apparently did not exist.

This universal neglect made her more self-conscious; she began to suspect that she looked out of place, that she was eating clumsily, that her every movement was being watched and despised by those hard blue eyes. To fortify herself she drank four or five glasses of champagne (the waiter filled up her glass as soon as it was empty) and felt no better for it. Her face became hot and angry; her feet were like ice and the silver slippers pinched them, while within her muddled brain there smouldered a revolving series of hot resentments—against Muriel, who sat there flirting complacently with that slow-witted oaf Joseph Astill; against the formal stick Hingston; against Mr. Morris, who looked and ate like a large black pig and had not even the sense to control his partner's behaviour; against Teddy Egerton, whose hungry face grew always more flushed and her husky voice louder; especially against Harry Levison, who had once been her friend, yet appeared unaware of the vulgarity by which he was surrounded. "If this is Society," Susan thought, "then I've had enough of it. They're the rudest people I've ever met in my life."

At the end of the dinner, postponed by Muriel's passion for ices, another magnum appeared, and Miss Egerton insisted on rising to propose Harry Levison's

health. Even then, Susan thought, Harry's eyes deliberately avoided her, as well they might, for sheer
shame, when that unspeakable woman kissed him full
on the mouth. The others, particularly Muriel,
applauded this gesture loudly, and Susan was thankful
now that Harry had never kissed her.

They were all of them, Susan included, the least bit
the worse for liquor, but that didn't, thank heaven,
affect her sense of propriety. On the contrary, it made
her more critical, more restrained, more aware of her
own unique (if relative) soberness. She was the only
person at that table, it seemed—except Miss Egerton—
who realized how grossly she, Susan Pennington, was
being insulted. Miss Egerton knew it quite well. That
was why her glance was so furtive, her smile so
malicious. The sight of that flashing smile, those loose
lascivious lips, that abandoned body, those glittering
ear-pendants, affronted Susan. They were in keeping
with the hateful scene in which she had been trapped
—with the gilt, the glass, the cascading candelabras of
crystal, with the clatter of high-pitched silly talk that
hurt her ears. She suspected now that Harry's behaviour was deliberate. He was "showing off" in the
hope of making her jealous. "I'll show him that two
can play at that game," she thought. If she had had
the courage of her disgust she would have stalked right
out of the room and left them to it; but by this time
her head had begun to ache vilely and her legs were
not to be trusted.

"I shall slip away quietly as soon as they move," she told herself.

They were moving already. Mr. Morris offered her his arm, which she thought most tactless: "I can walk quite steadily, thank you," she said, with dignity. She pulled herself together by a conscious effort of will as the party moved slowly from the private dining-room to the Grand Salon, where couples were already dancing.

Mr. Morris, beckoned by Muriel, left Susan's side. Mr. Hingston formally offered himself as a partner to Lady Astill, whose husband drifted like a dismasted vessel towards the bar. Harry Levison was still involved in the toils of the siren. Susan gave him one glance of appeal, but it never reached him. At that moment Miss Egerton abandoned herself to his arms and they slid away over the floor together, caught up by the music. Susan stood and gazed after them for one moment in jealous agony. She could see at a glance that Miss Egerton danced better than she did. As exponents of sheer virtuosity those two were worth watching; they drifted away on the smooth swell of sound as swiftly and lightly as floating thistle-down. It evidently wasn't the first time they had danced together. With rage and unwilling admiration in her heart Susan resumed her purpose. The rest of the party, it seemed, had already forgotten her. If she wasted no time she might still catch the last bus to Tilton. She made her way, with all the dignity she could command, to the dressing-room where she had left her fur coat.

It was empty. For that at least she thanked heaven as she sat down heavily in the chair in front of the dressing-table and contemplated her own flushed face with acute disgust. She was glad to be alone with the rage and humiliation that so deformed it, away from the noise and the lights and the empty chatter. The music of the Grand Salon now came to her ears in thin wailing snatches as though borne on a fitful wind. Though she hated those sensuous sounds by which she had once been ravished they still asserted their power over her imagination, interposing between her eyes and the face in the mirror a vision of the dancing-floor and Miss Egerton, a silver wraith, in Harry Levison's arms. And though she assured herself passionately that she didn't care, that a man who preferred a woman like that was beneath her contempt, her heart grew as hot with jealousy as her blotched and flaming cheeks, to which, as the music stopped, her attention returned.

"My God, what a sight!" she thought. "No wonder he wouldn't look at me!"

She repaired the damage as best she could by dabbing her brow with the eau-de-Cologne and her cheeks with the powder so generously supplied by the hotel management. The spirit gave momentary ease to her splitting head, though the excess of powder made her look even more ghastly than she felt. "But that can't be .helped," she thought, "nothing really matters as long as I can slink away safely. If I needed a lesson I've had one! Never again!"

She rose to her feet once more; her legs were steadier now, and her head, though it still ached abominably, grew clearer with the fading of anger. She glanced at the clock on the wall and was relieved to find that she still had just enough time to catch the bus; so she wrapped a scarf round her head, pressed her hands to her burning temples, and searched for her coat among the masses of others that hung on the opposite wall. As she slipped it over her shoulders a knock on the door made her jump.

"Yes?" she called back irritably. "Who is it?"

"Thank heaven! Is that you, Susan? It's me. Harry Levison."

"Yes. . . . What do you want?" she asked coldly, trying to control her voice.

"You, Susan. May I come in?" he demanded eagerly.

"Of course you can't. This is the ladies' dressing-room."

"Is anyone else in there?"

"Yes. . . . No. . . . But that makes no difference."

"In that case I'm coming in." He entered the room as he spoke. The sight of her standing there in her fur coat shocked him. "My child, what's the matter?" he cried. "You've given me an awful fright. Are you ill? What is it?"

"I'm quite well, thank you," she replied. "I'm just going home."

"Going home? What d'you mean? The evening's hardly begun."

"I can see when I'm wanted," she answered sulkily, moving to the door. He stood in her path.

"Susie, Susie, my child. . . . What's the meaning of all this nonsense?"

She shook her head obstinately. "It means nothing. I'm tired. Let me go, Harry."

He caught her arm and detained her. "You can't go like this. Why on earth don't you say what's the matter? You must be ill. You look ghastly."

She smiled wanly. His genuine anxiety softened her. "Oh, don't worry yourself about me," she entreated. "Go back to your party."

"And leave you like this? Not I, my dear! Don't be foolish."

He held her arm now so firmly that she could not escape. His distress was rather touching.

"Don't worry about *me*," she repeated. "I've a ghastly headache, that's all. I felt faint, and this place is stifling. The fresh air on the top of the bus will soon put me right."

"On the bus, Susan? Not if I know it! What a damnable shame! If you're feeling as rotten as that I must drive you home."

"And leave all the others? My dear boy, don't be ridiculous."

"The others?" he answered contemptuously. "You're all that matters to me. They'll look after themselves!"

His vehemence moved her. The pallor of his agitation made him unusually handsome. This moment of triumph—for triumph it was—was unimaginably sweet to her; yet the bitterness that lurked beneath impelled her to say: "You'd much better go back and dance with your lady friend."

He laughed. There was no mistaking her meaning. "Don't be naughty, Susie," he told her. He took command briskly. "Look here, if you'll just wait a moment, I'll tell them you're ill and that I'm going to take you home. Sit down here and keep quiet. I'll be back in a couple of seconds."

She assented feebly. "I'd much rather you wouldn't," she said; but when he was gone and she found herself sitting once more in front of the mirror, her face reflected the elation that quickened her heart. "I've won," she told herself proudly. "They can think what they like of me. I'm all that matters to him. He said so himself. Though they think that I'm nobody and treat me like dirt, he's mine—not theirs. When he tells them he's going with me they'll have to admit it." She examined her face. "No wonder he said I looked awful! It's this horrid white powder." She removed as much as was possible, closed her eyes to rest them, ran a wet finger-tip over her eyebrows and re-reddened her lips. "That's more like it," she said, with a sigh.

Harry bustled in anxiously with his coat flung over his arm. "It's all right," he assured her, "I've told them. Feeling any better?"

"Much better, thank you. My headache is nearly gone. I can manage to get home alone now, really and truly."

Her tone was less convincing than her words. Harry Levison did not miss the discrepancy. He slipped his arm round her. "Come along, that's all settled," he said. His voice was tender; his arm supported her gently yet firmly; she felt that he was sorry for what he had done and was trying to make amends. No other man in the world could have coaxed her out of her hard mood so quickly. Now that she came to consider it, Susan was forced to admit that her own behaviour had been theatrical; yet nothing in his manner hinted that he realized this or demanded the apology she owed to him and his guests. There was no need for her to explain. Yes, Harry understood women.

None the less, as she took her seat beside him in the Bentley, Susan knew that the incident was not closed. In spite of the caressing tones in which he whispered to her and his sedulous care in treating her as a delicate, overwrought creature, thoughtlessly wounded, she became increasingly aware of the power that his presence exercised and of his own consciousness of that power. The silence through which the great car shot out toward Tilton was not empty, but charged with a high emotional content which a word or a look or the

most trivial contact might release with incalculable results. It behoved her, for her own safety, to keep their
relationship matter-of-fact; so, although by this time
her headache was nearly gone, she sat mute and
apparently helpless: a frail, innocent woman whose
mood exacted an exhibition of perfect chivalry. She
could only admire the way in which, whatever he felt,
he adapted himself to this convention. His attitude
was solicitous, even tender, yet strictly formal. He
said nothing, did nothing, but what might have been
expected from a trusted friend. He was behaving, in
short, like a "perfect gentleman."

They arrived at "Chatsworth," Miss Maples noted,
at exactly two minutes past ten. Though this reasonable earliness relieved Miss Maples in one way, since
it promised her the chance of going to bed much sooner
than she had expected, she was disappointed in
another: the glimpse she had caught of Susan's splendid attire had awakened great expectations. She
noticed that Susan declined Harry Levison's arm as
they walked up the garden path. It looked, indeed,
as if they were going to say good-night on the door-
step. She saw them hesitate for one moment in the
shadow of the porch, and strained her eyes in the hope
of surprising a kiss. Then Susan opened the door and
they passed inside. A light bloomed suddenly in the
living-room window, and revealed them facing each
other on either side of the fireplace. Though she could
hear no sound, Miss Maples knew by the rapid move-

GG

ments of his hands that Levison was speaking urgently. Susan shook her head and flung her arms wide in a gesture of impatience. Then, as though becoming aware of the threat to their privacy, she moved swiftly toward the window and pulled down the blind. Miss Maples, though tensely excited, was compelled to cultivate patience.

Inside, Susan turned from lowering the blind to face Harry Levison. He smiled. "Yes, that's prudent," he said. He seemed quite at his ease, yet excitement coloured his voice—the same excitement which a moment before (as Miss Maples noticed) had made him employ a Jewish excess of gesture when Susan suggested he ought to go back to North Bromwich. Susan, too, caught his mood's infection. She felt uncertain of herself, as if between dizzy alternations of triumph and humiliation, of anger and gratitude, she had momentarily lost her sense of direction, her position in space. Though the headache had gone and the fumes of champagne dispersed she was oddly lightheaded. When she spoke, her words seemed somehow not to belong to her; when she laughed, her laughter had a ghostly, unreal sound. She saw herself from a distance, with uncritical interest, and wondered what in the world this rash creature, who most certainly was not herself, would say or do next. She saw their surroundings indeed—that cheap little room with its reminders of everyday life in the shape of Dick's pictures of Brunstone, her own books and Captain

Small's shell-case, all dramatically compressed and isolated by the drawn blind—as a scene in process of development in a toy-theatre. She saw the two leading characters—a flashy (yet so handsome) young man in evening dress and a dark-haired excited girl, so slim and silvery, with a similar detachment. But for once in her life she was unable to dramatize herself. The threads of the drama were held in a more powerful hand.

She saw herself, with a semblance of superb composure, taking a box from the mantelpiece and offering him a cigarette. She heard him decline it. "Not that kind, thank you. I'd rather have one of my own." As he lit it his fingers trembled. She smiled; so he was nervous, too.

"Very well. Don't you think you'd better be going back?" she heard herself saying with wise persuasiveness.

"You're not very hospitable, Susie."

She laughed with faint scorn. "Hospitality sounds the wrong word for you at this moment. What about all your poor guests?"

"Many thanks for the kind enquiries. They're probably enjoying themselves. So am I."

"Without Miss Egerton?" some devil tempted her to ask.

"Miss Egerton can go to hell for all I care."

"Is that how you usually speak about your old mistresses?"

He took up her challenge quickly.

"So that's it, is it? You're jealous."

"Of a woman like that? Well, really!"

"My dear child, you're as jealous as a cat. Look here, Susie, don't you think it's just about time we two understood each other?" He tossed his half-smoked cigarette into the empty grate with an air of clearing for action. The gesture scared her.

"I think I understand you perfectly," she said, "but I'm afraid you don't understand *me*. If you did, you'd go, Harry."

He laughed uneasily, but held his ground none the less.

"I can't turn you out, you know," she said. "Do you want me to make a scene?"

"I want you to be natural for once."

"That's just what I will be. Honestly, I'm tired out. I'm going to bed."

She moved to the door; he watched her with a smile of malicious amusement, but did not stir. His refusal to speak embarrassed her. "Do be reasonable, Harry," she pleaded. "I can't stand here like this. Look, I'm going to turn out the light." She stood with her hand on the switch, but he did not move. "Very well, then . . ." The strained silence was broken by a click, and the room went black.

(*At ten twenty-two*, Miss Maples noted, *they turned out the light.*)

"I shouldn't have done that," Susan thought. "It was far too dramatic."

What was more important, the gesture had failed in its effect. Harry Levison made no sign of moving. "Can you see your way out?" she enquired in a voice that trembled.

"I can see all I want," he said softly, coming toward her.

She retreated hurriedly now, but he was too quick for her. "You little devil!" he whispered. Midway in the hall he caught her.

"Let me go," she pleaded. "Don't, please . . . for God's sake let me go, Harry!"

"Don't be foolish, Susie! I'm not going to hurt you. You know how things are with us."

"But you mustn't, Harry. . . . You mustn't. . . . Oh, you're spoiling everything," she wailed.

"Spoiling what? We're not children. We know our own minds. Don't be cruel."

"Leonora . . ." she whispered.

"Oh, damn Leonora! That's just what I mean. It's our only chance."

"No, no. . . . Let me go. I can't, Harry. You mustn't. . . . Not here. . . ."

With an effort she wrenched herself free and made for the bedroom door, but once more when she tried to close it he was too quick for her and wedged his foot in it.

"You're mad!" she cried, "you're mad! Oh, what can I do?"

As midnight approached Miss Maples's excitement became intolerable. Since the moment when the sitting-room light went out the house had been wrapped in silence and darkness. The bulk of the big yellow Bentley still blocked Ada Road, and from her window it was impossible to see whether lights were still burning at the back of the house. This was extremely unsatisfactory; so having pulled on some rubber-soled snow-boots and moving on tiptoe for fear of waking mamma, Miss Maples slipped out of the scullery door, climbed the fence of the kitchen-garden, and made a wide cast through the field in the rear of "Chatsworth." Not a glimmer of light enlivened the bungalow's squat shape; not a whisper broke the silence of the owl-haunted winter night. As she stood by the impassable quickthorn that hedged the back garden Miss Maples shivered, for she had neglected to put on a coat; but the virginal soul within that chill, desiccated frame, roared in wild conflagration at the thought of the enormity concealed behind those blank windows.

"How could such things be?" she asked herself passionately; but the fact that they undoubtedly were made her heart pound so violently against her thin chest that she scarcely knew where she was going as she groped her way back to "Welbeck." Nor, when she crept into bed, did the fire abate. She lay restless, wide-eyed; her heart never ceased its wild tumult. Far into the night that exquisite torture continued. At 3.30

a.m., when the whirr of the Bentley's self-starter ripped the silence like tearing silk, Maud Maples was still awake.

II

Mr. Bulgin, striding down to his office through the crisp morning air, having slept the sound sleep of a quiet conscience and being at peace with the world, was astonished to hear that a lady awaited his convenience, and even more surprised when he learned that her business was confidential and that she preferred not to give her name. For one moment it crossed his mind that Susan Pennington might have come to her senses at last, in which case. . . . But the lady, his secretary said, was neither young nor attractive. On the contrary. So he sighed, and allowed Miss Maples to come in.

"I'm afraid that the worst has happened," she told him breathlessly. "In fact, it's so bad that I'm almost ashamed to speak of it. Mamma and I both agreed that it would be far wiser not to telephone, so I came here at once."

Mr. Bulgin courageously steeled himself to hear "the worst." "What exactly . . . ?" he asked.

Miss Maples blushed. Since last night she had been blushing continuously. Mr. Bulgin, with a sorrowful air, made notes on a scribbling-pad, and uttered, from time to time, a tut-tut of encouragement.

"Ten minutes past ten, did you say? The same car? Quite so: young Levison. They put out the light in the front-room half an hour later. *And* the back? Dear, dear. . . . I'm afraid there's no shadow of doubt."

There was none, Miss Maples agreed with emphatic reluctance.

"It's a very sad business, this," Mr. Bulgin declared, "a human tragedy. I had my doubts from the first. I blame myself, Miss Maples."

Miss Maples disputed this strongly; he had acted splendidly; but Mr. Bulgin would not be consoled; he couldn't help thinking, he said, of that poor young man.

"Perhaps we are not too late after all," he continued charitably. Miss Maples wished she could think so, but shook her head. "In any case," Mr. Bulgin wisely insisted, "the matter is so delicate that it needs to be handled carefully. The person we have to consider first is poor young Pennington. I don't even know that we should be justified in telling him the truth—the whole truth at any rate. The obvious course is to bring him home as quickly as possible and prevent any more of these scandals which, I'm sure, you feel deeply."

"Poor mamma's even more upset than I am," Miss Maples affirmed; "it's such a disgrace to the neighbourhood that she can't get over it."

"So you've told her?" Mr. Bulgin asked quickly.

"I always tell mamma everything; she noses it out in any case."

"I think," Mr. Bulgin said, "for poor Pennington's sake, it would be wiser to keep this private. You may rest contented that the kindly interest you've taken in this lamentable case has not been wasted. I'm most grateful to you for his sake. You may have been the means of preventing the breaking-up of a happy home. Not a word, please, Miss Maples, to anyone else! I'll think the whole matter over and deal with it personally. Just a hint, perhaps . . . perhaps nothing. We must work for the happiness of both of them. Poor young people! Married life is not easy in these unprincipled days," he said with a sigh.

Miss Maples sighed too. A thing like this made her only too thankful to have escaped the perils of early matrimony.

That evening, as soon as the office was empty, Mr. Bulgin removed the cowl from his secretary's typewriter and set himself to the composition of an anonymous letter on a plain sheet of paper. It was a wise, kind anonymous letter, composed without spite or heat. While the writer hoped for the best and was unwilling to put any unpleasant construction on the facts he related, he felt it his duty, prompted by local reports, to assemble those facts for Dick Pennington's information. A young man named Levison (business address: 64, Sackville Row) had been a frequent visitor (dates and times enumerated) to "Chatsworth" during Dick's absence. It was possible, of course, that Levison was an intimate friend of his—in which case the less said the better; no harm was done, anyway. His last visit, however, on the night of Tuesday, October the twenty-eighth, appeared, on the surface, to have overstepped the bounds of propriety. Levison had entered the house at two minutes past ten and left it at three-thirty precisely. In the interval all lights had remained extinguished. Any comment was unnecessary. Perhaps Mrs. Pennington had a perfectly good explanation. That was as it might be. The one thing the writer felt was that Dick ought to *know*. Mr. Bulgin remained (out of habit), his faithfully, Well-wisher.

Having typed Dick's address in capital letters, Mr. Bulgin carried the letter into Halesby to make certain of catching the evening post. As he dropped it into the letter-box he almost collided with George Lorimer, who had run up the High Street on a similar errand. Their eyes met; Mr. Bulgin's face lightened into a benignant smile.

"Why George," he began—he was going to add "I haven't seen you for months. How's things going?"

But no sooner had George Lorimer caught sight of him than his face went crimson. He jammed on his bowler hat and scurried across the road like a bolted rabbit. "Now I wonder if he's calling a meeting of his creditors," Mr. Bulgin reflected; "and I wonder what he'll think of his precious niece when he hears about this! And I wonder what *she'll* have to say when her husband comes home!"

He didn't wonder, curiously enough, what Susan was feeling then. She had been wakened that morning by the knock of the postman bringing Dick's daily letter to memories that seemed entirely divorced from reality. Her recollection of what had happened was painfully clear; but she had a strange feeling that it had not happened to herself—that it belonged to the fantastic life of the detached figure whose movements and dialogue she had followed last night with such dispassionate interest. That she, Susan Pennington, had actually taken part in that scene and the deplorable (if romantic) sequel seemed entirely incredible. It was like a bad dream conjured out of the stuff of the books she had been reading or the heated imaginations she had cherished in Picture Theatres.

After all, it wasn't a dream. When she opened her eyes with reluctance—for her head ached dully—the daylight revealed unquestionable details of that dark adventure which she recognized with an odd confusion of pride and revulsion. She was sick with herself, she was terribly sorry for Dick; her heart overflowed with shame and penitence, with the desire, whatever it might cost her, to make amends for this unamendable wrong. Yet, even as these emotions brought tears to her eyes another self cried: "At last! You've lived dangerously; you've expressed your true self and resolved all your inhibitions. They may call Harry what they like—he remains a Great Lover. *Your* lover—and you're his mistress. You have *given yourself!*

You've sinned magnificently! You have actually committed adultery!"

That word she had read it often lately with mingled awe and excitement; but now, when she breathed it to herself, it took on an ugly sound, and the thing that it represented when stripped of its mystery was no longer alluring—much less magnificent. The setting of her blind escapade—that disordered room, Mr. Bulgin's walnut bedstead, her rumpled clothes, her untidy dressing-table—was mean enough to destroy the last shreds of illusion. These inanimate witnesses of her lapse appeared to be gathered in judgment on her; their verdict was reinforced by the deep-rooted instinct of propriety which her mind had inherited from many generations of respectable middle-class ancestors.

So, accused by these outward reminders of former virtue and these inward promptings, she began to wonder whether, after all, she was a spectacular heroine in the grand tradition of passion or not, rather, a loose little fool who had weakly followed the way of least resistance. Not even the Great Lover himself could escape this tribunal. Was he really so richly romantic as she had supposed? Wasn't he just, on the contrary, a common-place, cheap seducer, who habitually exploited his handsome face, his smooth tongue and his glittering possessions to "get what he wanted" from gullible fools like herself? It was easy enough to see how Muriel O'Brien or the Egerton woman had succumbed to him; such creatures were his natural prey. But that she, Susan Pennington, who had boasted of being fastidious, should have fallen at the first essay, was a bitter reflection. "I might have done better than that!" she thought contemptuously.

With intense disgust she examined herself in her dressing-mirror. It surprised her to find that the glass reflected no trace of the degradation she felt. Her face, indeed, showed a curious freshness and innocence, which made her loathe it the more. As she gazed at it there arose in the back of her mind a strong desire to remove from her sight all reminders of what had happened. It was with the sense of performing some arbitrary lustral rite that, when she had bathed and cleansed herself, she collected all the clothes she had worn on the night before—the silvery frock, the fur coat, the grey stockings, the slippers, even her underclothes—and ruthlessly crammed them into the fire beneath the scullery boiler.

The task was less easily accomplished than she had imagined. Though the tinsel of the dress and the cellulose silk went up in a crackle, the French heels of the slippers and the pelt of the coat resisted the flames. There seemed something symbolical, she felt, in this resistance. She knew, for a moment, the panic of a murderer thwarted in the disposal of his victim's remains; amid the black ashes these fragments protruded like bones. After searching the house in vain for paraffin to quicken combustion she drew off a can of petrol from the tank of Dick's motor-bicycle and rashly flung it on the embers, which burst into a gust of flame that singed her eyebrows.

"Perhaps it would have been better," she thought, "if my clothes had caught fire and I'd been burnt to death. An easy way out of it! Nothing matters really after this."

Some things mattered a great deal, she discovered, as the day wore on and she began to think more clearly. The person who mattered most, after all, was Dick. The abasement of her own bodily and spiritual pride was a negligible matter. The tears that brimmed her eyes as she sat thinking of him in the little front-room which had now become so hateful, amid such reminders of his boyish innocence as the Brunstone photographs and the tasselled football-cap, sprang, for once, from her heart and not from her imagination. If she drama- tized her guilt (as she did) the rôle which she assigned to herself was no longer heroic. She had known humiliation before, but never humility. "If I lie till I'm blue in the face," she told herself, "poor Dick mustn't know."

Why should he know, after all? They were already separated by half the width of England. Even when he returned there was little likelihood of the poor innocent's encountering anyone who was aware of her Grand Midland existence. Captain Small had seen her in the Bentley with Harry Levison; but surely a motor- drive was an innocent thing? Should she warn Captain

Small not to mention it? That might look suspicious. Far better allude to the encounter frankly and casually when next she saw him. She had treated him rather badly during the last few months, and this only showed how blind her illusion had made her. That poor, blasted figure was worth a dozen of Harry! What other witnesses could spite gather against her? Dick's friend, the Inspector? She hated that man; he noticed everything. It was lucky that he had never caught sight of her, as far as she knew, in Harry's company. Miss Maples? That dry old spinster! She had seen Harry's car of course; but she had seen Mr. Bulgin's as well. After all, "Chatsworth" wasn't a convent.

It seemed, indeed, as if all the facts told in her favour—much more, she was ready to admit, than her conduct deserved. Unless. . . . There ran through her mind a new possibility—a possibility so damning in its implications that her body went cold and sick. Supposing . . . No, that couldn't happen. . . . Yet Jews were notoriously fertile; only look at their families! Her scared mind began to work swiftly. There was only one way of forestalling that awful emergency. Though it added unutterable meanness to her guilt she had no choice left but to take it.

"I must go down to Pandypool for a week-end to make certain of that," she thought grimly.

In the middle of the afternoon Captain Small "rolled up" gaily for tea. She was glad of any diversion that could prevent her thinking of herself; but each word that he spoke was charged with a bitter significance, for he deemed it his duty to talk about nothing but Dick. Whenever she answered him Susan felt she was on her defence.

"It's rotten for you to be cooped up here all alone," he said sympathetically. "My old leg's been playing up lately like the very devil or I'd have taken you out on a bit of a spree myself, though Lord knows I'm poor company for anyone. I suppose old Dick wouldn't mind?"

"Dick? Of course not. He's always bothering me to go out more. But I'm quite happy here."

"By Jove, what a wife! Lucky devil! They're not all like that."

"As a matter of fact"—Susan snatched at the opportunity—"I've had one or two motor drives lately. A friend took me out. The autumn colours are marvellous."

Captain Small coughed nervously. "Do you know," he said, "I'm glad you mentioned that. I thought I saw you out driving one night, but I wasn't quite sure, so I hardly liked to speak of it. Who's the friend, by the way?"

She laughed. "I don't think I'll tell you; you'll probably be angry. As a matter of fact there's no earthly reason why I shouldn't. It was Harry Levison."

"Harry Levison? My eye! Don't think much of your company, Susan."

"I know you don't. After all, he's amusing and . . . harmless."

Captain Small shook his head. "Well, with you, I dare say it's all right. But with ninety-nine women in a hundred . . ."

"As a matter of fact I'm not going with him again."

"I say, Susan, he didn't . . ." Captain Small began indignantly. His hand clutched his stick; he looked murderous.

Susan laughed. "Of course he didn't. Do you think I'm so easily approachable?"

"No, no. As you were! But I do think it's a bit rough on old Dick never seeing you for months at a time."

"Yes, it's been rough on both of us," she told him. "That's why I've decided to give him a surprise and run down to Pandypool this week-end or the next."

"Now isn't that topping?" Captain Small's face glowed with benevolence. "You know, Susan, old Dick and you are my ideal of a married couple. Whenever I think about getting married myself the picture of you two puts the wind up me. I know jolly well my marriage could never be anything like yours. You're unique; that's the truth; and, by gad, there's no getting beyond it! When I think of you two, sitting here round the fire of an evening . . ." He broke off suddenly. "I say . . . there's somebody knocking. Shall I go to the door?"

There was no need for him to go. The knock was

followed by a rapid step in the hall. Harry Levison stood smiling in the sitting-room doorway.

"Hello, Susan," he said. "I apologize. I thought you were alone."

She pulled herself together. "Do you know Captain Small?" she said.

"No, I don't think we've met," Harry Levison answered graciously. He held out his hand. Small shook it with obvious distaste. He had the air of a shaggy watch-dog who snarls with bared teeth, to its owner's despair, at a friendly visitor.

"I was just on the point of going," he said. "Good-bye, Susan."

"Oh, don't go!" Susan pleaded. She really meant it this time. She felt that when once he was gone she would have lost the only protection that stood between herself and . . . what? She followed him into the hall, still begging him to stay.

"I can't stick that blighter," he whispered; "he makes me see red. If I don't clear out I might go in off the deep end. Take care of yourself, Susan," he said as he limped away.

"Take care of myself!" she thought bitterly. She returned to the living-room. Harry Levison stood firmly planted in front of the fire, as though in possession. He smiled as she entered.

"Another admirer!" he said. "Congratulations!"

Susan scanned him from head to foot, from his sleek, wavy hair to his beige cloth-topped patent-leather boots. In that glance the last of her illusions withered away. She saw him now as, a moment before, Captain Small had seen him: as an overdressed, shoddy, vulgar provincial "blood." He stood with one hand jingling keys or money in his trouser-pocket; she noticed the rings on the other, his big diamond tie-pin, and the thought of his money sickened her. Why, now that she came to examine him, he wasn't even good-looking. His nose was too big; the skin of his clean-shaven cheeks was coarse-textured and sallow; all the grossness of the middle-aged Jew was inherent in his carefully-tailored figure. When he said the word "Congratulations" he lisped. She was consumed with hatred and rage, not so much against this mean pinchbeck creature as against herself for having been taken in by his Brummagem glitter. He was clever in his way . . . No, she wouldn't even say that for him. A man with any perceptions would surely see what she was thinking now.

Harry obviously didn't. His face still wore the masterful air of a Pasha condescending to visit his latest favourite. The satisfied smile with which he surveyed her was lazy, possessive.

"Well, thank God he cleared out," he said condescendingly. "That's a mangy customer, anyway."

He laughed lightly. That laugh released a hair-trigger in Susan's brain. All her scorn and distress and hatred exploded with surprising suddenness.

"How dare you—how dare you say that?" she heard

herself crying. "He's worth twenty of you. Why, you're not fit to black his boots, you . . . you rotten, mean little Jew!"

Harry Levison winced as though a blow had just missed his eyes. Then he fingered the diamond pin in his Old-Harrovian tie and, swallowing the insult, returned her a fascinating smile. He laughed nervously.

"H'm . . . feeling as strongly as that? Chuck it, Susan. Come here and be sensible. You've never said how you are, and you haven't kissed me."

Susan shuddered and stood motionless. Was he deaf, then, as well as blind? If such insults as those failed to wound him. . . ! Still smiling, he threw back his head in a commanding gesture. "Come here!" he repeated. "It's no use showing off with me." As she trembled and stood her ground he advanced toward her.

"Don't!" she gasped. "Don't touch me . . . Leave me alone. I can't bear it."

Harry laughed unpleasantly. "You bore it all right last night, and appeared to enjoy it, if you don't mind my saying so. Look here, you'd better cut out this injured innocence, Susie. That won't wash with me. Come on! What the devil's the matter with you?"

She shook her head passionately. "Everything's the matter. You've no right to come here. I didn't ask you. Please go."

He smiled caressingly. "I say, that's a bit thick, isn't it? When you've slept with a fellow . . ."

She wrung her hands in despair. "That's all over," she said.

"All over, is it? That's all you know. My dear kid, it's only beginning. Tender conscience . . . is that it? I've heard all about them before. It'll soon be better. Face the facts. We're in love with each other, Susie. Why pretend that we're not?"

"I'm not in love with you. I hate the sight of you. I hoped to God I'd seen the last of you. Is that plain? Don't you understand? Must I say it all over again?"

His fixed smile became ugly. "Rather a quick change of feeling, isn't it?" he said, with an easy insolence.

"I mean it. I despise myself more than you. I don't even blame you."

"That's a great relief. Thank you for nothing! I wish you could tell me the meaning of this sudden delicacy. I don't remember you being so delicate when you wanted money. You didn't mind taking it either. Thirty-six quid!"

"That just shows what he's like," she thought fiercely. "It was a business arrangement," she said. "You suggested it yourself. I never asked for it."

"Oh, yes, we know all about that," he broke in bitterly. "A business arrangement! The good old kind: heads I win, tails you lose. That's *your* sort of business!" He changed his tone suddenly. "I'm sorry I mentioned that, Susie. It was rotten of me. Forget what I've said. Let's be good friends, anyway. Of course I don't grudge you the money; you can have as much as you want. You looked topping last night in that silver frock."

"I burnt it this morning." She shuddered. "The fur coat—everything! That shows how I feel."

It showed him she was even madder than he had imagined, unless she were bluffing. The thought of this wilful waste really shocked Mr. Levison. "You've burnt them? Is that the truth!" he demanded incredulously.

She was calmer now. "I've told you nothing but the truth. It's no good your staying here arguing. It's finished. I've no more to say. If you don't leave the house, I shall. If you've any decency. . . ."

"Well, you've not done so badly out of it, have you?" was all Mr. Levison could say.

The interview, according to Miss Maples's timing, had lasted exactly ten minutes.

As soon as Levison had gone, Susan sat down and wrote a tearful letter to Dick. She was so miserable, she said, and she loved him so much that she couldn't stand being alone at "Chatsworth" any longer. "So, whatever you say, and whatever it costs," she went on, "I'm determined to come next week-end. I shall never be happy till I've seen you again, my darling . . ." The writing of this letter gave her some satisfaction, for she meant every word that she wrote; but it took her so long to phrase what she meant satisfactorily that it missed the post which Mr. Bulgin's wise, kind anonymous letter had caught.

III

Dick Pennington always came home from work to
his diggings tired out. Pandypool, as Mr. Bulgin had
said when he talked of taking Susan with him, was not
exactly a health resort. It lay in a mighty trough of the
millstone-grits, the biggest of a series of squalid mining
villages that thickened a mineral-line running north
and south like knots on a piece of dirty string. At the
head of the valley and on either side of it rose bald
masses of mountain, resembling the flanks of sleeping
mammoths that had lost their hair. On those grim
lower slopes no living thing throve or had thriven for
a century; for the south-west wind scoured them with
hot fumigations of sulphurous vapour that hung there
like gas in a retort, perpetually settling in a slow downward drift of grime, save when rain, unclean and acrid
to the tongue, fell in sheets that gurgled through blue-
brick gutters and culverts to befoul a stream already
polluted by waste from the tinworks.

In all this sad valley Mr. Bulgin's new works showed
the only signs of healthy activity. Already the Pittsburg presses and rolling-mills had begun their task of
meeting the demands of the Venezuelan contract. Day
and night, under those lowering skies, Dick could hear
the muffled shrieks and grunts of shunting-engines;
the clank of couplings that clashed like gigantic cymbals
from end to end of the long trains of mineral-wagons;

the stutter of hammers riveting plates and girders; the
thunder of rollers, the long-drawn cries that were
wrung from the travail of metal, and the hiss of escaping steam that perpetually rose from the huge works'
simmering activity. If he saw nothing of the scene's
monstrosity, it is equally true that its dark, savage
beauty missed him: those moments of swarthy splendour when the smoke-screen lifted, revealing, on the
barren slopes, long white farms that at midday seemed
washed in moonlight; the nocturnal flowers of flame
that were sprayed from black furnace-throats; the
billows of foam-white steam-jets thrown insolent and
inviolate against cliffs of curdled smoke or black walls
of mountain. Indeed he regarded this seventh circle of
hell as a mildish purgatory, the price of the sweet
heaven that awaited him at "Chatsworth."

He faced the test with enthusiasm. It was a matter
of pride with him to "clock in" at the earliest moment;
to grudge nothing of his abundant physical strength
and his laboriously-exerted intelligence. That, indeed,
was much more at home in the works than in a
merchant's office. He had for machinery the instinctive
understanding that is born of affection. He handled its
details lovingly; he venerated its huge, silken efficiency,
and worshipped its shapes with more imagination, perhaps, than he had ever given to any living thing.

All his life was centred in the works. At his diggings
he merely existed, cheerfully swallowing the fried
supper that his landlady threw at him, grateful for

the lumpy mattress on which he slept, and reading again and again, whenever he felt "blue", the letters that came from Susan. Of late that spiritual refreshment had been scanty and flavourless. It wasn't merely, he decided, a matter of distance. It seemed rather as if Pandypool resembled one of those silent zones in the ether which wireless waves cannot penetrate. Susan complained that the letters he wrote to her had the same defect. He preferred, indeed, to dwell on the visions his memory supplied. When he closed his eyes in the dark and rain spattered or whipped the window-panes, he could see her snugly ensconced in the warmth of "Chatsworth," curled up on the sofa reading in front of the fire and smiling to herself, now and then, when she thought of him. He could see her rise and stretch her arms like a lazy kitten, and switch off the light, and lock the front door, and make her way to their bedroom. When he thought of her lying there lonely, his heart would grow full of ineffable tenderness.

It was not lack of faith but an ardent desire to refresh these lovely memories that occasionally made him restless and compelled him to ask the engineer to whom he was attached what the firm meant to do with him. The head-office gave no new instructions. He was told that this silence was propitious, and advised to leave it at that—which was all very well, Dick thought: his boss was a bachelor!

On the Wednesday evening when Susan wrote

suggesting that she should come down for a week-end to Pandypool Dick had reached the limit of endurance and was planning to write to her on the very same subject. Susan's letter, addressed to his lodgings, missed the post and did not reach him; but as soon as he arrived at the works next morning the time-keeper gave him Mr. Bulgin's.

As he read it Dick's head went giddy. Apart from the enormities it suggested, the fact that it was anonymous was enough to make him indignant. Of course, he told himself, he didn't believe a word of it. It was the work, no doubt, of some poisonous, jealous female. Miss Maples. . . ? No, not even Miss Maples could have been guilty of such a dastardly act. After one awful moment his fiery faith triumphed over it. He would treat it with the contempt that their love demanded, as though it did not exist. He threw himself into the morning's work with bravado; but even as he worked, the letters of Mr. Bulgin's typescript ate into his heart like acid. Whatever he did, wherever he went, they burned on his inward eye. By eight o'clock, when the gang knocked off for breakfast, he could stand it no longer. He sought out his boss and demanded two days' absence.

"Can't you wait till Saturday?" the engineer asked gruffly.

"I should like to catch the next train."

"Why, what's up? Nothing wrong at home, I hope?"

"No, no. Nothing wrong. I've just had a letter." Dick trembled. "It's rather disturbed me . . . a matter of urgent business."

"Well, whatever it is, I can see it's turned you up a bit. You look sick as a cat. Yes, of course you can go. Clear out and come back on Monday. If I were you I should take a spot of brandy to steady me."

Dick hardly waited to thank him. There was a train, he knew, leaving Pandypool at five minutes past nine. He was so obsessed with the necessity of getting to "Chatsworth" that the thought of cleaning himself or changing his clothes did not even occur to him. He threw his overalls into his locker and ran for the station, where he caught the nine-five train by the skin of his teeth.

Of the journey northward to the Midlands he remembered nothing. He sat staring in front of him, his grimy hands clasped on his knees, in a strained, eager attitude as though, by sheer force of will, he could make the train go faster. It was a peerless October morning, though Dick did not know it. Great mountains rose blue on his left; brown rivers raced tumbling past; farmers' dog-carts, loaded for market, waited at level-crossings. In Herefordshire men were ploughing red fields for winter corn; gulls wheeled in the air at the tail of the plough, the hedges were shaggy with clematis. A covey of driven partridge went past in a flurry; two brace checked in the air, then fluttered and fell like stones; men with guns in their hands stared mildly at the passing train.

Dick saw them, yet saw not. In his breast-pocket, next his cold heart, lay Mr. Bulgin's letter. That folded paper, the vehicle of an evil will, had power of its mere existence to nullify every other sensual impression. It was almost as if the ink in which it was typed possessed penetrative qualities transcending those of any rays known to science; it burned through the mortal tissues of skin and bone and flesh to brand its message indelibly on Dick's innermost soul. HARRY LEVISON. Again and again the letters glowed and faded. HARRY LEVISON . . . HARRY LEVISON . . . HARRY LEVISON . . . The words were caught up in the regular rhythm of the rails—a rhythm that quickened now, for the train had crossed the watershed betwixt Wye and Monnow and was racing downhill between mellow cider-orchards and hop-yards. In a roll of hollow thunder they crossed the Wye bridge. The river flowed sullenly here, bank-high. In its tawny mirror the sandstone tower of a cathedral appeared and was gone.

"Hereford, Hereford," porters were calling as the train slid past them. "Change for Worcester, North Bromwich and the North . . . for Worcester, North Bromwich and the North . . . for Worcester . . ."

Dick got out of his carriage mechanically. "By your leave, sir!" A trolley of empty milk-cans rolled clattering past. A bothered old lady with two baskets caught his arm. "Does the Brecon train leave from this platform?" she demanded urgently.

"I really don't know, ma'am," he told her.

"Well, you ought to. You're a railwayman, aren't you?" she answered indignantly. Her words reminded him that he was wearing his working clothes.

Fifteen minutes to wait. Why need they waste time like this? He found himself facing a poster with the old parrot-cry: *Come to Breezy Brinton on Britain's Bluest Bay.* "It was there that she first met Levison," he thought. "But of course it's all a damned lie."

Fourteen minutes to wait. There must be something wrong with that clock. The bookstall confronted him with a row of variegated news-sheets. *New Low Record for Copper* . . . *Famous Film-Star's Confession.* . . . *Husband Strangles Unfaithful Wife and Shoots Lover* . . . The last words suddenly lit a red spot in his brain, like the glow of black-hot metal under the jet of a blow-pipe. The spot reddened quickly, then went dull and dead. "That's not England," he thought. "We've no time here for that Unwritten Law stuff. Besides, he isn't her lover. Lover be damned! The person who wants shooting is the woman that wrote that letter—and by God, if I find out who wrote it . . ." The red spot lightened again—like one of those warning lights, he thought, on a Yankee car's dashboard that tell you when you've left the ignition switched on. Red for danger! At his feet the levering-gear of a signal made a metallic sound. They were clearing the line.

"Train for Worcester, North Bromwich and the North!" a ticket-inspector was bawling. As he shouted Dick's bothered old lady with the baskets bobbed up in front of him. "Is this train the one for Brecon?" she eagerly enquired. "No, madam, it isn't. It's what I said it was," the inspector answered haughtily. "Keep back, please!" he cried. The train snorted in.

It was three minutes late already. They were wasting no time. The guard blew his whistle. They were off. .

HARRY LEVISON . . . HARRY LEVISON . . . HARRY LEVISON . . .

These exact dates and hours . . . *L arrived at five-thirty and left at seven. L arrived with Mrs. P. at two minutes past ten; lights put out at ten-thirty.* It must have taken a devilish mind to invent those details. If Levison had called at the house, Susan would certainly have mentioned it in her letters. Why, she even took the trouble to tell him when Captain Small came to tea. If there was one thing he could be sure about in Susan it was her absolute straightness. The rhythmical beat of the rails grew slower; the train panted up the gradient that crossed the flank of the Malverns. The might of those great green engines: he had always loved them! The rhythm quickened. They went banging through Colwall tunnel.

"Poor kid!" he thought, "she'll be scared to death when she sees me. I ought to have sent her a wire to warn her I was coming. And what shall I say when I get there? What *can* I say? Better show her the letter, I suppose. What a damnable business! The truth of the matter is I should have taken no notice and torn it to pieces. That's what it deserves. It isn't as if she didn't know all about Levison. She knows what a blighter he is from the way he behaved at Brinton with that little bitch Muriel O'Brien . . ."

Another cathedral tower and a tapering spire. Another great river, bank-high. "Next stop North Bromwich!"

The train pulled up at the platform on which he had met Susan when she came home from Chapel Green. He remembered walking beside her up the station steps, out of breath with excitement and the weight of her bulging suit-case. It all might have happened yester-day—even to-day. The same bustling, ill-dressed crowd thronged the noisy booking-hall; the same tram-cars jolted and jangled and whirred in the street out-side; the same people jostled him on the pavement with the same unconcern. A red Tilton bus was just moving away as he reached the terminus. Dick ran for it, at the risk of his life, and swung himself aboard.

"That was a near shave, young man," a familiar voice informed him. "What are *you* doing here?"

The voice was Inspector Frome's.

"Just home for the week-end," Dick told him.

"It's Thursday," the Inspector remarked.

"Yes. I've got to be back at Pandypool on Sunday night, though."

"Pandypool. That's in Monmouthshire, isn't it?"

"Yes, it's not very far from Glamorgan. I'm giving my wife a surprise."

"Left in rather a hurry, didn't you?" the Inspector asked, with a glance at Dick's clothes.

"Yes, I only got a letter this morning."

"A letter: then it can't be exactly a surprise," said the Inspector reprovingly. "And that can't be the letter I saw her posting last night. I remember noticing she was just too late for the mail-van. About six thirty-three, I should call it. What time did you say you left?"

"Oh, somewhere about nine o'clock," Dick answered impatiently.

"But you went to your work first thing?" Dick was silent. "Well, I hope you'll find everything all right when you get there," the Inspector said gloomily.

"He knows something," Dick thought. "I can't bear any more of this." He excused himself: "I'm going up on the top to get some fresh air."

At the Tilton cross-roads he dismounted before the Inspector could catch him. With every yard that carried him nearer to the awful moment his heart had gone colder and colder. As he hurried through Tilton he had the impression that his movements were being followed by curious eyes. The October sun which had gilded the Herefordshire orchards no longer shone; the air of the high Midland plateau was dank and sodden, its chill bit into his bones. At the corner of

Ada Road he stopped to pull himself together. It was no use. His cold heart kept up a terrified gallop. White as death in his oil-befouled work-clothes he passed through the garden wicket and entered the hall of "Chatsworth."

"Susan, Susan!" he called. His voice was shrill with agony. "Where are you?" he called.

"Dick . . ." Her voice was a terrified whisper. "Dick . . . What's the matter?"

She stood in the kitchen doorway, her face whiter than his. She did not move forward to kiss him, though he held out his arms.

"Then it's true . . . My God, it's all true," he thought, his heart turning to stone.

"There's a letter," he said. "I got it at the works this morning. I came home at once. Please read it."

She recovered herself first.

"Come in to the fire," she said calmly. She passed into the room in front of him. "A letter? What do you mean?"

He gave her the letter; then sat down, his head clasped in his hands. With each labouring pulse-beat the danger-light throbbed and waned in his brain. She stood still as a statue, holding the letter to the light. Her face, though he did not dare look at it, showed no sign of emotion.

"An anonymous letter," she said at last. "I suppose you believe it?"

"Of course not. I can't," he cried.

"Then why did you come here . . . like this?"

"I don't know. It half killed me. I had to see you. For heaven's sake say something, Susie!"

She sighed. "If I said it was nothing but lies I suppose you'd believe me?"

"I believe in you utterly, Susie, utterly . . . You know it."

"And if I told you it was true?"

"Don't be cruel. This means too much to me."

"I'd rather you heard the truth from *me*, Dick," she said. "If you don't they'll be sure to invent a whole lot of lies."

"You don't mean . . . ?"

Her face gave him the answer.

"My God!" he whispered.

She spoke urgently. "Dick, listen to me. I don't want to hide anything. I shall tell you the absolute truth, the whole of the truth. This boy, Harry Levison—you know he was a pal of Muriel's. I liked him. I'd always liked him. That was partly your fault: when people show violent prejudices against anyone I always swing to the other side. Then . . . I'm going too fast, though . . . Dick, you've no idea how lonely it was being here without you. It's a rotten thing for a girl who's got used to being married like me to be left alone. Men jump at the chance and take it for granted you've no objection." He made a gesture of violent dissent. "Yes, they *do*," she insisted. "*You* know nothing about men, Dick; you're different. Why, as soon as you'd gone, Mr. Bulgin tried . . ."

"Mr. Bulgin?" he cried. "Then Levison isn't the only one?"

"Oh, wait till I've finished! You surely don't think . . ."

"I don't know what to think."

"Well, at any rate you might guess that I turned *him* down. That's the cause of this letter. If he didn't write it himself he made someone else write it. I was terribly scared at the time; I felt simply awful. I wrote to you, Dick—don't forget that!—I wrote to you. I *begged* you to let me come down to Pandypool, but you wouldn't."

"I couldn't."

"I know. That's the awful part of it. If you had . . ." She paused.

"Go on, please."

"Very well. Then one day I ran into Muriel with a man called Morris . . ."

"Another?"

"No, he's nothing to do with it. I went to lunch with them both and met Harry Levison. We—oh, how shall I put it?—we liked one another at sight. He was awfully good to me. Remember, I'd nobody to talk to. We lunched in town once or twice and had dinner together and danced. He brought me back here in his car, I can't say how often; the person who wrote that letter knows far more about it than I do. There was nothing wrong in that anyway; we were just good friends; he never once hinted—I promise you that—at anything else. If he had . . . well, I really don't know what I should have done then, and it doesn't matter now . . .

"Then, last week—no, I'm wrong, it was Tuesday, the day before yesterday—Harry gave a birthday party. We had dinner in a private room at the Grand Midland. I think there were eight of us. For some reason or other I felt rotten that evening; everything went wrong. Yes, I know what it was—you'll laugh at me—there was a beastly woman who had on a dress exactly the same as mine and I drank a lot of champagne to make me feel better. When dinner was over I loathed the whole thing so much I tried to slip away quietly. Harry missed me and caught me in the dressing-room. He was awfully decent about it. When I told him I felt ill he insisted on leaving his party and taking me home. I tried to persuade him not to, but nothing could stop him; and it *was* rather flattering for him to leave all his party like that. . . ."

She paused, but Dick made no comment; he still sat with his head in his hands. Susan sighed, and went on:

"When we got here I thanked him and told him I felt much better, and then—this is terribly difficult, Dick—then I think I said that he ought to go back to them. But he wouldn't. He stayed there"—she shuddered—"in that chair where you're sitting now. So I said, 'Well, I'm tired out, anyway: I'm going to bed,' and I turned out the light."

Lights put out at ten-thirty: the words of the letter came back to him. He heard Susan's voice, a weak, level voice, continue:

"I laughed. It seemed rather a joke. I said: 'Can you see your way out?' He said he could see all he wanted. Then I think he caught hold of me. I forget what he said exactly—something about me and him being in love with each other. I wasn't in love with him: I swear by God, darling, I've never loved anyone but you. I told him he was spoiling everything. He said, 'We're not children. We know our own minds.' But I didn't; I didn't know anything. I was just tired and helpless and sorry for him in a way. Then he went raving mad. I tried to shut him out of the bedroom, but he put his foot in the door. I thought after all it was no good fighting against it. I must have been mad too. I felt as if nothing mattered. Nothing does matter now. Dick, why don't you speak?" she cried. He was dumb.

"Why don't you kill me? I suppose you've a right to. I wish to God that you would. I've no wish to live. I can't bear any more . . ."

Dick was thinking: *Husband Strangles Unfaithful Wife and Shoots Lover.* The danger-spot reddened and waned again in his brain. His clenched fingers tightened and tore at the hair on his temples. This quick stimulus of pain, self-inflicted, released the mad tension. He gave a loud, shuddering sob. Susan saw that he was crying. His agony found vent in paroxysms of dry, awful sound. She fell at his feet, weeping too, and kissed his rough oil-stained hands. The gesture was natural and unpremeditated. She knelt, crushed and humbled. They were crying together, their hands clasped; but their stricken minds were utterly separate.

At last Dick recovered himself. The fingers that had automatically tightened on hers released their pressure. He took out his handkerchief and wiped his hands, which were wet with her tears. He stumbled to his feet so suddenly that if she had not clutched him she would have fallen.

"Where are you going?" she gasped.

He did not answer; he did not even look at her. He staggered towards the door.

"Dick!" she cried in a white alarm. She scrambled to her feet and followed him. It seemed that he himself had no clear idea where he was going. He opened the bedroom door and stared inside. His face wore an awful blankness, more terrifying than passion.

"Dick . . . Don't do anything desperate," she pleaded. "I'm the only person to blame. I'm ready to pay for it. Dick . . ."

He pushed past her roughly, slamming the front door behind him. Susan fell on the linoleum floor of the hall and shivered with fright.

IV

At five-thirty that afternoon, the business of the day
being over, Harry Levison sat in his uncle's sound-
proof office, enjoying a late cup of tea. He was not
much pleased with himself at the moment. His private
affairs were not shaping any too well. To begin with
he felt sore at having been "sold a pup" by that Pennington girl. The climax of the affair had worked out
according to programme, but just at the point when it
appeared to be reaching its most interesting and profit-
able phase the damned little fool had lost her nerve
and gone soft. That served him right for getting mixed
up with a woman of temperament. The stupid sort
were invariably a safer investment. But though he had
learnt his lesson, the sense of frustration remained;
his mind was still pestered by memories of Tuesday
night.

That wasn't the only thing that made him uncomfortable. He had hoped to repeat the *coup* he had
made in Transvaal Platinum with Rhodesian Copper,
and heavy selling in Paris had played the deuce with
that market. In addition to the Bwanas which he had
bought, so to speak, for Susan and still held, he had
staked the best part of twenty thousand pounds, which
he did not possess, in that speculative stock. He wasn't
alone; Solomon Magnus too had been stung; all their
best information pointed to a steady rise and they knew

that the copper was there in millions of tons; but the fact remained that Rhodesians continued to go down— he had lost, at the moment, approximately two thousand five hundred—and settling day was coming uncomfortably near. All day long anxious clients had been ringing up to ask what the sudden slump meant. He had told them, airily, to hang on. But Paris continued to sell.

What with one thing and another he had never felt quite so nervous in his life. And now, just to complicate matters, his uncle had returned, like a dog with its bone, to the old vexed question of his marriage with Leonora.

"I've told Dr. Haskard that I'll go to Nauheim after all," he announced. "When you've paid through the nose for advice it seems a pity to waste it. He went off on a holiday to Shropshire or somewhere yesterday and I've promised to report myself when he comes back in three weeks' time. Now I've been thinking, Harry; that seems to work out very well. I'll call in for the night and make arrangements with old Marx on the way out to Nauheim—that'll save a hotel bill—and meet you in Frankfort for the wedding on my way back three weeks later. If we arrive in Frankfort the same morning and I catch the night-mail there'll only be one day or two at the outside when one of us isn't in charge at the office. It's a beautiful building, that *Hauptsynagoge* at Frankfort: all red sandstone, Arabesque, or whatever they call it. I forget what it cost."

Harry Levison answered him less evasively than usual. He knew he would have to be married sooner or later. Since the Pennington fiasco he had had a revulsion of feeling against Gentiles and in favour of his own race. In his present financial uncertainty it would be unwise to obstruct his uncle. As a married man he would need a larger allowance—he might even demand a partnership. Leonora Marx implied Leonora's marks; and, unless things looked up, he must find the money somewhere.

"I'm glad you've decided to try Nauheim, anyway," he said. "You and old father Marx can fix the other thing up between you."

Mr. Magnus spoke fervently. "I'm glad to hear you say that. I've a strong wish to see you settled, Harry, my boy."

He leaned over the table and grasped Harry's hand dramatically in a most un-Harrovian way. As he did so they heard a tap on the door. Mr. Magnus grunted "Come in!" and his secretary entered. "Yes?" Magnus demanded brusquely.

"There's a man asking for Mr. Levison downstairs," she began.

"A man? What sort of a man?" Mr. Magnus asked. "What's he want?"

"Well, he looks like a workman, sir. He's made no appointment."

"I expect it's a man from the garage," Harry broke in. "That old Bentley's in trouble again. When I come back from Frankfort I think we'll get a Hispano."

Mr. Magnus nodded approvingly. His mood was generous.

"He asked me to give you this card, sir," the secretary continued.

Harry Levison took it. It read *Mr. and Mrs. Pennington;* but the *and* and the *Mrs.* had been crossed out and the address, *"Chatsworth," Ada Road, Tilton,* added in pencil. He went white as he read it. "Tell the fellow to wait, Miss Lewis. No, look here . . . say I've left the office."

"I told him you couldn't see him after hours, sir, but he wouldn't go. He said he knew you were still in because of the car outside."

"Well, tell him to wait, then."

Miss Lewis went. "What's the trouble, Harry?" Mr. Magnus asked anxiously.

"It's about a woman. I'm afraid I'm in a bit of a hole. I don't quite know what to do."

"Tell me all about it: the truth," Mr. Magnus said calmly.

Harry did so. Mr. Magnus listened judiciously. "This woman," he said. "I suppose she's that sort— I mean you're not the only one?"

"I believe I am. That's the deuce of it. The little fool's probably lost her head and told him. My God, what a mess!"

"We can't have any scandal before the Frankfort affair," Mr. Magnus said gravely. "What's the husband? D'you know him? Lewis said he looked like a workman."

"Oh, a clerk or something. I don't know exactly. He's been working for Bulgin."

"Hard up?"

"Yes, I think so. She's just touched me for thirty-six quid."

"H'm. In that case it looks like blackmail. You'd much better leave it to me; we can't take any risks. I've told you a dozen times, Harry—but that's neither here nor there. What's done can't be undone, but we mustn't risk any scandal. I'll have him sent up. You can go down the other staircase and get away in the car."

"I'm awfully sorry about this, uncle . . ."

"Just leave it to me," Mr. Magnus replied as he pressed the buzzer on his desk.

When the secretary returned, he said casually: "Show Mr. Pennington up," and unlocked the drawer in which his cheque-book was kept, to prepare for emergencies.

A wild-looking fellow, Mr. Magnus thought, as Dick entered. He looked deathly white in his soiled working-clothes; the sleeves of his coat were too short, exposing white wrists and enormous clenched hands. He glanced round the room like an animal caught in a cage.

"Mr. Pennington?" Magnus asked suavely.

"I don't want to see *you*," Dick answered. "I asked for Levison."

"My nephew's unfortunately away," Mr. Magnus replied.

"That's a lie. His car's at the door. I've seen it before."

"No, no, you're mistaken there," Mr. Magnus answered truthfully. "The car's mine, though it's perfectly true my nephew sometimes uses it. Please sit down and be calm. I think I can deal with your business."

The habit of years of subservience in offices compelled Dick to sit. His knotted hands writhed on the table. Ugly hands, brutal hands, Mr. Magnus thought. He was glad he'd sent Harry away.

"Look here, it's no good, Mr. Magnus," Dick broke in suddenly. "I've got to see him. You can't help me. It's very nice of you; but it's no good."

He rose violently. As he did so, his sleeve was caught in the arabesque work of silver inkstand and pulled it away. It fell to the floor with a thud and the ink was spattered not only over the chair and the Turkey carpet, but on the walls and wainscot. Mr. Magnus rapidly calculated the cost of the damage. Dick stared at it blankly.

"I say, sir, I'm sorry," he said.

"Never mind about that," Mr. Magnus answered calmly. "Sit down and listen to me."

Dick sat, in a pool of red ink.

"I've been told," Mr. Magnus continued, "about this unfortunate business. Unfortunate for all of us.

I don't apportion the blame. No doubt there are faults
on both sides. You and I are the principal sufferers.
But you know, quite as well as I do, being a man of
the world, that there's nothing to be gained by crying
over spilt . . ." He was going to say "milk," but
suddenly substituted "ink."

Dick writhed impatiently. "It's no use talking, sir.
I've told you already . . ."

"Now be calm for one moment," Mr. Magnus insisted. "What's done can't be undone. Neither you
nor I are going to gain anything by creating a scandal.
Even if I admit my nephew's in the wrong . . ."

"Excuse me, sir," Dick burst in, "I'm wasting time
here. If Levison's not here . . ."

"Sit down, sit down, Mr. Pennington. Now I speak
as one gentleman to another. You say, talk's no good.
I agree. So let's try to be practical. I admit my boy's
in the wrong; he says so himself. It's particularly
awkward for him because—I'm quite candid with you
—he's just on the point of being married. We don't
want any scandal, I repeat, and I'm prepared to do the
handsome thing to avoid it."

Mr. Magnus stretched out his podgy hand and
opened the drawer from which he extracted his private
cheque-book. He performed these movements impressively, but the gesture was lost upon Dick, whose
mind, at that moment, had sunk back into a chaos of
frustration and misery. Mr. Magnus winked kindly
as he crossed out *"Order"* and inserted *"Bearer."* Next

he filled in "One hundred pounds" and appended his signature. On the counterfoil he wrote *"Pennington— debit H.L."* Then he blotted his cheque on the clean pad in front of him and handed it to Dick with a flourish.

"There!" he said. "I think you'll agree this—er— compensation is handsome."

Dick stared at the slip of paper for a moment without comprehension. His thoughts were still fluttering and beating like bats in a darkened room. When he read what was written and grasped its import the control he had exercised all day gave way like a broken dam and the mad contents of his brain burst forth in a havoc that deafened and blinded him. There was a roaring in his ears as his helpless reason went under.

"You damned scoundrel!" he shouted. "You rotten swine! Do you think you can buy my wife with your dirty money?"

As he spoke, he sprang to his feet. Blind fury augmented his stature. He towered above Magnus, a wild and terrible figure. He appeared to be laughing; his teeth were bared; his eyes burned with a berserk frenzy. In his left fist he clenched Mr. Magnus's cheque; with his right hand he seized the chair on which he had been sitting; he raised it and whirled it above his head like a battle-axe. This outburst of physical violence acted as a safety-valve. At the height of his fury his brain went suddenly clear. He saw himself with the murderous weapon uplifted; he saw Solly

Magnus's sagging face, dirty white with fear, his gross body cowering to meet the blow he could not escape. And the blow never fell, though the unloosed strength behind it sent the heavy chair crashing to matchwood against the ink-spattered wall. Dick stared at the splintered mahogany as though he were puzzled to account for the crash and the wreckage. Then he gave a horrible laugh and made straight for the door by which he had entered.

Mr. Magnus's pale eyes watched him go. All the colour had left them. He continued to cower, as though still awaiting the blow, hunched up in his chair. He reached out his hand to press the buzzer on his desk, but the muscles refused to move it, its weight was like lead. He went suddenly giddy. The walls of the room seemed to waver and slide together; all the air was sucked out of it. There was no air to breathe. Suffocation. . . . He supposed he was going to faint. His body was sliding down. With a supreme effort he regained command of his hands. They were pulling at his collar and shirt-neck. He heard the bone stud snap and the linen tearing. Air . . . air . . . ! He gave a great gasp and slid to the floor with a bump. As he fell, the sharp edge of the desk cut his forehead. Black blood oozed slowly from a vein. It made no difference whatever to Solomon Magnus.

Miss Lewis was waiting impatiently in her little private cubby-hole on the floor below. The Art Gallery clock had struck six. There was nobody left in the offices but Mr. Magnus, herself, and the young man Pennington. She had covered her typewriter and her dictaphone and locked up her correspondence; but, although she had an appointment with another responsible young lady, it was against her principles to leave Sackville Row before Mr. Magnus. Even though it was after hours he might need her services at any moment; and he had a right to them—not only because he paid her an unusually high salary and made her his confidante, but because she had worked with the firm for fifteen years and knew more about its business than anyone employed in the office, Harry Levison not excepted, and because she regarded Mr. Magnus himself with a respect that amounted to veneration and a loyalty more satisfying than love. It was a pity, she thought, that so important a man should waste his valuable energies on interviews of this kind, and she was glad when, at five minutes past six precisely, she heard rapid steps descending the stairs and gathered that the interview was over. So she pulled on her plain black hat and her plain brown gloves, then ran upstairs quickly and tapped at the office door.

Not a sound. That was odd. Mr. Magnus always recognized her knock. She tapped again, more loudly. Still no answer. She became alarmed. Though she always smiled tactfully when Mr. Magnus scoffed at his doctors, she had not liked the look of him lately. With a fluttering heart Miss Lewis entered the room, and saw, with surprise, that Mr. Magnus's chair was empty. Then her eyes caught sight of the other wrecked chair, the spilt inkstand lying where it had fallen, and a pool of red ink that looked like blood on the Turkey carpet. She uttered a shrill cry and ran to the directors' table. Behind it she saw Mr. Magnus's heaped body and grey face. His mouth was wide open, a ragged wound gaped on his forehead. She caught him by the shoulder and tried to lift him, but her strength could not manage it. She knelt down beside him and rubbed his plump hands. "Mr. Magnus, Mr. Magnus!" she gasped, but he neither moved nor answered. Then, crying like a child, with tears running down her cheeks, she flew down the stairs and dashed out into Sackville Row. The chauffeur sat reading his *Sporting Buff* on the seat of the double-six Daimler. Miss Lewis threw herself on him.

"Martin, fetch the police! And a doctor . . . quick! He's dead! He's been murdered!"

The chauffeur gaped. " 'Oo's been murdered? 'Oo's dead? What'yer talking about?"

"Mr. Magnus. Go quickly. Get hold of that constable on point duty. Where's the nearest doctor?"

"There's scores of them round the corner."

But Miss Lewis had not waited for an answer. She set off running without any precise sense of direction into one of the squalid streets that still, regrettably, clustered within a stone's throw of the North Bromwich town-hall. She ran, risking her life in the traffic a

KK

dozen times, till suddenly she saw in front of her a
blue lamp with the word "Surgery." It was attached
to what looked like an ordinary shop-window, made
opaque, to the height of six feet from the pavement,
by black paint on which a sign-writer had inscribed a
florid legend in gilt: *Dr. Altrincham-Harris. Consulting Hours:* 9—12. 6—8. It was one of those lock-
up surgeries, the medical equivalents of Woolworth's
Stores, that do a thriving, if undignified, trade among
the poor at sixpence a consultation and sixpence extra
for medicine. A partition of varnished deal divided
the single room. On the wooden benches of the outer
compartment a number of shawled women and awe-
stricken children sat listening to the consultation that
was taking place within.

Miss Lewis swept past them ruthlessly. Behind the
partition she surprised a bashful young man who was
stripped to the waist and the doctor himself, a mean
little figure with a straggling beard in an alpaca
jacket.

"You can't come in here, madam," he shouted indignantly and quite ineffectually.

"Are you the doctor?" Miss Lewis panted.

"Yes, I am. But you can't come in here. Kindly
wait your turn."

"You must come with me at once." Miss Lewis was
accustomed to command. "There's a murder in Sackville Row."

"A murder?"

"Yes, put on your hat," Miss Lewis gasped.

"Who's murdered?"

"Mr. Magnus."

"Not Magnus the stockbroker?"

"Yes. Please hurry up."

Dr. Altrincham-Harris snatched up his hat. A murder meant an inquest (two guineas) and a probable post-mortem (two more), and the two together represented exactly a hundred and sixty-eight consultations at sixpence a time! It was just like a gold rush, a matter of getting in first; and Dr. Altrincham-Harris, in spite of his smoker's heart and his acid dyspepsia, ran like a hare with Miss Lewis panting behind.

When they reached Mr. Magnus's office the police were already in possession. A ponderous young constable was taking particulars from Martin the chauffeur and making notes. Mr. Magnus lay where he had fallen in an enormous heap. Dr. Harris, triumphantly sure of being first on the scene, dropped down on his knees with a stethoscope at Mr. Magnus's side. The others stood staring down at him with the gaping stupidity that mortals generally exhibit in the presence of death.

"Yes, he's gone," he pronounced. "This looks pretty ugly, officer. There was evidently a struggle. Someone must have gone for his throat. The stud's broken and his collar's all torn."

"There's a wound on his temple, too," the constable remarked.

"Well, he might have got that when he fell. It may be *post-mortem.*"

"So you reckon it's strangulation?" said the constable.

"Looks like it. That remains to be seen. Have you phoned headquarters?"

"Yes, the super'll be round in a minute, sir."

"Then we'd better wait for him. I suppose nobody's any idea who's done this?"

"Yes, *I* know who it was," Miss Lewis broke in eagerly. "His name's Pennington. He sent in his card. The address was Ada Road, Tilton. I noticed it particularly."

CHAPTER XII

JUSTICE

I

THE room occupied by Detective-Superintendent Whittaker on the first floor of the block devoted to the Criminal Investigation Department in the Victoria Law Courts at North Bromwich resembled its occupant in many of its most obvious qualities. It was large, it was solid, it was pleasant, it was human; it gave an impression of conscientious efficiency; its outlook covered a wide range of the city's activities: from the lying-in hospital, through slums, factories, shopping streets, business-centre, churches and theatres, to the skylights of the new, refrigerated mortuary in which the remains of Mr. Magnus were lying, immediately beneath its windows.

Superintendent Whittaker sat at a large desk covered with orderly files and papers. He wore a decent brown suit and steel-rimmed reading-spectacles, and a casual observer might have written him down as a sober North Country manufacturer or business-man, kindly, unostentatious, but shrewd and tenacious to a degree.

Though his clean-shaven face was habitually serious, the Superintendent's eyes had a glint of humour. At the moment they were grave. On his left sat his principal assistant in the C.I.D., Detective-Inspector Parrott, a thin, melancholy man, all rugged protuberances from his beetling brows, bony nose and cleft chin to his Adam's apple. On the other side of the desk, very red in the face and self-conscious, the young constable whom Martin, the chauffeur, had summoned, stood to attention. All three were silent; but the Superintendent's lips moved. He was reading to himself the *précis* he had made of the Magnus case. When he had finished reading he nodded solemnly.

"Yes, I think that's all we've got up to the present," he said. "At five-fifty, according to Lewis, this young Pennington turns up and asks to see Magnus's nephew Levison. He refuses to say what his business is, but hands in the card that was found on the desk. He looked wild and agitated, Lewis says, and had no hat. Levison isn't expecting him, but apparently knows his name. Magnus says he's to wait, and a few minutes later rings for him to be sent up. That's at five-fifty-five, let us say. After showing him in, Lewis goes to her office on the floor below and waits. She hears nothing at all . . ."

The young constable coughed. Superintendent Whittaker looked up.

"Yes, Poultry?"

"She wasn't very clear about that, sir. I asked: 'Did

you hear anything out of the way?' She said: 'No, the room's sound-proof.' Then, later, she said she might have heard someone shouting, the deceased being in the habit of raising his voice. I pressed her on this, but could get no satisfied answer."

The Superintendent nodded. "Very well. At five minutes past six Lewis heard someone running downstairs, and concluded that it was Pennington. She went up to the office, knocked twice without answer, and entered the room. She found Magnus lying unconscious and ran for the chauffeur, who got hold of Constable Poultry while she herself went for Dr. Harris. In the meantime the chauffeur and Poultry entered the office and Poultry telephoned headquarters.

"Now we come to the office. First of all, there are signs of a struggle. We've an inkstand lying on the floor and red and black ink scattered everywhere as far as the wall. There's a solid mahogany chair, with red ink on the seat, that has been violently thrown against the wall and smashed to splinters. Finger-prints on the chair. On the blotting-paper there's the impression of a bearer cheque for a hundred pounds. Last counterfoil in the cheque-book says 'Pennington. Debit H.L.' The deceased is lying in a heap at the foot of his own seat behind the desk. His linen collar and shirt neck-band are torn and stud broken. No obvious finger-prints. There's a wound on his forehead, an inch and a half long, but very little bleeding. Dr. Harris, after examining the body *in situ*, refuses to commit himself without a *post-mortem*. (Wants to make sure of his fee, in other words. You can't blame him for that.) Says the blow on the head might possibly have been inflicted either by the chair or by the edge of the desk, and that the appearance of the torn neck-band and the face of the deceased are consistent with death by strangulation. Know anything about this Altrincham-Harris, Parrott?"

The Inspector agitated his Adam's apple. "Not much. Nothing definite against him. These sixpenny chaps sometimes sail pretty close to the wind. Illegal operations and suchlike."

"H'm. . . . It's a pity they didn't fetch somebody more reliable. However, we can't help that." The Superintendent drummed on the table. "It's an important case, this. Solly Magnus was a well-known man. The papers will be full of it. I shall have to give 'em something to chew. The curious thing is, Pennington didn't ask for Magnus or expect to see him. He was after young Levison. It looks like extorting money under threats. There's the blotting-paper and the cheque counterfoil that says 'Debit H.L.' Know anything about Levison?"

"A bright young spark. Fond of the ladies. Two convictions for exceeding the speed limit."

"A good job he exceeded it this time," said Whittaker sardonically. "We shall have to go into this question of motive at once. Put Frome on to it. He lives out at Tilton. See everyone who lives in their road; get the local gossip. Make Levison identify the body and question him afterwards. See Bulgin, Pennington's employer, and Pennington's wife, if he has one. From the way things look, I don't mind betting he has."

The Inspector nodded significantly. "That's about it. What about Pennington?"

"Well, you know I don't like making arrests in a hurry; but the evidence in this case seems good enough. If Pennington's our man, I doubt if he'll go home to-night. But you never know. We may as well go out to Tilton on chance. We can pick up a man in the village. We shan't need you, Poultry."

The constable saluted and retired. The Superintendent took out his pouch and methodically filled his pipe.

"Give me twenty minutes," he said, "to finish signing these papers. In the meantime, make certain that the doctor's informed the coroner, and get all these notes on the case typed in triplicate. I'll send on one lot at once to the D.P.P. with a covering letter, and you might let the prosecuting solicitor have a copy as well. You needn't worry about a car. We'll go out to Tilton on the bus and drop in at Frome's house on the way. He may tell us something."

Superintendent Whittaker lit his pipe reflectively. In a firm, bold hand, that betrayed the man's spiritual essence, he proceeded to sign the routine papers that lay on the desk in front of him. In all the bright heart

of North Bromwich, where the street-lamps now shone
on crowds queueing up for the theatres and news-boys
ran shouting *"Tragic Death of Prominent Business
Man!"* there was no spot more peaceful than his office,
dead silent now save for the rhythmical scratching of
his pen.

In the terra-cotta-faced block of the C.I.D. no other
light was visible. Ten minutes later the skylight in the
roof of the mortuary beneath showed white, as a
policeman, with turned-up shirt-sleeves, switched on
the electric light to admit Dr. Harris, who looked
seedier than ever, and now smelt strongly of whisky,
and a hearty young athlete, the pathologist from the
infirmary, whom the coroner had ordered to assist at
Mr. Magnus's *post-mortem.* It was an oblong chamber
with walls of bilious glazed brick and a concrete floor,
as clean as an operating-theatre and as cold as ice. In
the midst of it stood three narrow tables faced with the
same glazed tiling as the walls; on the central one of
the three Mr. Magnus's body bulked monstrously; but
neither Dr. Harris, nor the policeman, nor the pathologist seemed moved by Mr. Magnus's presence.

"I say, it's damned cold in here, officer," the
pathologist protested.

"Very sorry, sir. No heating in here. There's the
refrigerator, too."

"Well, you've got a cold billet, I must say."

"It works out much the same in the end, sir. Point
duty's no joke at this time of the year."

"Got anyone else in?"

"Just a couple of motor accidents. Want to see 'em, sir?"

"No, thank you." The pathologist shivered. "Well, doctor, I suppose we'd better be getting on with this job of work. D'you know anything about it?"

"Not a damned thing," Dr. Harris cheerfully replied.

In the office, above, Superintendent Whittaker continued his clerical labours. With his reading-spectacles on he looked a picture of gentle benevolence. Inspector Parrott tapped at the door and came in. His chief looked up and smiled.

"That you, Parrott? I shan't be a moment. This letter's the last. Now I wonder where our young friend Pennington's got to by this time?"

It was the question that Dick Pennington himself had lately been asking. He had left Mr. Magnus's office at a run, two hours earlier, with neither direction nor purpose, only desiring to escape from the storm of his own anger and the awful blackness of Susan's confession which still hung over him. He had blundered away, first of all, into the teeming quarter at the back of the Art Gallery, which Miss Lewis, a few minutes later, had penetrated in search of a doctor.

In those streets Dick's wild face and gait attracted no attention. They were so crowded with men hurrying homeward from work and women buzzing like angry wasps round stalls and shop-windows that he could make no headway on the pavement and took to the road. This degraded thoroughfare was the city's main avenue of approach from Dulston and Wednesford. Down its centre two lines of double-decked trams went bouncing and clanging. They hissed on the rails whenever they quickened their pace; crackling sparks made momentary lightning as they jumped the junctions of overhead wires; their great lighted bodies, charging down on Dick as he ran, seemed to exult in a deliberate, ruthless intent to crush and destroy him. At one moment two monsters, converging, missed him by inches. Their draught sucked his breath. Dick laughed out loud. It wouldn't have mattered much, he thought wildly, if the hurtling masses of metal had struck him. Nobody knew who he was, he thought, and nobody cared. Not now . . .

He staggered on recklessly, but his pace soon began to slacken for sheer lack of strength. Though he did not realize it, his parched mouth had tasted no food since supper the night before. "But I've got to walk it off," he thought, "I've got to go on."

The pavement was empty now. There were no more shops. The road became a canyon running straight between towering shapes of blank-walled factories and warehouses. Wet paving-stones reflected bleared street lamps like slimy ponds. This region, unknown to him, was as desolate at that hour as a plague-stricken city. Apart from the people huddled on the trams, which

screamed through in either direction as though in
terror, it seemed that he was the only living creature
abroad. The solitude began to excite his fancy; the
empty road had no end. He strained forward, forcing
his strength, to escape from its emptiness, and found
himself panting at last on the verge of one of those
patches of cindery waste which marked, like old scars,
an abandoned industrial area.

This expanse was dumb as a graveyard; in the
distance beyond it, like noiseless luminous shuttles, the
brilliantly-lighted lengths of suburban trains slid past.
Dick found himself leaning up against a high brick
wall, and gradually becoming aware of his surroundings observed that it was surmounted by a wicked
chevaux-de-frise of spiked iron. The discovery gave
him a shock. For the first time since his mad pilgrimage
began he realized where he was—that the wall against
which he leant was that of the City Gaol.

He gazed up at the unscaleable coping with awe-
stricken eyes. It was inside that wall, he remembered,
that Garside, the Wednesford murderer, had been
hanged. He had seen the gaol-wall before; but the
spectacle had never before made him shudder as it did
now. It brought back to his empty mind with shattering vividness the last moments of his angry scene in
Magnus's office. He saw himself, a potential murderer,
with the chair uplifted and whirling about his head.
He saw Mr. Magnus, pale-eyed, as he cowered behind
his table. He heard the crash of the splintered chair

as it hit the wall. "I might easily have killed him," he thought, "that's how murders happen; but thank God, he's all right."

This sudden realization of the peril from which he had escaped had the effect of a cold douche on Dick Pennington. He gasped and came to himself. The black cloud which had shadowed his mind defined itself; the mad confusion of fluttering thoughts stood still. He saw Susan standing before him in the "Chatsworth" living-room with her hard white face; he heard once more the incredible things she had said. And now, his rage having spent itself, his mind worked almost reasonably. He thought of Susan and himself with more compassion than anger as equally helpless victims of dastardly circumstance. She was young, she was inexperienced, she was lonely, entirely unequipped to deal with the devices of a professional seducer like Levison. An instinct of self-protection had compelled her to write and implore him to let her join him in Pandypool; and he, thinking only of money, had refused to listen. If he had followed the dictates of his heart this would never have happened. Though the guilt was hers, the responsibility was partly his own, and God only knew she had suffered as much as he had. She was suffering now. He had left her without a word. . . .

"Of course I shall never get over this business," he told himself. "Things can never be the same again. I can hardly bear to look at her. We shall both of us go through hell. All the same, I've no right to desert her—particularly now. She's weaker than I am." (*For better, for worse.* This was worse with a vengeance . . . !) "She'll be wondering," he thought, "what's happened to me at this moment, and probably imagining I've done something desperate to Levison. The poor kid must be terrified. Quite right. She deserves to be terrified . . ."

His brain blazed up again, but before the new anger had faded he saw Susan lying, as he had left her, on the hall linoleum. His Susan . . . Levison's Susan . . . Lord, what a mess!

Her words came back to him, the cold, careful words she had spoken. Thank heaven, at least she had had the courage to tell him the whole of the truth. There was a proverb about knowing everything and forgiving everything. Though he couldn't forgive her —when one's mind was full of a dull pain like that of an aching tooth, such a word as "forgive" had no meaning—two wrongs didn't make a right. She was his wife, and marriage was a sacrament, he still had a duty toward her. What was more, you couldn't decently hit a man when he was down—much less a woman.

Under the pressure of these vague convictions, which sprang from his established moral attitude rather than from the present emergency, Dick found himself moving again, not blindly as before, but in the direction of Tilton. Whatever suffering might await him there, he knew that he had to go home. He walked slowly, doggedly now, for his first wild rush, like that of a hooked sea-trout, had taken the steam out of him. It was a quarter-past eight when, drenched to the skin, he staggered at last over the ruts of Ada Road and reached the porch of "Chatsworth."

For a moment he stood there, breathing heavily, to regain his wind. This second interview with Susan promised to be even more devastating than the first. Though the lights were up and the blinds pulled down the house was so quiet that he wondered if "something had happened." An impulsive creature like Susan might easily have done something desperate. With a heart cold as lead he entered the little hall. A strained voice called: "Who's there?"

"Dick? Oh, where have you been? I thought . . ."

He passed into the living-room and stood blinking at the light. She was there, but he could not look at her.

"Why, you're soaked," she cried. "You must change your clothes at once. I've put out your best suit on the bed."

He was glad of any excuse to get away, and moved mechanically to the bedroom. The blue serge suit which she had put out for him was the one in which he had been married. Since that day he had only worn it once or twice on Sundays. He sat down miserably on the side of Mr. Bulgin's bed and began to change. "I shall have to sleep here to-night," he thought, and once more he was seized with an overwhelming desire to escape somewhere . . . anywhere. "But I can't go anywhere else," he thought miserably. "I shall have to go through with it."

When he had stripped to the skin he began to shiver violently, yet he was almost too tired and dazed to get into his clean woollen under-clothes. Susan tapped at the bedroom door. That showed the distance between them.

"I've made you a cup of hot Bovril," she said. "Will you have it in here?"

"Yes. Thank you." He answered her with an odd formality.

She brought him the cup. He took it with trembling hands. If it had been strychnine he would have drunk it willingly. Then she went away quietly. The hot liquid refreshed him. As he sipped it, warmth stole back into his limbs. It gave him strength to continue his mechanical dressing. He took up the Brunstone necktie and arranged it in front of the glass. The sight of his haggard, unshaven face distressed him. "Well, what can you expect?" he thought. "Fancy bothering about the shape of a knot at a moment like this!" He smiled, and the smile was ghastly. He supposed he must go back to the living-room. He would have to speak to her. Why?

As he stood there, lost, undetermined, a sharp knock on the door made him jump. "I can't possibly see any-one," he thought. It relieved him when he heard Susan's soft steps moving in the hall. He listened intently. A man's voice said: "Are you Mrs. Pennington?"

"Yes."

"Does your husband happen to be at home?"

"Yes. What do you want?"

"I should like to see him for a moment."

"Please come inside. I'll tell him."

Heavy steps in the hall. There must be more than one of them. "The furniture," Dick thought. Susan showed them into the living-room. She came to the door and spoke. "Two men want to see you."

"Did they say who they were?"

"I'm afraid I didn't ask them. They walked right in."

"I suppose I'd better see them."

The two visitors were standing. One wore a brown suit. He was a big-featured man with a kindly, clean-shaven face. The second, bony and melancholy, remained in the background while the other spoke.

"Good evening, Mr. Pennington," he said. "You *are* Mr. Pennington?"

"Yes, that's my name," Dick replied. "Won't you sit down?"

"No, thank you, I'd rather stand," said the Superintendent benevolently. "I've come from police headquarters and I want you to answer one or two questions. First of all, did you happen to be in Sackville Row this afternoon?"

"Yes."

"Somewhere about six o'clock?"

Dick hesitated. During the last twelve hours time had meant nothing to him.

"Yes, somewhere about that time," he answered at last. "Why?"

"This afternoon, Mr. Solomon Magnus the stockbroker was found in his office . . . dead."

"Dead?" Dick gasped. "But . . ."

Inspector Parrott stepped forward. "It has been ascertained," he said slowly, "that you visited the deceased about 6 p.m., and that during that visit some violence took place. I arrest you for the wilful murder of Solomon Magnus . . ."

"But I never . . ." Dick began.

The Inspector held up his hand. "Wait a moment," he said. "I caution you that you need not say anything, but if you do it will be taken down (his notebook was out) and may be given in evidence."

"I can swear that I never touched him," Dick cried. "This. . . . It takes my breath away. I know nothing about it."

"I'm afraid you'll have to come with us, Pennington," Whittaker said smoothly. "Your wife had better give you an overcoat. It's a chilly night."

Dick turned to the door. He saw Susan enter and stand there rigid. Her small face was white with horror, her hands were clasped in front of her.

"What is it, Dick?" she said. "Who are they?

What do they want?"

"It's . . . it's nothing. A misunderstanding." His dead broken heart went out to her—so white, so little, so helpless. He gulped. "Someone's been killed. It's nothing to do with me, Susie. Don't worry. It'll all come right. But I've got to go with them. Will you fetch my overcoat?"

The Superintendent appeared to be examining Watts's picture of Hope. Susan sprang towards him. "Of course it's a mistake!" she cried. "My husband . . . He couldn't! It's ridiculous!" A memory of her reading of fiction came to her aid. "Where's your warrant?" she demanded fiercely. "You can't take him without one."

The Superintendent shook his head slowly. "We don't need any warrant," he told her. "There's no need to distress yourself now, Mrs. Pennington," he went on kindly. "The less said about it the better. If he's innocent it'll all come out right. You just get him his hat and overcoat." He turned to the Inspector. "You might whistle for that taxi, Parrott."

Susan scarcely heard him. She was gazing at Dick with doubtful, anguished eyes.

"Dick . . . you didn't . . ." she began.

"Of course I didn't, Susie. Don't worry. That makes it worse. I've told them the truth."

"Thank God!" She grasped the Superintendent's arm. "Can I come with him?" she pleaded. "It's my fault. . . . If you arrested *me* . . ."

"Susie, Susie," Dick cried. "Be quiet, for heaven's sake!"

"Take me, too," she persisted. "I'd much rather tell you everything."

"Oh, be quiet," Dick groaned. "Don't listen to her."

"Now look here, Mrs. Pennington," the Superintendent gently intervened, "we can't take you with us, you know, and even if we could, there'd be nothing gained by it. You come down to the Law Courts to-morrow morning about ten and ask for me. My name's Superintendent Whittaker. Now be a good girl, get his coat."

Inspector Parrott appeared.

"The taxi's waiting, sir," he said.

"All right. Tell the man who's watching the back that he needn't stay. I'll leave you behind to carry on here." He took Dick's arm. "Come along, young man," he said.

II

For the last few days Captain Small had felt unhappy about Susan. The trouble had begun some time before, on the evening when he had been nearly run down by the yellow Bentley; it had been somewhat assuaged only yesterday when Susan had innocently alluded to the incident; but no sooner was he reassured than in bounced Levison himself without as much as a

"by your leave." Though Captain Small had known
the Penningtons ever since they were married, he
would never have presumed to enter the house with
so little ceremony. Levison's action implied an intimacy which he himself had never attained. It was
true, of course, that this generation of young men who
grew up when the war was on had no manners to speak
of; but, manners or no manners, the method of
Levison's entrance continued to offend him. The
fellow was a blighter, and a blighter of the blackest
description.

Not that he suspected Susan of any indiscretion.
Captain Small would have been furious if anyone had
suggested that. Guiding stars do not falter in their
courses. He continued to worship her as a creature
entirely immune from all human frailty. The thing
that he feared was not any lapse on her part, but the
mere possibility that the "blighter" might affront her
innocence by "trying to take liberties." She had not,
he was thankful to say, appeared to be particularly
pleased by Levison's visit. Still, ever since he left
"Chatsworth" that evening, he had been asking himself whether he had been justified in leaving them
together. *Desertion in the face of the enemy.* That
was what it amounted to. After all, he had promised
Dick that he would look after her.

It was some consolation to remember what she had
told him before Levison's arrival. She had made up
her mind, she had said, to join Dick in Pandypool this

week-end or the next. Though the mere fact of
Susan's living so near him at Tilton had inspired him
in his attempts to "go straight"—he was much more
dependent on her than she on him—he was only too
thankful to think of her leaving "Chatsworth." By
this time, probably, she was already in the train for
South Wales and well out of harm's way.

Even so, all that Friday afternoon, a vague uneasi-
ness had distressed his dog-like intelligence. He could
settle to nothing; his mind was so disorientated that he
began to wonder whether her departure hadn't, in some
mysterious way, affected his strength of will—whether
he wasn't, perhaps, on the verge of another outbreak.
He found himself over-smoking to soothe his nerves.
Once, dozing after lunch on his bed, he had wakened
with a start. He could have sworn that he had heard
Susan's voice—a cry of distress; and the illusion was
so real that, still half asleep, he jumped off the bed
and pulled on his boots, determined to hurry along to
"Chatsworth" and help her.

When he came to himself he realized how foolish
he had been; he had probably over-eaten at lunch or
smoked too heavily. Yet, all through the rest of the
afternoon and the evening that followed, the echo of
that cry continued unreasonably to haunt his ears. He
found it so difficult to forget that he was tempted to
break through his rule of "drinking nothing" in the
house. He surprised himself actually standing, with
the key in his hand, before the cupboard in which a

bottle of brandy was kept in case of emergencies. "No, no, my boy, that won't do!" he told himself firmly. "That's the beginning of the end. Cut it out! Go to bed and sleep. That's all you want."

Yet no sooner was he in bed and asleep than the same dream returned. He dreamt he was lying in bed and asleep (which seemed extremely plausible) and that, as he lay there, he heard Susan's voice in the distance. She was calling him by name. Again and again she called: "Captain Small ... Captain Small!" "Yes, I've heard that before," he told himself. "You don't catch me this time! It's only a dream." But the calling grew so insistent that it finally forced him to wake. In addition to the calling he heard a knock at the door. He sat up in bed and challenged the ghostly voice. "Who's there? What d'you want?" he shouted, expecting no answer. But an answer came:

"It's me, Captain Small. . . . It's Susan. . . . Susan Pennington."

He pulled on his ragged old trench-coat and limped to the door in bare feet. He flung the door open, expecting to find nothing but darkness and rain, and in a moment Susan was clinging to him like a drowning woman.

"What is it?" he gasped. "Susan, Susan, tell me, what is it?"

"They've taken him away," she cried. "They've taken him away to the lock-up." She burst into a wild fit of sobbing. Captain Small, astounded, half picked her up in his arms and carried her to a sofa in his sitting-room. She was crying too bitterly to speak. He groped on the mantelpiece for a match and relit his lamp. Then he saw her, and the anguish of her face destroyed him. It was small and white and utterly expressionless. The huge, black, dilated pupils stared not at him, but past him. He limped over toward her. Once more she clutched at his hand. "He's gone. They've taken him," she repeated.

"Susan, Susan, what's frightened you? You've been dreaming. Who's taken away who?"

She answered in jerks:

"The police. . . . They've arrested Dick. . . . He's been charged with murder. . . ."

"No, no, Dick's at Pandypool." He tried to soothe her.

"He came home to-day. They've taken him to North Bromwich." She shuddered. "He's killed Harry."

"Harry? Do you mean Levison?"

She nodded. "And it's not his fault. They should have taken me. I'm responsible. Oh, I wish I were dead!"

Captain Small gasped. "Your fault? You don't mean . . ."

"Yes, I do," she cried. "He was my lover. Only once, though. We went mad, both of us. I'm going mad now. I can't bear it. . . . I tell you I can't bear it!"

"Young Levison. . . . My God!"

Captain Small could utter no more. Her words hit him with the crash and concussion of an exploding shell. Their effect was more awfully shattering than that of any terrestrial catastrophe. It was like the bursting of a star. His heaven as well as his earth was convulsed and riven. All the sublime ideals with which he had patched together his broken life had crumbled to powder. If he couldn't believe in Susan that life became meaningless. He stood there aghast and cheated, all hope abandoned.

"That's not true," he protested. "Susan, tell me it's not true."

She shook her head piteously. "I had to come to you," she said. "However much you hate and despise me, there was nobody else. I couldn't stay there."

Her hand tightened wildly on his. He sank down on the sofa beside her. And suddenly, above the bitter resentment he felt toward this woman who had first rebuilt and then shattered his world, he became aware of her pinched, white, suffering face, no longer innocent and exquisite, but in its agony moving beyond words. If she were no longer a guiding star, she was human and pitiful. He grasped her hand and pressed it. It was cold and limp. The sense of manly protective strength that this contact gave infused his mind with the new and militant loyalty due to a woman—any woman—who, being guilty, confessed her guilt and was down and out. The old soldierly habit of precision reasserted itself. He was an officer in a tight corner. Other lives depended on him.

He began to question her narrowly. She answered between her sobs. Dick had left her at half-past five after she had told him everything. As soon as he had come back, about nine, and had changed his clothes, he had been arrested and taken away. Had Dick denied it? he asked. Yes, of course he denied it. But that made no difference. She knew, she *knew* it was true.

"We must get to work on this job," Captain Small said briskly. "We must do something at once. We ought to get hold of a lawyer—a barrister, the best we can find. We mustn't consider the cost."

"I've no money—not a penny," she told him.

"Never mind about that. I can scrape up a few pounds somewhere. I've a nest-egg of sorts. Come, pluck up your courage, Susie. We'll go over the top together, never you fear!"

He looked at his watch—he had no idea of the time —and discovered it was half-past ten. That was rotten bad luck; it meant that they could do nothing till daylight; you couldn't knock lawyers up at that time of night. He stroked her cold hand. "Look here, Susan," he said; "it's no earthly good attempting to do anything now. I'm going to get you a good cup of tea— you lie here while I make it—and then, when you feel a bit better, I'll dress and take you to 'Chatsworth.'"

"To 'Chatsworth'?" she cried out in horror. "I couldn't bear it. I stood it as long as I could. I sat down while that man searched Dick's clothes—he was looking for something. When he'd gone I nearly went mad. No, I couldn't go back!"

"Well, you can't stay here, can you?" he said.

She gave a strangled laugh. "Why not, if you'll have me? *I've* no reputation to lose."

"Well, we'll talk of that later," he said, going off to make her tea.

When he returned she was calmer. She spoke even with a bitter humour that puzzled him. "Do let me stay here," she pleaded. "I know Dick would wish it."

As if poor old Dick mattered now! His shocked eyes spoke for him.

"Don't you understand?" she cried passionately. "I love Dick. I adore him. The other was nothing. If Dick stamped on my face I should worship him just as utterly. I'm the murderer, not he—and I wish to God I could die for it! That's the only way I can pay for the harm I've done him. And he. . . . Even when they were taking him away he tried to protect me. As if *I* mattered!"

In the end Captain Small allowed himself to be persuaded.

"You had better sleep on my bed," he said. "I can find some clean sheets. I'll turn in on the sofa. I'm a soldier; I'm used to rough quarters."

He would take no denial. Between them they made up the bed. When everything was ready he retired and would have closed the door, but Susan cried out in alarm when he touched the handle.

"Leave it open," she said. "If you shut it it'll feel like a prison."

They both winced at the word simultaneously, thinking of Dick.

It was a strange night for both of them.

.   .   .   .   .   .

And even stranger for Dick. . . .

Superintendent Whittaker stepped into the taxi first. As a precaution Inspector Parrott kept guard on the other side until the door was closed. The taxi crawled slowly over the ruts of Ada Road, then drove swiftly through the rain to a door at the back of the police headquarters. During all that drive Dick sat mutely staring in front of him. The caution, so solemnly uttered by Parrott, impressed his mind with the need for silence.

"Here we are," the Superintendent said cheerfully as the car pulled up.

It was almost as difficult, it seemed, to get into the lock-up as out of it.

In addition to the door that opened on the street there was another locked gate of iron grating inside. The Superintendent passed Dick through both with the air of an actor-manager admitting a privileged guest to the mysteries of the world behind-stage. The policemen on duty treated Whittaker and his guest with equal respect. One of them took out a charge-sheet and proceeded to fill in details of Dick's personal appearance and ask him questions as though he were preparing a passport: "What is your name? Your address? Occupation?" Then the Superintendent said: "We're just going to charge you, Pennington." He said it as a dentist might say: "I'm just going to have a look at this molar. If it hurts, please tell me."

His assistant spoke, as though reciting a formula: "Richard Pennington, you are charged with wilfully murdering Solomon Magnus at his office in Sackville Row, North Bromwich, supposedly by strangulation. Do you wish to say anything in answer to this charge? You are not obliged to say anything unless you wish to do so, but whatever you say will be taken down in writing and may be given in evidence."

"Is he speaking to me?" Dick thought. It sounded like a rhetorical question, demanding no answer; but the eyes of the others were fixed on him; he supposed he had better say something. After all, there could be no harm in telling the truth. He cleared his throat and gulped. His voice came thin and husky. Its tones were as unreal and remote as the three listening men and these strange surroundings.

"I can't say anything," he said, "except that I'm innocent and know nothing about it. When I went to the office I didn't expect to see Mr. Magnus. I wanted to see his nephew Levison on a private matter. Magnus told me that Levison wasn't there. It was a lie—I'd

seen his car in the street outside—and that made me
see red . . ."

"Steady, Pennington. Not quite so fast!" the Superintendent interrupted. "We want to get everything
correctly," he said—as an anæsthetist might have told
a patient to breathe deeply and slowly.

". . . and that made me see red," the policeman with
the notebook repeated ponderously. "After that," Dick
went on. . . . "Well, to tell you the truth, Magnus
offered me a cheque. It was an insult. I suppose I went
mad for a moment. My sleeve caught in the inkstand
and pulled it over on the floor. No . . . that happened
before. I'm sorry. I'm getting this wrong. Cross that
out, please. I can't quite remember . . ." Dick put
up his hand to his forehead.

"Take your time; there's no hurry, Pennington,"
Whittaker encouraged him. Dick stared helplessly in
front of him. His mind had struck work. Behind the
desk, at the level of his eyes, hung a printed notice:

North Bromwich Police Force.

Notice to Prisoners.

*Friends.—A prisoner will be allowed facilities for
    communicating with his friends or legal
    advisers. He will be supplied on request
    with writing materials, and his letters will
    be sent with the least possible delay. If he
    so desires, telephone and telegraph messages
    will also be sent . . .*

These printed words imposed themselves on his brain to the exclusion of everything else. *"Notice to Prisoners,"* he thought. "Good Lord, I'm a prisoner! *Friends* . . . I haven't any friends. I haven't a friend in the world."

"That inkpot?" Whittaker reminded him. Memory came back suddenly.

"Yes, that happened before he offered me the cheque," Dick said slowly. "It was the cheque that made me go mad. I picked up the chair. When I'd got it in my hand I didn't know what to do with it. He was sitting there, all huddled up, as though he expected me to hit him. I didn't want to. I didn't want *him*. I wanted Levison. I chucked the chair at the wall. I had to do something. Then I got out as quick as I could. That's all I remember. Honestly, I never touched him. Never . . . I can't understand . . ."

"All right, all right. That'll do. Just read through the statement and sign it."

They handed him the statement. It wasn't exactly what he had said—the sergeant had improved on his style—but the essentials were there. He signed it clumsily, blotting the paper with ink.

"I'm afraid I've made a mess of this," he said, timidly smiling at Whittaker, whom, for some obscure reason, he now regarded as his friend.

"That'll do. Don't worry," the Superintendent answered consolingly.

"But the whole thing's a mistake, you know," Dick

protested, "a ghastly mistake."

The Superintendent pursed up his lips and nodded sympathetically.

"Better search him, Walters," he said.

The sergeant ran through the pockets of the blue serge suit which Susan had laid out on the bed. There was nothing in them but crumbled tobacco-dust and a grimy pink tram-ticket from Brinton-le-Sands. They removed his wrist-watch and made him sign a receipt.

Then they took his finger-prints. It was a leisurely affair. He followed the process with impersonal interest. They put five dabs of printer's ink on a long slab that looked like rubber and smoothed them out with a squeegee. "Don't try to do it yourself," the sergeant told him, "just leave it to me." He took Dick's right thumb and fingers and rolled them, one by one, in the spaces provided for them on a printed form. (*MALE*, Dick read: *This space is reserved for use in the Finger-Print Bureau, C.R.O. No. 653. Name in which charged . . . Aliases . . .*) Then the sergeant did the same thing with the left hand and made two new impressions of the four fingers of each bunched together. "Now sign this paper," he said, "and put the print of the right forefinger in the space below. That's A1." *This form must be completed in every detail*, Dick read, *before the Officer concerned begins to take finger-prints of any other person. On no account . . .*

"Come along, Pennington," Whittaker was saying.

The cells at the Central Police Station were arranged in three storeys about an oblong well. The middle storey was separated from the one above and below by thick wire-netting, which gave the whole space the appearance of a horizontally-divided cage. It smelt clean as a hospital ward; the close air was impregnated with disinfectant. The brick walls, painted buff above, were encircled below to a height of four feet by a skirting of tarry black varnish, and the absence of all bright colour, save in the faucets of hydrants, which were painted a bright vermilion, gave the place an aspect that was grimly appropriate. In the door of one of the cells on the left-hand side a flap had been opened, and through it protruded the body and arms of a man. He was a small, dark man, with close-set eyes and a cunning gypsy face. He watched Dick's entrance with a smile of malicious satisfaction. He peered round the door and winked at him, then burst out laughing.

The sergeant turned on him. "You stow that, Richards," he said severely.

Dick gazed at the degenerate smiling face with horrified interest. "Good Lord, he's a criminal," he thought; "a prisoner . . . how awful!"

The sergeant walked over and shut up the flap, but the man inside continued to laugh insanely. Dick wished they could stop him. That laughter got on his nerves. He reflected, with awe, that he had never seen a criminal before. Another constable opened the door of a cell on the opposite side. It was a narrow compartment, seven feet by ten, illuminated by an electric bulb in a stout iron cage. Along the wall that faced the door ran a wooden bench; in the corner next to it stood a wooden water-closet. They gave Dick a roll of bedding that smelt faintly of carbolic. Then the door closed behind him with a business-like click. He was alone, and in prison . . .

The soft click of this closing door was the first unquestionable reality in all that Dick had experienced since he left Pandypool that morning. He heard it with the shudder of a man coming out of a nightmare. He stood staring at the blank door, the whitewashed walls, still dazed and incredulous.

"This is a cell," he thought. "I'm in prison! Why? What have I done? It's all wrong . . . It's impossible!" But the futile question was rapidly overborne by another emotion—sheer, mindless panic, the insensate horror of a free animal suddenly caged. He had an impulse, hardly repressed, to shout at the top of his voice, to beat with his useless hands on the metal door, to fling himself madly against the unyielding walls. He wanted to cry: "Let me out! Let me out! It's all a mistake. I'm Dick Pennington. I haven't explained . . ." He stood panting and faint, then reeled backward, to save himself, to the bench where the bundle of bedding lay still unfolded.

"I can do nothing . . . nothing," he thought. "But it's bound to come right. They can't do anything to me without evidence, and I'm innocent." He spoke to himself: "Be calm. Pull yourself together. You've nothing to fear." But dread answered. "What about that statement you signed? What did you say? For all you know you may have committed yourself."

He couldn't remember. It was no use trying to remember. He felt sick and dragged himself to the water-closet in the corner. "Sick with fear," he told himself, "Don't be a fool. You've nothing to fear."

Nothing to fear, indeed! He remembered the various stages by which he had finally arrived at this awful predicament. The whole mechanism had worked with such terrible, deadly smoothness: the first questions, the arrest, the taxi, the cautioning, the finger-prints . . . then *this!* And what next? He recalled an account he had read in a magazine of the Chicago stockyards; of a smooth-moving platform, like the escalators in London Tube stations, on which terrified, helpless animals were carried to their doom; of piteous ululations and the smell of blood. He saw himself tied, like those predestinate beasts to the deadly smooth-moving mechanism of the criminal law. No power on earth could check that machine when once it was in motion. He smelt blood already. . . .

He might have smelt it before. He saw himself standing propped up against a high brick wall whose coping was surmounted by an iron *chevaux de frise*, the wall of North Bromwich Gaol—the place where Frome had hanged Garside. *A prisoner will be allowed facilities for communicating with his friends or legal*

advisers . . . Writing materials . . . It would be no
use asking for those at this time of night. What time
was it? They had taken away his watch. What friends?
Only Susan. . . . A vision of Susan rose to torment
him. She was standing rigid in the doorway of the
"Chatsworth" sitting-room, her small face white with
horror, her hands clasped in front of her, detached,
frail, pitiable. A wave of compassion, more irresistible
than any love he had ever felt for her, broke over
him. He was a man, he told himself, equipped by
nature to meet this disaster and fortified to bear it by
his knowledge of his own innocence; while she, poor
kid, was a delicate, fragile creature, inured to no
greater distress than that caused by a jelly that refused
to set or a colour that wouldn't match, now harassed
by possible doubts as to his innocence and crushed
by the weight of her own guilt—the prime cause of it
all. Fate hadn't intended this weak, warm creature for
huge, tragic rôles. She was made for her own small
life of feminine cares and little excusable vanities;
and now, in this monstrous emergency, he, Dick Pennington, her natural protector, had been snatched away
from her.

The thought of her lonely helplessness disarmed
him completely. Beneath its pressure the last tinge of
bitterness faded from his generous heart. What were
the trivial rights and wrongs of human sexual behaviour beside this new, vast complication involving
life and death? What were guilt or innocence, for-

giveness or the refusal to forgive, compared with the awful weight of suffering, the agony of uncertainty she was forced to bear now? Her dear name dragged in the mud and thrown to the snouts of the guzzling public! She, poor child, in her innocence would have told those men everything. He must stop that somehow. God knew she had suffered enough already.

A prisoner will be allowed facilities for communicating with his friends. He must write to her at once, not only to comfort her by insisting on his innocence and telling her that she was forgiven, but to warn her urgently against giving herself away.

"If I write, they'll read my letter," he thought. "And I can't write now, anyway. I must wait till tomorrow morning. If only I knew what time it is!"

He had no means of knowing. Time no longer existed. The only appreciable dimensions were those of space, defined by the cell's white walls, and of anguished suffering. Once, indeed, heavy steps had rung on the concrete floor when a couple of constables had marched in a blaspheming drunk. Once a prisoner had shrieked out in a nightmare. Once a new guard, coming on duty, had turned on a hydrant and sluiced the water-closets. Once, again, the cover of the peephole in the cell door had been pushed aside and a shaft of yellow light had fallen on him like the stare of an accusing eye. "I must sleep," he told himself. "I must have all my wits about me."

Though the very word "sleep" was a mockery, he

unrolled the bedding and spread it out on the wooden
bench. As he stretched out his heavy limbs he became
aware that something important in his ordinary mode
of life had been neglected. He sat up again, wondering what it was, and suddenly realized that, for the first
time in his life, he had forgotten to pray. He knelt
down on the concrete floor beside his bench and said the
Lord's Prayer; and, being a simple soul, he was greatly
comforted.

III

Inspector Frome was up early next morning, though
he had been busy long after midnight collecting statements and general information on the Magnus case.
He had passed an extremely fruitful half-hour with
Miss Maples and her mamma, who had always feared
it would "come to something like this." After that he
had spent ten minutes waiting in Mr. Bulgin's front-
hall and two with Mr. Bulgin, who could say no more
than that he was grieved and shocked beyond words,
but only knew the young Penningtons slightly. Next
he had hurried over to Mawne Hall, where Harry
Levison, just returned from identifying his uncle's
body in the mortuary, gave an extremely evasive
account of his nodding acquaintance with Susan which,
in view of the precise observations Miss Maples had
given him, appealed strongly to the Inspector's
saturnine sense of humour. Finally, returning to Ada

Road, he had thought of dropping in for a few sympathetic words with Susan. When he knocked at "Chatsworth" and received no reply, he concluded that she was in bed, and decided that she would be more fit to answer questions after a good night's sleep.

On the following morning, when he renewed his quest, every door at "Chatsworth" was unlocked and the house untenanted. Its emptiness was a little sinister. In situations of this kind hysterical women were apt to do desperate things. "But if she's not done away with herself," he consoled himself, "she's bound to turn up in court."

Though Susan had not slept a wink she was anything but hysterical that morning. Captain Small, limping round in his socks for fear of waking her, tapped timidly on the door at seven with a cup of tea. A firm voice bade him enter. He found Susan already dressed and marvellously composed. Her composure was positively frightening. She was no longer, indeed, the frail, fluttering creature who had clung to him on the night before, but a hard-faced, capable, unemotional woman whom he had never known. Her face had not only the pallor but the rigidity of marble; her eyes, her chin, her mouth showed determination; even her voice had a hard, inflexible, metallic quality.

"I'm going to Halesby to see my uncle," she said. "We must find a lawyer at once, and I must have money."

"I'll come with you," Captain Small suggested.

She rejected his offer instantly. "I can go quicker than you. There's no time to waste. I must be in court by ten."

"You must have some breakfast."

"I'll get that at Halesby," she said; and almost before he had time to answer her she was gone.

Hurrying down the hill to Great Cornbow Susan passed through the outskirts of Halesby. The newsagents' shops were already gay with placards. "*North Bromwich Stockbroker Found Dead. Young Man Arrested*," she read. The words distressed her surprisingly little. She had gone through all that. What was past did not concern her. All the energy she possessed must be concentrated on the present. Regrets and recriminations were now as futile as shame or sorrow. Her stony exterior was no more than the envelope of an inflexible will, a strong intelligence tightened to the uttermost efficiency, determined, at whatever cost, to save the man she had wronged, the man she loved.

She entered the house without knocking. George Lorimer, shattered, sat staring at the *Daily Courier* which had just told him the news. Aunt Edna, her face drawn and awful, stood behind him. As Susan entered, George Lorimer sprang to his feet.

"Susan, Susan," he cried. "I was just coming up. This is dreadful. I can't believe it. Tell me, what happened?"

"They've arrested Dick," she said calmly. "They say he's killed Harry Levison."

"Harry Levison? What do you mean? It's Mr. Magnus who's dead."

"Mr. Magnus?" Susan gasped. "Mr. Magnus? There's some mistake."

"It's here in the paper. Look . . ."

"Solomon Magnus . . ." she read. The paper glided from her hands. "Mr. Magnus . . . that's different," she said, as though talking to herself. "He never killed Mr. Magnus. He couldn't. An old man like that. He was speaking the truth. I thought he was trying to let me down lightly. This alters everything." She turned to George Lorimer. "I want you to come with me at once. To a lawyer. Who is there?"

"Mr. Price always acts for us."

"No, no, he's too old. We want somebody smart and vigorous."

"There's young Hadley."

"Yes, he will do. And I want my money. Come along. He won't be at his office yet. We must go to his house."

George Lorimer picked up an old fishing-hat in the hall. His choice offended Aunt Edna's sense of propriety; but before she could protest they were out of the house and hurrying along Great Cornbow. By the time they reached the lawyer's George was flushed and panting; but Susan, it seemed, was beyond such human weakness. She was a cold will, barely incarnate. When she enquired from the maid at the door for Mr. Hadley her voice never wavered.

Mr. Hadley was at breakfast, the maid said. They entered a frigid drawing-room. George Lorimer knew no more where he was than if he had been dragged there on the tail of a tornado. His confused mind was thinking: "She wants money! My God, she wants money. This is the end of everything."

Mr. Hadley came in with excuses for keeping them waiting. He was carrying the *Daily Courier* and had read of the arrest. With an air of professional tact he began to give solemn condolences. Susan broke in on them ruthlessly.

"I want to know what we're to do," she said. "We want your advice. My husband's been arrested. He's innocent. We ought to act quickly. Isn't there something called bailing him out?"

Mr. Hadley shook his head. "In cases of this kind they never allow bail. The first thing they'll want to do is to establish a motive. Of course I know nothing of the circumstances . . ."

"There's very little to know, Mr. Hadley. I'll tell you all there is. Harry Levison, Mr. Magnus's nephew, was my lover."

Mr. Hadley blinked at her frankness. At the same moment the bottom fell out of George Lorimer's world. He clutched at the arms of his chair. Susan went on coldly:

"He spent Tuesday night with me at our house in Tilton. Somebody—I think I know who it was—kept a record of when he came and when he went. My husband was in South Wales. They sent him an anonymous letter with all the details. When he got it he came straight home. That was . . . yes, it was yesterday. He showed me the letter and I . . . well, I told him the truth. It would have been very much better if I hadn't—but that can't be helped. He left the house without speaking to me. He was terribly broken . . ." Susan's voice, too, cracked for an instant; but the will of steel forced her on. "I was broken as well. I saw what a mess I'd made of it. I was terrified to think of his doing something desperate. If he *had* killed Harry, I shouldn't have been surprised. But he didn't kill Mr. Magnus. I'm certain of that. He said he didn't, and I believe him." She stopped.

"So you saw him again?" Mr. Hadley enquired encouragingly.

"Yes. He came home about nine o'clock. He'd been walking in the rain. He was drenched. I gave him a change of clothes—you see, he'd come up from South Wales in his working things."

"He said nothing?"

"No. He only thanked me for a cup of Bovril. He hadn't finished dressing when two policemen came to the door. When they took him away the stout man said I couldn't go with him. He told me to come to the court at ten this morning. What time is it now?"

"We've plenty of time. This looks pretty bad, Mrs. Pennington."

"Pretty bad!" George Lorimer thought. For him,

oddly enough, the major tragedy was as nothing at that moment compared with the enormity of Susan's confession. That she, Susan, *his* Susan . . . His reason refused to believe it. Yet there she stood, with that awful, unnatural calmness, uttering those unbelievable words in a voice as matter-of-fact as if she were describing a picnic! Her hard voice broke in on him:

"Of course it looks bad. Will you take on the case, Mr. Hadley?"

"Most certainly. We shall have to brief counsel as well. This is a serious matter. What we need, of course, is a first-rate criminal lawyer. I think Cronshaw's the man. You've heard of Sir Edward Cronshaw? This is going to cost a mint of money, of course."

"Money doesn't matter. My uncle has two thousand pounds that belong to me. If you use every penny it won't matter. He'll let you have it at once. Won't you, Uncle?"

"Yes, yes, of course," George Lorimer murmured. Two thousand pounds! The idea was so fantastic that he could almost have laughed.

"Well, that's very good news," Mr. Hadley said. "He ought to be represented by counsel at the inquest."

"The inquest?" Susan enquired.

"Yes. The usual procedure is this. Your husband will appear before the Stipendiary this morning. The police, in all probability, will ask for a remand until the day of the inquest . . ."

"How soon will that be?"

"In five days at the outside."

"Five days?" Susan's heart fell like lead. "Can I wait?" she thought, "can I possibly keep it up? I *must* keep it up if I die."

The lawyer was speaking: "I think I had better come with you to the court this morning, just in case anything should be said that oughtn't to be said. I don't think the police will make any slip, but you never know. If they do, it may come in useful. We ought to be starting." He rose from his chair at the spindly teatable where he had been taking notes. His face showed acute embarrassment. Apparently he wanted to say something but couldn't find words. Then he spoke in a solemn voice:

"Mrs. Pennington," he said. "I want you to know how much I appreciate your frankness and your whole —er—attitude. It's not every woman who would have had the courage to speak like that. I appreciate it and —er—admire it. If you've made an unfortunate mistake you've atoned for it by this splendid—er——" He stopped and blushed violently. "Well, you know what I mean. To put it shortly, I'm proud to act for you. Shall we go?"

The dull compliment, as compliment, entirely failed to move Susan; but she clutched at what it implied with eagerness. This young man, whatever his value might be, was now on her side, she had won him over. She realized that the frankness she had shown out of

complete disregard for her own modesty or conventional sensibility was a negotiable asset. It had proved
its effectiveness with one man. Why not with others?
With their own counsel, the Public Prosecutor, the
judge, the jury? This modest initial success of her
own immodesty filled her heart with wild hopes. If
needs were, she could humble herself further. There
was no personal humiliation she would not court willingly if only Dick might be saved. In her hard, white
face the desperate eyes grew brighter. With this, and
with money . . . Yes, money; that was equally important. She turned to George Lorimer.

"You'll see that Mr. Hadley has all the money he
wants?" she demanded.

"Yes, yes. I'll see about that at once," said George
Lorimer miserably.

.   .   .   .   .

Dick Pennington awoke, at some hour unknown and
unascertainable, amazed to find that he had slept. It
was impossible to judge what time it was by the light
that entered his cell, but a new flush of the hydrant,
combined with a tread of heavy boots and scraps of a
conversation which seemed to refer to the North Bromwich Albion's fixture against the Arsenal that afternoon,
suggested that the free world was awake. Of a sudden
the cell-door was thrown open and a policeman whom
he had not seen before commanded him to "gather" his
blankets and make his toilet. The new constable was a

friendly, well-fed young man with a brick-red face and a Shropshire accent. Dick had known dozens like him in his country boyhood. He asked him the time. "Seven o'clock," the constable told him. "Want your breakfast? I bet you do. You'll be getting it in a moment."

The atmosphere, on the whole, was informal, almost friendly. It surprised him. He didn't realize, at that moment, the difference between a lock-up and a gaol. Though the law would do its damnedest to prove him guilty, in its eyes at that moment, he remained an innocent man. The bread-and-butter and tea that they brought him was hardly appetizing, but he did his best with it. Then, remembering the *Notice to Prisoners*, he asked for writing materials and was given pencil and paper. Behind the closed door he composed a short letter to Susan. It was difficult to write, for the very syllables of her name had a softening influence (which must not be encouraged, he thought) and reduced him to tears.

My darling, he wrote,

I have been thinking of you all the time. That's the worst of the whole thing, leaving you to face it alone. Whatever they say I want you to trust me and believe that I never touched Magnus. If you and I stick together we shall get through all right. That's all that matters. Don't forget I've forgiven you utterly and completely. (He underlined this three times.) *I have done no wrong, so they can't touch me, Susie. Slept well, in spite of everything. It is just after seven, they say, but they've taken my watch. So keep up your courage. Your loving husband. R.P.*

When he read over what he had written it seemed wholly inadequate, so he added a postscript. *P.S. Don't forget I've forgiven you. Say nothing.*

The completion of this letter, which expressed so little of what he felt, lifted a weight from his mind. It was as though, in the spirit, the words had been actually spoken to her. The fact that the paper was still in his hands made no difference. Unfortunately the "facilities" given to prisoners did not include any means of summoning the guard. He supposed his letter to Susan must await their convenience. After an interval that seemed almost as long as the night, his cell-door was opened again. The sergeant who had filled in the charge-sheet was standing outside, very smart in his silver buttons and stripes.

"Going up to the court in a minute or two," he said. "If you want to do anything . . ."

Dick shook his head. Now that the dreadful moment approached he was so agitated that he crammed the letter he had written into his pocket and forgot all about it. He felt singularly helpless again. All through the night that stockyard-platform had continued to move without his being aware of it. It seemed to give a sudden lurch forward when, sitting with the cell-door open, he heard the word "Pennington" and the sergeant beckoned him out with a turn of his head.

They passed through an iron gate into a long sub-
terranean passage made gloomy by the same funereal
skirting of black paint; a series of black-painted pipes
of large calibre attached to the ceiling made it resemble
an alleyway in the bowels of a ship; little cages, con-
taining a volatile disinfectant, failed to sweeten the air.
They paused before another door, at the foot of a staircase. Dick heard another echoing voice call: "Richard
Pennington." "Come on," said the sergeant. Obediently Dick climbed the stairs.

He found himself standing on a platform surrounded by wooden rails, like a miniature horse-box:
above, a high rafted roof; below, rows of benches
and desks, where a number of men—they were lawyers,
he supposed—sat writing, crouched over their papers.
Full in front, at the level of his eyes, rose an imposing
dais, in the centre of which a frail, refined-looking man
with a patient face sat in lonely state. Behind and beneath, though he could not see them, the court was
crowded with the inquisitive, ill-dressed mob that seeks
free entertainment and warmth in a Stipendiary's court.

They were wasting no time that morning. Bewildered by his sudden transference from the under-
ground cell to this open space, Dick scarcely knew what
was happening until the charge had been read. He was
scanning the benches below him, eagerly, searching for
Susan. Superintendent Whittaker stepped forward and
began to outline the case. Looking more benevolent

than ever, he spoke slowly and confidentially, as though this were a small personal matter that he wished to explain to the magistrate without any fuss or delay.

"Your worship," he said. "Detective-Inspector Parrott will prove the arrest, and on his evidence I shall ask for a remand for five days—till next Wednesday. The coroner will commence his inquiry on that day."

The Stipendiary nodded. "Of course you know best, Superintendent," his manner implied. "Detective-Inspector Parrott!"

Inspector Parrott gave evidence slowly. He stared full in the magistrate's face as though challenging him to dispute a word of what he uttered. "At eight-fifty p.m. last night," he began, "I proceeded according to instructions to Ada Road, Tilton . . ."

"We've heard all this before," Dick thought. "Why don't they get on with it? She's not here. They haven't told her. Thank heaven for that! But if only I could see her for a moment . . ."

"I then cautioned him," Parrott was saying.

". . . for one moment, poor darling," Dick thought.

Parrott had finished and stepped down. The Stipendiary spoke deliberately in a thin, cultured voice. "Remanded for five days," he said.

And then Dick saw her. She had entered the court during the final phrases of Inspector Parrott's evidence and was moving, shepherded by the solicitor Hadley's arm, to the lawyers' benches. She was dressed all in black, a tight, brimless cloche on her head, and her profile beneath it had a hard, white purity. He wanted to cry: "Susan, Susan . . . I'm here. . . . Quick! Look at me!" But already they were calling the name of the defendant in the next case, and the sergeant, standing beside him, laid his hand on his arm. Then suddenly Susan turned. For an instant their eyes met. Susan's heart broke to see his face. At that moment it showed her nothing but bewildered distress. And he, on his side, saw nothing but the tragic mask of suffering in which her features were frozen. It was not Susan's face, but that of an older, desperate woman, incapable of expression. Dick tried to smile, but his features no longer obeyed him. In his brief glance she read: "He hates me; he will never forgive me. Why should he? I've broken his life." And Dick, as he gazed at her impotently, was thinking: "This business is killing her. It's I who have done this. This is worse than murder. It's all wrong; she doesn't deserve it. My Susie . . . my little Susie!" His eyes blinded with tears. If the sergeant had not supported him he would have stumbled down the stairs of the dock.

"Pick 'em up, old chap," he said kindly.

In spite of Mr. Hadley's endeavours to arrange an interview the black van was carrying Dick to the City Gaol before they could reach him.

· · · · · ·

As George Lorimer stood in the High Street at Halesby and watched Susan and Mr. Hadley hurrying to catch the bus he felt himself imprisoned by black walls of misery. His love for Susan and his faith in her absolute goodness, together with his obstinate passion for the Dingle Works, had constituted the main-spring of his slow-moving life. That outworn piece of clock-work had been past regulation for years. Now the spring had snapped; the mechanism had ceased to move; the leisurely, subdued ticking had ceased, and in the silence that followed, he knew, for the first time, that the wretched thing was past mending. He saw himself not only as a bankrupt felon, but as the owner of a name that had now been smirched beyond any recovery.

At first, driven by sheer habit, he found himself making his way mechanically in the direction of the Dingle. For all the trade that came to it in these days, now that Bulgin's New British Nail Company had swept it away from him, he might just as well have locked the place up and deserted it. As he trudged down the hill he felt a sudden repugnance for its empty solitude. This lonely little man became frightened of being alone and, paradoxically, even more terrified of being seen—for by now the whole small world of Halesby must be buzzing with the news. Within sight of the smokeless chimney-stack he checked, like a fox that is headed, and ran back, like a hunted fox seeking its earth, toward the house in Great Cornbow.

Mrs. Lorimer anxiously awaited his return on the doorstep. She looked at him with enquiring eyes. He shook his head vigorously; for the moment he could not speak.

"I saw you hurrying down the road and called after you," she said, with her usual severity. "Come in and have breakfast, George. There's no point in starving yourself."

He took his place at the table obediently. Curiously enough, at this instant, he found her severity heartening. Here, at last, was a person with enough strength to face the disaster. She was treating him as a rather harsh mother might treat an unhappy child. He sat down at the table, listlessly stirring his tea.

"Come, drink it up, George," she said, "or it will go cold."

He was glad to be commanded like this. When he raised his eyes and saw this strange creature, whom he had married in a moment of negligence, sitting there, so calm and collected, his shrinking mind was filled with sudden admiration.

There was something superb about women. This amazing composure, resembling—yet different from— the stony determination he had already witnessed in Susan, impressed him as the most stable thing in his reeling world. Would she be so composed, he wondered, when she heard from his lips the story of their personal ruin? Would she be equally steadfast and capable of bearing the secret burden under which his weak conscience had staggered for many months? As he gazed at the worn, determined face of this woman

who, though his wife, had been so remote from him,
a wild gleam of hope illumined his spirit's night. He
had wronged her as deeply as he had wronged Susan.
Would she ever forgive him? Would she help as well
as forgive?

With an heroic effort he pushed back his untasted
cup.

"I've something to tell you, Edna," he said with
tremulous lips.

"Yes, Georgy?" she replied, almost meekly. She
had never called him "Georgy" since the days of their
stiff autumnal courtship.

"Hadley says they'll have to brief counsel—the best
they can find. He mentioned Cronshaw. Susan wants
her money, her capital, you know."

"She must have it. If Dick's innocent, as she says,
it's the very least she can do. You must make arrangements at once."

"I can't," George gulped. "It . . . it's gone!"

"Gone? What do you mean?"

"I've used it." He shook his head. In spite of the
gravity of the occasion he was smiling weakly. "I'm
afraid it's what they call fraudulent conversion. I've
. . . I suppose I've stolen it."

"George. . . . What are you saying?"

"It's the truth, Edna. Just the truth. I meant to re-
pay it. Then John Bulgin. . . . Oh, everything went
wrong."

He collapsed with his head in his hands and began

to cry. The gaunt woman moved swiftly to his side and knelt beside him. She caressed his bald head. "Georgy, Georgy," she whispered. "My poor lamb, why didn't you tell me? If you'd only told me before!"

"I couldn't." His plump little body shook in her arms. "First of all I thought it would all come out right. When I saw that it couldn't, I was ashamed . . ."

"Tell me everything, darling," she said, her voice strangely tender. She gathered him in her bony arms and hugged him to her breast as though he were nothing but a naughty, disconsolate child, while, coaxed by the strength and consolation that her unquestioning love infused into him, George Lorimer poured out the tale of his weakness and pride.

"If only you'd told me!" she cried, again and again.

He had told her now, told everything from the beginning to the end; and, such was the virtue of confession, his suffering soul was freed—if not from the burden of his crime, from its intolerable loneliness. When he had finished his story she continued to hold him in her arms, whispering words of endearment which were as strange to her ungracious tongue as to his ears; and while she soothed him the face of this woman, habitually so forbidding, became transfigured with a tenderness that made it beautiful. The very tones of her voice were enriched by the radiance of a spiritual fulfilment; yet, when next she spoke, the old, hard definiteness of thought reappeared.

"We must put this right at once, George," she said,

"for our own sakes as well as Susan's. We shall have to cut our coat according to the cloth. If I had known how things were I should have made you do that long ago. I've a little money of my own put by—about four hundred pounds in War Savings Certificates. We must realize that and hand it over immediately. I suppose I could borrow more from Eleanor's husband—I'm sure he would lend it—but I'd much rather not do that: it's only putting things off. What we ought to do, of course, is to sell this house and all the superfluous furniture. Some of the old things may possibly be valuable. I've no idea what they're worth. In any case we're not justified in staying here a moment longer than is necessary. We must find a small house that I can run single-handed. I'm not frightened of work, and people in our position have no business to be keeping a servant. Poor Mary will hate leaving us after all these years, but that can't be helped. I'll go round to the auctioneer's offices to see Mr. Barret—he knows all about furniture—and get him to take an inventory and arrange the sale. Then as to the business . . . I'm afraid I know nothing about that. You see, Georgy, you never told me," she added reproachfully.

George Lorimer shook his head sadly. "I couldn't," he said. "It's been going back steadily for years, and Bulgin's competition has finished me. Now there's practically nothing left."

"He offered you the chance of going in with him, George," she reproved him mildly.

"I know. It wasn't so much an offer as a threat. He's a bully, Edna. He wanted me under his thumb. When I think what Lorimers' have been . . ."

"We can't think of the past. Is the business saleable, George? Would Bulgin buy it?"

"Not now. He's got all he wants." His mind wandered. "Do you know, Edna," he said, "I've a sort of idea that John Bulgin has something to do with this . . . other business?"

"Never mind about that," Mrs. Lorimer answered firmly. "I suppose the Dingle's worth something?"

George Lorimer writhed. "It's worth something to Bulgin," he said. "That's what he's been after from the first."

"Thank heaven for that! You must make him buy it, George."

Even in these desperate straits his small obstinate mind resented the idea; but the relief of resigning himself to her colder, more reasonable intelligence, of surrendering his limp will to her direction and support, overcame his instinctive rebellion. She took his submission for granted. With a final kiss and an encouraging pat on the back she rose from her knees.

"I shall put on my hat," she said determinedly, "and go to see Barret at once. You had better go straight to John Bulgin and see what you can do with him."

George Lorimer made his timid way to the Tube Works with the air of a condemned man walking to the scaffold. He approached Mr. Bulgin's offices by a circuitous route, to avoid the painful condolences of his acquaintance in Halesby and, even more, the sight of his beloved Dingle. Mr. Bulgin was in but, characteristically, kept him waiting. "What the devil does *he* want?" he wondered. His conscience was not quite clear of the part he had played in the "Chatsworth" tragedy, and Inspector Frome's shrewd enquiries, though skilfully evaded, still troubled him. Mr. Magnus's death, in itself, had somewhat embarrassed him, for his investments were large and in the present state of the market he did not trust Harry Levison's judgment.

George Lorimer found him sitting at his desk with a stony face. Bulgin rose and shook hands. "Sit down, George," he said. "This is a terrible business . . . terrible. No need to say what I feel."

George shook his head helplessly. It was true. He hoped that he wouldn't. As Mr. Bulgin looked at him he couldn't help thinking the shabby little man had shrunk physically. He made this observation without pity or satisfaction.

"I've come to you, John," George Lorimer began, then stopped suddenly.

Mr. Bulgin encouraged him. "I take that as a compliment, George, old fellow. You never know who your friends are until you're in trouble," he added sententiously.

"I've come about the Dingle," George said abruptly.

"The Dingle?" Mr. Bulgin repeated with a puzzled

air. But, though George who was gazing at the carpet did not see them, his small eyes hardened. "So that's it," he thought. "At last!" "I'll do anything in my power, George," he said sympathetically.

"Do you still want it?" George asked.

Mr. Bulgin spoke carelessly. "Why, to tell you the truth, old fellow, I've never given it a thought since the new company was formed."

George Lorimer's heart fell. "You wanted it a year ago," he said.

"Did I mention it? Yes, of course. I remember. But that was before we opened up the new works at Pandypool. The position's altered since then. Times aren't any too good, George."

"The Dingle's for sale," said George Lorimer. Even now the words cost him an effort. "I want money immediately."

"Yes, I bet he does," Mr. Bulgin thought. He said sadly: "It looks to me as if you'd missed your market. The whole country's full of factory-sites going begging."

George rose. "In that case," he began, "I'd better not keep you."

"Sit down, George. Sit down. I'm hard-hit at the moment myself, but if I can possibly find you a buyer . . . What about price?"

"I raised money on it once," George confessed.

"Dear, dear, is that so?"

"I had a mortgage for two thousand pounds."

"Well, you must have been lucky! Two thousand pounds? That's a damned lot of money in these days."

"What do you reckon it's worth?" George asked bluntly.

Mr. Bulgin considered. "For a man who wants it," he said—"and, mind you, you've still got to find him —I'd say twelve hundred pounds."

"I'd take fifteen," George Lorimer answered eagerly.

Mr. Bulgin shook his head slowly and smiled. "I should darned well think you would, George," he said, "but you'll never get it. Of course you might try an advertisement . . ."

"I've no time for that. If the proposition doesn't interest you personally . . ."

Again Mr. Bulgin implored him to sit. He himself, on the other hand, rose from his chair and paraded the room with slow steps and knitted brows. On his inward eye there flashed a vision of that Naboth's Vineyard, so perfectly adapted to the secret purpose he had cherished. "He'll take anything," he thought. He returned to his desk and resumed his seat.

"Look here, George," he said, with the air of conferring a favour. "I don't want the Dingle, that's straight. But we're old friends and you're in a hole, and I'm anxious to help you. I'll give you twelve hundred and fifty."

"I'll take it," George Lorimer gasped thankfully.

("Twelve hundred and fifty and four hundred

make sixteen hundred and fifty," he was thinking. "Sixteen hundred and fifty from two thousand leave three hundred and fifty. The house, the furniture . . .")

"If you could give me a thousand in advance," he suggested humbly.

"A thousand? Of course," Mr. Bulgin lightly replied. "I'll ask my secretary to make out a cheque at once."

When George Lorimer, having paid his cheque into the bank, returned to Great Cornbow Mrs. Lorimer was impatiently awaiting him. Her usually sombre face wore an air of excitement and triumph. "Have you sold it?" she asked.

"Yes. Twelve hundred and fifty," he told her.

"Thank heaven! I've good news, too."

"From the court? They've released him?"

"No, no. I've heard nothing about that. But I've seen Mr. Barret. I made him come home with me and look round. It's about the furniture. You know that old set of mahogany chairs with horse-hair seats that we put in the morning-room? Well, they're ladder-back Chippendale—I think that was what he called them—and they're worth at the very least three hundred and fifty! And those two high arm-chairs, George, the ones with embroidered backs, in the attic . . ."

"Three hundred and fifty," George Lorimer was thinking. "That makes two thousand. Two thousand

. . . I'm saved! I shan't go to prison after all!"

"Well those, it appears," Mrs. Lorimer went on triumphantly, "are walnut, Queen Anne. Mr. Barret says Americans are mad on them. They mustn't go into the sale on any account, he says. We must send them to Sotheby's. And that's only the beginning! All the rubbishy old stuff in the attic . . . Oh, *why* didn't you tell me before, Georgy dear? You've been suffering alone so long—and all quite needlessly. Don't you *see?*" she cried. "Now sit down and have your dinner."

George Lorimer saw. He shared her generous enthusiasm. But it was not enough. "I don't want any dinner," he said. "I must go and see Susan."

Aunt Edna's face clouded momentarily, but her ancient jealousy had less power to move her now than her pitiful love for him.

"Eat something first, darling," she persuaded him tenderly. "You can go up to 'Chatsworth' afterwards."

"Thank you, Edna," he said.

"Like a child," she thought. "He's never been anything else."

She had no other child; her tenderness for George was maternal.

"When you go up to 'Chatsworth,'" she said, "you'd better tell Susan that I'd like her to stay with us till Dick comes home."

George Lorimer blushed with pleasure. "Thank you, Edna," he repeated, humbly.

IV

It was just a bit of bad luck, Mr. Hadley admitted to
Susan, that they had missed seeing Dick at the court on
Saturday morning. Even Superintendent Whittaker,
whom they interviewed later, was most sympathetic
about it. Dick had been whisked away to the City Gaol
because, at that precise moment, a police-van happened
to be starting. It would be the easiest thing in the
world, he said, for Mr. Hadley to arrange a meeting between his client and his wife; after all, Dick
was not a convict but a prisoner remanded in custody. The easiest thing in the world, Mr. Hadley
agreed. He would see to it at once. By to-morrow,
possibly . . .

It wasn't the easiest thing in the world for Susan.
She had hurried to the court that morning in Hadley's
company with her courage screwed up to the tautest
degree short of breaking. The brief glimpse she had
caught of Dick in the dock had been almost too much
for her. It was only when she saw him isolated in
those solemn surroundings, then suddenly marched
away by a policeman in uniform, that the utter helplessness of a man in the grip of the law became real
to her—that she, too, realized the ruthless efficiency
of the machine that had taken charge of him.

And that wasn't all. The brave smile of encouragement which Dick had intended for her had died on its

way to his lips. Susan had seen nothing but the agonized face and hollow eyes whose message she could not
interpret. He was hardly gone before another prisoner
stepped into the dock. She could not believe that Dick's
case, for the moment, was suspended. When Hadley
told her that he had been taken from the Court to the
gaol she broke down completely. It took him the best
part of an hour to coax back her self-control. Though
a married man, he found this spectacle of beauty in
distress extremely moving, and considered it his duty
to escort Susan home in a taxi; but later on, when he
told his wife what had happened, her attitude proved
to be considerably less sympathetic than his.

At "Chatsworth" Inspector Frome was awaiting
Susan's return. His manner was considerate; one might
almost say neighbourly. He just wanted, he said, to
ask her a few little questions. He sat down on the sofa,
with his notebook on his knees, and asked a great many,
pertinaciously—and, as Susan thought, stupidly—for
a large number of his questions seemed to her pointless
and trivial. When he made a casual allusion to Harry
Levison Susan adopted the method of abandoned
candour which had made such a strong impression in
her favour on Mr. Hadley. On Inspector Frome it
made no impression whatever. The romantic implications of her confession apparently left him cold. He
received her statements as facts, and took them down,
word for word.

"H'm, thank you very much, Mrs. Pennington," he

said. "If you've no objection, I should like to go through the house."

Susan consented willingly—if she had refused it would have made no difference—though she little knew what the words "go through" implied. The dimensions of "Chatsworth" offered scanty opportunities for concealing anything; but Inspector Frome "went through" it as thoroughly as if he were straining its contents through a fine hair-sieve. No corner or cranny escaped the minutest scrutiny; even Captain Small's shell-case gave up its secret hoard.

"By the way," the Inspector said, when he had finished his search, "did your husband happen to mention such a thing as a cheque?"

"A cheque?"

"Yes, a cheque. A cheque for a hundred pounds," he repeated slowly.

Susan shook her head. "He mentioned nothing," she told him.

"Oh . . . He mentioned nothing." The Inspector shut up his notebook. "Much obliged, Mrs. Pennington. Good afternoon. I'm sorry to have troubled you."

Alone and bewildered, she began to repair the disorder created by Inspector Frome's search. She set herself to the miserable task without enthusiasm, her mind weighed down by an uncertainty more distressful than the fear she had felt before. Again and again the vision of Dick's face in the dock returned to her, his parted lips, his blank inexpressive eyes. Again and again she asked herself what that long gaze signified; but memory, however tormented, could give no answer. For want of positive evidence her imagination supplied one. "He was too dazed at first to think anything," she told herself, "but since then he's had time to realize the wrong I've done him. He's thought it all over coldly and now he hates me. He couldn't do anything else, and I love him so," her heart cried.

Captain Small limped in—"just to have a dekko," he said. His marred face was so deeply overscored with suffering that if she had had any feeling left she would have tried to comfort him. Yet her heart was icily incapable of giving anything. She accepted his help in putting things straight as a matter of course; but the sound of his uneven steps on boards and linoleum nearly drove her mad. His face, in spite of its forced cheerfulness, reproached her continually; he reminded her of Dick, and she wished to God he would go.

In the middle of the afternoon George Lorimer appeared. He carried in his news and laid it at her feet, for all the world like a spaniel who has caught a small rabbit.

"Your money's all right," he proudly declared. "I've given Hadley *carte blanche*, so there's no need to worry any more about that." Then, equally proudly, he gave her his wife's invitation. "It'll be much better for you than moping up here all alone," he said.

Susan thanked him mechanically. "But I'd rather stay here," she told him.

As if it mattered where she went with her misery! She couldn't understand why George was so proud of having secured the money. That seemed to her the most natural thing in the world. After all, it was hers. And what was money, anyway? The only thing that mattered to her now was Dick's forgiveness. And he hadn't forgiven her. He would never forgive her. How could he?

She left Captain Small and George Lorimer talking together, repeating, again and again, what this or that person had said. She went into the Baronial dining-room and closed the door quietly behind her. She was standing there, gazing out of the window at nothing, when the lights of Mr. Hadley's car threw two beams across the dusk.

Mr. Hadley looked worn and excited. She heard him telling George Lorimer that it had been a devil of a day. He, too, dragged in his news and laid it triumphantly at her feet. He had had, it appeared, a long interview with the Superintendent and another with Dick. From what he could gather—the police were as guarded as usual—old Whittaker wasn't any too happy about his case. The police had managed, he guessed, though Whittaker wouldn't admit it, to get hold of the pathologist's report. He suspected that the cause of Magnus's death wasn't half as clear as they had imagined. After that he had had the extraordinarily good luck to catch Edward Cronshaw at his chambers and had talked with him for over half-an-

hour on the telephone. Now that Cronshaw had
accepted the brief they should all feel much happier.
More than that, he had promised to run down for the
inquest on Wednesday. It was common knowledge in
legal circles that the police were afraid of him as a man
who had never yet lost a murder-case in which he
defended.

Captain Small and George Lorimer listened ecstatically, nodding their heads and exchanging significant
glances. Susan heard Mr. Hadley's account of his
activities unmoved. All the time she could think of
nothing but the mystery of Dick's inexpressive eyes.
The lawyer turned to her:

"I've kept the best news till last, Mrs. Pennington,"
he said. "I've arranged with the Governor for you to
see your husband. I'll call for you in my car and drive
you over to the gaol to-morrow morning at ten."

Susan thanked him; but as she did so her heart sank
like a stone. Her mind was torn between eagerness and
deadly fear. It seemed to her that everything depended on that encounter. "To-morrow at ten," she
thought. "Can I live till to-morrow? Oh, why can't
I see him now and get it over?"

George Lorimer left her reluctantly. He seemed
really hurt, poor dear, that she wouldn't accept Aunt
Edna's olive-branch and come with him to Great Cornbow. The three men went together, for Mr. Hadley
insisted on giving the others a lift. A frigid November
night descended on Susan's loneliness. She lay cold

and brooding and sleepless on the sitting-room sofa; for she could not enter the bedroom—it was haunted by too many ghosts. Lovers' nights were short, they said. For Susan that night was endless. Again and again she found herself starting up in sheer desperation.

"I can't bear it . . . I can't bear it!" she cried.

But she had to bear it. In the end she cried herself into a state of numb exhaustion resembling sleep.

She awoke in a panic. Daylight had come; but, like Dick, she had no means of knowing the time, for she had forgotten to wind up her watch and the clock in the kitchen had stopped. It must be past eight o'clock, she decided, for Mr. Duke's man had left a bottle of milk in the porch.

"Only two hours," she thought. "I must pull myself together." With the aid of the mirror above the kitchen sink she completed a hasty toilet. Her face, she saw, was incredibly thin and white; but she made the best she could of it—so successfully that when the susceptible Hadley arrived, at ten precisely, her neatness and composure amazed him.

"What a woman!" he thought. "What courage! She's wonderful! She may have made a bad slip, but, by Jove, that's hardly to be wondered at. You can't blame anyone for falling in love with a girl like that!"

"Had a good night?" he tactlessly enquired.

Susan smiled and nodded. She was thankful to know that she didn't look as she felt. The last ounce of her will had been spent in attaining that false composure.

"I've got to hold on," she told herself, "until I've seen him." But her shallow breath came and went so fast, her faint heart pounded so sickeningly, that she began to wonder if she could.

"We're in plenty of time," Mr. Hadley told her consolingly.

In less than a quarter of an hour they approached the gate of the gaol. She saw the blank wall with its iron *chevaux-de-frise*, against which Dick had leant in his agony. She shivered at the sight. Inside there, she thought, with a high brick wall and that wicked iron between him and the sky, a man must have twisted thoughts. So much time to think! And no man could think sanely or justly in a place like that. However sweet his nature might be, it would turn to bitterness. He would brood on his wrongs until they became obsessions: fluid anger cooling and thickening into stony hate. Sometimes they went mad, people said . . .

"A quarter-past ten to the tick," Mr. Hadley remarked with acute satisfaction. He pointed to the prison-clock.

She agreed; it was indisputable.

"I told you we'd do it." He surveyed his small car with affectionate pride.

"Only nine horse-power," he said, "and four years old; but she'll do forty-five on top and more than thirty to the gallon."

Two nights and a day to brood over it, Susan

thought; two nights and a day in which to realize what I've done to him!

"Now come along. Keep your pecker up," Mr. Hadley said cheerfully. "I hope to goodness I've not left the order behind! No, no . . . here it is. They're awfully strict in these places. The lock-up's quite different."

They passed through the gate of the gaol. There were certain formalities; but Mr. Hadley explained in a loud voice just who they were and produced his order.

"A lawyer gets more consideration than ordinary visitors," he whispered. "More or less the same line of business, you know," he added with a wink, "so they won't keep us waiting. O.K.?"

The warder assented.

Susan entered a long room shaped like a corridor: on one side a blank whitewashed wall, on the other a series of alcoves, separated by partitions, resembling the screened shelves in a post-office where people write telegrams, into one of which the warder directed her. The wall that faced her, instead of being of wood provided with a box of telegraph-forms and a chained stub of pencil, was of thick plate-glass; and in place of the counter on which telegrams are written there was an iron grill.

"Speak downward through the grating," the warder instructed her. "You needn't raise your voice; he'll hear you all right."

She wondered what he meant. There was apparently no one to hear.

"They'll bring him along in a jiffy," he told her kindly.

Susan gazed through the glass into the corridor corresponding to her own. It was empty. Would he never come? She heard, through the grating, a sound of steps on the concrete floor. Her heart checked, fluttered, stopped, then began to beat wildly. "I'm going to faint," she thought, "but I mustn't . . . I mustn't." Two men advanced quickly. One was a warder and the other was Dick. But he wasn't, as she had imagined him, in convict's clothing or handcuffed. He stepped out like a free man, his cheeks shaved, his hair neatly brushed. Though his face was paler than usual he looked almost smart in his wedding-suit. It seemed that he didn't realize Susan was there awaiting him till the warder touched his elbow and pointed to her compartment.

Then, suddenly, he saw her. That moment of recognition was the most terrible in Susan's existence. Her very life seemed to hang on the expression of his eyes and his lips. He moved forward rapidly and held out his hands. She could see his eyes now. There was no vestige of hate in them—only joy and excitement and love. She drew a deep breath of relief and clutched at the grill. He was speaking quickly; his voice sounded strange coming upward.

"Is it you?" he said. "I hoped, but I didn't dare . . ."

She shook her head helplessly. The power of speech had left her.

"Susie, Susie," the voice went on. "Take off your hat. Take off your coat. Let me see you if I can't touch you."

She obeyed him hurriedly, feeling unaccountably shy —much shyer than when she had undressed on their wedding-night.

"That's better, my darling . . ." Again he reached out his arms, as though momentarily unconscious of the barrier of glass between them. He laughed at the futility of his own gesture. "Did you get my letter?" he asked.

She shook her head.

"They promised to post it yesterday."

At last she was able to speak. "It's Sunday to-day."

"Sunday? Really? Good lord! I'd forgotten. I hoped you'd had it. It killed me to think of your being there all alone . . ."

"Oh, Dick, Dick!" her heart cried.

"You see," he went blundering on, "it's all a mistake. I never touched Magnus. You *do* believe me, don't you? If you and I stick together that's all that matters. There was only one thing I wanted you to know. Listen, darling, remember—I've forgiven you utterly . . . utterly. It was all my fault. I've been thinking it over in here. I should never have left you like that . . ."

"Oh, my darling," she whispered.

"And as for this wretched business: they can't touch me, Susie. I've done nothing wrong; they don't ever punish an innocent man in England. So you mustn't worry. It'll all come out right in the end and none of this matters to me as long as you believe in me, Susie . . ."

"Of course I believe in you, Dick."

"Yes, I knew that you would. I've told myself so again and again. We must go through this business together, you and me, Susie. Don't worry, my sweet, and don't forget I've forgiven you. Don't cry, my darling . . ."

He was too late. She was crying already. Tears streamed down her cheeks and fell on the iron grill. Dick's face quivered too.

"Dick, I love you so dreadfully," she sobbed.

The warder, who had been strolling up and down, came up from behind and touched Dick's arm. He started; then turned away helplessly. Susan, weeping with bowed head, did not see him go.

For several moments she went on crying brokenly. Then, her body still shaken by sobs, though her eyes were dry, she methodically put on the hat and coat which lay on the grating in front of her. She emerged from the visiting-room no longer pale and stony. Her cheeks were flushed; her eyes shone; her body and spirit seemed to have taken on a new lease of strength and vitality. The cold statue had come to life. She was like a flame. Mr. Hadley, who had whiled away time in chatting to the gatekeeper, was startled by this burning transfiguration. One couldn't be gallantly tender with a fiery creature like this; but he did his best.

"So it's over?" he asked sympathetically.

"No, it's only beginning," she flamed at him. "I know where I am, I've got to fight now. I've got to fight till I drop!"

"And, by Jove, she looked like it!" he told his wife that evening. "You may take my word for it: that woman's a positive tigress. Fight? She'd take on the Bench and the Court of Criminal Appeal and the blessed Home Secretary himself with one hand tied behind her!"

v

The information which Superintendent Whittaker had given the journalists to "chew" was not extensive, though they spun it out with the skill and assiduity of silkworms chewing a mulberry-leaf. On Monday morning, however, the *North Bromwich Courier* let itself go as far as the law allowed in a highly-coloured account of Dick Pennington's police-court appearance and a flattering obituary notice of Mr. Magnus which brought tears of pride to Miss Lewis's eyes. The *Courier* reached Lesswardine by motor from Ludlow at half-past eight. The morning was crisp and clear and propitious for grayling: on such days, in late autumn, the grayling rise on the fords of Teme toward midday. Dr. Haskard, smoking his after-breakfast pipe and waiting for his waders, was selecting a number of dry-flies that Teme grayling appreciate—such as Wickham's Fancies, Red Tags and Green Insects, when the landlord appeared on the porch of the Bridge Hotel and handed him the *Courier*. The first thing that caught his eyes was Solomon Magnus's name.

The news shocked him.

Dr. Haskard was interested in Magnus not only as a patient, but as a man. He admired his shrewdness and courage, if not his obstinacy. He was even more interested, professionally, in Mr. Magnus's heart. It was a mysterious heart: neither cardiograph nor stethoscope had satisfied his curiosity about it. Now, that heart, with all its mysteries revealed, lay exposed in the City Mortuary; while he, Charles Haskard, sat out in the sun, prepared to catch grayling. His wife came on to the porch with packets of lunch to join him.

"Solomon Magnus is dead," he told her.

"Not the stockbroker, Charley? Wasn't he a patient of yours?"

"Yes."

"What did he die of?"

"The *Courier* says he's been strangled. The police have made an arrest. He *ought* to have died of Auricular Fibrillation."

"Let me see." Mrs. Haskard took the paper and scanned it eagerly. She was a little dark woman, taut with passionate energy. "Who's this man they called in? Dr. Altrincham-Harris, it says."

"An old chap with a sixpenny surgery behind the Art Gallery. Pretty shady customer, I imagine. *I* wouldn't give sixpence for his opinion, anyway."

"Then perhaps he *did* die of Auricular what-do-you-call-it? If you were the only person who knew, this man may have made a mistake. Who's Richard Pennington?"

"I haven't the faintest idea."

But the landlord, who heard them, had. "We reckon it must be Miss Pennington's nephew," he told them. "You know Miss Pennington, madam: a tall, thin lady; you saw her out ottering last year."

Mrs. Haskard nodded: "Of course!"

"We can't make it out, none of us. He's a nice, quiet fellow, young Dick is. Married, too. The Penningtons have always been greatly respected round here."

Dr. Haskard yawned. Mrs. Haskard, however, persisted. Her imagination was aroused.

"Was this thing Mr. Magnus suffered from the kind of disease that might kill him at any moment?" she asked.

"Yes, certainly. It's a wonder he lived so long. I told him to go to Nauheim to keep him quiet."

"It says there was a quarrel."

"Yes. That would be quite enough."

"Without any strangling? They've only this man Harris's word for it, and you say that's worth nothing."

"Why are you getting so excited, my dear?"

"Supposing this young Pennington didn't kill him after all? It's too awful to think of! Mr. Shipley says that he's married."

"Lots of murderers are. There'll be a *post-mortem*, anyway."

"But they won't know what you know?"

Dr. Haskard sighed. The persistence! "I'll write to the Coroner if you like."

"The inquest's on Wednesday. A letter might go astray."

"Don't be foolish, darling. They never do. If you prefer it, I'll wire him."

"Yes, write it out now. I'll take it along to the post-office."

Dr. Haskard laughed. "You'll be saying next that you want me to go to the inquest."

"I'm not sure that you oughtn't to," she replied.

"Well, of all the ridiculous nonsense!"

Now, grayling or no grayling, he found it impossible to get the bee out of her bonnet. "The police," he told her, "don't arrest a fellow on a charge like that without pretty good reason. You know nothing about it."

"Of course I don't *know*," she replied. "It's a matter of feeling. And I *feel* . . ."

"Do you seriously want me to break up our holiday and go back to North Bromwich?" he asked.

"Yes, seriously. I can't tell you why," she said, "but I feel it's our duty. Besides, it's great fun doing things on the spur of the moment. I'll drive you, darling. Let's go. We can come back on Thursday. If we don't, I believe we shall regret it."

After that he knew that the grayling would rise in vain. "Very well," he sighed. At least there was one compensation. He would have the opportunity of examining Solly Magnus's heart without being inconvenienced by the remainder of Solly Magnus. He not only saw it, with the Coroner's permission, that evening, but also the wound on Mr. Magnus's temple and the sections the pathologist had made from the skin of his neck. Dr. Haskard, as a physician, had not much belief in the rightness of feminine instincts. But his wife was a remarkable woman. He was inclined to think that, for once, her instinct was right. On Tuesday morning he telephoned to the Coroner and arranged to have lunch with him; and the Coroner, being a medical man himself and alive to the precise value of Altrincham-Harris's opinion, was glad to accept his friend's offer to give expert evidence. When a man of Haskard's standing abandoned his well-earned holiday, he could hardly do less.

"It's an odd case," he said. "We shall have to go very carefully."

"This is rather a tricky case . . ." Sir Edward Cronshaw was thinking as he took off his reading-glasses and gazed unobservantly through the windows of the two-o'clock train from Euston to North Bromwich. As a very young man he had practised on the Midland Circuit; he knew that grim city intimately. In those days he had often done business with Hadley's father. The best type of country solicitor: very few of 'em left. That was why he had treated young Hadley's telephone-call so sympathetically and accepted the brief which he had just finished reading. There was another excellent reason for having accepted his brief: young Hadley's assurance that there was plenty of money to back it—for though Cronshaw's success in criminal cases had been spectacular, though his appearances were always "news" and his fine head and commanding figure a prize for every press-photographer, there wasn't, to tell the truth, much money in murder. One worked like a horse and pleaded like an angel and got them acquitted and . . . that was that! It was the habitual insolvency of murderers that made him grateful, in this case, for the chance of appearing (and possibly saying nothing) at a mere Coroner's inquest.

"An unpleasant case," he reflected, replacing his glasses. On the surface it looked like an ordinary crime of passion. This Pennington, a decent young man with nothing against him, tolerably educated and intelligent, goes to work in South Wales and leaves a gay wife behind. The wife, a girl of the same class, makes hay while the sun shines. The most ordinary thing in the world; modern girls had no morals. Pennington gets an anonymous letter—from some other admirer probably—and comes home. She confesses. He flies off to see Levison and finds Levison's uncle instead. There's the story of the cheque. The police, of course, say "Blackmail!" With a man of Pennington's sort and in his state of mind that seemed wrong psychologically. Pennington says that he lost his temper at the idea of being offered money. That sounds more probable. Pennington admits that he lifted a chair. It was a good thing he did admit it: the police would have fingerprints. But Magnus's collar was torn as well; there was a wound on his forehead. If the chair had been used as a weapon it would show signs of that, and then, God help Pennington! Then the collar . . . If that were of highly-glazed linen it would carry fingerprints too. That remained to be seen: a matter of vital importance. And the brief didn't mention it . . .

The brief, in short, was a well-meaning but a most inadequate document. These country solicitors were the devil! There was nothing in it, for instance, about Magnus's previous health. Hadley ought to have got hold of every doctor he'd ever consulted. He ought to have said more, again, about Pennington's psychological state. Had he forgiven his wife? Did anything in his behaviour suggest the possibility of a plan, contrived between them, to extort money from Levison? The brief told him nothing. He folded it and put it away. At the moment everything seemed to depend on the medical evidence. Expert evidence, even the most distinguished, was often assailable; the only good thing about experts was their eagerness to disagree. Supposing that failed, he would use his well-tried methods of appeal to a jury's sentiment, which depended not only in his own histrionic power and the timbre of his voice, which stirred men's emotions to the complete abandonment of reason, but on his client's appearance and behaviour in the dock and—possibly—in the witness-box. He hoped to goodness that Pennington was a good-looking fellow. If the wife was beautiful and contrite it might help matters too. But one never knew with a jury.

Mr. Hadley met him at North Bromwich and escorted him to the Grand Midland, and Hadley was exactly what he would have imagined from the brief: well-meaning but inadequate. Mr. Hadley, it appeared, was most deeply impressed by the behaviour of Pennington's wife. Cronshaw listened to his raptures cynically. He knew a good deal about women. It wasn't only learned counsel who could act. Still, the wife might be useful—provided she kept her head, as they rarely did.

They drove out to the gaol together and interviewed Dick. "Yes, he'll do," Cronshaw thought, "a decent clean-looking lad." What moved him even more was Dick's Old Brunstonian tie; for Cronshaw himself, though he forgot to mention it in *Who's Who*, was an Old Brunstonian. Dick told his story with patent disarming candour. The poor devil didn't appear to realize what a deadly mess he was in.

"You believe I'm innocent, sir, don't you?" he asked pathetically.

"Of course I believe you're innocent. I'm defending you," Cronshaw replied.

And the odd thing was that he did. With a man like Cronshaw that meant a great deal.

"We must have this fellow in the box," he told Hadley afterwards. "What about the wife?"

Mr. Hadley had arranged for Susan to meet them in a private room at the Grand Midland after dinner that night. Cronshaw ate an excellent dinner, enhanced by a bottle of *Nuits St. Georges*—the last thing in the world he expected to find at North Bromwich. He felt sleepy after it and extremely benevolent. He had heard a great deal about Mrs. Pennington while they were drinking it. To tell the truth he was getting rather bored with Hadley's tale of her perfections when Susan and the coffee appeared simultaneously.

Curiously enough, this pilgrimage to the Grand Midland had been one of the hardest penances imposed on her by the disaster. It was there that her association with Levison had begun and run its course, and she would have been happier had she never seen it again. As she slunk into the entrance-lounge and enquired at the office-counter for the number of Cronshaw's room, she felt herself running a gauntlet of eyes that had once been friendly, but now surveyed her with scorn. She was out of breath and tremulous when she reached Sir Edward's room on the second floor. Mr. Hadley came forward and fluttered round her. The man on whose skill Dick's fate depended was introduced to her.

As Cronshaw rose from his chair and bowed, rather stiffly, Susan looked him full in the eyes. She held out her hand and he took it. They still continued to gaze at each other. And as they did so Susan Pennington blushed. Not for shame. On the contrary, her heart leapt high with triumphant excitement and laughed within her. In this heavy-jowled man with full lips and fiery eyes and rebellious hair, she recognized a victim far worthier of her steel than poor provincial Mr. Hadley, who continued his flutterings un-noticed. Edward Cronshaw, in fact, had something of the quality of Harry Levison. He was a little ornate, a little romantic, a little theatrical, as superbly confident in his powers as a professional "charmer"—but all on a nobler scale. She could have sworn that, like Harry Levison, he "understood women." He was at liberty to develop that understanding in her case by any means that pleased him—provided that he saved Dick's life.

As Susan sat down opposite him, warmed by her conquest, her quick wits told her to exploit the method which had so successfully flattened out Mr. Hadley. She threw her modesty, as before, on the mercy of his chivalrous nature; but with Cronshaw she was not the cold, contained woman whose disarmed and disarming frankness had won Mr. Hadley's enthusiasm, but a passionate, palpitating creature, all softness and fire, who, if she had generously sinned, was burning to make an equally generous atonement. In this rôle—which was nothing indeed but an intensified presentation of her genuine feelings—she succeeded magnificently. Edward Cronshaw listened to her with rapture. An emotional man by nature (to say nothing of the Burgundy), he was, for once, in the position of a criminal jury being addressed by himself. When Susan had finished her story he felt oddly moved—not so much by the story itself as by Susan. His theatrical sense acclaimed a fellow artist. "My God!" he thought, "what a pair of witnesses!"

He said: "Mrs. Pennington, this story has affected me deeply. Your disregard for yourself. Your candour . . ." he paused.

"Can you save him?" she broke in hurriedly.

"If it's humanly possible. I'm sure you can help me," he said.

"I . . .?"

"Yes. In the witness-box. If you speak as you've spoken now."

"I'd do anything . . . anything. I shall die if he doesn't get off. You see, I . . . love him."

Edward Cronshaw nodded approvingly. It was done to perfection: the rapid phrasing, the fall on the final words. He took her hand firmly. They were charming soft little hands and pleasant to hold. His voice—that voice which had often melted twelve hearts at a time—took on an emotional tone and his fine eyes shone liquidly.

"Cheer up, little woman," he said. "We're going to fight this together, you and I and your husband, all three of us . . . *and* Mr. Hadley, of course," he added tactfully. "I'm going to tell you something: your husband may have found you a poor sort of wife in the past, but if we get through this you'll be a much better wife to him than he ever dreamt that you were when he married you. Isn't that so?"

Susan blushed and was silent. He pressed her hands and released them. When Hadley fluttered back from seeing Susan downstairs, Edward Cronshaw was thoughtful.

"That's a damned clever woman, Hadley," was all he said.

VI

The North Bromwich Coroner's Court was housed in the same building as the Stipendiary's and the Police Headquarters. In its size and general arrangement it resembled that in which Dick had made his first appearance; but the space which in the Stipendiary's was occupied by the dock contained, in the Coroner's, nothing but desks and benches. By the time that Dick reached it in custody on Wednesday morning the space allotted to the public was already full; for the Magnus case had caused a sensation, and the rumour of Sir Edward Cronshaw's appearance was enough to attract a crowd. From this crowd, as Dick entered, a sinister buzzing arose. It was a threatening, inhuman sound; he instinctively turned his back on it.

He sat down between two warders and scanned the court eagerly for familiar faces. He saw Cronshaw, magnificently at home in his element, limelight, and chatting friendlily with the City's Prosecuting Solicitor, who represented the police. He saw his old friend, Superintendent Whittaker, resplendent in uniform. He was aware of the ponderous imminence of Inspector Frome. On the witnesses' bench, among several strangers, he recognised Miss Lewis. She was wearing deep mourning and looked deathly. Dick felt sorry for her. At the desk behind Cronshaw and the Prosecuting Solicitor he perceived the round shoulders of George Lorimer, George Lorimer's pink tonsure fringed by fluffy white hair, and, beside him, the dapper form of young Mr. Hadley.

It was Hadley who first noticed Dick's presence. He moved over to greet him, his face set in an encouraging smile. "Now who would have thought of meeting *you* here?" that smile seemed to say.

"Where's Susan?" Dick whispered.

"Oh, not *here*," Mr. Hadley said sagely. "She's waiting outside till it's over. Small's taking care of her. There's no question of *her* giving evidence in this court, you know."

"Thank heaven for that!" Dick thought. He said: "How is she?"

"Splendid, splendid!" Mr. Hadley replied enthusiastically.

"Is Levison here?" Dick asked.

"No, they haven't called him."

"When will they begin?"

"The Coroner's not come yet, and the jury haven't been sworn. Here he is . . ."

The door at the back of the dais opened. The City Coroner entered and took his seat. He was a comfortable, middle-aged man, clean-shaven, with a shiny bald head. The court rose and bowed to acknowledge his presence. Sir Edward Cronshaw performed the movement superbly, his silk-robed figure looming like a magnified shadow in front of George Lorimer. The Coroner nodded curtly. "That sort of thing's wasted here," his nod implied. "Keep that for the Old Bailey."

"I declare this court open in the King's name," he quietly remarked. "Are the jurors all there, Superintendent. Get them sworn in at once."

The jurors, who, up to this point, had been scattered anonymously all over the court, immediately coalesced in a single group, like globules of mercury, and became a jury. They then separated by simple fissure into two rows, one above the other, like the manuals of an organ. Cronshaw ran his eye over them, as a musician might run his fingers over the keys of an unfamiliar instrument to test its quality. The keys, in this case, appeared to be a selection of average middle-class citizens: Dick could have taken his place among them with perfect propriety. Instructed by the clerk they repeated the oath one by one in a Midland accent of varying density:

"*I swear by Almighty God that I will well and duly enquire* . . .*"

"It is your duty to choose a foreman," the Coroner directed them.

They chose one, wisely, Dick thought: a smartly-dressed business-man, with a big, red face, a heavy moustache and a flower backed by asparagus fern in his buttonhole.

They passed through a door at the back of the court to "view" Mr. Magnus's body and returned, a few moments later, with solemn faces.

"Now it's really begun," Dick thought, and his heart beat faster.

"*Georgiana Lewis!*"

The black figure crept forward silently and swore by Almighty God that the evidence she would give to that court would be the truth, the whole truth, and nothing but the truth. Her name was, actually, Georgiana Lewis. She was aged forty-nine and secretary to the deceased, whose body she had identified. At five forty-five on Thursday last . . .

She gave her evidence and identified Dick with an admirable, collected precision. P.C. Poultry entered the box and rapped out the oath like a maxim. As he gave his testimony, uninterrupted, the faces of the jury grew graver; they nudged one another and whispered and nodded their heads together.

Dick's heart went colder and colder. As one witness succeeded another, indisputable fact linked with fact appeared to be gripping him in an iron chain: the signs of violence; the spilt inkstand; the shattered chair with its damning, identified, inky finger-prints; the torn collar . . .

Cronshaw rose slowly.

"Is it suggested," he asked smoothly, "that the chair was the weapon with which the wound on the temple of the deceased was inflicted or that that wound caused death?"

That remained for the medical witnesses to prove, the Coroner suggested.

Quite so, Cronshaw agreed. His client did not challenge the finger-prints. The chair had evidently been examined very minutely. The finger-prints were inky and oily and easily identified. He would like to know—and he put the question deliberately—if the chair showed any traces of human blood or hair. None were found? Of course the witness expert had looked for them with an equal care to that which he had displayed in identifying his client's finger-prints? Would it not have been fair and in the interests of justice, he asked mildly, if that negative result had been included in the evidence?

Now as to the collar. It was a starched collar, with a high glaze. He would like the jury to look at it, but begged them to handle it carefully. Had the expert discovered similar finger-prints on that? On a surface of that kind, the witness replied, fingers might not leave an impression. Cronshaw shook his massive head reproachfully: would he kindly answer the question. The answer was "No"? Very well . . . Now supposing the fingers that touched—let him put it more strongly—that grasped that collar with sufficient violence to cause strangulation were inky and oily, like those that had grasped the chair, did the witness suggest that they would leave no impression? It was difficult to say? He would have thought it extremely easy. Did the witness agree that the outer side of the collar, being more highly glazed, would show finger-prints much more clearly than the inner, which was less highly glazed? He did? Very well . . .

Again . . . It was maintained by the police that the deceased had been strangled. If the witness desired to strangle a man, in other words to compress his throat until he could not breathe, would he exert that pressure outwards or inwards? Would an inward pressure have torn the stud-holes of the collar in the manner in which the witness and the jury could see for themselves it was torn? Wouldn't the tearing of the collar in that manner have the effect of relieving pressure rather than exerting it? That was a question for the medical experts? Wasn't it rather a question of common sense?

No questions . . . Cronshaw sat down. James Altrincham-Harris was called. He hurried toward the

box with quick, nervous steps. Cronshaw rose immediately. His client, Richard Pennington, he said,
wished to tender evidence as allowed by the Coroners
Act, 1887. With the Coroner's permission he would
prefer his client to give evidence before the medical
witnesses. The Coroner granted it. The clerk called:
"Richard Pennington."

Dick stepped forward. Behind him he heard once
more that sinister buzz of excitement. His clenched
hands were clammy and icy cold. He repeated the
words of the oath in a dull, hushed voice. He was
asked his name, his age, and his occupation. He turned
to hear Cronshaw speaking.

"Now I want you to tell the jury—the jury, not me
—exactly what happened in Magnus's office last Thursday. Let them hear what you have to say, and take
your time over it," he said sympathetically.

For a moment he could not speak. He found himself fascinated by the twelve solemn faces watching him
so intently.

"Come along, just put it in your own words," Cronshaw told him.

It was almost impossible to explain himself, Dick
thought, without mentioning Susan. He must avoid
that at all costs.

"I went to the offices in Sackville Row," he began,
"to see Mr. Levison, Mr. Magnus's nephew, on private
business . . ."

He stopped. The eyes of the jury fixed him stonily.

The mellifluous voice of Cronshaw encouraged him to continue.

"On private business," he repeated . . . All the twenty-four eyes became concentrated in the heavy, red face of the foreman. Dick began to address him personally; and now that his tongue was loosened his words gushed out in a spate.

"Take your time, take your time!" Cronshaw warned him.

It was easier now. The foreman's face looked intelligent, not merely a mask like the others. He listened to Dick most carefully and must surely realize that he was telling the truth. Dick seemed to himself to be making his story endless. It came as a surprise to him when he found he had no more to say. There was a pause: no sound but the scratch of the Coroner's pen and the muted buzz that came from the back of the court. Cronshaw spoke:

"Now answer my questions carefully and address the jury. I can hear what you answer. Did you know the deceased before this?"

"No."

"Did you go to Sackville Row intending to see him?"

"No."

"Had you any feeling against him?"

"None whatever."

The Coroner looked up uneasily.

"This is not a criminal court, Sir Edward," he began. Cronshaw bowed. "I submit that these questions reflect on the contention that the deceased met his death by violence."

"Well . . . Continue your examination."

Cronshaw turned again to Dick.

"You say that you became agitated during this interview. Why?"

"He offered me a cheque."

"Yes. The jury has heard about that."

"Did you ask for this cheque or demand it?"

"Most certainly not."

"Why did Magnus offer you a cheque?"

Dick was silent.

"I want you to answer."

"I'd much rather not answer."

"You needn't answer," the Coroner quietly interposed.

"For your wife's sake as well as your own I want you to answer," Cronshaw persisted.

"Is this really material to the matter the jury is investigating, Sir Edward?" the Coroner inquired. "This is an inquest, remember, to determine the cause of Magnus's death."

Dick Pennington's mind clutched eagerly at this avenue of escape. Cronshaw closed it.

"I submit that this question is not only material but of vital importance. If my client refuses to answer it I shall ask you to call Henry Levison," he replied. "Let me ask you another question, Pennington. Was the cheque that Magnus offered you in the nature of compensation? You have sworn to speak the whole truth."

Dick capitulated. "Yes."

"For a wrong that Levison had done you?"

"Yes. I suppose so."

"Through your wife?"

There was no escaping it now. He answered: "Yes."

"Very well . . . You refused it indignantly?"

"Of course I refused it."

"Tell me this. Are you a man who ordinarily loses his temper "

"I don't think so."

"Neither do I. Have you ever laid violent hands on a man in your life?"

"No, never. I'm not made like that."

"When you picked up that chair had you any intention of attacking Magnus?"

"I had no intention of doing anything. I just picked it up. When I realized what I was doing I chucked it away. I was letting off steam, so to speak. I recovered myself immediately. I was angry with Magnus, but not as angry as that."

"Exactly. Now answer this question carefully, Pennington. Did you use that chair to strike Magnus?"

"Most certainly not."

"Did you lay hands on Magnus's throat?"

"No. The width of the table was between us all the time. I couldn't have done so."

"Were your hands, as the prints on the back of the chair suggest, stained with ink and oily?"

"Yes. I left the works in a hurry, without washing, that morning."

"Two more questions. When you left the office at five minutes past six, was Solomon Magnus alive?"

"I'm certain he was alive."

"He was alive when you left him. Now . . . Did you, or did you not kill Solomon Magnus?"

"I never even touched him."

"Thank you. That will do, Pennington."

The Coroner turned to the jury: "Do you wish to ask any questions?" The foreman shook his head ponderously. "Very well. Step down."

"James Altrincham-Harris!"

Dr. Harris slipped forward again. The Coroner questioned him. He was a medical practitioner and had been on the register for thirty-five years. He had been called to the case at thirteen minutes past six. He had examined the deceased and come to the conclusion that he had met his death by violence. He had used the word "strangulation" on the spur of the moment. It was justified, as he thought, by the fact that the collar was torn, and by the colour of Magnus's face, which appeared to be cyanosed. Death had taken place, in his opinion, a few minutes before he arrived. It was impossible to say exactly when. The same evening he had been present with the pathologist at the *post-mortem*. He was not a pathologist himself, but, as a man of practical experience, he adhered to his first conclusion as to the cause of death. As he had urgent cases waiting for his attention he would be grateful if the Coroner would release him as early as possible.

Cronshaw rose again.

"One moment, doctor," he said. "You say you have been on the medical register thirty-five years and are a man of practical experience. Have you ever, in your practice, seen a case of death by strangulation?"

Dr. Harris considered. He couldn't say that he had. But he knew the signs of it.

"From what you learnt as a student, thirty-five years ago?"

Dr. Harris replied that he tried to keep up to date.

"You are what is commonly known as a sixpenny doctor?"

"I conduct a working-class practice to the best of my ability."

"An extensive practice? No chance of your getting rusty?"

"I see as many as a hundred patients in a day," Dr. Harris said proudly.

"And have plenty of time left over for reading, of course. You admit you are not a pathologist?"

"No."

"In which case your evidence as to the *post-mortem* findings cannot be of much value."

"That's a matter of opinion."

"Exactly. Thank you very much."

Any questions from the jury? None. The reply, in this case, was emphatic. Cronshaw smiled.

Arthur Sherwell, aged twenty-seven, was Assistant Pathologist at the North Bromwich Infirmary. He was a brisk and confident young man, a lively contrast to Dr. Altrincham-Harris. His evidence had the orderly succinctness of a scientific document. He had made a *post-mortem* examination of the deceased in collaboration with the last witness, and proposed to make use of the notes he had made at the time and subsequently in the hospital laboratory. Externally there was nothing to remark but the wound on the temple, undoubtedly inflicted after death, and a slight ecchymosis on the front of the throat . . .

"The jurors are not medical men," the Coroner reminded him. "I think you had better . . ."

Ecchymosis meant bruising, Dr. Sherwell explained enthusiastically. The bruising was quite superficial and *ante-mortem*. (The foreman whispered to his neighbours that this meant before death.) Internally, the liver was enlarged and all other abdominal organs affected with a considerable degree of fatty infiltration. The heart was hypertrophied, dilated and also infiltrated and the vascular system generally atheromatous."

"Atheromatous . . ." The Coroner smiled a soft protest.

"The blood-vessels, in other words, were brittle and calcareous—the arteries of an aged man. The heart itself showed an old valvular lesion, aortic stenosis. The brain . . ." Dr. Sherwell's enthusiasm continued to expend itself in a series of fluent technicalities that

left the jury bewildered and raised a laugh at the back
of the court.

"Do you agree with the last witness's opinion as to
the cause of death?" the Coroner asked.

"Strangulation? No. I do not. The bruising at the
root of the neck was not caused by violent handling.
If you remember, sir, I stated just now that the deceased's blood-vessels were generally atheromatous.
That fragility applies to the whole of the vascular
system: he was a man who bled and bruised easily.
Apart from that the lungs showed no signs of asphyxiation."

"Then what, in your opinion, was the cause of
death?"

"Heart failure. Syncope."

"As a result of shock?"

"Possibly. It could have happened without any shock
with a heart like his. If I may go into details . . ."

"I think you may leave it at that for the present,
Dr. Sherwell," the Coroner said without smiling. He
glanced inquiringly at Cronshaw. Cronshaw nodded
and rose.

"I want the jury to have this quite definitely,
doctor," he said. "First of all: the wound on the
temple was inflicted after death?"

"Yes."

"In falling, possibly. His head might have hit the
desk?"

"I know nothing about any desk. If he did hit a desk,

819

"Exactly. But the desk, it appears, has not been examined. Now secondly: you are definitely of the opinion that this man did not die from strangulation?"

"There are no physical signs to justify such an opinion."

"And that the condition of his heart was such as might cause sudden death at any time?"

"Decidedly."

"Either with a shock or without it?"

"Either with or without it."

The foreman rose clumsily. "We should like to know," he said, "if Dr. Sherwell has ever examined a case of death by strangulation."

Sherwell answered promptly. "Yes. Five, to be exact."

The foreman nodded and sat down.

"Charles Haskard!"

The Coroner treated this witness with patent deference. He was aged fifty-three, a consulting physician on the honorary staff of the Prince's Hospital, a Fellow of the Royal College of Physicians, and Professor of Medicine in the Medical School of North Bromwich University. The deceased had consulted him seven times during the last twelve months. He had last examined him five days before his death. He had communicated with the Coroner on his own initiative, having read an account of Magnus's death in the morning paper. It was perfectly true that he had been away

on a holiday and returned to North Bromwich for no
other reason than to give evidence. During life he had
examined Magnus with the greatest care; he had diag-
nosed his complaint, and last evening the *post-mortem*
results had confirmed his original diagnosis. He had
frequently warned the deceased that his end might be
sudden. Death was due, beyond possible doubt, to the
condition of his heart: an uncommon disease of the
heart-muscle known as auricular fibrillation. Yes, a
shock might have precipitated the event. On the other
hand, the man might have died at any moment without
it. He would say nothing of Dr. Harris's diagnosis of
asphyxiation, or strangulation as he called it, except
that he disagreed with it. There were no signs, external
or internal, to justify that conclusion. Cronshaw rose.
He treated the witness with a deference exceeding that
of the Coroner.

"Dr. Haskard," he said. "I am not going to embarrass you by any questions regarding your eminence
as a physician. (Dr. Haskard was obviously relieved.)
"But I think I am correct when I say that you are an
authority on diseases of the heart?"

"I have made a special study of them."

"You are very modest. This case interested you
particularly?"

"Yes. The condition was obscure."

"I understand it is obscure no longer?"

"No. The condition of the heart is quite evident."

"And Solomon Magnus died of it?"

"That is my opinion."

"He did *not* die of strangulation? I am sorry to make you repeat yourself, but I want this made clear."

"No."

"Nor yet of a blow on the temple?"

"No."

Cronshaw paused. "I hope you will forgive me if I ask you a personal question. I want you to tell the jury exactly why you returned from your holiday."

"I wished to give evidence in this case. It was my duty as Mr. Magnus's medical attendant."

"We appreciate that. I gather that you had read an account of certain police-court proceedings. Was there no other ethical reason for your return?"

Haskard hesitated. As he did so, he thought of his wife. "Yes," he answered at last, "I think it would be true to say that I realized the grave implications of the case and was anxious"—Cronshaw nodded—"that no mistake should be made which my special knowledge might prevent."

"Thank you. That's exactly what I wanted. I have no more to ask."

The Coroner began to sum up. He wanted, first of all, to impress the jury with the fact that they were not empanelled to bring in a verdict on a criminal charge; they were simply there to inquire into the cause of Solomon Magnus's death. Their verdict must largely rest on the medical evidence; and in this case, as often happened, that evidence was at variance. They would almost certainly have formed their own judgment of the relative value of that evidence. In his own opinion Dr. Harris's original diagnosis of strangulation appeared to have been hasty. It was not borne out by the pathologist's findings or the evidence of Professor Haskard, who had offered his testimony out of a laudable sense of duty and at considerable inconvenience to himself. There seemed to be little doubt but that the cause of death was the condition of the heart. Whether that condition had been aggravated by shock was for them to decide—as also whether the shock in question was due to any particular act of violence during the stormy interview which had taken place. On that point they had to rely on the evidence of the only living person present at that interview: Richard Pennington. He was glad that Pennington had elected to tender evidence. They had heard Pennington's evidence, on oath, as to what took place. Pennington had stated, on oath, that he had used no physical violence towards Magnus. If they believed he was speaking the truth they would be justified in bringing in a verdict of Death from Natural Causes. If they disbelieved Pennington's evidence it was their duty to say that Solomon Magnus met his death by violence. In coming to a decision the possible consequences of their verdict must not weigh with them. He asked them to retire and consider it, reminding them that the verdict of a Coroner's jury must be unanimous.

The jury retired; and now it seemed to Dick as though the buzzing released in the back of the court increased in volume and malignancy. Was it possible, he wondered, that the jury should not believe him? Surely people must know when one was speaking the truth, and he had never told a lie that mattered in all his life. But one never knew. Perhaps some obstinate juryman . . .

He sat there, beating a restless tattoo with one hand on the other. A policeman in uniform was making the various witnesses sign copies of their evidence; the clerk was paying their fees. He saw, for an instant, the determined, set face of Miss Lewis. It was bitter, implacable. Supposing one of the jurymen felt as she did? He saw the enormous black bulk of Sir Edward Cronshaw. Cronshaw lounged in his seat and was talking to Hadley just as if nothing were at stake. He saw, behind Cronshaw, the immobile hunched shoulders of George Lorimer. George Lorimer seemed to have grown smaller and smaller during the last two hours, and his tonsure, which had been pink at the beginning, was now ashen white like his hair.

Five minutes . . . Ten minutes . . . Fifteen . . .

The jury trooped in with the foreman in front. The Coroner looked up from his papers pleasantly. The buzzing stopped.

"You have considered your verdict?"

"Yes, sir."

"And you are all agreed?"

"Yes, unanimous, sir. We bring it in Natural Causes."

The Coroner nodded. The back of the court exploded in a roar of talking.

Young Hadley was wringing Dick's hand while Cronshaw towered over him, smiling complacently and nodding his head. Only George Lorimer did not move.

"Can I go?" Dick asked suddenly.

Hadley laughed. "Good lord, no. I hope the Stipendiary's still sitting."

Superintendent Whittaker appeared. He smiled wryly at Cronshaw. "You've done it again, Sir Edward." Cronshaw patted his back good-humouredly.

"Come along with me, Pennington," Whittaker said.

He went, still in custody. They entered the magistrate's court. It was empty except for the Stipendiary on his dais, as calm and ascetic as ever, the clerk of the court, and a couple of sergeants of police who were busy with documents. Superintendent Whittaker spoke in a whisper to the clerk; the clerk passed on his message to the Stipendiary. Dick found himself again in the dock with the wooden rail in front of him. Superintendent Whittaker stood up on the Stipendiary's left. Dick vaguely heard him speaking.

"Your Worship, with regard to the case of Richard Pennington, remanded in custody on the thirtieth of last month on the charge of wilfully murdering Solomon Magnus. The City Coroner has completed his inquiry on the death of Magnus this morning and the jury has brought in a verdict of Death from Natural Causes. Under these circumstances I propose to offer no evidence against the accused."

The Stipendiary listened attentively and nodded.

"Very well, Superintendent," he said. He looked kindly at Dick over the empty gulf that separated the dock from the bench. His tired eyes smiled behind their glasses, his thin lips smiled faintly.

"You are discharged," he said. "You may go."

.   .   .   .

It was a nuisance that all these people insisted on crowding round him and shaking his hand. He only wanted Susan. She was coming, they told him; Hadley had gone to fetch her. Cronshaw, looming over him, laid a heavy hand on his shoulder. Dick felt guilty; realized that he hadn't even thanked him. But that wasn't what Cronshaw wanted.

"Yes, yes, it was a narrow thing," he admitted. "It was Haskard's evidence that told. If you'd stood your trial for manslaughter at assizes it would have been touch-and-go. You were lucky in your jury too. I could see that from the very first. But that's all over. What I want to talk about, Pennington, is your wife. She's a remarkable woman. She may have been weak in one way, but through this particular business she's turned up trumps. I suppose you know that she's fond of you . . . that she loves you, in fact. The other

MR. AND MRS. PENNINGTON

thing was an accident that might happen to anybody.
When you get to my age you'll probably realize that.
Now look here. This isn't a case for half measures.
Either you wash out the whole wretched business or
else you don't. If you do—and you will if you're wise,
in my opinion—I see no reason why you shouldn't be
happy people, a good deal happier than you've ever
been before. It's like when you crash in the air. The
only thing for your nerves is to go up again as soon as
possible. But you've got to cut loose. Understand?
You've got to get away from all the people and circumstances that can remind you of what has happened.
Leave the house! Leave the district! Go hundreds of
miles from anyone who's ever heard of it! I gather
your wife's got money enough for you to carry on with
until you find a job. So clear right out of it. Go to-
night. Take no notice of anything or anybody. Do you
see what I mean?"

"Yes, I do, sir. Thank you. I'll take your advice."

"Well, God bless you both! Here she is."

She came hurrying in with Captain Small limping
behind her. Small was flushed in the face; there had
been an excuse for his hip-flask that morning. Susan
was wearing the dress she had worn at the gaol on
Sunday. Dick reached out his arms to her. No plate-
glass separated them now. It was the first time they
had kissed since Dick went to Pandypool. Susan clung
to him fiercely, but neither said anything, though the
rest of the group with instinctive delicacy had turned

their backs on them. When the others came up to congratulate Dick Susan still clung to his arm, as tightly as if she felt that once she let go she might lose him. Cronshaw bade them good-bye. He was catching the next train for London. He smiled as he took Susan's hand. "Well, young woman, what did I tell you?" Then he whispered to Dick: "Don't forget what I said. To-night!"

He moved away, smiling. "What did he say, to you, Dick?" Susan asked.

"He wants us to shut up the house and clear right away somewhere to-night."

"He's quite right, I'm glad he said that. We can't go without luggage, though."

"I shan't want much, Susie. Small can get all that I want."

"I should have to go too. I hate leaving you alone, Dick. He'd much better stay with you. Mr. Hadley can drive me out and I'll meet you both later. Where are we going, darling?"

"Heaven knows! It depends on what time we've got. I was thinking of Ludlow."

"As long as I'm with you nothing whatever matters."

They left the court arm in arm. When they reached Hadley's car Dick surrendered her. The only interested person left in the building was little George Lorimer, who had somehow got left behind.

·　　·　　·　　·　　·　　·

Two hours later Susan joined Dick and Captain Small in the station refreshment-room, where Dick had been watching Captain Small drink beer: a healthy beverage, he insisted, which never hurt anyone. She had a porter outside, Susan told them, with two small suitcases. Captain Small immediately gave the porter two shillings and insisted on carrying both: he was feeling A1 and up to anything, he laughed, and Dick couldn't prevent him.

"I've got the tickets for Ludlow," Susan whispered.

Captain Small, walking rapidly in front, with a suit-case in either hand, found an empty carriage. He tipped the guard half-a-crown on the sly to keep it empty. "Looks more like the end of an 'oneymoon than the beginning," the guard thought. Susan gave Captain Small the keys of "Chatsworth" and asked him to stop Mr. Duke delivering milk. Though she spoke to Small, her eyes never left Dick's face. Captain Small watched the long train steam out, with Susan waving. It was very unfortunate, he thought, that the refresh-ment-room bars closed so early.

Susan lay close in her husband's arms all the way to Ludlow. It was a pitch-black inhospitable evening out-side; but that made no difference. They turned out of their train in the dark. Dick carried the two suitcases up the long hill from the station. As they reached the centre of the town a sweet sound of bells met their ears. Dick paused, panting. "Listen, Susie," he said. "I told you about those."

They listened. The lovely, melancholy music hung on the air like still smoke, then drifted away.

They turned into an hotel. The smart girl in the office pushed a register in front of him.

Dick wrote: *Mr. and Mrs. Pennington. North Bromwich.*

"Double room, I suppose?"

"Yes, please."

"Two beds or one?" the young lady inquired. "You can have whichever you prefer."

"It's all the same to us," Dick answered awkwardly.

Montreux: Esthwaite Lodge.
　　1-1-31—25-8-31.